CREATURES OF LIGHT

BOOK ONE

THE AWAKENING

JOHNNY RAYE

Creatures of Light: Book One—The Awakening

Published by Wheatmark®
2030 East Speedway Boulevard, Suite 106
Tucson, Arizona 85719 USA
www.wheatmark.com

ISBN: 978-1-62787-923-1 (paperback)
ISBN: 978-1-62787-924-8 (ebook)
LCCN: 2021920306

Bulk ordering discounts are available through Wheatmark, Inc. For more information, email orders@wheatmark.com or call 1-888-934-0888.

Special Thanks to
Barbara Allen, and the Barbara Allen Writer's Service.
Without your help, dedication, and friendship,
this book would have been next to impossible to complete.

Before time was, we were,
and He That Is Three
ruled with an iron hand.
One, however, would not be ruled,
and many followed the One,
They were Legion.
But He That Is Three rallied
his Host against The Legion,
and there was war.
The Legion was cast out,
but the war continues...

PROLOGUE

Nelson Jordan wore a slight smirk as he pushed his new Mercedes S Class along a winding riverside road, its headlights cutting through the low-lying fog, and glistening off the rain dampened asphalt. Nelson loved this car, and ever since it had been delivered, he grabbed every opportunity that came along to open her up along this challenging stretch of highway.

His beautiful wife, Emma, twenty years his junior, sat next to him. She accessorized the car well, her flowing elegance giving the front seat of his Maybach the look of a glossy sales brochure. It was picture perfect, and that was how Nelson Jordan liked his life to be.

Nestling into his seat Nelson took a deep, self-satisfied, breath. He did so love that "new car smell". And the aroma of Emma's perfume, mingling with that of the soft leather seats, made it all the more intoxicating to him.

In the back seat sat his seven-year-old son, Chance, sipping from a juice box and giggling as his doting mother made faces at him in her vanity mirror. The scene was idyllic, and it had been designed that way...for the most part anyway.

Nelson Jordan, a middle-aged, self-made millionaire, had achieved all the material wealth he had ever dreamed of. He had discovered, however, that the age-old adage that money could not buy happiness was indeed true, but he consoled himself with the discovery that it could buy him a boat, so he could sail up next to it for a few hours. As a result of this revelation, he had purchased a yacht, and christened it the "Happiness".

Yes, life was going as planned for Nelson Jordan. His checklist of success had thus far been completed methodically; M.B.A. from Harvard, check. Millionaire by age thirty, check. Expensive house, expensive cars, and an expensive super model trophy wife, check, check, and double check.

Conventional measures of success also called for 2.5 children, but Nelson was content with just one, and even that one had been an accident. Nelson had never wanted children. He considered them a burden that would diminish his quality of life. He admitted without any equivocation, that his opinion of children was driven mostly by materialistic selfishness, and he was unapologetic about it. Nelson Jordan wanted to live his life as he wanted to live it, without being responsible for anyone but himself. It was just that simple.

Upon learning of his wife's pregnancy, Nelson had wanted the child to be aborted. In fact, he had strongly advocated for it. But Emma would not hear of it, forcing Nelson to become the father he had never wanted to be.

Because Nelson did not like being forced into anything, he chose to rationalize the situation by admiring what he perceived as Emma's shrewd tactical maneuvering in securing her financial future. He even found that it gave him a modicum of respect for her.

There was, of course, an upside to having a child that he had not considered. It gave Emma something to do that kept her occupied, and out of his hair, but it didn't always go as planned.

In fact, that he found himself that night behind the wheel of his Maybach, racing down the old river road, was the result of one of those moments that was supposed to have kept his lovely young wife and child occupied. An event that Nelson had unexpectedly, and unwillingly, become entangled in, the boy's birthday.

Nelson had hoped for a quiet evening at home with some cake and ice cream. Nelson did so love birthday cake. But Emma had other plans. Instead, she had insisted on taking Chance to Richmond to see The Lion King.

Nelson had eventually given in. A nice dinner in Richmond, and an opportunity to take his S Class out and stretch its legs along the river road, being the most compelling factors. Now he was enjoying the fruit of his capitulation.

The Maybach was amazing. It felt to Nelson as if he were not just driving it, but wearing it. The car seemed to respond to his every command, almost at the moment he thought it. He was completely enraptured by the experience, and that is why it was odd that his attention should be drawn to the silence of his son in the back seat.

Emma was now paging through a fashion magazine in which she was featured, when for no reason other than silence, Nelson looked into his rearview mirror at his son. When he did, he saw Chance sitting with his head laid back on the seat, staring transfixed into the sky, through the car's rear window.

Adjusting his side mirror Nelson tried to see what Chance was looking at, but saw nothing in the moon silvered, foggy night. Dismissing it as another one of his son's many eccentricities, he returned his attention to the road.

But Chance did see something. A grotesque humanoid shape, soaring above the car, just far enough away to be dismissible as nothing more than a shadow in the mist. But this shadow was uncomfortably familiar to the boy, as if calling to him.

As he watched, the creature faded in and out of existence, there, but not there, as if made of smoke. It was hypnotic, and Chance was drawn to it, as eyes that glowed like burning embers, fanned by a breath, pierced through the mist and locked onto his.

A shock ripped through the boy's body causing him to jerk and spasm as his mind, and the mind of the creature above him, melded into a singular thought. He clinched his teeth, his eyes glazing over, and rolling back in his head.

The beast came into view as it pressed closer to the car. Held aloft by broad leathery wings, its heavily muscled body rippled with each beat as it moved fluidly through the fog, moonlight glistening off its dagger-like teeth.

Burning brightly from its dark silhouette, the creature's eyes intensified, and as they did visions of murdered children flooded Chance's mind. He could see their faces, and hear their screams as if he were there, watching through the eyes of the killer, while at the same time hovering above the gruesome scenes like some kind of macabre drone.

The images were horrifyingly vivid, like memory induced nightmares that flashed from scene to hideous scene, with each stroke of the beast's massive wings.

As the creature's heavy wings churned the air, Chance's body convulsed and seized. Then the image of a boy swimming in a pool filled his mind.

The pool was indoors, but sunlight poured in through large greenhouse style windows that enclosed it on three sides. The boy splashed happily, an inflatable mat holding him buoyant, as his mother sat poolside reading from a tablet computer. On the poolside table was a birthday cake with several pieces missing, a large candle in the shape of the number seven stuck in its center.

As the boy played, and the woman read, neither noticed that eight feet below the screws that held down the pool's drain cover had begun to turn and pop free. Once all the screws were out the cover slid aside and a massive, inhuman hand crept from the drain pipe, twisting and expanding as it did.

It was hideous, and impossibly large to be coming out of such a confined space. Its fingers, thick as baseball bats, were covered with scaled, mottled skin, each tipped with a ragged yellow claw.

As the hand reached upward toward the surface, and the boy swimming there, Chance convulsed. He tried to scream a warning, but choked as if the hideous hand were at his own throat.

The boy played unaware as the enormous claws rose from the water behind him. It wasn't until its shadow fell over him that he turned to look, and when he did, his eyes grew wide in terror.

As the thing seized the boy, a wave of water broke over the reading woman like a tidal wave, drenching her and causing her to jump up angrily. Standing she tried in vain to shake the water off herself, and her soaked computer.

"Bobby!" she screamed, "If this thing is ruined, I'm gonna kill you!"

When the boy didn't respond, the woman turned. Scanning the surface of the water she saw nothing, only its rippled surface, and the boy's now deflated air mat floating in a red cloud that drifted in an expanding plume. Looking more closely she finally saw the boy, his crumpled body motionless at the bottom of the pool.

Diving into the water the woman was immediately with the boy. Frantically she pulled on his arms in a futile effort to drag him to the surface, but his tiny body would not budge.

Unable to hold her breath any longer, the woman surfaced, gasping and screaming. In a panic she looked down into the water and saw that the boy's body had been broken, folded back at the waist, then pulled down into the drain pipe. His feet beside his head, his arms reached toward the surface as if trying to embrace her. His head was thrown back screaming a silent scream, as a trail of blood rose like smoke from his open mouth.

The vision faded, and Chance's body was racked by another convulsion. Looking up into the moon-soaked fog he saw the winged creature was still there, soaring above him, keeping pace with the car. As its wings pounded the air, his mind, and the mind of the creature, bonded once again, and Chance stared horrified as another vision wrenched him.

A bright moon shone above a lakeside beach and sparkled off the wind whipped water. Unusually large waves, more appropriate to a coastal setting, broke upon the shore.

At first the scene seemed deserted, but through the howling wind, Chance heard the sounds of panicked voices as a man and woman struggled to pull their seven-year-old twin daughters through the soft sand.

They were frightened, continually looking back into the darkness at some unseen pursuer when, inexplicably, the roar of the wind died away, and the surface of the lake turned to glass. In the relative calm that followed, Chance heard what sounded like a pack of wolves just out of sight in the tree line. The sound of the snarls and growling was blood chilling, and the twin sisters were crying from both fear and confusion as their parents pulled them along.

"Get the girls in the house!" shouted the man as he handed off one of the girls to his wife, "I'll slow them down."

"Brad, no!" pleaded the woman

"Go!" he screamed.

The woman pulled the two girls down the beach as the man picked up a heavy tree limb and turned to fight for his family's life. But as his wife and children ran toward safety, he was swarmed by the pack, and torn to pieces, his screams piercing the chaos.

The sounds of her father's cries caused one of the girls to stop and look back at the gruesome scene. As she did, she stumbled and fell, the doll she was carrying flying from her hand and landing several feet away.

As her mother stopped to help the fallen child, the other little girl ran to her sister's doll, but as she stooped to pick it up, her mother called out, "Run baby, run to the house as fast as you can!"

Grabbing the doll by its arm the girl ran up the walkway and into the house. Turning to call out to her mother, she screamed as she watched a crazed pack of huge black dogs swarm over her mother, eliciting hideous cries of agony as flesh was ripped from bone.

She watched in horror as one of the dogs snatched her sister in its jaws. It dragged the little girl away, screaming, into the dark forest, a cohort of dogs following behind to join the feast.

The child in the doorway began to scream, her wails drawing the attention of one of the Hell Hounds. With eyes glowing like burning embers, it stalked toward her. But when the dog attempted to cross the house's threshold, it yelped and recoiled in pain, smoke rising from its flesh as if it had been burned. Its face momentarily transformed into the same gruesome visage as the creature that stared at Chance from the mist above his father's car, and the little girl screamed.

Once again Chance jolted, and the vision faded. He watched as the terrified little girl hugged her sister's doll tightly to her chest. Turning her back, she hid her face from the scene of her family's slaughter just feet away, the doll now the only witness, the gruesome scene reflecting in its blue glass eyes.

Another seizure jolted Chance's body and he found himself once more in the backseat of his father's car, gazing out its rear window. The great beast hovered there for a moment, then staring back at Chance, it pounded its wings against the air and streaked away, shaking the car violently with its passing.

As the winged creature pulled away, and vanished into the mist, Chance's body began to relax. He became limp and dazed as if heavily sedated and the juice box in his hand slipped through his fingers, spilling its contents on the car's seat.

Feeling his car shudder, Nelson's head began to swivel. He checked his mirrors, but saw nothing. Then he saw his son's face and was startled to see that the boy's eyes were rolled back in his head, his tiny body shaking in intermittent spasms. Turning Nelson looked into the backseat and was horrified by what he saw.

The horror that struck him was not the sight of the winged beast in the mist, nor was it the sight of his son's obvious distress as he strained and relaxed in successive convulsions. No, what filled Nelson Jordan's heart with panic, was the sight of Chance's juice box draining onto his hand stitched Italian leather seats.

"Damn it, Chance! Pick that up!" he shouted. But Chance did not respond. He just sat there, his head rolling on his shoulders as if he were drunk.

Nelson didn't notice his son's distress however, as his full attention was focused on the leaking juice box. He tried to reach it, but his seatbelt restrained him. Unbuckling his belt, he reached for the juice box again and this time he got his hand around the offending...

"Nelson, look out!"

Emma's scream was just in time to allow Nelson to look up and see a massive stag standing in the road. Dropping the juice box, he grasped the steering wheel with both hands and swerved sharply to avoid the huge animal, causing the car to skid on the dampened asphalt.

Slamming broadside into the guardrail the car was launched, barrel rolling through the air until it came crashing down hard on the rocky river bank. The impact threw open the driver's side door sending the unrestrained Nelson flopping from the car like an overdressed crash test dummy.

After Nelson was ejected, the car continued to roll violently until it smashed into the icy river. The car began to sink almost immediately until only the trunk was visible protruding above the surface. The car bobbed there momentarily, slowly turning in the river's current until, at last, it slid beneath the churning water, only the glow of the tail lights attesting to its presence.

Up on the road, the great stag stood watching as the lights of the submerged Maybach finally failed. The cold black water returned to darkness, leaving only the light of the moon flickering peacefully on the slow-moving river.

The stag waited, scanning the water with its red, pulsing eyes, its breath bursting forth in clouds of steam that fell to the ground as frost. After a moment, red electric arcs began to crawl over its body until the great stag twisted and transformed into the winged beast. Spreading its leathery wings, it crushed the air as it rose into the sky, and once airborne, it turned to mist, dissipating like a pot of boiling water thrown into frozen air.

Silence fell over the scene like a heavy blanket. The only audible sound was that of the river lapping at its banks, when an anguished groan sounded from behind some rocks.

Nelson Jordan lay bloody and shattered amongst the boulders. He tried to move, but screamed as white-hot pain shot through his leg. Looking down, he saw that the bone of his lower leg was jutting out through his flesh, his limb twisted in an unnatural and obscene angle.

Lying back, he panted as the cold closed in on him. Feeling for his phone, he pulled it out of his coat, but when he tapped the screen, he found that he had no signal.

Lifting his head, Nelson looked for his car and family, but saw nothing. Resting his head on the rocks he began to search through his possible options.

Out on the river a bubble burst on the surface of the viscus black water, and it was quickly followed by a juice box, and then the body of a small boy. Face down and motionless, the tiny body drifted in the undulating current.

Up on the embankment a bright flash, like a lightning strike, lit the road. Moments later a figure dressed in black jeans and a hoodie, pulled up over its head, stepped up to the damaged guardrail.

The mysterious figure surveyed the scene, then leaping over the railing it bounded down the embankment to the river's edge. Diving into the frigid water the hooded figure pulled Chance's limp body up onto the shore.

Chance was not breathing, his pale skin glowing morbidly in the moonlight. His eyes, unnervingly half open, were nothing more than a glassy lifeless stare that focused on nothing

The hooded figure knelt over Chance and placed a hand on the boy's chest. Immediately a soft light began to emanate from beneath its palm, casting an eerie blue hue. Then the figure spoke. It was more of a whisper, barely heard, but it was clear.

"Don't be afraid, Sari'El."

The glow of the light caught Nelson's attention as he lay helpless in the rocks. Looking up he saw a person in a dark hood kneeling beside Chance, a bright blue light issuing from what Nelson assumed was a flashlight.

"Hey! Help me! Please!"

The mysterious figure stood and turned toward Nelson; its face hidden in shadow. For a moment Nelson thought he saw eyes, pulsing with blue electricity staring back at him. Then the eyes winked out, and the shadowy figure fled, running up the embankment and out of sight. At that moment Nelson's phone chirped and had full signal. Nelson dialed 911, then passed out from the pain.

On the river bank, Chance coughed, water spouting from his mouth as he sat up, confused and cold, but very much alive.

ONE

Chance Jordan sat up in bed gasping, rivers of sweat running down his face and chest. Gripped by panic he clutched at his bed sheets, but quickly calmed as he realized that it had only been a dream.

Only a dream. That was a bit of an understatement. It was a nightmare to be more exact. A terrifying nightmare of the night his mother had been killed over eleven years earlier. A nightmare that was, for some reason, recurring with disturbing frequency in this his final year at Wellington Preparatory Academy.

Chance had no direct memory of that horrible night. His last mental image was of leaving the theater where he and his parents had just attended a performance of The Lion King for his Birthday. Where his imagination had come up with winged gargoyles, and fire eyed stags, he didn't know, and yet the hideous creatures seemed so real to him, so...familiar. Pulling off his sweat-soaked sheets he headed for the lavatory of his dorm room.

"Same dream?" came a pillow-muffled voice.

The question had come from Chance's roommate, and best friend, Eric Easton, still half asleep in the other bed. The two friends had shared this room since they were freshmen. Now in the final months of their senior year, they had no secrets from one another.

"Yeah, same dream," answered Chance as he splashed water on his face.

"Dude, you gotta get some help," said Eric sleepily. "I'm getting bags under my eyes."

"I'm sorry," said Chance, sincerely. "I'll see what I can do."

"I don't do bags, Chance."

"I know Eric," said Chance patiently.

"I have a reputation to consider, you understand."

"Of course you do," said Chance dryly.

At that moment Eric's cell phone began chiming a wake-up call. Shutting it off Eric sat up, sleep still clinging to him. Getting out of bed, he pulled on some sweatpants.

"Get your shit together, Chance. Coach wants us in the weight room early."

Chance did not reply, he just looked into the bathroom mirror as the images from his dream loosened their grip on him.

"You okay, Chance?" asked Eric poking his head in.

"Yeah," said Chance, taking a deep breath, "I'm good."

The morning was cool and calm as the boys made their way across campus to the Wellington Sports Complex. With their senior year winding down, and graduation looming, Eric and Chance had become proud Spartans, even if Wellington Prep had not been either boy's first choice four years ago.

Being sons of wealth, Chance and Eric had hoped to attend a "normal" public high school, with "normal" kids, not the children of congressmen, diplomats, and celebrities that typified the Wellington student body. So, when they had moved onto campus their freshman year, the two boys immediately bonded over the fact that neither of them wanted to be there. But now, after four years as Wellington Spartans, they both had to admit the place had grown on them.

For Chance, attending Wellington had at least one upside from the very beginning. That upside being that Wellington was a boarding school, and its live in, year-round, dorms were something Chance was looking forward to.

Life with his father had always been somewhat strained. That strain being fed by both Chance's resentment of his father due to his belief that Nelson had been responsible for his mother's death, and Nelson's resentment at having been forced into a parental role he had never wanted in the first place.

But time heals, and distance facilitates that healing. Over the last four years Chance had matured, and his feelings for his father had evolved into a tolerant acceptance. Nelson Jordan was still the self-absorbed and childish, boy in a man's body, he had always been. Over the years, however, his selfishness had expanded to include his son, who he had grown to love despite himself.

Another major advantage of attending Wellington, other than the internationally recognized academic curriculum, was the exceptional quality of its athletic program. It was unrivaled in both its resources, and especially its coaching staff.

Every Spartan coach had, at the very least, Division One university experience. Many had been professional athletes, or coaches and their expertise had directed the design and development of the school's facilities. And those facilities were exquisite.

This was nowhere more obvious than when one walked into the four thousand square foot strength and conditioning center. It was a state-of-the-art temple to the gods of victory, and through their sacrifices there, Spartan athletes had become accustomed to being champions.

Chance and Eric hustled into the weight room a bit winded. They had hurried because they knew better than to be late. If coach McCune said to be there at 0600 hours, that meant he expected you to be sweating at 0600 hours. Stragglers were dealt with severely.

As the boys walked in, it was clear that most of the team had already arrived and the last few were streaming in. Dropping their bags against the wall, they began warming up. Coach McCune entered a few minutes later and blew his whistle.

"Circuit stations! Move!" he bellowed.

The players scattered, taking up positions at the various training stations around the room.

"Who are we?" shouted McCune.

"We are Spartans!" responded the team in unison.

"No surrender!"

"No retreat!"

The whistle sounded again.

"Exercise!" barked McCune.

Iron began to clank, and young men strained, as the Spartan baseball team began making its daily sacrifice to the gods of victory.

TWO

Nowhere on campus was the history and tradition of Wellington Preparatory Academy more on display than in the school's Grand Foyer. The academy was founded prior to the Revolutionary War, and had been educating the children of the landed gentry ever since. The Grand Foyer was a time capsule of that history.

Chance loved history, and often took time to examine the various artifacts on display in the numerous glass cases around the ornate room. Artifacts that, sadly, many of the students paid little attention to.

Today, Chance pondered the class of 1861. In one of the glass cases were two Civil War officer's uniforms, one Union, and one Confederate, each worn by Wellington alumni. There was also a cavalry sword, and next to it an antique silver frame containing one of the earliest Wellington class photos.

"What were their dreams?" he wondered as he looked at their boyish faces. "Did any of them live long enough to realize them?"

Chance took a deep breath and looked around the foyer. At moments like these, when he was surrounded by all this history and art, and the ghosts of Spartans long dead whispered to him, he would take in the vaulted ceilings, oak paneling, and marble floors, feeling truly fortunate to have had the opportunity to write his name into Wellington's history.

The Grand Foyer was also the place to meet before classes, and today was no exception. The vast space was filled with students chatting animatedly as they waited for first bell. Amongst them, a group of uniformed cheerleaders hung hand painted posters congratulating the Spartan baseball team for having won the Regional Championship the night before.

Chance looked out over the crowd. The members of the Spartan baseball team were easy to find in their Letterman's jackets, the red leather sleeves standing in bright contrast with the black blazers worn by the other students.

The "Wearing of the colors" by victorious Spartan teams was an old Wellington tradition. On the first day of school following a victory, the members of the winning team, as well as the cheerleaders that had supported them at the game, were permitted to forego the required school uniform and wear instead their distinctive jackets and sweaters. The school spirit, and pride, in the room was palpable.

"Talking to ghosts again?" teased Eric as he walked up and stood next to his friend. Eric was more than aware of Chance's fascination with the faces in the old photos.

"Yeah, they told me you're an asshole," retorted Chance without looking.

"Why must dead people be so rude?" said Eric, feigning insult. Stepping up he rapped on the glass, "Hey, dead guys, come out and say it to my face."

"You'd shit if they did," came a voice from behind them.

Turning they saw that they had been joined by Conor Jackson, another member of the baseball team.

As the three friends stood chatting, Eric noticed that a group of freshman girls was staring and whispering as they walked by.

"Jeez, you guys will never stop being a freak show," said Eric.

What Eric was referring to was the fact that Chance Jordan and Conor Jackson, though unrelated, were almost spot on twins. Only their eye color spoiled the effect. Where Conor's eyes were brown, Chance's eyes were green. Other than that difference, it was difficult for most people, especially those who had just met them, to tell them apart.

The confusion was amplified on days like today when they wore their Letterman's Jackets that were decorated with exactly the same awards. If they wore sunglasses, which they often did, only the embroidered name on the front of their jackets made it possible to tell who was who. But their similarity in appearance is where the similarity ended.

Conor and Chance had grown up in vastly different worlds. Conor Jackson was an "Army brat". His childhood had been spent bouncing around the world from one army base to another, living in the various third world countries in which his parents were stationed. His father, a Green Beret Colonel, and his mother an army Intelligence officer had some prestige but no wealth. They could provide Conor with a comfortable, loving home, but could never afford the tuition for a school such as Wellington.

No, the reason Conor was at Wellington had nothing to do with his parents. Conor was there by his own hand...or arm to be precise. To put it plainly, the boy could throw a baseball.

When head varsity baseball coach Phil McCune first saw Conor pitching in the Little League World Series, he knew the kid was special. Coach McCune lobbied hard for one of the coveted full scholarships that Wellington offered each year to be awarded to Conor. Fortunately, Conor scored high enough on the school's academic admissions exam to silence the few critics, and so Conor was in, and he did not disappoint.

Conor reported to spring training his freshman year with a 94mph fastball and a change-up that had opposing batters swatting at flies. In his first game as a Spartan, he threw a no hitter, earning him the nickname of Zeus from the local sports writers, and the legend only grew.

Consequently, pro scouts had been crawling all over the Wellington Sports Complex for the last four years. That Conor was going to be playing professional baseball was a foregone conclusion.

"What got into the coach this morning?" said Conor, wincing as he rubbed his sore muscles, "I'm pretty sure he was trying to kill us."

"He just wants to make sure we don't lose the fire before the state championship," said Chance.

"He doesn't need to worry," said Eric, smiling as he patted Conor on the back. "Zeus gonna drop some lightning bolts on their asses."

"I can't do it alone" said Conor humbly.

"You know we got your back," said Eric, "and we'll be ready."

"Speaking of ready," said Chance, changing the subject. "Are you ready for Miss Hotchkiss' chem test?"

Conor grabbed his head as if in pain, "Crap, I totally forgot."

"Dude!" exclaimed Eric, "How could you forget anything to do with Miss `Hotcakes`? I dream about her, and I'm not even in her class."

"She can be quite distracting," agreed Chance.

At that moment their attention was drawn to a workman driving a lift into the foyer. Alongside the lift walked three students carrying a large rolled section of canvas some twenty feet long. Along the length of the roll was affixed a heavy golden rod.

Walking along with the canvas, escorted by one of the cheerleaders, was a boy. He was extremely pale, yet oddly beautiful, his long white blond hair framing his angelic face. His diminutive stature made him seem almost frail as he walked with the group. He avoided making eye contact with anyone, preferring to keep his eyes fixed on the floor.

As the lift came to a halt, the three students handed up the rolled canvas to the workman. Taking the roll, he balanced it on his lift, then slowly began to ascend toward the ceiling. There he attached the rod to chains anchored from the foyer's large wooden beams. When he was finished, he released the roll and it unfurled with a flourish.

A susurration rolled through the assembled students as they stood awestruck by the beauty and intricate detail of the baroque style painting that had been revealed. Greek and Nordic gods danced on silvery clouds, pierced by fluted columns that supported the heavens. Apollo danced with Aphrodite, Odin with Frig. Off to one side a man with long white hair seduced a beautiful blond girl with his harp, as Thor raised his horn of ale in salute. Above their heads galaxies sparkled in the velvet black of space, as stars burst to life within colorful nebula. The painting was, quite simply, a masterpiece.

It was a shocking and unexpected level of art, considering that it was an advertisement for the upcoming prom. The fact that the words "A Night Amongst the Stars" were painted across it, was a desecration boarding on the obscene.

"It's so beautiful," said Chance to no one in particular.

One of the cheerleaders nearby heard him. "Isn't it amazing?" she sighed.

"Incredible," he said softly. "The stars, they look like they're twinkling. Where did they get it made?"

The cheerleader pointed at the small blond boy. "Jäger painted it," she said.

Chance looked at the strange boy. Some students stood next to him, a few giving him congratulatory pats on the back, from which he seemed to be made uncomfortable and shied away.

Looking back at the painting, it struck Chance again. He couldn't explain his emotional reaction to it. As he tried to decipher what he was feeling, the one emotion that kept forcing its way to the surface was...homesick.

Disquieted by this feeling, Chance forced his eyes away and once again looked down at the odd little artist. This time Jäger was staring directly at Chance, seemingly through him, with intense unblinking eyes.

Just then Conor appeared over Chance's shoulder, breaking into the moment. "Listen to 'em plotting," he said, indicating a group of coeds chattering excitedly nearby. "This prom is gonna cost a fortune."

"Ah, the price of love," laughed Chance.

"An escort would be cheaper," said Eric, wryly.

A soft chime sounded calling the students to class.

"Saved by the bell," said Chance, shaking his head as the students began to disperse.

"See you at lunch," said Eric laughing as he walked away.

Chance and Conor waved as they slung their backpacks over their shoulders and headed for their first class of the day.

⌐

The bell chimed as Miss Vanessa Hotchkiss, or "Hotcakes" as many of the boys in the student body called her, but never where she might hear it, was finishing writing the instructions for her chemistry lab exam on the Smart Board. Now that her first year at Wellington Academy was coming to a close; she was finally feeling like she had a handle on her classroom management.

It had been a tough first year for two major reasons. The first being the high expectations from staff, and especially from herself. Miss Hotchkiss was a Wellington alum, that had graduated with honors as her class valedictorian. She had gone on to Cornel University on a full ride academic scholarship and had earned a B.S. in chemistry, and a Masters in biochem, as well as being twice published in route. She was more than qualified to teach the honors chemistry class at Wellington.

The other issue was, unfortunately, something she could do nothing about, and that was that she was drop dead gorgeous. She hadn't always been so. In high school she was awkward and rather nerdy. What a difference six years had made. Now at a statuesque 5'10", with long wavy brown hair, and striking hazel eyes that mesmerized anyone who dared to gaze into them, she commanded every room she entered, driving the boys in her classes, and even a few of the girls, quite literally to distraction.

In an attempt to compensate, Miss Hotchkiss had developed a no-non-sense style of maintaining focus on academic matters in her classroom, but it was too little too late. Being a hard ass just wasn't in her nature, and her overly stern scoldings, unconvincingly delivered, did nothing to change that.

As Miss Hotchkiss completed her class preparations, two boys worked setting out glassware at the various black topped science stations around the room. The boys, Travis Shelby and Martin Wellington, were well known, and well connected, trouble makers. On this morning they were serving extra duty for intimidating underclassmen. To put it simply, they were bullies.

When the bell rang, both boys moved quickly to collect their backpacks, but as they ran toward the door, they were stopped by Miss Hotchkiss.

"Are all the stations complete?" she asked.

"Yeah," they answered simultaneously.

"How much longer is your extra duty?"

"Two more days," said Martin.

"Okay, I need you both here after school to clean this glassware. You may go now," she said turning back to her desk.

Martin and Travis once again moved towards the door, but students had already started to stream into the classroom. Annoyed, Martin began to violently push his way through the crowd of unsuspecting kids, causing them to bounce off him like tennis balls, and then it was Martin's turn to bounce.

He stumbled backward from the unexpected impact, and was only kept from falling to the floor by Travis, who caught and held him up. Martin looked up in shock, only to find that the brick wall he had run into was Chance Jordan.

"Excuse me," said Chance as he extended his had in an effort to help Martin up, but Martin just slapped his hand away as he struggled to his feet, rebuking Travis for his help as he did.

"Fucking jocks. You think you own the school," spat Martin.

Conor, who was standing next to Chance, couldn't help but be amused by Martin's outburst. "Think we own it? We do own it. Didn't you get the memo?" teased Conor.

Martin shook with rage, but he wasn't stupid enough to act on it. Chance and Conor were two of Wellington's top athletes, and while Martin was a bully, he wasn't an idiot. Choosing discretion over suicide, he pushed his way past the two, once again bouncing off of Chance's solid stone physique, glaring at Chance and Conor as he did.

The two friends watched amused as the two trouble makers retreated. After they were gone Chance turned to Conor with a smirk on his face," There was a memo?"

"Yeah, you didn't get it?" said Conor seriously, "I'll have my assistant send you a copy."

"I'll have my people contact your people," said Chance laughing, as they entered the classroom and hurried to their station just in time for the final tardy bell.

"Everyone, take your seats. The exam will begin after the morning announcements," said Miss Hotchkiss as she went to her desk to take attendance.

As the students settled into their seats, and quieted, a large screen monitor came on and a slick, highly produced intro for the school's student news program started. As it concluded, a student announcer came on screen.

"Happy Friday Wellington Academy," the young talking head began,

"Today's announcements will be very short. First, as you may have seen from the banner in the Grand Foyer, the prom is here. Tickets for 'A Night Amongst the Stars' are now on sale..."

As the announcements continued, Conor leaned over and whispered to Chance, "Do you know who you want to take to the prom?"

"I don't think I'm gonna go," replied Chance.

Chance had been dreading this event. There was always so much social pressure to go, but it had been his experience that asking a girl to the prom was the high school equivalent of a marriage proposal, and if you weren't that into the person you asked, it never ended well.

"What?" responded Conor, incredulously, "You have to go, it's our senior year."

Chance did not reply other than to shake his head.

"Why not?" said Conor, almost shouting. The exclamation startled some of the students around him and drew the attention of Miss Hotchkiss, who did her best to fire a Medusa-like glare at him.

"This isn't over," whispered Conor relenting, if only for the moment.

"Lastly," said the student news anchor, "Congratulations to the Spartan Varsity Baseball Team, who last night won the Regional Championship. Next, they will march to the State Championship against the yet to be determined Eastern Regional Champions. Men of Sparta, you bring us great honor."

Polite applause broke out and a few students reached over giving Chance and Conor congratulatory pats on the shoulder. The announcements then ended and the room's lights came on.

"The exam begins now," barked Miss Hotchkiss, doing her best to appear perturbed by the interruption. As she watched her students scurry to boot computers, and light gas burners, she hid a satisfied smirk behind her coffee mug.

"And I will accept no late results," she added for effect.

THREE

Douglas Callister, the President of the United States, sat at the Resolute Desk in the Oval Office awaiting the arrival of Andre Lugenet, the man responsible for his presence in the White House. Opening his humidor, he was annoyed to find it empty. Slamming down the lid in disgust, he spun in his chair and looked out into the Rose Garden as his mind drifted back on the night his expected guest made him the most powerful man on Earth.

Douglas Callister's rise to power had been meteoric, and a surprise to all. After two terms as a member of Virginia's State House of Representatives he realized that his political career was on life support. It became clear to all that Douglas had ascended to his level of incompetence, and would eventually fail there.

As a last resort he had taken a run at the U.S. House of Representatives, only to be defeated by no less than thirty percentage points. Yes, 'The fat lady' was singing on the political career of Douglas Callister. Then one day, all of that changed.

While hosting a mid-term fundraiser, that was costing more than it was raising, Callister met Andre Lugenet. Lugenet was a French businessman who was looking to expand his empire to the United States. His many holdings included: the mining of rare earth minerals, renewable energy research, military weapons development, and a monstrous worldwide private security apparatus that rivaled even the United States in intelligence gathering. Up until that moment Lugenet had studiously avoided any U.S. entanglements, despite numerous overtures from recent administrations to conduct "investigations" into that president's political rivals.

As much for his business acumen, Lugenet was known for his command of the art of quid pro quo. Favors for him were famously repaid. His influence in international affairs was legendary, and his leverage, once obtained, was always perfectly applied. He was widely perceived as a 'King maker'.

Andre Lugenet also had a very intimidating presence. He was tall, fit and strikingly handsome. His was a rare mixture of youthful glow and seasoned experience. His black hair, elegantly frosted at the temples, framed dark eyes that seemed to shine with a light of knowledge and ancient wisdom. He was power personified, so when he told Callister that he could deliver to him the White House, there was never any doubt.

On Lugenet's instructions, Callister submitted paperwork to run for the U.S. Senate the following day, and as Lugenet promised, Callister's war chest began to swell. But money alone wasn't enough to put a man like Callister in the Senate, and so Lugenet began to pull on the strings of American democracy.

Callister's opponent was a vulnerable incumbent, and all Lugenet needed to do was drop a few well-placed bombs to clear the field. He dropped the bunker buster a month before the election.

Out of nowhere the media began to report that a sixteen-year-old volunteer was accusing Callister's opponent of sexual misconduct. It wasn't true, but accusation is often all that is needed to destroy a person, and accusation did its work. The overzealous media, always looking for the next Pulitzer Prize winning scandal, smelled blood in the water and went into a feeding frenzy. By the time the truth had been sorted out, Callister was a U.S. Senator.

Senator Callister's run for the White House began, officially, just eighteen months later, and it was flawless. Lugenet and his machine worked quietly in the background, putting out fires on one side, while starting infernos on the other. It was surprisingly simple.

Lugenet had the ability to look into the soul of the American people and see their dreams. More usefully, he could see their hate and fears, and he played on them with a practiced finesse.

Using Douglas Callister as a mouthpiece, Lugenet began to whip up a fanatical base by feeding them what they wanted to hear. He gave them validation of their fears, and justification for their hatred.

It was a time-tested formula, and this wasn't the first time he had used it. Ultimately the lambs fell in behind their new shepherd, and Callister swept into the White House in a landslide.

The "quid" had been paid. The "pro quo" came due on the night before Callister's inauguration.

After a day of preparation for the inaugural festivities, Janine Callister, the soon to be First Lady, primped at her mirror modeling new lingerie that she had purchased just for this evening. She was in a celebratory mood, but much to her disappointment, her preparation was interrupted by a Secret Service agent notifying her husband that there was a visitor downstairs.

She hoped the meeting wouldn't take long. She knew that if Douglas got too tired, her amorous plans for that evening would end with her in the tub alone with her favorite shower massager.

When Callister entered his study, he had found Andre Lugenet waiting. The Frenchman extended his hand in congratulations and Callister took it in thanks.

"What is this?" asked Callister, indicating an ornate silver box that Lugenet had tucked beneath his arm.

"A gift," said the Frenchman.

Lugenet handed the chest to the President, then went the wet bar to pour himself a drink. As he did, he held up the bottle of Bourbon to Callister as an offering, but the new President declined.

"Look inside," urged Lugenet.

Callister lifted the lid and a look of mild puzzlement crossed his brow. Inside the box, nestled in black velvet, was a gleaming cut crystal bottle, capped with an ornate silver stopper that was engraved with runic symbols.

"It's beautiful," said Callister, lifting the bottle from the box. "What is it?"

The lights in the room sparkled off the facets in the crystal. Through the glass, Callister could see what looked like surging black clouds, glowing red from a fire that burned deep inside them, as webs of red lightning crawled across their faces. The whole scene reminded him of ash clouds he had seen over erupting volcanoes.

"It's a tempest in a bottle," smiled Lugenet, "and it has waited thousands of years to be set free. Open it."

Callister looked doubtful, but he had no reason to question the man who had personally tied a ribbon around the White House, so without further thought, he pulled out the stopper. As it clinked free, the bottle inhaled deeply, a throaty, rasping breath like a man gasping for life. Red electric charges crawled out of its elegant neck and swirled over Callister's hand, startling him. With a slight shriek he dropped the bottle, and stepped back, letting it fall to the carpeted floor.

The room grew deathly cold as a billowing mist began to issue from the bottle, ice crystals forming a glittering crust that crept across the carpeted floor. The cloud of mist expanded outwards from the bottle's mouth, growing and heaving as it began to take form, finally congealing into a massive winged monster. When at last its eyes opened, they glowed like embers in a fire.

Callister opened his mouth to scream, but with a slight gesture from Lugenet's hand, the President Elect choked, his scream becoming nothing more than a silent puff of condensed breath in the frigid air. He rasped as the unseen hand at his throat lifted him until only his toes touched the floor. Eyes wide with horror, he struggled helplessly against the unseen force that held him.

The creature crouching at Lugenet's side watched him intently. It appeared ready to lunge, but it held back, its burning eyes shifting from Lugenet to Callister and back, as if waiting for permission.

"Is he not beautiful?" cooed Lugenet, stroking the beast almost lovingly. "So powerful, so patient."

Lugenet looked at Callister and saw the confusion and fear on his face. He sighed.

"You don't understand," said Lugenet, almost sympathetically. "Allow me to explain."

The Frenchman finished his Bourbon in one large gulp, then spoke. "This beautiful yet pathetic being, is a fallen Creature of Light. In the lore of your shamans and religious wizards he is often referred to as a demon, but that is just superstitious nonsense invented by ignorant fools. And while he does have a frightening appearance, I can assure you it is not because he is 'Evil'. It is in fact a vindictive punishment inflicted by He That Is Three. A punishment for the crime of desiring freedom."

Lugenet stepped back, then continued. "He has waited untold ions for his turn to feel the pleasures of the flesh that were denied him. And now my Fallen child, need wait no longer."

At Lugenet's words, red electric arcs began to erupt from the creature's flesh, increasing in number and intensity until its entire body was surrounded in a web of surging celestial power.

"You may take him," said Lugenet at last.

Permission finally received, the electric arcs cocooning the winged beast flashed, then fired across the room encircling Douglas Callister in crackling arcs that burned into his flesh. Had he been able to, he would have screamed.

Later that evening, President-elect Douglas Callister bounded up the stairs of his home, taking them two at a time, to join the First Lady in bed. Sweeping the unsuspecting woman up in his arms, he threw her roughly onto their bed.

Janine had no idea what had transpired down in the study. All she knew was that her husband of thirty years was behaving like the twenty-three-year-old grad student she had married in college.

His passion burned hotter with every tear of her new lingerie', and as he parted her legs and drove into her, he was like a man possessed. She clinched the bedsheets in her fists, swooning as she felt his passion pulse to climax, ebb, then surge back to vigor, over and over again.

The next morning Janine Callister was tired and sore. Looking down at the tattered remnants of her Victoria's Secret camisole, she smiled and let out a contented sigh.

Yes, something had certainly gotten into Douglas last night, and all things considered, she wasn't complaining. Sliding out of bed she walked with a lilt, and a crooked little smile, to the bathroom, a satisfied woman.

———

The intercom on the President's desk buzzed, jolting him from his reminiscence. Reaching over he pressed the button,

"Yes?"

"Mr. President," the female voice chimed, "Mr. Lugenet is here."

"Please send him in."

The door to the Oval Office opened and a young lady wearing a stylish blue jacket and matching skirt entered. Her young eyes sparkled in the direction of the President with obvious familiarity. Directly behind her was Andre Lugenet.

"Thank you, Monica," said Lugenet, his French accent like dripping honey as he took her hand and kissed it. "You look lovely today."

Monica blushed. Smiling shyly, her eyes once again sparkled as she glanced at Callister. Lugenet couldn't help but notice her affection. There was an awkward pause until she realized that the two men were waiting for her to leave. Embarrassed, she backed up toward the door.

"Andre, how have you been?" said the President as he came out from behind his desk to shake his guest's hand.

"Mr. President, it is good to see you again."

The president glanced furtively at Monica as the smitten intern backed out of the Oval Office, closing the heavy door behind her. When the latch clicked shut, Lugenet's charming demeanor vanished. He circled around the president's desk and seated himself in the chair of the most powerful man on earth.

Callister was visibly annoyed by this. His eyes turned black, his irises to burning embers, as rage surged up in him. In response, Lugenet's eyes turned to pools of black, centered by red and blue electric arcs. They locked onto Callister's in a withering stare.

Recognizing his place, Callister looked down in submission, his eyes returning to normal. Satisfied that the order of things had been reestablished, Lugenet relaxed. His eyes became human again and he leaned back in the chair.

Running his hands over the desktop, his eyes fell upon the cut crystal bottle he had brought to Callister on the eve of his inaugural. Leaning forward he picked it up and held it to the light. Pulling the stopper, he sniffed it and smiled.

"You kept it? How...sentimental."

Lugenet spun the bottle slowly casting tiny rainbows on Callister's face as sunlight refracted through it. "So, what news?" he asked without taking his eyes off the gleaming crystal.

Callister collected himself with great difficulty. He had become accustomed to having his orders followed, not to standing at attention before his own desk. But he understood his place, and that any power that he had was minuscule compared to the powerful entity that was seated before him.

"The project is progressing," he finally said through clenched teeth.

Lugenet's attention shifted from the bottle as he once again held Callister in a cold, lifeless gaze. "I have heard otherwise," he said evenly.

Lugenet replaced the stopper in the mouth of the bottle, placing it carefully back where he had found it. "It has come to my attention," he began smoothly," that the Catalyst is unstable, especially in water, and that due to this, its effectiveness is extremely limited. Or have I been misinformed?"

Callister was taken aback by the comment. Not because it was untrue, but rather because he had himself only read the reports that morning.

"No, you have not," admitted Callister.

Lugenet pursed his lips in contemplation, "And what of the delivery system?" he continued.

In an effort to regain some level of control, Callister walked to his wet bar and poured himself a drink. Downing it in one gulp he poured himself another, this time dropping some ice into his glass.

Callister had found liquor to be one of the more satisfying sensations he had experienced since his taking of a human vessel. The way its warmth burned his throat and stomach, then spread to the rest of his body was so soothing, the lightness it gave his mind, liberating.

Since occupying this body a little over a year before, he had experienced many other wonderful sensations. His senses were overwhelmed by the complexity of gourmet food, the exhilarating power of signing a lethal finding to terminate an enemy of the state, and especially the explosive feeling of sex, particularly if that sex was with a young and enthusiastic intern.

Shaking off his momentary distraction, Callister returned to the topic at hand. "Aerosol delivery is the most effective, but inefficient. It would require production of ten times more of the compound than our current capacity is capable of. Not to mention the need to develop the equipment to deliver it."

Lugenet pondered for a moment, "How then do we target a large city?" he asked.

"At this point, dispersal via water supply is the only reasonable method," said Callister as he returned to the desk, ice tinkling in his glass as he walked.

"So, then the catalyst's solubility in water looms as a fatal flaw," pressed Lugenet.

"It would seem so," said Callister, "However..."

But Callister was not permitted to finished his sentence as Lugenet slammed his hand down on the desk cutting him off. Rising to his feet Lugenet leaned across the desk, his eyes once again becoming red and blue electric arcs crawling over black pools, their intensity so fierce that they cast a purple glow on Callister's face.

When Lugenet spoke, his voice took on an ominous booming, "Let me be as clear as possible. Once the celestial shift is set in motion, there will be no stopping it. The seven seals will fracture and open in rapid succession. A celestial machine designed for one purpose: to return my fallen children to their rightful place. For this to happen, each piece must work in perfect timing with the next. The catalyst is a vital part of that machine. I will leave none of my children behind, and none of it to chance."

As he stared at Callister, his eyes increased in intensity, "And if it is not ready when I call for it..."

Lugenet's face went blank, his eyes returning to normal as the fury of his presence subsided. The charm that had manipulated leaders of state around the world returned. Sitting back down he took a deep cleansing breath, then found himself distracted by the pen on the desk. Picking it up he scribbled on the blotter. Apparently impressed by its quality he slipped it into his coat pocket, then standing he walked to the door without regarding Callister. "Solve the problem," he said, reaching for the door.

Callister choked back his anger saying nothing.

"And Douglas?"

"Yes sir?"

"If you ever call me Andre again, I'll rip you out of that meat suit and scatter your Light to the edges of this universe." Then pulling open the door, he walked out without waiting for a response.

Callister stood looking at the door as it clicked shut, his knuckles white as he clenched his fists in rage. After a moment he composed himself and walked to his desk. Draining his cocktail, he sat down and pressed his intercom.

"Linda?"

"Yes, Mr. President?"

"Please get Dr. Bains on the phone."

"Yes sir."

"And would you please ask Monica to bring in a fresh box of cigars?"

FOUR

Chance's stomach growled. Looking up at the clock on the classroom wall he saw, with relief, that his fourth period physics lab was almost over, and lunch would soon be served.

The cause of his hunger was easy to explain. The intensity of coach McCune's early morning strength and conditioning sessions had ticked up considerably once it had become clear that the Spartans would be going to the playoffs. Consequently, Chance's hunger never seemed to be quite sated, and at this moment it gnawed at him. When the dismissal bell finally chimed, he quickly grabbed his backpack and headed out the door.

The hallway was already filled with students on their way to lunch. As Chance followed the crowd, he could smell the culinary aromas of the kitchen wafting in the air, which only served to sharpen his hunger. Walking into the dining hall he saw that it was already half full. Hanging his backpack on a coat hook near the door, he turned and walked down a short hall to the washroom.

As Chance came around the corner, it was just in time to see Martin Wellington hand a small plastic bag of white tablets to a female student. The girl looked at Chance nervously-the proverbial "deer in the headlights"- then bolted, pushing past Chance to make her escape. Martin, on the other hand, had the look of a cornered animal, that didn't mind being cornered.

Regarding Chance with an expression of supreme arrogance and con-tempt, Martin withdrew a butterfly knife from his pocket, and opened it with a flourish. But his bravado faded when he saw Jäger standing behind Chance, watching intently. Jäger's stare unnerved Martin, the boy's eyes boring into him with an uncharacteristic intensity.

Martin's eyes flittered from Jäger to Chance, and back as he calculated the situation. Coming to the conclusion that this was not the time or place to settle any scores, he flipped his knife closed, then pushing past Chance he fled down the hall.

Chance watched Martin go, then turned to Jäger only to find that the boy was gone. Finding himself alone, he made his way to the washroom.

As Chance washed his hands, he contemplated Martin. It was easy to see that the kid was out of control. Over the years Chance had grown accustomed to the youngest member of the Wellington family taking advantage of his legacy status to avoid the consequences of his actions, and Chance couldn't really blame him. But lately Martin had changed. His usual anti-social personality had become tinged with an angry malevolence, and now Chance saw a possible reason why. Martin was selling drugs, and was probably using them himself.

The reality of drugs on campus was just that, a reality. As long as there were students who wanted them, there would be opportunists like Martin that would provide them. The fact that Chance didn't like it, changed nothing.

Walking out of the washroom Chance headed for the dining hall, looking forward to being with his friends. The dining hall at Wellington was an ornate affair, more suited to a meeting of Parliament, than the feeding of high school students. The hand carved wood paneling, thirty-foot arched ceilings, and massive stained-glass window at one end of the room, created an environment of unsurpassed splendor. For this reason, and much to the chagrin of the stodgier members of the faculty, the students referred to the elegant facility as 'Hogwarts'.

Normally the room was filled with round, six-foot, carved oak tables, covered with white linen tablecloths. But today was a 'Day of Champions', and so the middle of the room was dominated by a long banquet table reserved exclusively for the Spartan baseball team. As Chance moved through the line, he saw that most of the team was already seated, the crested Spartan helmet emblems on the backs of their Letterman's jackets looking like a phalanx of ancient Greek warriors.

"Hey, there he is," called out Conor, smiling as Chance approached.

The other boys at the table also shouted their greetings. As Chance took his seat he smiled and waved to his teammates seated up and down the table, clasping the hands of those nearby.

Chance found it difficult to articulate the comfort he took in just being in the presence of this group of young men he thought of as family. And while he loved them all, there were two, Eric and Conor, that he knew would always be there for him, as he would be for them. Sitting back, he relaxed, enjoying the playful jabs and trash talk of this band of brothers.

"So, what did you think of the Chem exam?" Chance asked.

Conor put his hands to his head and mimed his brain exploding. "If the final exam is anything like that, I'll have to go to summer school just to graduate," he snorted.

"Dude, relax," chimed Eric, "with all of the pro scouts looking at you, you could fail the whole semester and still be a millionaire before you're old enough to buy beer."

"He could always hire someone to buy it for him," suggested Chance.

"Great," said Conor, "I'll be a wealthy, drunk, high school dropout."

"Your parents will be so proud," said Chance, dryly.

"Okay, okay, Conor's questionable academic success is not at the moment my concern..." said Eric. A comment which resulted in Conor to flipping him the bird.

"Yeah, right back at ya," said Eric. "Anyway, what is my concern at this moment, is the party I'm planning tonight at haunted beach." Placing his arm around Chances shoulders he smiled at his friend, "You're coming, right?"

"I'm so there, I need to decompress," replied Chance.

"That's my boy," said Eric satisfied that his event was coming together as planned. "That leaves just one final detail to nail down."

As if on cue, a sweetly melodic voice, with a strong Italian accent, interrupted their conversation, "Hello Eric," the voice said.

Eric smiled broadly as he winked at Chance. "I do believe my final detail has arrived," he said.

Turning in his seat, Eric's eyes fell upon Isabella Di'Amecci, a beautiful Italian foreign exchange student. "Well, hello, Bella," he said as he took the girl's hand and kissed it tenderly. "What can I do to make your life worth living?"

Bella giggled.

Conor rolled his eyes, "How does he get away with that shit?" he whispered to Chance.

Chance smile and shook his head, "I don't know bro, but he does."

"I heard that the team is having a party tonight," said Bella.

"I may be planning a small, exclusive soirée," said Eric in a mock snobby English accent. "Would you be interested in attending?"

Bella and Eric had been dating for a few weeks, and she was well aware of his eccentricities, so folding her arms she played along. "Yes," she said, with slight smirk.

Well, I don't know," said Eric, still in character. "I mean, the guest list is already set, and the caterer would have to be called..."

Bella began to pout. Taking Eric's hand in hers she began to nibble and kiss his fingertips. "Please Eric, I promise, you will have so much more fun if I am there," she cooed.

"Well, my dear, you do make a compelling argument. I guess you will just have to be there," said Eric tapping his phone. "There, I just sent you a text with all the information."

"May I bring a friend?" asked Bella

"You may bring anyone and as lovely as you, my dear."

Bella blew him a kiss then turned and walked away, giggling as she joined arms with her friend.

Conor watched them go, his eyes making contact with those of the Japanese girl with Bella.

Chance was amused by it all, and shook his head smiling, but his smile faded as his attention was drawn across the room to where Martin and Travis had just walked into Hogwarts.

Martin scanned the room like a predator, but like every successful businessman, he was multitasking.

"We're almost out of Oxy and Adderall," said Martin, his eyes moving over the room.

"I don't work again till Monday," replied Travis warily, "but don't worry, I'll be able to get my dad's keys for sure. He's working on some project for the government, so he'll be there late."

"Just get it," snapped Martin threateningly.

"Yeah, yeah. No problem," said Travis in a worried tone of voice.

But Martin was no longer listening. The predator's eyes had found what he was looking for, and he began moving across the room with purpose.

Jäger had no idea what was coming. He was sitting off to the side of the dining hall in his usual place, and as always, alone. Many wondered why he even bothered to come to Hogwarts at all, since he only ever picked at his food, his beautifully androgynous face moving almost imperceptibly as he ate.

Jäger never spoke unless directly addressed, and then only enough to answer a question with as few words as possible, before falling once again hauntingly silent. As a result, no one knew much about him, but almost everyone at Wellington knew who he was.

Jäger was a senior, but looked like a young freshman. His social interaction was nonexistent. He had no friends that anyone knew of, and what family he had, if any, was a mystery.

It was widely known that Jäger was at Wellington on a full ride academic scholarship due to his perfect scores on the school's entrance exam, but what people knew most about him was the power of his art.

His first pieces were just pencil sketches on the back of his homework. These sketches were eye-popping not only for their technical skill and artistry, but also for their subject matter. Almost every figure in his drawings was a nude. And not just nude, but nude at a level of realistic idealism that caused those who saw them to feel uncomfortable, and in many cases, inadequate.

It was this reaction to his art that resulted in an investigation being initiated during the first few months of his freshmen year. Upon discovering the provocative drawings on Jäger's homework, an anal-retentive teacher took them to an anal-retentive counselor, who called the police. After an anal-retentive sex crimes detective saw them, they all had a collective anal-retentive hissy fit.

It was their collective opinion that no child could render the naked human form in such intimate detail, without that child having been the victim of sexual abuse. But as hard as they tried, nothing could be found, or even contrived, to support such an allegation. In the end the administration, and law enforcement, were forced to concede to the only conclusion left to them. Jäger's art was the result of genius, not abuse.

For Jäger, his aptitude in mathematics and science only served to alienate him from the other students, but his art, on the other hand, caused many to try to engage with him. Unfortunately, no one had much luck. ultimately, most just gave up, politely ignoring his oddness.

To Martin, however, Jäger's passive nature made him appear weak and defenseless. It made Martin furious that this weird little kid had insinuated himself into his personal business, and this was, at least in Martin's mind, a gross display of disrespect. A display that could not go unpunished.

Martin moved up behind Jäger, looming over him like a panther in a tree, eyes cold and fixed on the helpless boy. Reaching down he picked up Jäger's glass of milk and emptied it over the unsuspecting boy's head.

"Whoa!" said Chance when he saw Martin's bold cruelty.

"What?" asked Conor looking up, but by the time he turned around, Chance was already moving around the end of the table. Seeing this Conor pushed back his chair and followed his friend.

Conor's sudden movement attracted Eric's attention. "What's going on?" he asked, rising from his seat and moving up beside his friend.

"Not sure," said Conor as he observed Chance making a direct line toward Martin and Travis, "but we had a run in with these two shitheads first period, so stay frosty."

Martin stood looking down at Jäger as the small boy sat motionless, hands pressed flat on the table, fingernails white from the pressure. He kept his eyes cast down, his hair hanging about his face, dripping with milk.

In a flash of anger, Martin slapped the back of Jäger's head, causing it to snap forward. "You need to mind your own business, freak," said Martin, intoxicated by his power over the boy.

But Jäger did not respond. His face remained expressionless, his demeanor calm and unflinching, and this infuriated Martin all the more.

"Hey, retard, he's talking to you," taunted Travis, feeling the rush of the violent scene, and wanting to join in.

Anger surged through Martin as he looked at Jäger in disgust. He could not, would not, allow this pathetic weakling to ignore him. In a rage he drew back his hand to strike Jäger yet again, when he was violently shoved away, falling over the chairs of an unoccupied table nearby.

"Leave him alone, Martin," said Chance as he positioned himself between predator and prey.

Martin scrambled back to his feet and squared off with Chance, just as Eric and Conor stepped up beside him.

"Mind your own business, jock," snarled Martin.

"I'm making it my business," said Chance through clenched teeth.

"What gives you the right to tell me what to do?" said Martin.

"Dude, don't you remember?" quipped Conor. "We own the whole school."

"You're pretty brave with a little kid," menaced Chance. "How about you mess with someone who'll break your jaw for ya?"

Martin looked from Chance to Conor, then Eric and lastly to the table where twenty-two jacketed Spartan athletes sat watching the exchange intently. "And you're pretty brave as long as you got a pack of apes backing you up," he finally spat.

Hearing this, Eric pressed in close. "Then how 'bout you and me take a walk over to the stadium so we can have some alone time?"

The boys stared at each other, violence on a hair trigger, when the tension was broken by a voice.

"Is there a problem here?"

Everyone turned as coach McCune positioned himself in the midst of the confrontation, his booming voice reverberating in the room, its tenor defusing the situation completely.

"No, sir. Just promoting a safe educational environment," responded Conor, smiling at his own cleverness. But then he always cracked himself up.

Coach McCune, on the other hand, was in no mood. Unblinkingly, he stared at Conor until all humor had drained from the boy's face.

Next McCune turned and glared at the rest of the team watching from the table, which caused those boys to turn away, becoming suddenly fascinated by the food on their lunch trays. Burying their faces in their mid-day meals, they tried hard to look like they weren't looking.

"Uh-huh," dead-panned McCune as he scanned the group of boys. "Martin, you and Travis are late for trash duty. Since you seem to be finished with your lunch, you can move out."

Inwardly, Martin was relieved to be able to get out of the situation intact. Outwardly, he stared aggressively at Chance as he walked away, Travis trailing behind.

"You three go finish eating," McCune said, then looking Conor in the eye he added, "And you, leave the educational environment to me."

"Yes sir," came their unison reply.

As Chance turned to leave, he noticed that Jäger had once again vanished. On the table only his tray of mostly untouched food still remained, along with two scorch marks, as if someone had left two small, hand shaped, irons burning on the white linen too long.

FIVE

Ribbons of low-lying fog crept across the roadway, like boney fingers, as a government-plated S.U.V. cut through the early morning mist. The road was damp, and as droplets accumulated on the windscreen, the windshield wipers came on intermittently to wipe them away.

The driver was U.S. Army Corporal Jeremy Winters. He had been assigned to this detail for the last four months, and every morning, Monday through Friday, he would wake up at 0430 hours, dress in his class A uniform, then draw a vehicle from the motor pool. At 0600 hours he would arrive at the home of Dr. Sabine Bains, walk to the door and ring the bell. What happened next, was nothing less than magical.

First, he would hear her delicate heels clicking on the hardwood floor as she came to the door, and his heart would begin to race as the seconds crept by. When at last he heard her hand on the door's latch, he was sure his heart stopped.

As her front door opened, the experience was overwhelming. Her scent, her... essence, rolled over him, surrounded him, teased him. He found it sensuous, intoxicating, and intensely arousing.

Sabine Bains always took Jeremy's arm as he escorted her to the waiting vehicle, her full breasts straining against her blouse as they reacted to the cool morning air. Jeremy could feel their weight against his arm as they strolled together, and he often lamented that her walkway wasn't longer.

When they got to the S.U.V., Jeremy would open the door for her. Before releasing her hold on him, Sabine Bains would smile sweetly and give his bicep a playful squeeze.

As she slid into the back seat, the young soldier would inhale her. He was sure he could taste her in the air, both sweetness and spice rolling on his tongue. Finally, she would pull her legs into the vehicle, causing the slit in her skirt to fall open just far enough to be unprofessional.

His eyes would travel over her body, caressing her with his gaze, and when their eyes met, he knew she had caught him looking once again. Embarrassed, he would close the door and hurry around to the driver's side, hoping his arousal wasn't obvious.

For the next hour, as he drove Dr. Bains to her destination, Jeremy was in sweet agony. And while he understood why, he was at a loss as to how to explain it rationally.

True enough, Dr. Bains, or Sabine as she preferred to be called, was a beautiful woman. But her appearance alone was not enough to justify Jeremy's reaction to her. Whenever he was near her, she drove him completely insane with desire.

Jeremy Winters had been in love before, and he had been in lust before, but neither of these two emotions came close to describing what he felt for Sabine Bains. Not love, not lust, but something so much more base, more primal, even...visceral.

He had shown a photo of her to his buddies in his army unit, and universally they had opined that while yeah, she was an attractive woman, she wasn't all that hot. At least not hot enough to justify Jeremy's reaction to her. For Jeremy, however, the opinions of his friends were irrelevant because he knew that from the moment Sabine opened her front door, until he returned her to her home at night, he would be consumed by her.

For the moment at least, Sabine Bains sat quietly in the back seat, her reading glasses, which Jeremy was pretty sure she didn't actually need, perched adorably on the end of her nose as she typed on her laptop.

The black S.U.V. wound its way along a rural mountain road, Jeremy's attention flittering between duty and desire as he stole glimpses of Bains in his rearview mirror. During one of these flirtations with desire, while lost in his painful longing, Jeremy failed to notice that his vehicle had drifted toward the shoulder of the road. When the right-side tires dropped off the pavement, the unexpected jolt startled him, but he quickly brought the S.U.V. under control.

Looking into his mirror, Jeremy's eyes met those of his obsession sparkling back at him and she smiled, amused and flattered by his loss of concentration. Jeremy turned a deep red. He vowed to himself to keep his eyes on the road and avoid distraction, but a few minutes later, he once again glanced back at Dr. Bains, hopelessly distracted.

When at last the car began to slow, Dr. Sabine Bains peeked up over her glasses and saw that they had arrived at their destination. Corporal Winters turned his vehicle onto a nondescript, paved forest road that disappeared into a dark tree line. Easing along the road, they passed a sign that read simply, "Restricted Area, U.S. Army Military Facility, White Mountain."

A hundred meters further the S.U.V. entered a clearing and approached a checkpoint at a gate in a ten-foot security fence that surrounded the complex. Beyond the fence loomed a massive concrete building patrolled by soldiers in black fatigues, its appearance so stark that it would have been easy to mistake it for a prison.

The S.U.V. came to a smooth stop at the facility's security checkpoint and a black uniformed soldier, with an assault rifle slung across his chest, stepped out of the guard shack. Thick necked and barrel chested, the guard was an imposing figure that looked like he had fallen out of an Army recruiting poster.

Jeremy mockingly called him, Captain America, but never to his face. As he approached, Dr. Bains leaned forward and handed her ID card to Jeremy, who then lowered his window. The guard took both I.D.s, but didn't look at them. Instead, he lowered his smiling, ruggedly handsome face to look through the window and into the back seat. Ignoring Corporal Winters, he instead focused all of his attention on Dr. Sabine Bains.

"Good morning, Sabine. You look beautiful as always," said Captain America, flashing his toothy smile.

"Good morning, Brian. And you look handsome as always," replied Bains, flirtatiously.

Jeremy watched Bains through his mirror, jealousy surging through him. But when Bains looked up at him and met his eyes, he looked away, embarrassed and confused by his emotions. After a long moment, the guard returned the I.D.s and waved the vehicle through.

"You have a wonderful day Sabine," he said.

"And you as well, Brian."

Jeremy sped away through the checkpoint, more aggressively than necessary, and immediately felt foolish for doing so. Bains just smiled.

The S.U.V. pulled up to the front entrance of the monolithic-looking building and parked. Getting out, Jeremy ran around to the rear door and opened it for Dr. Bains. He watched as she slid out off of her seat, the slit in her skirt seemingly to have inched even higher than when she had gotten in. The length of exposed thigh that extended from the door was breathtaking as Jeremy offered his hand to her.

"Your identification, ma'am," said Jeremy holding out her credentials.

"Ma'am?" said Bains, noting his uncharacteristic formality.

His formality did sound odd, but he couldn't help himself. He was still a little miffed at the attention she had given Captain America, but his upset withered as she looked at him, her lips pouting.

"Oh Jeremy, you know how I hate that word," she said as she touched his face lovingly. "I will be in the building all day, but I look forward to seeing you this evening. I will call you when I'm ready to leave. Now you be sure to keep your eyes on the road."

She winked and he melted, blushing as he forgot why he had been upset. "I will...Sabine."

Bains smiled and walked into the building, leaving Corporal Jeremy Winters standing by the S.U.V. feeling like a lovesick idiot.

SIX

Dr. Sabine Bains entered her office and immediately her eyes focused on an ornate floral display sitting on her desk. It would have been hard to miss, even if it were only a single blossom. Bains' office did not reflect her warm and flirtatious public facade. It was empty and cold, the only furnishings being a desk and a high-backed office chair. There was no guest chair, as Bains did not invite visitors to linger. She did not want anyone to be comfortable in her space.

To the right of her desk was a small steel tea service. Other than that, the room was bare, no art, no plants, no personal touches, nothing. For this reason, the shock of color brought by the bouquet of two dozen roses on her desk was especially startling.

Setting her briefcase and purse aside, Bains strolled to her desk and plucked the card from the display. 'Always thinking of you.'

Bains puzzled for a moment, then called out, "Mama?"

"Yes, my dear?" replied Mrs. Sybil Ross as she entered the office.

Mrs. Ross was an elderly woman with a pleasant, nurturing disposition. She spoke with a slight English accent and dressed in an almost matronly style, her only eccentricity being that she always wore long gloves that reached up to her elbows.

Bains called her 'Mama', but they were not related. Everyone else called her 'Mrs. Ross' though no one could recall ever hearing about a 'Mr.' Ross.

As Mrs. Ross approached, Bains just pointed at the flowers with a question in her eyes.

"Dr. Shelby," explained Mrs. Ross. "He seems quite smitten."

Dr. Bains smiled as she gently smelled the colorful arrangement. "Take them away, please," she said.

Without comment Mrs. Ross picked up the vase full of roses and strolled out of the office.

Dr. Bains dropped the card into the waste basket and walked to her tea service. Scooping loose leaf tea into an antique silver tea strainer she placed it in a porcelain cup and added boiling water. Her face took on a peaceful expression as she inhaled deeply the aromatic steam rising from her cup. Dipping the strainer, she walked to her desk, sat down, and began to read her emails. As she read, a window opened on her computer, and the face of Mrs. Ross appeared.

"Yes, Mama?" said Bains.

"You have a video conference call from Dr. Shelby."

Dr. Thomas Shelby was the owner, administer and CEO of the Havenhurst Psychiatric Hospital. As a private, for-profit facility the prestigious hospital was widely perceived as being on the cutting edge of psychiatric research. So, when the U.S. Army, and specifically Dr. Sabine Bains, had offered a lucrative government contract to Havenhurst to assist in some next level psychological warfare research, Dr. Shelby had jumped at the opportunity. Jumped not only for the sake of the science, but also because it would require his spending many hours in close work with the intoxicating Sabine Bains.

"Put him through, please," said Bains.

The window showing Mrs. Ross instantly vanished, only to be replaced by the face of Dr. Thomas Shelby. His broad smile beaming through his beard, along with his signature bow tie, gave him a goofy appearance that caused Bains to smirk.

"Good morning, Sabine," he said brightly. "Did they arrive?"

"Good morning, Thomas. Yes, they did."

Dr. Shelby's voice took on a conspiratorial tone as he looked around the room where he was seated to ensure that he was not overheard. "I hope you liked them."

"They are beautiful," cooed Bains. "I have them right here on my desk."

She gestured out of view of the camera to the empty space on her desk where the flowers had once stood.

Upon hearing this, Dr. Shelby beamed like a school boy that had just learned that he was the teacher's pet.

"So, how can I help you?" asked Bains.

Slightly embarrassed, he shook off his lovesick stupor and got down to the purpose of his call.

"Ah, yes," he stammered, "Have you reviewed the notes and data for the latest round of tests yet?"

She clicked on an email titled 'Batch 237 Results'. Looking it over she leaned back and sipped her tea. "I see them here, but I just got in, and have not had an opportunity to read them," she pouted. 'Would you be a dear and summarize them for me?"

Dr. Shelby was always willing to do anything to please his Sabine. He would sacrifice anything for her. The fact that he had been married for over twenty years was an inconvenient truth that seemed to flitter out of his consciousness whenever she was near him, or even spoke to him from a distance, as she did now.

"I would be happy to," he replied, settling into his seat. "As you know, batch 237 was administered to a cohort of twelve subjects ranging from eighteen to fifty-one years of age. All subjects, with the exception of one anomaly succumbed to the compound immediately upon aerosol application."

"An anomaly?" said Bains, scanning the data.

"Yes," replied Shelby, clearly excited by a result that created a new mystery. "Subject seven, an eighteen-year-old female, showed complete resistance to the compound."

All pleasantry drained from Bains' face. "No effect at all?"

"None whatsoever," confirmed Shelby.

"Did you increase the dosage?"

"Yes, I doubled it, then administered an intravenous dosage, but there was still no effect."

Bains looked at the screen, tapping her fingers rhythmically on her desk, thinking. "I want to examine this anomaly myself," she finally said.

Shelby smiled. "I thought you might, so I have arranged for an examination room this evening."

Upon hearing this, Bains relaxed. Her normal, affable expression returned as she once again leaned back sipping her tea, much to Shelby's relief. "Excellent, I will see you at eight then," she said, not bothering to ask if that time worked for him.

"Shall we meet for dinner first?" asked Shelby hopefully.

"I'm sorry, my dear, but I will be in the lab all day, and will be writing reports until then."

"Oh, okay...well..." stammered Shelby, obviously disappointed.

"I will see you at eight, Thomas," said Bains, gently but firmly.

"See you then," he said, forcing a smile just as Bains closed the call.

Bains sat quietly, watching steam rise in twisting tendrils from her cup as she contemplated her conversation with Shelby, and the data on her screen. She did not like the presence of an anomaly. True, it was only the first subject in these trials to be resistant, but in such a small sample, it was statistically significant. Beyond that, just the very idea that this human would not do as she desired, infuriated her. But before her fury could spark, her thoughts were interrupted by the sound of Mrs. Ross at her office door.

"Dearie, they are ready for you in the lab," she said, cheerfully.

"Thank you, Mama. Tell them I'm on my way."

Bains rose and removed her jewelry, placing it in an ornate silver box on her desk. She primped for a moment in the reflection in the window, then taking a deep breath, walked purposefully out of her office.

As she walked past Mrs. Ross' desk, she saw Dr. Shelby's flowers adorning it. Mrs. Ross was arranging them, humming softly to herself. Bains smiled and winked at the woman as she passed by.

Mrs. Ross smiled back cheerfully. "You two have fun," she said, her eyes sparkling.

Turning into the hallway, Bains strolled along, her heels clicking rhythmically on the tiled floor. Stopping at a thick glass door, she entered a six-digit code into a touch pad. The door buzzed open, and she walked through.

On the other side was a bank of elevators and a guard in black fatigues. He stood at an elevator with a red door, watching as Bains placed her hand on a palm scanner. She waited patiently as the scanner glowed for a moment. When a green light came on that read 'Access Granted'; the elevator door slid open.

Bains entered the elevator, giving the guard a seductive sideways glance as she walked by. He smiled uncomfortably, resisting the impulse to reach out and touch her. He always wanted to touch her it seemed. As the door closed, he stepped back lightheaded, both grateful and disappointed that she was gone.

When the elevator opened again, Bains stepped out into a short corridor. At its end was an intimidating steel door that looked more suited for a bank vault than a research laboratory.

Beside the door was an optical scanner which Bains approached and peered into. The device hummed as it crisscrossed her eye with beams of light. After a moment there was a whirring sound followed by a heavy metallic clunk as the door swung open, hissing as the pressure inside equalized.

Passing through the imposing door she entered a small stainless-steel room and pressed a red illuminated button on the wall. The heavy door closed behind her and the room began to pressurize. After a few seconds the red light on the wall turned green and a second door at the other end of the small room opened.

Beyond that threshold was a dressing room, and Bains began to disrobe, placing her clothes on a steel valet. Once she was naked, she walked to the shower room. Steam rose from the extremely hot water as she scrubbed her body and washed her hair with antibacterial soap. When she was finished, she toweled dry, then dressed in a disposable paper gown and slippers. Pressing a call button on the wall, she sat down on a stool in the middle of the room and waited, her long wet hair tied back tightly.

After a few minutes two technicians in Hazmat suits, wearing rubber gloves and respirators, entered the room. Bains rose as they approached. Taking hold of her by the arms, they escorted her out of the dressing room.

Flanking her, they walked wordlessly down a bright white hall to a glass wall with a door that slid open as they reached it. As they entered, the door slid shut. Extending their arms from their bodies and slowly turning in what looked like a bizarre piece of performance art, they were enveloped by stiff streams of air. After a few seconds the airflow stopped, and a door at the other end of the room opened.

The trio proceeded down a long corridor to a pair of stainless-steel doors, each having a large round window at its center. Beyond the doors seemed to be only darkness.

Pushing open the doors, the technicians led Bains into a laboratory dominated by what looked like a high-tech operating table. The lab was like a black hole. The walls, ceiling, even the floor were covered with a black rubberized material making the room so dark that only the lab equipment and the various medical devices around the room, stood in contrast. Highly focused beams of light illuminated the various work stations arranged around the room, and the light sparkled off their polished metal surfaces like a thousand tiny suns.

Personnel in scrubs were moving about the room consulting monitors, lost in their preparation checklists. Technicians in white lab coats could be seen through the window of a large control room twenty feet above the laboratory floor going through preparations of their own. None of them seemed to pay the slightest attention to the half-naked woman and her Hazmat-suited escort entering the lab and walking to the table.

As one of the techs knelt and eased Bains' slippers off her feet, the other untied her paper gown and slipped it off her shoulders. Once again naked, Bains padded to the table, her footfalls undetectable on the black rubberized floor.

With the assistance of the two techs, Bains eased herself up onto the table and reclined. Extending her arms, she rested them on the small platforms that protruded from the sides of the table. Lying there she looked like a convicted murderer awaiting a lethal injection. She waited patiently as she was secured to the table with thick metal shackles. But while her demeanor was calm, it was clear to all that she was becoming more and more agitated. Her breathing was rapid and short, her muscles taught. As an EKG was attached to her, it immediately began to register a heart rate of nearly 200 beats per minute, and increasing.

Once Bains was secure, her attendants signaled the control room, and the lights in the lab immediately changed from white to ultraviolet. In the purple cast of the U.V. lighting, an opalescent, smoky haze could be seen hovering around Bains' body. It rose in twisting fingers of eerie yellow iridescence that swirled around her and clung to the technicians as they worked.

A cannula was placed under her nose, then the techs stepped back, nodding again to the control room. As they did a clear plastic cowling, molded in the shape of a human body, lowered from the ceiling.

The human shaped shell was sealed to the table, completely encasing Bains. The techs then began to attach an array of hoses and data cables to the contour hugging form. When this was completed, a vacuum began to pull at the yellow mist around her body, drawing it into the hoses.

When all of the attendants had completed their tasks, the table began to tilt up until it reached a forty-five-degree angle. As the table locked into position, an electric motor came to life and one wall of the lab began to open. Behind it was a second laboratory, identical in every way, but for one. In the second lab, the subject encased in the clear shroud on the table, was a man.

He was young, in his early twenties, and shockingly handsome. His long, wavy blond hair, wet and pulled back, his perfectly muscled body glistening. At first, he appeared to be unconscious, his nude body motionless in the purple hue of the U.V. lights. From his body rose a blueish fog that encircled him in wisping eddies across the surface of his skin, until it was vacuumed away through the hoses attached to the shroud encasing him.

Sabine Bains stared across the room, intensely aware of his presence. Her eyes locked on him, hungry and yearning. She watched in rapt anticipation, as the cannula under his nose began to fill with the glowing yellow mist that had been harvested from her, waiting for the reaction she knew was coming. And she was not disappointed.

When her essence reached his nose, his eyes flew open, wild and burning with passion. His body tensed as his manhood became engorged, pointing accusingly across the room at her. He strained as he fought against his restraints, trying to reach her.

Next the cannula under Bains' nose began to fill with the blue mist of his essence, and again her anticipation was obvious. When the blue vapor hit her nose, her body lurched and undulated, goosebumps dotting her flesh as evidence of her arousal ran in silvery trails down the inside of her thighs.

As they breathed in each other's essence, the colorful florescent clouds surrounding their bodies intensified, growing brighter and thicker before being vacuumed away. Around the lab, technicians scurried about, monitoring their equipment and making adjustments.

The male roared his frustration, his eyes pools of oily black, with irises that glowed like burning embers bound by a web of crackling red electric power. Bains roared back at him. Her eyes as his, her desire as his. She strained, pushing her hips towards him in a vain attempt to touch him.

In the control room above, the technicians ignored the erotic argument taking place before them. Instead, they watched their monitors as the florescent blue and yellow vapors were collected, condensed and loaded into a centrifuge. All indicators were showing green. Another successful harvest had begun.

Hours later, Dr. Sabine Bains was led naked, down the hall to the dressing room. She was in an obviously weakened state. Wobbling unsteadily on her feet, she had to be assisted by her two attendants. Across her back and buttocks were deep scratches and welts, as if she had been mauled by a tiger.

Arriving in the locker room, the attendants walked her into the shower and left her there alone. Gripping the wall for balance, she let the water wash over her.

In another part of the lab, a technician peered into a sealed chamber. Using robotic arms, she lifted a glass vial containing a bright green fluid from a centrifuge, and carefully placed it in a liquid nitrogen storage unit. Wisps of white vapor poured from the device as the vial was dropped into an empty slot, filling the first of seven spaces. Behind it, five empty racks sat waiting. Beside it one full rack of seven vials sparkled in the frost.

SEVEN

The walls of the great edifice groaned under the strain of the immense pressure bearing down on them. It was palpable and increasing, as the empty space awaited the deluge to come. And then, with a pleasant chime, it broke.

As the classroom doors of Wellington Preparatory Academy burst open, a flood of students poured into the hallways. Chattering excitedly, they rushed toward the exits and the joyous freedom of the weekend beyond.

As the students surged through the imposing facade of the school's main entrance, they began to shed their formal school attire as if by doing so they would escape the oppressive control those symbols imposed.

Blazers were removed, ties pulled down, hair unbound and allowed to hang unfettered. Some students gathered in groups planning their weekends, while those with plans best kept private slunk away whispering conspiratorially.

A line of expensive cars and limousines waited at the curb to whisk away those who would be going home for the weekend. Some students were embraced by a loving parent, others were met by the emotionless gaze of thick-necked bodyguards, annoyed by the fact that all of their training had only prepared them to be little more than well-armed babysitters.

In the distance the metallic ring of an aluminum bat hitting a baseball, could be heard as the Spartan baseball team was put through their afternoon workout. The practice was relatively light due to the team having played the night before. Still, Coach McCune was not the sort to take his foot off the gas completely, so he was running his boys through an infield drill. Not so much because they needed it, but rather, because he just loved to watch them work, and there was one member of his infield that he enjoyed watching the most.

McCune had been a student of the game of baseball since he was a boy. In all that time he had never seen such fluid grace and skill as Chance Jordan working the infield.

Nothing got by Chance. If a ball was hit anywhere near him, grounder or line drive, he would haul it in. Once he did, he would display the dexterity and shear grace of Baryshnikov as he flipped it to Eric Easton at second base, or turned in mid-air and fired a cannon shot to first.

McCune was also impressed by the intuitive interaction Chance displayed with Eric Easton at second base. It seemed to McCune that Chance and Eric were of a single mind, each instinctively putting themselves into position and having blind faith that the other would be exactly where they needed to be. Even the pro scouts looking at Conor Jackson had noticed.

Satisfied by what he had seen, McCune called the team in and walked to the pitcher's mound. Standing with his hands on his hips he waited until the boys had taken a knee around him, ready to hear his analysis of the day's work.

As the boys expected, McCune began to pluck the psychological strings needed to mentally prepare his warriors for the challenge ahead. This daily preaching of baseball philosophy was lovingly referred to by the team as McCune's "Sermons on the mound."

When his sermon was done, he called his faithful to their feet and in a display of unity and pride they shouted, "Spartans!" then jogged off the field toward the locker room. As they did, plans were being finalized.

"You got everything?" asked Eric as he jogged beside Conor.

"Yeah," replied Conor, "The truck is loaded with wood, I got the ice tub, and Rheinhard is bringing the ice."

"Excellent," said Eric. "Danny is bringing a pony keg, and I procured four cases of Dos Eques from my dad's cellar while I was home last week. Those are just for our fire."

Chance looked at Eric, dubious, "Four whole cases?"

"Yeah," confirmed Eric.

"You didn't drink any?"

Eric's lips pressed into a tin line. "A few," he finally confessed, smiling his pirate's smile. "It was a transport tax."

At this the group laughed and horse played their way to the locker room. Once there they began to shower and dress. The whole locker room was buzzing about that evening's plans.

"Hey, Conor!" shouted Chance above the din, "Is anyone riding with you?"

"Yeah, Kimiko," said Conor, smiling broadly. "She said she would bring some sandwiches."

Eric's phone had been blowing up with last minute texts regarding the party, but upon hearing this news, he paused for a moment and looked up at Conor. "Kimiko, huh?" he said with a devilish grin.

"Are you impressed yet?" said Conor.

"I'll be impressed if you can stay on for the full eight seconds," said Eric, shaking his head. "There is something wonderfully twisted about that girl. She comes off all sweet and shy, but I sense a dark side in her that I don't think she can keep quiet for long."

Eric went back to his phone, but Conor just stood there, looking at him dumbly.

"What's twisted about her?" he asked with trepidation, but Eric had returned to his phone, absorbed in party preparations.

Eric was the social center of Wellington. If there was a party of any consequence going on, it was a safe bet that he was pulling the strings. And if there were girls around, you could be sure he would be laying down his game.

Eric's panache for social planning came from his mother who was a respected member of Boston's high society. He had grown up watching his mother put together hundreds of major events, so for him, planning was second nature. Not that Eric's experience was unique at Wellington.

At Wellington, the rich came in two flavors: old money and new money. Old money was America's financial and social royalty. Wealth handed down and grown by each generation, until their wealth became the source of their wealth.

New money, on the other hand, had not in the eyes of the old money, put in the work, nor developed the culture, to be 'wealthy'. These included entre-preneurs, Dot Coms, entertainers, and the biggest abomination of them all, lottery winners.

Eric Easton came from the former. The Easton family had been growing its wealth and influence in the Boston area since the Revolutionary War. His family's business in mercantile, textiles, and – prior to the War of Independence – rum running, had grown into a massive import/export empire, as well as a substantial international shipping company that had been operating out of Boston Harbor since the time of tall ships. Just the liquid wealth of the Easton family was estimated to be in the hundreds of millions.

Consequently, Eric had grown up in pampered luxury. His upbringing filled with innumerable high-profile events, dinners and cocktail parties that had made alcohol a social element not considered 'strictly adult'. Such things were a part of Eric's normal, and his friends knew it.

Eric also loved his ladies, but he had no patience for childish high school games. As a result, he tended to gravitate toward more mature, independent and socially sophisticated female companionship.

His last long-term relationship had been when he was sixteen. It was with a twenty-three-year-old professional photographer named Annie Corcoran. He had met Annie on the sidelines of a preseason football game his junior year. Eric and Annie had traveled to Europe, gone dancing often and attended parties together, but one of their most beloved activities had been going to the midnight B-movie horror shows. It was where they had seen, *The Rocky Horror Picture Show* for the first time. None of his friends or family thought anything of it. It was just part of Eric's normal.

Recently, however, Eric's attention had been captured by Isabella Di'Amecci, the daughter of an Italian businessman. She was beautiful with long, wavy brown hair and golden-brown eyes. Her musical Italian accent made every word she spoke sound flirtatious. But beyond being beautiful, Isabella was sophisticated, charming and bright, with a clever sense of humor. Not at all the typical high school girl. All of Eric's friends understood his interest in her completely.

The baseball team, cheerleaders, band members, friends and guests, were all assembled in the parking lot ready to go. Lining up behind Conor's truck in convoy, they waited to depart.

Conor sat looking back at the other cars. There were lots of Mercedes, BMWs, Caddies and of course Eric in his Porsche chatting with Bella. Conor felt a little self-conscious of his truck, but Kimiko loved it.

Kimiko had become jaded from the wealth wielding snobs she had dated in the past. When she had met Conor, she found him down to earth, unpretentious, and most adorably, humble. Which for Kimiko, made him irresistible.

Glancing over at Kimiko, Conor saw she was smiling as she watched him. Then she looked out the rear window and waved to Bella as Conor pulled out and the procession of cars fell in behind him.

A black limousine sat curbside at the entrance of the White Mountain Research Facility. The driver leaned against its fender, looking bored, as he waited patiently for his client.

Parked behind the limo was Corporal Jeremy Winters. He had seen the limo before. It had started showing up a few months ago. Always around the end of the month, it would arrive with its enigmatic passenger, but why it came he did not know. What he did know was that on the days the black limousine came, Sabine always worked late, and so he waited dutifully, as twilight's purple haze draped over the forest.

A sudden flurry of movement caused Jeremy to look up to see the limo driver rushing around his car to open the passenger door. Seconds later, the front door of the building opened and his passenger strode out, his silk Armani suit shimmering as he walked to his waiting car.

The man was supermodel perfect. He was young, no more than his early twenties, but he carried himself with the confidence of a much older man.

A woman walked beside him, consulting a phone as she spoke to him. Jeremy assumed she was his assistant. Jeremy had never spoken to the man, but he had overheard this monthly visitor speaking to his assistant in what sounded like German.

When the man reached his limo, he turned and a white coated lab technician presented him with a metal case, which he promptly handed off to his assistant. With a slight bow the tech turned and walked back to the building as the model in the Armani suit slid into his car. Seconds later the limousine pulled away.

Corporal Winters eased his vehicle forward just as Dr. Sabine Bains stepped out from the building. He noticed that she was carrying a metal case, just like the one given to the man in the limo. Jumping out, Jeremy opened the door for her and she gave him a pleasant smile.

"Thank you, Jeremy," she said

"My pleasure, Sabine."

Stepping up into the S.U.V. she took his offered hand and slid into the seat, wincing slightly.

"Are you okay?" asked Jeremy.

"I'm fine," she said with a pout.

He smiled and closed the door. Climbing in behind the wheel he looked up in his mirror. "Home?" he queried.

"No," she replied, frowning, "unfortunately I must go to Havenhurst and it may be a late night."

"Yes, ma'am," he said with a smirk.

She wrinkled her nose at him, and he eased the S.U.V. away from the curb, happy just to be with her.

EIGHT

The long shadows of the sunset had blended into the impending darkness, and a vespertine mist was building as twilight faded into night. Through it charged a convoy of cars, with team captain Conor Jackson leading the way.

Conor sat behind the wheel of his truck smiling as Kimiko made videos with her phone. The music from his truck's sound system provided the background for her impromptu films, and she danced in her seat as she posted them to her various social media apps.

As he drove, he would occasionally glance over at her, he couldn't help himself. She fascinated him. She was playful and flirtatious, and she loved to laugh. Her almond shaped, Japanese eyes, so brown they looked black, along with her cascading hair that fell to her waist like a black silk waterfall, created an exotic sensory experience that Conor found overwhelming.

Conor and Kimiko had been talking, sometimes for hours at a time, over the last few weeks. But Conor had, as yet, not worked up the nerve to ask her out on a date. So, when the Spartans had won the regionals and Eric had thrown together the lake party, Conor had taken the plunge. Now she was sitting in his truck, her legs stretched out on the seat, her bare feet resting on his lap as she wiggled her toes to the music. He was in heaven.

Kimiko's colorful, floral sundress rode up on her thighs revealing an enticing display of bare legs. When Conor stole a glance, she playfully lifted her foot to his chin and turned his face forward.

"Eyes on the road, lover," she purred, as she traced the line of his jaw with her perfectly pedicured toes.

He couldn't help smiling his subtle approval as he looked down at her wiggling toes. Kimiko noticed and her face took on her characteristic big-eyed naivety that Conor thought made her look like a human manga cartoon.

"Do you find my feet beautiful?" she asked.

Conor took a deep breath. "Yes, I do," he said, at last.

"Then you must want to kiss them," she continued, her face a study of her well-practiced innocence.

Once again, she lifted her foot so that her toes were only inches from his lips, and Conor shook his head in amused disbelief. 'Wonderfully twisted' he thought, finally understanding Eric's earlier comment. Gently cupping her foot in his palm, he pressed his lips to her tiny, perfect toes.

"Mmmmm," she purred, biting her lip. "I think you will work out just fine."

Corporal Jeremy Winters slowed and signaled for a left turn, but seeing the headlights of oncoming traffic, he decided to wait. As the first vehicle, a pickup truck, drove past, his brow furrowed.

He was not sure if he saw what he thought he saw, but it looked like a girl in the passenger seat had her foot in to the driver's face and he was kissing it. But the odd scene went quickly by. Dismissing it, he completed his turn into the driveway of the Havenhurst Psychiatric Hospital.

The hospital's main building sat looming at the end of a long driveway that rose abruptly up a grass-covered hillside. A layer of early evening fog had formed around the building creating the illusion that Havenhurst was resting on a cloud.

Havenhurst was a massive and imposing edifice. Built in the neoclassical style, it had a time-worn appearance. It's limestone facade had a roughhewn texture due to the damp mountain air, that wafted up the valley from the nearby lakes, having eaten away at its surface.

As Jeremy Winters drove toward the ominous looking building, a chill overcame him. The building had a darkness about it that made it difficult to imagine anything good coming from it.

Dr. Thomas Shelby stood outside the front door, a toothy smile radiating through his neatly trimmed beard. Tall, thin, oddly shaped and with a head that seemed too large for his body, he bobbed on his toes, obviously excited by the arrival of Dr. Bains. As her vehicle came to a stop, he opened her door.

"Hello, Sabine," he crooned

"Good evening, Thomas," she said, stepping down from the open door.

Shelby leaned in to kiss her, but Bains turned her head so that all he could manage was an awkwardly executed peck on her earlobe.

Jeremy smirked at this rebuke. Reaching into the back seat he collected the heavy metal case and presented it to Dr. Bains.

"Where is the anomaly?" said Bains, a mild annoyance slipping into her voice.

"Ah, of course. Right this way," said Shelby, sensing her displeasure.

Taking the metal case from Bains, he awkwardly pulled open the large wooden door of the hospital, clumsily hitting himself with it as he did. As Bains gracefully swept through the threshold, she rolled her eyes in Jeremy's direction, making the soldier smirk once again.

Bains didn't much care for Shelby. She found him weak, needy and far too willing to please. And, not to put too fine a point on it...old.

She preferred young men, like the one who was currently waiting outside with her car. But she needed Shelby and so she gave him just enough attention to keep him placated.

Bains and Shelby rode the elevator to the second floor where he directed her down the hall to a door marked 'Observation Room 1'. Opening the door for her, he followed her in.

The observation room was a small space. Except for an old desk and chair pushed up against a wall under a large window that looked out into the facilities day room, it was empty.

The day room contained several tables, and a few sofas. There was even a piano in the corner, but its lid was padlocked. Large painted cartoon characters adorned the walls on all sides. On the wall with windows, they curved around the steel security screens. The whole effect created an almost surreal atmosphere.

The only occupant of the day room was a rather plain and disheveled looking girl. Her physical development made it obvious that she was in her late teens or early twenties, but she sat playing with a doll, compounding the absurdity of the scene.

"Her file is on the desk," said Shelby, pointing to a folder.

Bains picked up the file and began to read. "Who is she?" she asked not looking up.

"Her name is Marina Robins," began Shelby, but Bains cut him off.

"Yes, so it says here," she said, tapping the file impatiently. "Tell me about HER."

Flustered, Shelby began to fill in the details. "A horrifying story really. She witnessed her entire family being slaughtered by a pack of wild dogs."

"Wild dogs?" said Bains skeptically, raising her eyes to him.

"That's how she described it, and apparently the forensic evidence supported her story."

"Go on," she said, returning to the file.

"Uh, yes...well, it happened eleven years ago and she has been institutionalized with us ever since." Shelby turned to the window and looked at the girl. "So sad."

"No family at all?" asked Bains.

"None," confirmed Shelby, still watching Marina. "When she first arrived, we hoped that her twin sister might be found alive. The remains of her parents were identified, but neither her sister, nor her sister's body, were ever recovered."

Bains' mind was calculating. The lack of family meant that the anomaly could be examined without the possibility of interference by next of kin. And then, if an explanation for the anomaly was not forthcoming, a more...invasive procedure could be conducted.

Returning her attention to the file, Bains read until her brow rose in interest. "Developmental stasis due to traumatic stress?"

Shelby turned from the window, excited that Bains had used a term that he had developed just for this case. "Ah, yes," he began enthusiastically, "as you can see, Marina...uh, I mean the anomaly, is a healthy eighteen-year-old female. Her mind, however, ceased to develop at the age of seven due to the emotional trauma she has suffered. She is mentally, for all intents and purposes, a seven-year-old child."

Bains stared at the girl intensely. She did not like this anomaly. It offended her sense of order. It represented a failure that mocked her with every breath it took. If she had her way she would just as soon kill it and be done with it, but she knew Callister would demand answers and Lugenet would want them before that.

She also realized that this was no small issue. A single anomaly in such a small sample was statistically significant. One immune subject, in this small of a group, could potentially translate to millions worldwide.

"I need to talk to it," said Bains at last.

When Bains entered the day room, Marina did not look up from her doll, or even acknowledge her presence. Bains walked up next to her and stood there for a moment, annoyed that this inferior being was ignoring her. Suppressing her disdain, Bains regained her composure and charm, then spoke.

"Hello Marina, my name is Sabine. May I speak to you?"

Marina turned and looked at Bains, examining her closely, her eyes pausing momentarily on the patient file she was holding. Marina recognized it as hers. She had seen the file hundreds of times before over the last eleven years, but always in the hands of Dr. Shelby.

After making her assessment, she shrugged then returned her attention to her doll. "I guess so," she said.

Bains sat down and watched the girl fidget with the doll.

"Is that your doll?" she asked.

"No," said Marina sharply, "it's my sister's." Marina looked at Bains curiously. "Are you a doctor?" she asked.

"Yes, I am," said Bains.

"Is Dr. Shelby watching?"

"I don't know," said Bains glancing at the mirror.

"He's watching," said Marina softly. "He's always watching."

NINE

Several small fires dotted lake side beach, as some sixty Wellington students relaxed together under the stars. The revelers congregated in small groups, warming themselves in the glowing radiance of their tiny pyres, unconcerned about anything other than the joy of friends. Some drank beer, others soda or sweet tea, but all laughed and mingled from fire to fire celebrating.

The weather was warm, but a cooling breeze was blowing, causing the trees that lined the beach to flutter as if gossiping amongst themselves over the scene taking place before them. Over the lake, the moon was rising, and it reflected in millions of tiny points of light on its agitated surface.

Just within reach of the light of the Spartan fires sat a neglected old house, the glow of flickering light through the leaves casting dancing shadows on its peeling walls. Around the house, staked at odd intervals, were no trespassing signs that had become faded over time by the damp air and sun. Some had fallen over, others had been graffitied by petulant children, but all went mostly ignored.

Locals told stories of the house being haunted by the ghosts of a family murdered there over a decade before, the stories only becoming stranger as time had gone by. There were numerous reports of sightings of strange lights emanating from the house, everything from flickering candles to bright flashes. Some said they had seen a girl looking out of the windows, watching families playing on the lakeshore. Still others reported having heard singing coming from the house, but each time the house had been searched, nothing had been found.

Despite these reports, no photos, videos or other evidence had ever been produced by any of the ghost hunter teams that had at one time frequented the house. Nevertheless, the house's notoriety had served to ensure that it would remain empty and deteriorating, and with each passing year, the broken windows and peeling paint, only served to help the legend grow.

But on this night, none of the Spartan faithful were much interested in paranormal investigations. Least of all, Eric Easton.

Eric trotted naked out of the water, walking up the beach to where he had left his clothes. As he slid on his jeans, he gazed out into the black water, the silvery moon shining off his wet body.

A look of concern momentarily crossed his face, but vanished as his eyes found the vision he had been seeking. Rising from the lake was Isabella Di'Amecci, her nude form shimmering as the cool fresh water sheeted off her flawless skin.

A breath caught in Eric's throat as he watched her pad, almost cat like, out of the sparkling lake. He was reminded of Botticelli's masterpiece, *The Birth of Venus*, and found himself thankful that Wellington students were required to take Art History, so that simple men such as himself would be able to truly appreciate moments such as this.

"Bella," he whispered as he watched her stroll casually toward him.

He held up a blanket, but she pushed it aside, instead wrapping her arms around him and kissing him passionately. Eric was fascinated by the taste of her lips, sweetness mixed with the earthly tang of the lake's water, her skin exuding the scent of Night Blooming Jasmine.

Eric gently wrapped her in the blanket, his lips never leaving hers. Bella shivered ever so slightly, and so he lovingly stroked her until her shivers subsided. When their kiss did finally break, she gazed up at him, her eyes limpid pools of passion.

"Feeling better?" he asked softly.

"Much better," she replied, embracing him tightly.

As they began to sway to unheard music, Eric kissed the top of Bella's head. Taking a deep breath, he sighed contentedly. After a few minutes, the two lovers kissed again, then Eric scooped up their clothes and holding one another, they made their way back to the warmth of their fire.

Chance sat tending the flames, the sounds of playful screams and laughter emanating from the darkness around him. In the distance he could see the silhouettes of his classmates dancing and chasing each other around their fires like pagan lovers.

Poking at the fire with a piece of driftwood, he stared into the flames with a faraway look in his eyes. Despite his flame induced trance, he was uncomfortably aware of Conor and Kimiko cuddled up on the other side of the fire as she caressed his bare feet with hers.

As Chance looked up, he made eye contact with Conor through the twisting flames. Chance smiled at his friend, shaking his head. Conor grinned broadly and shrugged as Kimiko bit his ear.

At that moment, Eric and Bella walked into the glow of the firelight both with wet hair, Bella wrapped in a blanket, and Eric in jeans and an open shirt that clung to his wet body. She found a place beside the fire as Eric went to the ice filled tub and extracted two bottles before returning to her.

"For you, my Bella," he said as he sat down and presented her with a green tea.

As Eric opened his beer and drank deeply, Bella wrinkled her nose. "I don't understand beer," she said sipping her tea. "It is bitter and ruins food."

Eric laughed, "It's an acquired taste."

"Besides," she continued, "you said you only drink German beer."

"This is German beer."

"Dos Eques?"

"Dos Eques was founded by a German Braumeister who came to Mexico to open a brewery. It IS German."

Bella smiled. "Your standards seem rather flexible," she said, opening the blanket just enough for Eric to slip in with her.

"I can be quite bendy," he said as the blanket closed around him and Bella snuggled up closer.

Chance looked down and noticed that Eric had dropped something beside him. When he realized that it was the dress that Bella had been wearing earlier, the situation got a bit awkward. No matter which way he looked, he was confronted by lovers in love, doing what lovers do, and all he could do was sip his beer, poke the fire and try to act like he wasn't noticing.

Chance didn't mind being alone. In fact, at this point in his life, it was his preference. Over their years at Wellington, he and Eric had developed, not unearned, reputations as players. Conor, on the other hand was too good a guy. More a goofy sidekick than a wing man.

But now things were changing. Eric seemed genuinely and uncharacteristically, devoted to the lovely Bella, and Conor had come out of his shell and appeared to have bitten off more than he could chew with Kimiko.

As for Chance, he had decided that he needed to be on his own for now. He wanted something meaningful and unique. The problem at the moment was that his friends were with their ladies and he was alone five feet away. He wanted to leave, but he knew that getting up would cause a disruption and he didn't want to be 'That Guy'.

So, Chance had resigned himself to staring at the fire until his eyeballs dried out. But then, salvation.

As Bella broke a very passionate kiss, she snuggled up to Eric's chest and purred, "I'm in the mood for smores."

We've got everything we need, but I forgot to bring skewers to roast the marshmallows," said Eric, looking apologetic.

Bella pouted and Chance saw an opportunity. "I'll go find some sticks," he said jumping up.

"Are you sure you don't mind?" asked Bella.

"It would be my pleasure."

"There's a flashlight in my truck," offered Conor, tossing his keys.

"I'll be right back," said Chance as Bella and Eric disappeared beneath their blanket, giggling.

TEN

A security guard escorted Marina down a darkened hallway, her slippered feet shuffling on the carpeted floor. He opened the door to Marina's room and she wordlessly walked inside, clutching her doll tightly.

Closing the heavy steel door, the guard peered through its small window. He watched Marina as she stood motionless in the center of the room, staring through the security-screened window at the world outside. With a loud metallic clunk, he turned the key, securing the door.

He continued to observe her, curious. He had seen this behavior many times before. Sometimes the girl would stand motionless like that for hours. On nights like tonight, when the air was still, and the other patients were quiet, he could hear the girl mumbling or chanting in a strange language that he did not recognize. He once tried using his Google Translate app to figure out what she was saying, but it didn't work, so for all he knew, it could just be gibberish.

Watching for a moment longer, he became bored and turned away. "Crazy bitch," he muttered, then continued his evening rounds.

Turning a corner, he walked past Shelby and Bains as they stood talking. They waited for him to walk out of earshot, then followed him chatting as they strolled.

"Based on my examination, and your notes, there does not appear to be any physiological reason for the anomaly to be immune to the compound," said Bains, talking more to herself than to Shelby.

"Is it possible that there is a correlation with our earlier tests on prepubescent children?" asked Shelby, tapping his chin with his finger. "As you may recall, the compound has never been effective on subjects under eight years of age."

Bains chewed on this information, her mind processing the problem. "Perhaps there is a correlation between psycho-social maturation, or brain development, and susceptibility to the compound," she postulated. "Continue your tests and keep me informed. In the meantime, I will bring you a new variant of the drug, one more refined. I will administer the test myself."

"I understand," said Shelby.

"I will need a baseline subject before I use it on the anomaly."

"I will set it up," he said.

Satisfied, she took his arm. Shelby felt like his feet were floating six inches off the floor as he strolled down the hallway with his Sabine.

ELEVEN

A sleek silver car rolled slowly into the Lake Side Beach parking lot. Its headlights turned off, it slipped without notice into a parking space facing the beach. The driver, Travis Shelby, shut off the motor and leaned forward scanning the activity on the moonlit shore.

In the passenger seat sat Martin Wellington. He observed the celebrating Spartans around their fires through a pair of high-powered binoculars, their polished lenses reflecting thousands of glowing embers as they escaped into the velvety night sky.

As Martin stared at the magnified image of joy in the distance, hatred frothed up inside him: Hatred of Wellington Academy, hatred of his peers, hatred of his family, but most intensely, a deep and unwavering hatred of himself.

Martin had never been at, or even near, the top of Wellington's social food chain. Always an outlier, he was avoided and frequently alone. Not that he was a bad looking boy, though at 5'6" and two-hundred pounds, with a prematurely balding pate, he was an odd sight, but far from repulsive.

No, what made Martin a pariah amongst his classmates was his volatile anger. What made him an untouchable, was his connection to power.

Martin was a direct descendant of the influential family that had founded, and now dominated the board of Regents of Wellington Preparatory Academy. As a Legacy, he was entitled to enrollment without question.

His father, Arthur Wellington, sat on the board as its Chair. Consequently, Martin's teachers and the school's administrators, were frequently reticent to take any aggressive disciplinary action against him, and Martin took advantage of this in every way possible.

The only member of the Wellington staff that wasn't impressed with Martin's familial bone fides was Coach Phil McCune. In fact, it was McCune that had placed Martin and Travis on the extra duty they were currently serving.

In McCune's world, who you were was unimportant – what you did was what mattered. "By your work will I judge you," he would often say.

McCune's lack of esteem for Martin's place on his family tree wasn't Martin's biggest problem. McCune had lately become far too frequent a pain in Martin's ass. All of his poking around had often created problems with Martin's nascent drug empire, and now McCune's jacket-wearing thugs were making it difficult to conduct business. Something had to be done. As Martin watched the revelry on the beach, a solution to his problem presented its self.

"Perfect, get to work," he said, taking out his phone.

Travis jumped out of the car. Producing a knife, he proceeded to move amongst the parked cars, slashing their tires as he went. Moments later Martin stepped out of the car, pocketing his phone and joined Travis.

"Who'd you call?" asked Travis, whispering.

"The cops," said Martin flatly.

"The cops? Are you crazy?" said Travis, looking at him stunned.

Martin just smiled. Maybe he was crazy, he mused, but crazy or not, he could see clearly how the dominoes would fall in this situation.

The police were most likely on their way, Martin had made sure of that by telling the 911 operator that he had heard a girl screaming for help. When the cops showed up, they would find the entire Wellington baseball team drinking, if not drunk, and committing various acts of sexual deviancy with under-aged coeds. An investigation would ensue, and of course it would become a media feeding frenzy as both local and national news outlets competed to spoon feed a judgmental American public the sexual titillation it craved.

Martin's father and the Board of Regents would be embarrassed, and they would look to save face, and the school's reputation, by rolling a head.

McCune's most likely. But the 'piece de resistance' would be that those asshole jocks like Chance Jordan and his goon friends would all be suspended, their precious state championship lost to forfeit.

At that moment Martin noticed a silhouette moving rapidly toward the parking lot from the direction of the campfires. Holding his finger to his lips, he motioned for Travis to follow.

Moving with stealth, the two boys took cover behind a parked car as Chance, fumbling with some keys, walked to the rear door of a King Cab pickup truck and opened it.

Upon seeing Chance, a bile of pure hatred rose in Martin's throat until its acrid tang burned in his mouth. Reaching into his jacket, Martin slowly and deliberately pulled out a large menacing looking knife, its steel singing as it was pulled from its scabbard.

Travis' eyes bulged when he saw the glimmer of the blade in the moonlight. But what terrified him more, was the wild look of malevolence in Martin's eyes.

Martin gripped his knife tightly as he readied himself, but before he could act, Chance pulled out a flashlight and turned it on. The sudden bright light forced Martin and Travis to hunker down.

Closing the truck's door, Chance turned and walked off into the trees, the flashlight illuminating his path. Martin watched him go, then rising he followed, motioning for Travis to come with.

"What are you doing?" said Travis, slightly panicked. "The cops will be here soon."

Martin regarded Travis with a cold, homicidal expression, his body shaking with rage. Travis hesitated, but when Martin took a menacing step toward him, it became clear that he would either have to help Martin, or become the focus of his wrath. Tentatively nodding, he moved to join Martin who turned and stalked off into the forest.

Chance was easy to find. His flashlight shown like a beacon as he collected and trimmed twigs. He was so focused on his work that he didn't notice Martin's approach until...

"Hey, Jordan."

Chance never saw his attacker. As the heavy tree limb smashed into his face, his whole world became an explosion of pain. Falling back to the ground his ears rang, as blood gushed from his shattered nose and mouth. Pouncing on his devastated victim, Martin began raining crushing blows down on the defenseless boy.

Chance was on the verge of losing consciousness. Realizing he couldn't last much longer, he reached up blindly with both hands. Searching for the face of his assailant he grabbed hold of Martin's head and drove his thumbs deep into his eye sockets, gouging at his eyes.

Martin howled in agony. Twisting he tried to yank Chance's hands away and pull free. Sensing Martin was off balance, Chance gripped his shirt and violently pulled Martin down hard, head-butting him. Martin wavered, and Chance pushed him off, rolling the stunned thug onto his back. Chance pressed him to the ground and began to crush him with powerful blows, blood and saliva hanging in sickening strands as it dripped from his ruined face. But before he could do any real damage, he was seized from behind in a Full Nelson.

Flailing at this new attacker, Chance grabbed handfuls of hair, but to no effect. He reached up again, but before he could strike, he was disabled by a sharp pain in his chest.

At first, he thought it was a cramp, but this pain was deep, and it took his breath away. He couldn't understand why his body had suddenly stopped working, shutting down as his arms fell limp.

When Chance looked down, he saw his attacker's fist pressed hard against his ribs. It was only then that he realized that the person he had been battling with was Martin Wellington.

Martin looked up at Chance, a sneering evil smile on his lips as he slowly withdrew a wicked looking blade from Chance's chest. Chance was shocked by the size of it. Watching it emerge from his body, he became nauseous as he saw his blood, glistening black in the moonlight, on the cold steel blade.

Travis felt Chance go limp. Lifting him off Martin, he heaved him to the side where his seemingly lifeless body tumbled grotesquely down a steep embankment to a narrow rocky shore below.

Lying on the rocks, small waves washed over him, and as they did, visions of the night his mother had died began to flash through his mind. He saw the tempered glass of his father's car exploding, the sparkling shards suspended in the air as the car rolled before his father's body was thrown from the open door. His mother, her face an iridescent blue in the icy water, was panicking as she struggled to open his safety belt, as her own life slipped away.

High on the embankment, Martin and Travis stood looking down at Chance, the blood-stained knife still in Martin's hand. Chance could see them there, but he didn't care anymore. Washed in the gentile surge of the lake he looked up at the stars, an overwhelming sense of peace passing through him, and he smiled.

"Oh man, this is crazy," said Travis on the verge of panic.

Martin at first said nothing, but after a moment he turned to Travis and said simply, "Let's go."

Travis didn't move. He just stood there staring at Chance's body, shock registering on his face.

"Come on," yelled Martin, pulling Travis with him.

Travis gave way, falling in behind Martin. As they ran through the forest Travis' head was spinning as the reality that he had just helped Martin kill Chance Jordan hit him. He was scared, and his adrenaline was pumping like mad, and then he realized that he had never felt so...alive.

Chance looked up and saw that Martin and Travis were gone. His mind was quiet, as the points of light in the night sky beckoned to him.

"Home," he whispered, as bubbles of pink, air saturated blood, frothed from his disfigured face.

"Not yet," came a voice, soothing and melodic.

More disappointed than startled, Chance tried to find the voice's source, but found he couldn't lift his head. He didn't have to.

As he looked into the night sky, a darkened face eclipsed the heavens above him. Featureless and shrouded in a dark hood, Chance could not make out who was looking down at him, but he was not afraid. In fact, the presence of the mysterious figure calmed him.

"You can't go home yet Sari'El," the hooded figure said softly. "You have work to do."

It started as a flicker of blue electric charges crawling over the hooded figure's eyes. They intensified until the entire iris was a web of surging blue electric energy that grew into a blinding flash.

TWELVE

Bella cuddled up to Eric, nuzzling against his chest, as others moved in and out of the fire's light. Conor kneeled, tending the fire. Next to him sat a jumbo bag of marshmallows, a box of Swiss chocolate, and some graham crackers waiting for Chance's return.

"Where the hell is Chance?" he wondered aloud, as he stood and peered into the darkness beyond the glowing fire.

Kimiko looked at him standing there and started to snap photos of him, then joining him, she stood next to him for a few selfies.

"Miko," called Bella.

Kimiko turned to see Bella begin to kiss Eric, biting his lower lip and pulling it out while still clenching it between her teeth. Giggling, Kimko started to video the playful display from several angles as if she were making a commercial for the next fashionable fragrance.

As the girls played, the roar of an engine, and the spinning of tires, drew everyone's attention. Conor craned his neck, trying to see the source of the sound, but all he saw was a dust cloud rising in a huge gray mass, tinted by the reverse lights of a car speeding, apparently backwards, from the parking lot.

"Who was that?" asked Eric, joining Conor.

"I don't know," said Conor, still watching, "let's go check it out."

Together the two friends trudged through the sand toward the parking lot. As they drew closer, they saw the glow of headlights approaching in the distance.

"I think he's coming back," said Eric. "Can you tell who it is?"

"No, I can't even tell what kind of car it is."

The unknown vehicle pulled into the parking lot; the beams of its head-lights made visible by the dust still suspended in the air. As the car pulled to the end of the lot it stopped, then activated its high beams.

Eric and Conor continued to advance, squinting into the bright light, when they were suddenly dazzled by two bright spotlights. They pierced the darkness, lighting up the beach like a pair of tiny suns, causing the boys to stop, frozen in the sand.

"Uh oh," said Eric.

The mystery vehicle removed any lingering doubt as to its purpose when red and blue police lights began to strobe from its roof, further illuminating the teens on the beach who were already scrambling to hide the evidence of their celebration.

"Well shit," said Conor taking a sip from his beer.

Uniformed deputies stepped out of their car, and into the cacophony of light. They added to it with the focused beams of their police Mag-Lights, which washed over Eric and Conor just as Chance came stumbling out of the darkness, soaked, disoriented, and without a scratch on his face.

"Coach is gonna kill us," said Eric.

But Conor wasn't listening. He had noticed the vacant, almost bewildered, look on Chance's face. Reaching out he placed a steadying hand on his friend's shoulder.

"Dude, are you okay?" he asked.

Chance did not respond. He just stood in the confusion of light, his teeth chattering, as he examined a large hole in the front of his letterman's jacket, his eyes searching Conor's for an explanation his friend could not provide.

The glow of fluorescent lighting shone brightly out of the front doors of the rural sheriff's substation, bathing the patrol cars parked outside in a sterile light. The front doors swung out, pushed open by a massive man with broad shoulders and no neck, wearing a suit that strained at the seams.

The huge man held the doors open as Isabella Di'Amecci and Kimiko Yamamoto walked out. Barefoot and wrapped in blankets they were escorted to a waiting town car. Bella looked contrite, Kimiko more amused, but both girls climbed into the car and were taken away.

Inside the station the members of the Spartan baseball team filled the benches and chairs in the small foyer to overflowing, forcing several of the boys to sit on the floor. Two uniformed deputies, under the supervision of their commanding officer, lieutenant Robert "Red" Redinger, sat at desks interviewing the last of the boys and typing reports as they did.

Chance Jordan sat on the floor in the corner, alone. Eric and Conor had tried to talk to him, but he was distant and distracted, oddly preoccupied with the hole in his jacket. Conor had examined the hole, checking Chance's body for a corresponding injury, but had found none.

"How much did he drink?" whispered Eric.

Conor just shrugged, looking at his friend, worried. In all the time he had known Chance, he had never seen him like this, staring expressionlessly as if at some incomprehensible vision a thousand yards away.

"OK, that's it," said one of the deputies handing the boy at his desk his I.D. "You can go have a seat with your friends."

"Yes, sir. Thank you, sir," said the repentant Spartan as he stood and gratefully rejoined his teammates.

The last boy quickly followed but before he could take his seat, the Wellington team bus pulled up and parked outside the door of the station. A susurration, followed by an oppressive silence, rolled through the room. Wrath had come, and they waited breathless for it to rain down upon them. They didn't have to wait long. Seconds later the bus door opened, and coach McCune stormed down its steps and into the sheriff's station.

"Get your asses on that bus, NOW!" he roared.

The terrified boys fell over each other as they scrambled to their feet and stampeded toward the bus. McCune gave no quarter as he positioned himself directly in the doorway, leaving only thin spaces for the panicking Spartans to squeeze by. He scorched them with his stare as they passed, daring someone – anyone – to so much as touch him.

None dared. Instead, the boys contorted themselves into impossible shapes in their effort to squeeze past unnoticed and gain the relative safety of the team bus beyond.

Lieutenant Redinger stood watching, a knowing bemused expression on his face as the last boy successfully negotiated McCune's gauntlet. When at last the station's foyer was empty, McCune's stern, stone face melted into a smile as he walked up to the lieutenant, his hand extended.

"Thanks, Bobby," said McCune, shaking Redinger's hand. "I appreciate you keeping this unofficial."

"No problem, coach," replied Redinger. "Having the boys here kinda took me back to my days at Wellington."

Redinger handed McCune a cup of coffee, "No surrender."

"No retreat," said McCune, smiling.

They clinked mugs and drank. "You guys were a pretty good group of kids," said McCune, reminiscing.

Bobby Redinger had played for McCune at Wellington ten years earlier. He had been one of the coach's scholarship athletes, and had stayed in touch after graduating.

"Those are some pretty good kids, too, coach," said Redinger nodding toward the bus. "Don't be too hard on 'em."

"You know me," said McCune with a wink.

"Yes, I do, coach. Yes, I do."

McCune put down his cup, "Well, I guess I should get this party started."

"One last thing, coach," said Redinger, walking to his desk and picking up an evidence bag.

"Here are their car keys," he said, handing the bag to McCune, "but there may be a bigger problem. Someone slashed the tires on most of the cars at the lake."

Redinger showed the coach some photos, then continued, "The reporting complaint call was anonymous, and it came from a burner phone. It smells like the boys were targeted."

McCune nodded his understanding, then shook Redinger's hand, "I'm grateful it was you looking after my boys, Bobby."

Redinger nodded.

The coach turned and, getting back into character, stalked out of the station and onto the bus. As the door of the bus hissed shut, McCune could be heard bellowing.

"Zero five hundred, practice field! Do you understand me?"

"Sir, yes, sir!" thundered the team in reply.

Redinger sipped his coffee as one of the other deputies stepped up beside him.

"They're in pretty deep shit, aren't they?" said the deputy, as the bus pulled away.

"Oh yeah," said Redinger chuckling, "they're dead."

―――

The sun illuminated the eastern sky, but had not yet peaked over the horizon. Coach McCune stood on his mound as the silhouettes of the Spartan baseball team ran the bases, visible against the nascent sunrise.

Some staggered, while others vomited the last vestiges of their celebration. Still others could only dream of vomiting as they heaved so hard to no avail that they would not have been surprised to see their shoes come out of their mouths.

McCune taunted them as they stumbled by. "Don't taste as good comin' out, as it did goin' in, does it?" he said as another boy bent over and heaved.

―――

Boys with flushed faces filled the steamy hallway of the Spartan locker room as they crowded around a bulletin board reading the posted lists.

"You're with me at Havenhurst," said Eric to Chance.

Chance rolled his eyes as his teammates teased and jostled him. Just then coach McCune's office door opened and he stepped out amongst the boys. He was holding a stack of envelopes, and his grave expression caused the noise in the room to drop to nothing.

"Each of you has fifteen hours of community service due by Saturday," he said as he distributed the envelopes. "Your assignments are on the board. These are your letters of introduction. You will report there today."

McCune looked his team in the eyes, but few dared meet his gaze. "And God help you if you embarrass me again," he added, then continued. "Failure to complete your community service will result in your being removed from the roster."

This announcement caused a murmur to ripple through the group as the consequence of failure set in. McCune exploded.

"You don't like my sense of justice? You think me unfair? Well, the only thing fair around here is the weather, and today..."

THIRTEEN

"...it looks like rain," chorused Eric and Chance, laughing as they completed their coach's oft-stated ridicule of the concept of 'fairness' as a light spring rain begin to spatter on the windshield of Eric's car.

Coach McCune was not a fan of 'fairness'. Eric recalled the first time he had walked into the locker room at Wellington, he had been shocked by a large sign over the door that read, "You are not all equal, and you will not be treated as though you were". He was at first offended, but as time had gone by, he had begun to understand that it was a statement that one's value was proportional to one's effort.

As the windshield wipers pushed aside the symbolic evidence of McCune's wisdom, Eric glanced at Chance. He was worried about his friend.

Chance had been acting strangely since the cops had broken up the party, but Eric had been reluctant to bring it up. Now that the mood had lightened, he finally worked up the nerve to ask about what was on his mind.

"So... what happened to you last night?" he asked tentatively. "I know you didn't drink that much, so, why were you so out of it?"

Chance had hoped to avoid this conversation. He vaguely remembered being attacked and hit in the face by what felt like a baseball bat. He remembered the flash of a knife, and a burning pain in his chest, but all of those memories danced on a line between dream and reality.

Looking in the car's vanity mirror, he saw no telltale marks of the vicious fight that his mind brought back to him in flashes. He had no explanation that made sense. And the presence of the dark hooded figure from his dreams about the death of his mother, made him pretty sure that it had all been only in his mind.

"I don't know," he finally replied. "I think I might have fallen and hit my head. I woke up lying in the lake at the bottom of a cliff. The next thing I remember is cops shining lights in my face."

Eric nodded, seemingly satisfied with this explanation, "But you're OK now, right?"

"Yeah, I'm cool," assured Chance.

Eric nodded again. "Cool."

Chance was grateful that Eric had accepted his explanation, as he had no other to offer. At least no other that wouldn't make him look like a mad man. It didn't matter anyway as Eric's ever frenetic mind had moved on to other issues.

"I can't believe are were assigned to Havenhurst for our community service," he complained.

"How bad can it be?" said Chance, trying to throw a positive light on the situation.

"How bad can it be? Just look at it," Eric scoffed, as he turned onto Havenhurst's long ascending driveway. "This place gives me the creeps."

The day had been long and filled with trivial tasks. The sort of tasks that typically fall to the bottom of honey-do lists just because they are so...trivial. For two young men, more accustomed to a faster paced lifestyle, the monotony of Havenhurst's honey-do list was mind numbing.

As the afternoon pressed toward the dinner hour, Chance found himself vacuuming a large cartoon-adorned day room filled with patients who were involved in various art and music therapies. Seated at one of the tables, he saw a teenaged girl scribbling with a crayon.

Hunched over her work, her disheveled hair formed a thick copper colored curtain around the drawing on which she toiled. From time to time she would reach out to a scattered array of crayons lying loose on the table, select one without looking, then return to her art work.

Chance watched the peculiar artist for a few moments, fascinated by her process. At first, he assumed that her color selections were random, but the more he watched, the more he became convinced that there was a deliberateness to her choices.

He would have watched longer, but he became aware of another girl in the room. She had long black hair, and wore heavy black lipstick and eye liner. She displayed numerous tattoos which covered her arms, and hinted at more beneath her patient's gown. She had been playing a guitar but had stopped. Now she sat, intensely staring at Chance, with obvious disapproval. Feeling a bit unnerved, Chance went back to his vacuuming just as Eric walked into the room dumping art scraps into two large trash bags.

"This blows," said Eric.

"It needs to blow a little harder. You kinda stink," teased Chance.

Eric held up both bags, one in each hand, and gave Chance a double middle finger salute before leaving the room.

Chance laughed and restarted the vacuum, but as he did a strange sensation overtook him. It crawled up his back in subtle resonating charges of electricity that spread across his shoulders. Thinking that he was being shocked by the vacuum he jerked his hand away, but the sensation continued to intensify, when a voice called out to him, like a whisper in his ear, breathy as if in a dream.

"Sari'El."

Chance stepped back. Startled, he looked around, certain that the source of the voice would be leaning over his shoulder, but no one was there. The closest person to him was a huge orderly, but he was some twenty feet away, leaning against the wall looking bored. He was ready to write it off as misunderstood white noise.

"Sari'El," came the voice again.

This time he was sure he heard it. It surrounded him as if coming from every direction. Spinning, he searched for the source, but he could find none.

Glancing around the room confused, Chance's attention was drawn to the girl who had been so engrossed in her art. She was now standing, staring at him as she clutched a doll. Her mouth hung open in stunned awe, as if looking at something impossible.

"It's you," she finally said, a joyous smile radiating from her face.

Baffled, Chance looked at her, then behind himself, expecting that perhaps a family member of the strange girl had entered the room, but he saw that that was not the case. When he looked back at the girl, he was surprised to see that she was slowly walking toward him. He glanced over at the orderly, but he was absorbed in his phone, unaware of what was happening.

"Sari'El" she said again, her hand reaching out to him as if she were still unsure that he was actually there. But Chance did not respond.

An uncomprehending expression washed over her. "Don't you recognize me, Sari'El?" she said.

Taking his hand in her's, she pulled him closer. Placing his hand over her heart, she held it there as she looked deeply into his eyes with an expression of hope and expectation.

"See, it's really me," she said.

As his hand came in contact with her, he was overcome by a feeling of intense joy, his heart exploding as if he had been reunited with a part of his soul long lost. And then it was gone, ripped from him like a plug from a wall socket, as the orderly pulled the girl back.

"What are you doing?" asked the orderly, accusingly.

"I'm not...," began Chance weakly, but his head was swimming, and he leaned against a nearby table for fear of falling.

Chance backed away as the intimidating orderly insinuated himself between him and the girl, pulling her away. Turning, Chance stumbled toward the door, the effect of the sudden emotional disconnect clouding his mind in a thick tenebrous fog.

"No!" screamed the girl, resisting as another orderly arrived to assist.

"Sari'El, don't go! Please don't go!"

The girl was on the verge of total panic as the orderlies moved her, struggling, toward the door. As they did, one of them spoke briefly with a nurse who had run into the room. Upon hearing his report, she locked her eyes on Chance, then moved with purpose toward him.

"You need to come with me, young man," she said sternly.

‸

"What the hell did you do?" asked Eric, exasperated as they drove away from the hospital.

Chance sat in the passenger seat, arms folded across his chest defiantly. "I didn't DO anything," he said emphatically. "I was standing there and then this girl walks up to me..."

"Whoa. Was she hot?"

"What?"

"Was she hot?"

"No... I mean, well...Shut up!"

"Hey, hey, just tryin' to get a mental picture here. Go on."

"Anyway," started Chance again, "she walks up and starts talkin' to me like she knows me, and the next thing I know is she's being hauled outta there, and I'm gettin' the boot."

"While I was waiting in the office, I heard them say that you touched her."

"She touched ME," protested Chance. "She grabbed my hand and put it on her chest."

Eric's eyebrows shot up as he considered the situation. He realized there were two ways he could play this: He could be the deeply concerned and supportive friend Chance needed in this moment of crisis or he could be the charming, yet sometimes crass, Eric Easton that he was known to be, and have a bit of fun at Chance's expense.

Eric wanted so much to be the former, but the latter promised to be so much more fun. And so, she dove right in.

"Uh-huh," he grunted, "So... were they?"

"Were they what?" asked Chance confused.

"Real. Were they real?"

"Fuck you, Eric."

"And what about size?" pressed Eric. "Some say that more than a mouthful is a waste, but I personally find that philosophy offensive."

Chance did not respond. He just sat silently fuming.

"I mean, think about it," continued Eric. "If you go to a steak house and order the one-pound prime rib, would you only eat one mouthful? Of course not. THAT would be wasteful. So, tell me my friend, were they a waste? Were they a horrible, horrible waste?"

Eric was smirking as he watched Chance sit brooding out the window. Satisfied that he had milked the situation for all its mirth, he finally relented, taking pity on his friend. "OK, Ok, so who was this girl anyway?" he said.

Chance looked at Eric, assessing his earnestness. Deciding he was most likely done, he took a breath.

"I don't know her name," he finally said. "They told me that she's been there since she was seven."

Eric whistled in astonishment. "So, you've never seen her before?"

When Chance hesitated, Eric pressed. "Have you?"

"No," said Chance a little too quickly. Then equivocating he added, "I don't know."

"You don't know? How could you not know?"

"I didn't recognize her, but I felt like I should. She felt so...familiar to me," said Chance, his confusion visible.

"Well after grabbing her boobies, she sure as hell should feel familiar."

Chance rolled his eyes and crossed his arms. Turning he looked out his window, sulking.

"Well, your new girlfriend got us fired," continued Eric. "Coach is gonna be pissed. I'm just glad I'm not you. You sure screwed the pooch."

Chance wasn't listening anymore. He was trying to make sense of the intense emotions he had felt. Feelings that were violently ripped out of him. He remembered feeling them, but now they were but a faint echo reverberating from a hole in his soul. He shook his head. It made no sense.

"Who was she?" he wondered to himself.

Chance shivered as Eric drove. He watched as the rain drops turned into tiny rivers and slipped across the glass in silvery webs. He pondered the name she had called him. A name he had heard before but only in his dreams.

"Sari'El"

FOURTEEN

Students in black Wellington blazers, boys in gray slacks, girls in pleated plaid skirts, moved quickly into the main building, and filtered through the Grand Foyer as the first bell began to chime. Chance strolled down the hallway with that confident, and slightly cocky gait of a senior classman, when Conor jogged up next to him. Chance was pretty sure he knew what was coming.

"Uh...so, I heard you got caught fondling a crazy girl," said Conor teasingly.

"I wasn't fondl... You're an idiot," said Chance annoyed.

"Denial is an ugly thing," chastised Conor playfully.

Chance stopped and glared as Conor swept past him and into the classroom, a restrained smile on his lips. Walking to their lab station, they settled in quickly, but Conor wasn't done.

"Is it true that Havenhurst told you not to come back?"

"Yep," replied Chance, attempting nonchalance.

"Well, that explains why coach was paying so much attention to you this morning at practice," said Conor, chuckling. "You were like his personal chew toy."

Their conversation was suddenly interrupted by the sound of a metal lab tray crashing to the floor. As every head turned toward the source of the noise, Chance's eyes were met by the shocked, and seemingly horror stricken, stare of Travis Shelby. Travis' reaction was not without cause.

After leaving the lake Friday night, Travis and Martin had fled to Travis' house, and secluded themselves for the weekend. Both were sure they had murdered Chance Jordan, so the two boys watched for any report of a Wellington student being killed, or even missing for that matter, but no such report materialized.

Monday morning, they had returned to Wellington expecting the student body to be abuzz over the death of Chance Jordan, but all was normal. Just the standard gossip, along with tittering over prom could be heard.

The only possibility was that Chance's body had washed out into the lake. If it had, then he would not be officially missed until he failed to show up for class. But surely his roommate, Eric Easton, would have reported him missing.

Then, beyond all reason, there he was. Not only undead, but seemingly in good spirits, chatting with his 'twin' Conor Jackson, and showing absolutely no sign of the beat down they had given him just two nights before.

The sight of him had startled Travis, causing him to drop the lab tray he was holding. Martin, who had had his back to the classroom, turned around, startled by the crashing sound.

"What the hell's wrong with you? he snapped.

When Travis didn't respond, Martin followed his eyes out into the classroom where he saw Chance Jordan looking back at him. Now it was Martin's turn to gape, his two blood hemorrhaged eyes, and broken nose giving him a fierce expression. He tried to contemplate the variables necessary for Chance to be standing alive, and unharmed before him, but it was inconceivable.

Travis picked up the tray and placed it on the lab bench, as Martin grabbed him and pulled him toward the door. Glancing furtively back at Chance, they both hurried from the classroom.

Watching them leave, Chance felt an odd aching twinge in his side, and he massaged the spot absentmindedly, but when he saw coach McCune enter the room, the aching he felt went to his stomach.

"Uh-oh," said Conor, elbowing Chance as McCune spoke to Ms. Hotchkiss.

Chance hung his head upon seeing his tormentor, then he hung it a bit lower when McCune turned, scanned the room, and called out.

"Jordan, you're with me," he barked.

"Shit," mumbled Chance, under his breath as he shouldered his backpack.

Conor gave his buddy a supportive clap on the back. "Hang in there, bro," he said.

As Chance walked to the front of the room, he saw McCune turn and walk out of the door, and his imagination filled with ridiculous fantasies of escape, and a life on the run evading Coach McCune's justice. But spending the rest of his life looking over his shoulder for a pissed off McCune was no life at all, still the idea of it gave him a chuckle.

He needed a laugh. It had been a tough morning, preceded by a disastrous weekend. The situation with the girl at the hospital had spiraled out of control. By the time he and Eric had returned to Wellington, late Saturday afternoon, the good nurse at Havenhurst had already called Coach McCune and told him that Chance was not welcome back, and why.

As Eric pulled into the parking lot of the sports complex, McCune was waiting, his stony face wet and unflinching in the light rain. Chance tried to talk to him, but the coach just raised his hand and shook his head. He was in no mood for explanations.

In an ominous monotone, McCune made his mind clear. "Enjoy your Sunday, Mr. Jordan. Get lots of rest. Get right with whatever God you pray to, because on Monday, your ass is mine."

McCune had then turned and stalked into the sports complex to await the passing of the Sabbath, at which time he would exact his pound of flesh. When Monday morning came, the coach was well rested and had had over thirty-six hours to design his retribution.

'The coach's chew toy," that about summed it up.

Chance hurried to catch up with McCune as the hulking man moved up the hall with surprising alacrity.

"What's up Coach?" he asked, hoping to soften him up with conversation.

"There are some people here to see you," was the only explanation he offered.

Upon hearing this, Chance fell back a few steps as his heart dropped into his stomach. Turning into the school's administrative offices, McCune led Chance into the staff conference room.

As Chance stepped through the door, he pulled up short when he saw the two people seated at the long table. The man he had never seen before, but the woman he recognized. She was the nurse that had kicked him out of Havenhurst on Saturday

The man stood and extended his hand to Chance.

"Good morning Mr. Jordan," he began politely. "Thank you so much for taking the time to speak with us."

"Um...sure," replied Chance, confused, but grateful that the conversation hadn't started with, 'You're under arrest'.

My name is Dr. Thomas Shelby, and I believe you have met my head nurse, Ms. Denali."

The woman just nodded.

"Please, sit," offered Shelby.

Chance and McCune took seats opposite their visitors, McCune placing a reassuring hand on the boy's shoulder. Chance glanced at his coach confused, not sure if his hand was for support, or to keep him from running.

"First and foremost," began Dr, Shelby, "Mr. Jordan, I want to apologize to you for any discomfort or distress this situation may have caused you."

Chance glanced at McCune, who smiled back. "I think he means me," he said with a wink.

Shelby looked at McCune slightly confused by his comment, but went on. "We have gone over the security video, and it is clear to us that you did nothing inappropriate."

Chance let out a deep breath as an oppressive weight was lifted from his chest.

"But we do have some questions," Dr. Shelby added.

The boy looked at his coach who nodded his approval.

"OK, sure. Whatever you need," said Chance tentatively.

"Excellent," said Shelby, smiling as he opened a leather case and withdrew a notebook computer. He tapped the screen a few times, then looked at Chance.

"Mr. Jordan...May I call you Chance?"

"Sure."

Shelby offered his best reassuring smile, then proceeded.

"Chance, the girl you spoke to at the hospital is named Marina. Can you think of any reason why she would react to you the way she did?"

Chance was surprised by the direction the conversation had taken. He had thought a lot about the strange girl he had met, and the tidal wave of emotion that had flooded through him when she had touched him. He had struggled since that meeting to gain control over those feelings and find some level of perspective.

Now, as he contemplated her openly, those emotions threatened to come rushing forward once more. Doing his best not to be obvious, he forced them down to a point where he felt he could control them.

"No," he finally replied, "I mean, other than she acted like she knew me."

"Does the name 'Sari'El' mean anything to you?" interjected Denali.

Hearing the name again struck Chance like a hammer. A name from his dreams. A name spoken so softly, almost lovingly, by his dark hooded savior as he lay helpless in the water at the bottom of the cliff. But this was not the time or place to confess to hallucinations, or voices in his head.

"She called me that," he said, deciding that it was the safest response.

Denali could see Chance's discomfort and grew suspicious. "Are you sure you've never heard it before?" she pressed.

Afraid his voice might betray him, he only shook his head, not looking at the woman. Sensing Chance's withdrawal, Dr. Shelby spoke up.

"The reason we ask," began Shelby, "is that since you left, there has been a remarkable change in Marina. Normally compliant and desiring to please, she has become argumentative, even defiant. She has left her room without her doll, something she has never once done in the last eleven years. She has even begun to complain about her lack of options with regard to wardrobe."

"Sounds to me like you have a normal teenaged girl on your hands," said McCune.

"But that's the point exactly; Marina is far from normal," said Shelby, taking a deep breath. "Allow me to explain. Marina's emotional development halted at age seven. In her mind, she has been seven years old for the last eleven years. We have tried numerous techniques to stimulate her arrested development without success. Then you came to Havenhurst and it's as if a dam has broken."

Denali opened a leather portfolio case and spread several crayon drawings on the table. "These are samples of Marina's art before Saturday," she explained.

The drawings were typical of a young child. Stick figures in a world of happy little houses, surrounded by misshapen animals under rainbows.

"Here are some drawings Marina did on Sunday," said Denali as she spread out another collection, which was clearly far more technically proficient, and with a subject matter startlingly more mature."

"As you can see," explained Denali, "Marina's art has shifted drastically in both theme and quality."

Chance looked closely at the drawings. Gone were the bunnies and flowers, having been replaced by idealized nude figures of a man and woman, walking hand in hand. The woman's long spirals of copper colored hair cascaded over her voluptuous form, contrasted with the man's brown hair that touched the shoulders of his chiseled torso, post-it-notes, strategically placed, provided modesty.

"She has also begun to groom herself much more purposefully," Denali added. "Your meeting with her has had a profound effect."

Chance was struck by what he had heard, and how it unnerved him. Pushing the drawings back across the table, he looked at his visitors.

"What does all of this have to do with me?" said Chance.

Dr. Shelby and Denali exchanged glances, then Shelby spoke. "We would like you to come back to the hospital and visit Marina."

Chance's heart raced, joy and fear clawing at his stomach, but he was also consumed with confusion as to why this conflict within him existed at all.

"Uh, I'm not sure that's such a good idea," he finally stammered.

"You wouldn't be alone with her," reassured Denali. "I would be with you at all times."

Chance sat silent, his eyes moving from face to face as he took measure of his feelings. After a moment, Dr Shelby got up and moved to a chair next to him.

"Chance, Marina is eighteen-years-old, but with the mind of a child. I have long feared that she would never show progress toward normalcy. But since meeting you, that appears to be changing. When you left Saturday, Marina was inconsolable. The only way we could calm her down was to promise that we would try to get you to come back. What we're hoping for is that this more... mature interaction will help her break through.

"More mature? What do you want me to do, take her on a date?" said Chance, disbelievingly.

"No, no, nothing like that," assured Denali. "Just talk to her. Be her friend. We'll be there. Please Mr. Jordan. We believe this could really help her."

The desire to see her again was overwhelming, and this terrified Chance. At the same time, the need to know more about her burned in his chest as if it were filled with hot coals.

"When?" he asked, trying to remain calm.

"We had hoped to start today after school," said Dr. Shelby, hopefully.

"What about practice?" said Chance looking at his coach.

"I think I can spare you today," said McCune.

Chance paused. He noticed that his hands were wet with sweat, as he took a deep breath. "Ok, I'll be there."

Dr. Shelby breathed a sigh of relief, "Thank you, Chance," he said sincerely as he extended his hand once again.

Rising, Chance quickly wiped his hands dry on his slacks and took the doctor's hand. Turning to Denali he shook her hand as well.

"I'm sorry for the misunderstanding," she said.

"I understand completely," said Chance.

"Will you need a ride?" inquired McCune.

"No, sir, I'll take my motorcycle."

"Very well, then, get your butt back to class," McCune barked.

"Yes, sir," said Chance, then nodding to the guests, he headed out the door.

As he walked down the hall, he softly spoke her name, "Marina. Her name is Marina."

He allowed himself a smile.

FIFTEEN

After his meeting with Dr. Shelby and nurse Denali, the bell for second period was chiming, so Chance headed to his A.P. English class. But as he sat at his desk, he found that he could not concentrate. He couldn't stop thinking about Marina. The connection he felt to her was powerful, and he couldn't explain it.

Her drawings haunted him. They spoke to him in a way he didn't understand. But more startling than any of that was the fact that she had called him, Sari'El, a name that carried a powerful meaning for him.

He knew he needed to clear his mind. His distraction was making him useless. So, as his English class was wrapping up, he began to ponder his options.

Returning to his dorm room was out of the question. The House Master would know he should be in class, so he decided to take refuge in the one place of comfort he had left, the baseball stadium.

Walking down the tunnel from the Field House, Chance emerged into the dugout and saw that the batting cages were set up for that afternoon's practice. Peeling off his blazer, he selected his prized maple-wood Louisville Slugger then grabbed his helmet and batting glove. With his bat tucked under his arm he walked into the batting cage and set the machine to send some heat.

Stepping up to the plate, he put on his helmet then slipped on his batting glove. Loosening his tie, he reached over and started the pitching machine. Raising his bat, he sank into his stance. His eyes narrowed, as his breathing slowed to a point where he could hear his own heartbeat. He was focused, and in the zone.

The pitching machine began to deliver fast-balls in what looked like long white blurs. As Chance looked at the oncoming ball, he could see it turning in its unique rotation. He could almost count the stitches, and smell its leather.

A breath, a swing, and the crack of the bat. It reverberated through the empty stadium, the vibration of the maple-wood slightly stinging his hands as bat met ball.

It was good.

Chance preferred to take batting practice with a wooden bat, even though high school teams almost exclusively used the more advantageous aluminum. He was drawn to its tradition, but he also reasoned that if he could put one over the fence with his Louisville Slugger, the same ball would end up in the parking lot off his Easton aluminum.

He worried for a moment that coach McCune would hear the crashing of his bat and send him back to class, but it was too late to worry about that now, so he crushed another one.

In the field house, McCune stood sipping coffee as he watched Chance from his office window, the boys bat thundering like Thor's hammer. Reaching for the phone on his desk, he dialed.

"May I speak with the attendance secretary please? Thank you...Hello Gail, this is Phil, I wanted to let you know that I have Chance Jordan with me... Yes, all morning...thank you."

Hanging up, he watched Chance crush a few more, then nodding his approval of the boy's form, sat down at his desk and returned to his paperwork.

Students poured into 'Hogwarts' for lunch as white-jacketed servers stepped forward to portion out the gourmet entrees.

Chance sat alone at one of the round tables, eating. He had stayed at the batting cage for a few hours, grateful for the distraction, but now was looking forward to being joined by his friends.

Looking up he saw Eric and Conor enter the dining hall, and he returned their waves as they cued up to get their lunches. In a few short minutes they were at his table.

"So, what did the coach want with you?" asked Conor as he threw his leg over the back of a chair as if he were mounting a horse.

"Some doctor from Havenhurst was here to see me," said Chance.

"What'd he want, a DNA sample?" said Eric, dryly.

"Fingerprints," theorized Conor in a matter-of-fact tone. "C.S.I. must have dusted the girl's boobs for prints."

"They can do that?" said Eric, amazed by the idea.

Conor nodded his confirmation as he bit into a French fry.

"How do you get THAT job?" wondered Eric, aloud.

"You guys suck," said Chance.

Eric and Conor chuckled as they watched Chance ignore them.

"OK, OK," said Eric, still laughing, "Tell us what happened."

Chance looked at his two friends, who were now looking back at him expectantly. Satisfied that he had their attention, he wiped his mouth and sat back, placing his napkin on the table.

"Well, first they apologized for falsely accusing me," he said, looking at them both to be sure that little factoid sunk in. Eric and Conor said nothing, so feeling vindicated, he continued. "Then," he said with emphasis, "they asked me to come back and visit the girl, because apparently just meeting me, has therapeutic value."

Eric and Conor looked at each other, perplexed, then back at Chance as they waited for an explanation.

"It would appear," continued Chance, "that after meeting me for just a few minutes, the girl has begun to show, heretofore, unrealized improvement. So, now they are hoping that if I spend more time with her, she will benefit even more."

Chance crossed his arms and smirked at his friends with smug satisfaction. It didn't last long.

"They set you up on a date with a crazy girl?" said Conor dryly.

"Hey, hey, hey," interjected Eric, raising his hands, "don't knock crazy if you haven't tried it. Crazy girls are an underappreciated demographic."

Chance rolled his eyes, but had to laugh. One of the best parts of having Eric and Conor as friends was that their irreverent approach to life made it impossible to take one's self, or one's problems, too seriously.

"So, when is this date supposed to happen?" asked Conor.

"Today, after school."

"What about practice?"

"Coach gave me the day off."

"Hmm," contemplated Eric, aloud, "What does one wear on a date with the criminally insane?" Turning to Conor he asked, "Does Victoria's Secret make a satin and lace straight jacket?"

Conor snorted, causing milk to come out his nose.

"You guys are such idiots," said Chance, shaking his head.

"Hello, boys," came the melodic voice of Isabella Di'Amecci.

All turned to great her, "Hey Bella," they replied.

Bella swept into a seat with her customary grace, quickly pulling out her computer with obvious excitement.

"You guys have got to see this," she said, exhilarated.

Activating the device, an image of herself and Eric cuddling in the glow of a fire, filled the screen.

Eric smiled. "You and me at the lake."

"That's right my handsome man," she said, leaning over and kissing him on the cheek. "Now look at this."

She slid her fingertips over the screen to enlarge the image. Zooming in, she centered the image on the old beach house near where the party had taken place.

"The haunted house, so what?" said Conor unimpressed.

"Look closer," Bella urged as she zoomed in again.

This time she centered the image on an upstairs window. There, in its lower corner, as if peeking over the window sill, was a distinct set of eyes, glowing as if filled with blue flame, staring out through the time-degraded wisps of curtain.

Chance stiffened in his seat. He was stunned to be confronted with photographic evidence of the hooded spectre from his nightmares.

Eric was beside himself. "Whoa, is that real?" he said, grabbing the computer. "That is so creepy."

Conor was more skeptical. He stood, leaning on the table analyzing the image closely. Shaking his head, he straightened and folded his arms.

"You Photo-shopped that," he declared.

"No, I didn't, lover," said Kimiko, joining the group. "That is raw video. Whatever that is, it was there when I videoed Eric and Bella."

"It's the ghost," said Bella, almost giddy.

The group stood speechless, staring at the screen, the haunting, glowing eyes staring back at them. It was Eric that broke the silence.

"We gotta go back," he said, turning to the others. "We gotta check this out."

"Are you outta your mind?" said Chance almost shouting. Then seeing several heads at nearby tables turn to look, he lowered his voice to a conspiratorial whisper. "If Coach McCune finds out, he'll cut our nuts off."

"No," said Conor thoughtfully, "we gotta go."

"I don't know, guys," said Chance.

"We won't stay late," Conor assured, "but we're going."

"I'm going," said Eric.

"We're going, too," said Bella, taking Kimiko's arm.

Now the group, as a whole, turned to Chance. He looked at their faces and caved.

"Shit," he exclaimed exasperated. "But I'll have to meet you there."

"Oh, that's right. You have a play date," quipped Eric. "Do you need my car?"

"No, I'm taking my bike," said Chance, "but I do need to borrow a jacket. Mine's got a hole in it."

"Yeah, I saw that," said Conor. "You can borrow mine."

Bella and Kimiko clapped and squealed, excited by the plans for the evening.

Chance sat back and sighed deeply as he watched his friends cluster around the computer offering various hypotheses on how the eerie glowing eyes came to be in the photo. Everything from fraud to poltergeist was being floated. For Chance, however, there was another possibility.

Even though he had no direct memory of the night his mother had died, his dream of that night was as real to him as if he had been there watching. Nevertheless, he had always discounted his dreams as just that, dreams.

But ever since the dark hooded figure had seemingly come to him again, as he lie helpless on that rocky lake shore, the line between what was real, and what was a dream had become blurred.

Now those glowing eyes – eyes that were etched into his mind – stared at him from the screen of Bella's computer. He could feel them looking into his soul and it frightened him.

Chance looked away, trying to break the preternatural hold the eyes on the computer screen had on him, only to find himself held in the curious gaze of Jäger, sitting alone at his customary table. The beautifully odd boy regarded him, studying him it seemed, then returned his attention to his lunch as he slowly lifted a spoonful of soup to his lips.

Intrigued, Chance rose from his seat, unnoticed by his friends, as they had become distracted by YouTube videos of ghost hunts. Stepping away from his table, Chance made his way across the dining hall to where Jäger was sitting.

As Chance drew nearer, Jäger clearly was aware of him. Jäger slowly put down his spoon and laid his hands in his lap, keeping his eyes cast down like an abused child waiting to be beaten. But Jäger did not tremble, nor was he tense. There was in fact a tranquility that surrounded him.

"Excuse me," began Chance. "Jäger, right?"

"Yes," replied Jäger.

"May I join you?"

"If you wish," said the boy.

Jäger remained motionless, without regarding Chance in any way. Chance could not shake the feeling that he was intruding on something more than just a bowl of soup, but nevertheless pulled out a chair and sat down.

What happened next was completely unexpected. As Chance lowered himself into the seat, Jäger lifted his head and looked directly at him, a warm smile spreading across his angelic face.

"Um...Hi," said Chance lamely, slightly startled by his gaze.

"Hello, Chance Jordan," said Jäger, his eyes now fixed on Chance's.

"I wanted to talk to you about last Friday."

Jäger only nodded.

"You left before I could talk to you."

Jäger's smile grew. "You seemed to have the situation well in hand. I was... in the way."

Chance was surprised by Jäger's sudden loquaciousness. In the few years he had been aware of the diminutive prodigy, he had never actually heard him speak a single word. Now to hear him speak, not only in full sentences, but while making eye contact as well, was nothing less than monumental.

"Uh-well," began Chance, composing himself, "I would like to invite you to come sit with me and my friends so we can make sure no one bothers you again."

Jäger looked at Chance with an almost loving expression, which Chance found both disarming, and a bit unnerving. "You have such a kind soul," responded Jäger.

An awkward silence fell between them as Chance tried to decipher what Jäger's response meant in the context of his offer of sanctuary. The two boys just looked at each other, Jäger's peaceful countenance unchanging.

"Well..." said Chance fumbling for words, "Please feel free to join us whenever you want to."

Chance waited for a response, but Jäger just looked back at him with a pleasant expression. Not sure what to say, Chance added, "Just think of me as your guardian angel."

Upon hearing this, Jäger smiled in obvious delight.

"Yes," he said without breaking eye contact, "I will do that."

SIXTEEN

The final bell had chimed and students filled the commons, chatting. Others headed for their dorm rooms, or athletic facilities. Still others shouldered heavy book bags and trudged toward the library to start hours of homework.

Amongst all this sat Chance Jordan on a bench outside the field house, his Harley Street Rod waiting in the parking lot nearby. During sixth period he had reminded Conor of his need to borrow his Letterman's jacket. Now he tried to relax as he waited for Conor to run up to his dorm room to get it.

As he waited, he became distracted by an ant as it struggled to move a crumb across the sidewalk. He leaned forward to watch, silently cheering the little guy on as he negotiated his treasure across the chasms of the walkway.

But his fascination was short-lived as, without warning, Kimiko slipped onto the bench behind him. Wrapping her arms around his chest, and her legs around his waist, she pulled him tightly to her.

"I repainted my toes," she said, extending her legs so that he could see the delicate artwork wiggling enticingly before him.

When the object of her affection did not respond as she expected, Kimiko grabbed a handful of his hair and pulled his head back firmly. Biting his ear she whispered in a sultry voice, "Do you not find them beautiful?"

Chance smiled as he realized what was happening, as this sort of misidentification had been occurring since he and Conor had been freshmen. While Chance and Conor were not "identical", their resemblance to each other was uncanny. Their hair color and style was the same, they were the same height and build, they even had the same slightly upturned noses and chiseled features.

It was easy to mistake one for the other, and the boys had at times used this fact to their advantage. So once Chance got over the surprise of having Kimiko's legs wrapped around him, the rest was automatic. Restraining a smile, Chance snuggled back as he began to massage Kimiko's naked feet.

"Mmm," she purred, as she encircled him with her arms and began trailing kisses along his neck. But this romantic, even slightly erotic, expression of love was quickly shattered by the droll, deadpan voice of Conor Jackson coming from behind the bench.

"Dude, I said you could borrow my JACKET."

Kimiko looked up, shocked and surprised to hear the sound of her lover's voice coming from behind her. Once again, she took hold of Chance's hair, and roughly turned his head so she could see his face. Chance winced as she stared, furious, into his eyes. His very green eyes.

Chance and Conor burst out laughing, but Kimiko was not amused. Jumping up, she began slapping at Chance's head and shoulders.

"How could you just sit there?" she scolded angrily.

"How could I not?" laughed Chance as he fended off her blows. "That was so hot."

"You should have said something."

"But your feet were so beautiful."

At hearing this, Conor roared with laughter.

Fuming, Kimiko grabbed her shoes, which she had discarded on the grass, and stormed away, embarrassed. Laughing, Conor tossed his jacket onto Chance's lap, and sat down beside him.

"She's a fascinating girl," said Chance, chuckling.

"She has...very specific tastes," conceded Conor.

"It would seem that your tastes have evolved a bit as well."

"A bit," agreed Conor. "You ready for your date?"

When Chance said nothing, Conor looked at his friend closely. "Something bothering you bro? You've been acting kinda strange since Saturday."

Chance looked at his friend, unsure if he was willing – or even able – to go into it. Finally, exhaling a deep breath, he decided to take a chance.

"You ever met someone you've never met before, but from the first moment you speak to them, you feel as though you've known them forever?"

"You mean like a soulmate?" asked Conor.

"I guess so. But since you've never met them before, you have no context to explain how you feel,"

Conor thought for a moment, "In my world religions class I read a creation myth that said every soul started its existence bound with its perfect other half, but jealous gods ripped us apart and scattered us into every direction of the universe, dooming us to forever search for our perfect other half."

As Chance considered this, a silence fell between the two friends.

"Who we talkin' about here?" asked Conor.

"You don't know her."

"So, what's her name?"

"Marina."

Conor looked at Chance with a 'Who the hell is that' expression. Chance hesitated for a moment, took a breath, then spoke.

"The girl at the hospital," said Chance, looking Conor in the eye to let him know he was serious.

Conor blew out a breath as he leaned back and spread his arms across the back of the bench, the gravity of the situation made clear by the look of confusion on his friend's face.

"Is this gonna be a problem for you, bro?" he asked.

"No... I don't think so," said Chance, unconvincingly. "I mean...I don't know...I'm not sure what it meant."

"What, 'what' meant?" asked Conor, picking up on Chance's subtle cue.

Chance knew that with his next words his friend could very well label him a head case, and be justified in doing so. But he also realized that he had said too much to stop now.

"She called me Sari'El," he said at last.

"What the hell does that mean?"

"It's a name."

"So... she called you a name. So what?"

"So, I've heard the name before," explained Chance.

Conor looked at Chance expectantly, "Where?"

"In my dream," said Chance seriously. "The one about the night my mother died."

"Whoa," exclaimed Conor, raising his hands, "ten out of ten on the creepy scale. Maybe you should hold off on this visit until you've got a better handle on this."

"No," said Chance, standing and putting on Conor's jacket, "I need to do this now."

Conor stood, patting Chance's back in support. "Ok, bro. I'll see you at the lake."

"I hope I didn't piss Kimiko off too much," said Chance.

"She's tough. She'll get over it."

Chance swung his leg over his motorcycle. "She does have pretty feet, though," he said with a wink.

Conor grinned, "That she do, Poot. That she do."

A ribbon of asphalt undulated under Chance's feet as he leaned on the throttle of his Harley. The white lane markers blurred, from intermittent dashes, into one continuous streak as his machine screamed through the relative calm of the emerald green, spring forest.

The two-lane rural road that led to Havenhurst, and the lakes beyond, was a scenic drive, its winding nature and banked turns making it a challenging test of a biker's skill. Even for the well initiated, it was an exhilarating thrill ride.

For Chance, riding his Harley was as much his therapy as it was a means of transportation. Chance imagined stress, anger and frustration to be like little creatures that clung to him, trying to pull him down. 'Getting in the wind', as it is referred to by the adherents of the church of the iron horse, peeled those creatures away, and after a good ride, he came out the other side clean and renewed. He realized that those minions of despair would eventually find him again, but as he leaned into another turn, he knew that at least for now, he was free.

Too soon for his liking, a sign indicating the driveway for the Havenhurst

Psychiatric Hospital appeared on the right. Throttling back, he pulled in his clutch and began to chunk down through the gears. As his machine slowed, the engine screamed its protest as he made the turn into the driveway.

Chance proceeded to the parking lot and parked. Unhooking the bungee that held his backpack to the rear seat, he let out a deep breath as he took in the building's imposing facade. Summoning his courage, he walked to the main entrance.

Entering the lobby, Chance was once again struck by the antiquated atmosphere. The room was dominated by burgundy, red and gold. It was a veritable turn of the century, 1800's time capsule. Antiques, many over two-hundred-years-old, filled the space and competed with the garish wallpaper and area rugs for the gaudiest piece in the room. It was a confusing mixture of baroque and rococo style that created an assault on the senses. If one were to add a few women of ill repute to the room, Havenhurst could have been a brothel.

Chance walked up to the reception desk and waited as the cheerful, round woman seated there finished her phone call. Hanging up, she looked at Chance, smiling.

"May I help you?"

"Yes, ma'am, my name is Chance Jordan..." but she cut him off.

"Oh! You're the boy from Wellington. Dr. Shelby is expecting you," she said excitedly as she punched numbers into the phone.

"He's on the second floor," she said leaning over the desk and pointing toward the elevators. "Go on up. I'll let him know you are on your way."

Chance thanked her, amused and flattered by her enthusiasm. Turning he walked to the elevator and rode it to the second floor. When the car's doors opened, he stepped out into a stark and clinically white, tiled hallway awash in the sterile glow of fluorescent lights. It was a shocking transition from the bordello on the first floor.

Sitting across from the elevator was a uniformed security guard. He was reading a *Batman* comic book that was unconvincingly concealed in a textbook titled *Passing the Basic Police Officer's Exam*. He seemed not to notice Chance's arrival.

He was an odd sight. His uniform, ill-fitting yet pressed, was highlighted by sparkling tactical boots and a radiant badge. His name, 'D. Dobos' was easy to read on his brass name plate that had also been polished to a high sheen.

Tall, thin and bow legged, with hips wider than his shoulders, he looked down at the comic book over a long, hooked nose that made him look like a bird of prey. He read with an obvious intensity that betrayed his desire to don a cape and cowl so he could right the wrongs of a society gone mad.

Now if only he could pass the Civil Service exam. 'Next time for sure' he promised himself each time he failed.

Stepping into the hall, Chance looked left, then right, not sure which way to go. Choosing left, he hadn't taken more than a step when a nasal voice squeaked from behind him, "Hey, Hold it right there!"

Chance turned and was startled to see the wanna-be caped crusader moving aggressively toward him, his left arm extended, as his right was unsnapping a pouch on his hip. At first Chance thought the guard was drawing a sidearm, so he quickly raised his hands. After a moment, however, he realized that while this devotee of the Dark Knight had every gizmo, tool and pouch a dedicated crime fighter could possibly fit onto a polished leather utility belt, a firearm was not among them.

"Drop the bag, then turn around and face the wall," commanded Dobos.

Dobos had been working on his 'command voice', but it was rendered somewhat less effective by his pronounced lisp. Nevertheless, Chance did as he was told, more out of reflex than from any sense of obligation.

"Now spread your legs and put your hands on the wall," Dobos continued.

Chance complied, and Dobos took an aggressive stance behind him beginning to pat him down, but as he ran his hand up the boy's inseam, Chance protested.

"Hey!" exclaimed Chance, pulling away.

Dobos pushed him hard against the wall. "What you got down there?" he snarled.

"My dick," shot back Chance angrily. "What you got down there?"

Chance had had enough, but before it could go any further, Dr. Shelby walked out into the corridor.

"That won't be necessary, Mr. Dobos," said Shelby, sternly.

Dobos appeared crest fallen by the rebuke. "But sir, the regulations say..."

"They say exactly what I say they do, Mr. Dobos," interrupted Shelby.

Without regarding Dobos again, Shelby crossed to Chance and shook his hand.

"Thank you for coming, Mr. Jordan," said Shelby, smiling. "Please allow me to apologize for Mr. Dobos'...overzealousness."

Chance nodded, "I understand completely. Obviously, he takes his job VERY seriously."

"Quite," agreed Shelby dryly. "Please, come... we have been waiting,"

With a sweep of his arm, the doctor indicated a door marked 'Observation Room 1'. Following Dr. Shelby's direction, Chance proceeded through the door, giving Dobos a sideways glance as he walked past the deflated crime fighter.

Dobos only glared.

SEVENTEEN

Entering the observation room, Chance walked over and looked through the large window. He quickly recognized the room on the other side as the cartoon-adorned day room where he had first seen Marina. As he scanned the room he saw her, seated at one of the tables, and his heart fluttered.

Just as the last time, Marina sat drawing, but gone were the greasy strands of unkempt hair, and the plain shapeless hospital gown. Her hair had been washed and brushed out so that it fell in glistening copper ringlets around her shoulders; the frumpy patient's gown replaced by a stunning white sundress that accentuated a rather lovely figure which had been completely obscured by the bulky gown.

"She looks different," said Chance.

"She IS different," said Shelby, joining Chance at the window. "She has been getting ready all day. Nurse Denali bought her the dress, and helped with her hair. Marina is very excited to see you."

Chance's stomach was in knots. Marina wasn't even in the same room with him, and already he was starting to sweat. His instincts were vacillating between toughing it out, and running like hell; the latter sounding better and better as the seconds ticked by.

"Dr. Shelby, I don't even know what to say to her," said Chance.

Shelby placed his hand on Chance's shoulder and turned the boy to face him. "You'll do fine," he assured. "Just talk to her. You don't have any agenda or goal.

You have already had a profound impact."

Chance looked at Shelby, nodding nervously. Realizing that if he was going to understand the feelings this girl was causing in him, it would begin with talking to her. Gathering his resolve, he reached for the door.

When the door opened, Marina looked up expectantly. Seeing Chance walk in caused her face to light up, and she sprang to her feet, jubilant.

"Sari'El!" she shouted excitedly, as she ran toward Chance.

Nurse Denali stood anxiously. "Marina," she called out, "remember what we talked about."

Immediately Marina stopped and looked back at Denali. Composing herself, Marina straightened her dress and brushed back her hair. Then walking calmly up to Chance; she extended her hand to him.

"Hello, it is so nice of you to accept my invitation," she said sweetly, her face shining with innocence and joy as she bobbed excitedly.

Chance was unsure what to do. The last time Marina had reached out to him, all hell had broken loose. Looking at Denali for guidance, he saw the formerly stern nurse smiling and nodding her head while mouthing, "It's OK."

Chance was caught a bit off guard by Marina's appearance. He had not realized how pretty she was during their disastrous first meeting. Reaching out, Chance took Marina's hand. It felt so soft and small in his. He marveled at its elegance, emotion once again threatening to choke him.

"Thank you for inviting me," he managed to croak.

Marina pulled him toward her table, elated by his presence. Her delight was infectious, and Chance found it impossible not to get caught up in it.

"Come, sit with me," she said excitedly. "You can look at my pictures."

Leading him to the table where she had been drawing, she practically shoved him into a chair. "Here, sit next to me," she said as she seated herself beside him, and scooted her chair closer.

Scattered about the table were crayons and various completed works of art. Chance sat patiently as he waited for Marina to arrange them to her liking, chattering away as she did.

Try as he might, he could not lose the uncomfortable feeling that any minute he might be snatched out of his chair by a pissed off orderly, but there was no orderly in the room. The only other person there was Denali, and she sat watching, apparently charmed by the scene before her.

Chance took a breath and relaxed. Looking more closely, he examined the drawings that Marina had laid out. He was immediately captivated by them.

The first was of a man who floated in the colorful clouds of a nebula. In one hand he held a sphere that glowed like the sun. In the other was a sword, or a lightning bolt, or maybe a staff of some kind.

"Who is this?" he asked.

"That's you silly," said Marina giggling. "In the before time."

"That's me?"

Marina looked at him, perplexed, then laughed as if he was joking. But when Chance didn't laugh with her, she realized that he wasn't joking.

"Don't you remember?" she said, not understanding.

Reaching out, she touched his forehead and her eyes began to dampen, as an expression of confused sadness washed over her face.

"You can't see anymore," she said disbelievingly.

As if to help him, Marina pushed another drawing toward him. This one he had seen before, during his meeting with Dr, Shelby and nurse Denali earlier that morning. It was a depiction of a man and woman as they walked through space. The post-it notes had been removed, so now the couple strolled in all their naked glory.

Marina watched him expectantly. Her insinuation that the figures were depictions of her and Chance was not subtle. Under her urging he looked at the drawings once more. As he did, she placed her hand on his.

He found her touch both reassuring and soothing, but it did nothing to help him 'remember' what Marina clearly thought he should. Marina seemed to accept this, and Chance was grateful for that.

"We can make some new memories," said Marina, pushing her drawings away and placing blank paper in front of each of them.

"That sounds perfect," said Chance.

Dr. Shelby stroked his beard as he watched Marina and Chance from the sequestration of the observation room. His calm demeanor incongruous with his excitement, and deep fascination, over Marina's sudden and unexpected progress.

It was easy for Shelby to see that Chance was enchanted by Marina, even though the boy tried desperately to conceal it. And if love were possible in such an absurd situation, then Marina was clearly in love with Chance.

Shelby was intrigued by the idea that Marina believed that she somehow knew Chance without ever having met the boy. He postulated possible explanations. Telepathy? Precognition? Maybe. There was plenty of research that made these plausible.

One thing he was sure of was that Marina had never physically met Chance Jordan before Saturday. After the incident, he had pulled all of the visitor logs for the last four years and confirmed that Chance had never visited Havenhurst. And while Marina had been on several field trips, none had been to Wellington or any event where she could have had an opportunity to meet him.

The easy explanation was that Marina was delusional, or just pretending in an effort to get attention. But Marina had never displayed such behaviors in the past, and Shelby felt he knew the girl well enough to be able to discount this potential out of hand. Her child-like mind just wasn't sophisticated enough to concoct, much less execute, such a plan.

One other variable to consider was the drug trials he was conducting for the military. Marina had received a double dose of the compound for the first time on Thursday, then experienced her breakthrough on Saturday. Were the two events related? Possibly, but finding out created a host of new problems, as that research was highly classified and from what Shelby had seen, highly unethical. The project reminded him of the mind control experiments conducted by the C.I.A. in the '50s and '60s.

As Shelby stood pondering the possibilities, the hallway door opened and Travis Shelby stuck his head into the room. "Dad, my keys are locked in the janitor's closet again," he said.

Dr. Shelby took a ring of keys from his belt and tossed them to his son. "Be sure not to leave those laying around," he admonished.

"I'll bring them right back," Travis assured, turning back into the hallway and closing the door.

Sorting through the bundle of keys as he walked, Travis headed to the janitor's closet. Reaching a door marked 'JANITORIAL SERVICES', he slid a key into the lock, and opened the door.

Travis had been working as a janitor at Havenhurst since he was fifteen. It wasn't because he needed the money. The Shelby family was wealthy, and Travis had a sizable trust fund waiting for him. But Dr. Shelby believed that Travis needed the character building that a menial labor job provided, and since his trust money wouldn't be available until after he graduated from college, if Travis wanted spending money, he would have to earn it by mopping floors. And that pissed Travis off.

So, when Travis met Martin Wellington, and Martin suggested stealing drugs from the hospital's pharmacy to supply Martin's fledgling drug empire, Travis saw an opportunity to finance the social lifestyle he felt he was entitled to.

Travis pulled on his coveralls and grinned. He called them his stealth suit. Travis had discovered soon after his first week on the job that when he was wearing it, he became 'The Janitor' and no one ever really noticed, The Janitor.

In his coveralls Travis was invisible. He could move, hiding in plain sight, anywhere in the hospital, and nobody would think anything of it. He was, after all, only The Janitor.

Travis pulled his cart out and began to push it down the hall. The last medication call of the day had been completed, and most of the administrative offices were empty. A few stragglers were just leaving, and they chatted amongst themselves as they walked by The Janitor without noticing him.

Travis knew he had a short window before his father would start thinking about his keys again, so he moved quickly to the pharmacy's door. Leaving his cart parked in front of the door, as janitors do, he entered the pharmacy's lobby.

Travis had done this numerous times in the last two years, and there had never been a question. He would slip in, skim some tablets from the bulk storage, then slip back out. It never took more than a few minutes.

Opening the door, he found the room mostly dark except for a few scattered security lights. As he proceeded past the main desk, he searched his father's keyring for the key to the Schedule II drug storage room.

Moving purposefully, Travis walked down the short aisle of non-controlled, over the counter medications, to the back of the pharmacy. As he cleared the end of the tall metal storage shelves and stepped into the narrow corridor along the back, he was startled by a booming voice from the office at the end of the hall.

"Hello Travis. Can I help you?"

The voice was that of Dr. Gregory Tallman, the pharmacy's supervisor. He was at his desk, which was stacked high with binders and files of medication orders, prescriptions, and receipts. Sitting mostly in the dark, he was barely visible, only a small desk lamp, and his computer monitor, illuminating his face.

Travis was surprised to see him. In the nearly three years the boy had been working for his father at the hospital, he had never seen Dr. Tallman work late, even once.

"Oh, hello, Dr. Tallman. I didn't see you there," said Travis, obviously shaken.

"Just doing some inventories," said Tallman, smiling even as stress showed on his jowly face.

His stress was not without reason. Due to recent changes in D.E.A. policy in response to a nationwide opioid crisis, unannounced audits were popping up with alarming regularity. So far Havenhurst had not been the target of one of these surprise visits, but Tallman doubted that their luck would hold much longer.

He had not been concerned that an audit would reveal any problems, but just to be safe, he decided to conduct a few spot checks. Almost immediately, discrepancies that he could not resolve began to surface.

A more in-depth sample revealed that the problem was much bigger and widespread than he had realized. At that point he had taken it upon himself to conduct a thorough and complete inventory, vowing to account for every tablet, cc, and capsule, but so far it wasn't looking good.

"How can I help you?" asked Tallman, taking off his glasses and rubbing his eyes.

"Uh," stammered Travis, attempting to collect himself, "Do you have any trash that needs to be taken out?"

Understanding at last, Dr. Tallman smiled and raised a waste paper basket that was overflowing with discarded documents.

"Always," he said.

"I'll come back later and vacuum," said Travis taking the can.

"Don't worry about it tonight," said Tallman with a wave of his hand. "I'll be here late working on this."

"What is all this?" asked Travis, cautiously curious. "I've never seen you here this late."

"I'm doing a full inventory of the pharmacy's stock, and as you can see," he said gesturing toward the stacks of binders on his desk, "it is rather involved."

"Oh, okay, well...I guess I'll see you later."

"Goodnight, Travis."

As Travis turned to leave, he glanced, frustrated, at the door to the Schedule II drug storage, then took Dr. Tallman's trash to his cart.

'Martin's gonna be pissed', was all he could think.

Chance and Marina hunched over their respective pieces of art, stealing glances at each other's work. The mood was light and happy as Chance's dilettante level stick figures drew giggles from Marina.

"Hey, no laughing," he admonished with a smile.

Pausing for a moment, he began to look through Marina's other drawings. He could see the rapid evolution of her work that Denali had spoken of.

His attention was captured by one of her earlier pieces. It was a depiction of a small girl outside of a two-story house, waving up at a sky with three suns.

"Why are there three suns?" he asked.

"That's my mom and dad, and my sister," Marina replied without looking up.

She said it in such a matter-of-fact way that at first the gravity of her comment missed him. When he realized that the conversation had just turned to the death of Marina's family, he was concerned that he may have opened an old psychological wound, but to his relief Marina just continued drawing, seemingly unperturbed by the question.

Chance looked again at the drawing, this time focusing on the house. It was a quaint two-story cottage with a porch, surrounded by trees. He had seen many such houses, but this one seemed familiar to him.

"Is this your house?" he asked.

"Yes," she said.

"It's very nice."

"It's not nice anymore."

"Where is it?"

"At a beach next to a lake."

"The beach off Lakeshore Drive?"

"I don't know," she said shrugging, "It's just a beach."

Chance glanced at Denali who nodded confirmation. "That's interesting because I'm meeting some friends of mine tonight at Haunt...Lakeshore Beach," said Chance lightly. "We're having a cookout."

"That sounds wonderful," said Marina, jumping up from her seat. "I need to get ready."

Chance was flummoxed. He looked to Denali, not sure of what to do.

"Marina, you know the rules," said Denali calmly. "You are not permitted to leave on unscheduled field trips."

Marina crossed her arms and stared at Denali defiantly. In a calm, empowered, and measured voice, she informed the Head Nurse that she would not be stopped.

"I will go, if I wish to go."

Denali was both shocked and thrilled. While Marina had thrown tantrums in the past, and engaged in argument in recent days, she had never openly defied a staff member, much less Denali. Marina's challenging of authority indicated maturation. The girl was growing up, changing, seemingly, by the hour.

Rising to her feet, Denali looked at Marina with a slight sparkle in her eye. "Ok, I think we've had enough for today," she said firmly. "Gather up your things, and say good night to Mr. Jordan."

"No," said Marina, putting herself between Chance and the nurse. "That's not fair. You said he could stay late."

Denali calmly spoke into a radio, and within seconds, two orderlies entered the room. When Marina saw them, she became visibly frightened.

Chance rose to his feet, his heart breaking as Marina's fear caused a flash of anger to shoot through him. His instinct to protect her, an instinct he was surprised to learn existed, surged, then subsided as he fought to control the impulse.

As the orderlies approached, Marina became panicked. She took cover behind Chance, and Chance's protective instinct surged again. He wanted to fight them off for her, to crush them and carry Marina to safety. Thankfully, discretion won out.

Instead of going to war, he turned and took Marina's hands in his. They were trembling as her eyes, wide with fear, locked on the orderlies.

"Marina," he said, but she did not respond.

"Marina!" he repeated forcefully, this time causing her to shift her gaze to him.

"Marina, I have to go," he said, sorrow soaking his voice.

"No, Sari'El. Don't go, Please, don't go."

Tears flooded her eyes, and he touched her face.

"Please," she whimpered.

"Marina, it will be okay. I'll come back to visit you again, but they won't let me if you make them mad. Please, do as they say."

"You promise to come back?"

"I promise, but only if you promise not to laugh at my drawings anymore," he said, wiping tears from her eyes.

Marina choked out a laugh, "But they're so bad."

"Ok, you can laugh at some of them."

Marina smiled. "Deal," she said.

Taking a deep, halting breath, Marina turned and walked to the waiting orderlies, who escorted her away. Denali went with them, but before leaving the room, she looked at Chance.

"Thank you, Mr. Jordan," she said before walking out the door.

Chance's heart hurt. As Marina had left with the orderlies, she had held his eyes with hers and he could see that all her joy was gone. He looked at his fingers, still damp with her tears and he couldn't get past the feeling that somehow, he had let her down.

Picking up his jacket and backpack, he walked to the observation room door, the cartoon characters on the wall seeming to mock him as he went.

As he approached the door, it opened and Dr. Shelby stood there inviting him in.

"I'm really sorry about that, Dr. Shelby," said Chance as he walked through the door.

"It wasn't your fault, Chance. You handled it extremely well," said Shelby reassuringly, as he closed the door. "We expected some choppy water at first."

"So, it's okay if I come back?" asked Chance, not sure what he would do if Shelby said no.

"Of course, it's okay. We look forward to your continued visits with Marina."

"Tomorrow then?" asked Chance, hopefully.

"Tomorrow will be fine."

"Sir, will she be okay?" asked Chance, looking through the window into the day room where nurse Denali was now collecting Marina's art supplies.

Shelby smiled. "Don't worry son, Marina just needs some time to reflect and get used to her new boundaries."

'Some time to reflect'. Chance was in need of that as well.

"Sir, would it be okay if I brought Marina some art supplies? You know, chalks, pencils, pastels, that sort of thing?"

"That would be very kind of you," said Shelby. "I'm sure she'll be thrilled."

Chance smiled, "Thank you, sir. Then I'll see you tomorrow."

"Until then," said Shelby.

As Chance walked out of the hospital, the sun was setting in the western sky, and darkness was inching its way up the valley. The cool vespertine air braced him, and he took a deep cleansing breath. He could smell the dampness of the lake miles distant on the gentle breeze.

Strapping his backpack to his seat, he closed his jacket and took out his phone, just as a big black S.U.V. pulled into the parking lot and stopped in front of the main entrance.

A uniformed soldier jumped out and ran around to open the rear passenger door. Chance watched curious, and was mildly surprised to see an attractive woman step out, her hand lightly gripping the soldier's as he helped her down.

The woman looked in Chance's direction and smiled, just as Dr. Shelby appeared and greeted her, taking from her a metal case as he did. As they entered the building, the mysterious woman gave Chance one more, almost flirtatious glance, then disappeared into the hospital.

EIGHTEEN

After baseball practice, Eric and Conor met up with Bella and Kimiko to make their final plans for that night's ghost hunting mission. Earlier that afternoon they had spread out across the campus to assemble the equipment they thought they would need.

Eric had slipped out of his physics lab with an electromagnetic field detector, and a laser thermometer. Kimiko had downloaded an audio analysis program designed by paranormal investigators, while Bella had borrowed a condenser mic and digital recorder from the audio-visual lab.

Conor had asked his dad if he could get some military grade night vision, but he couldn't get it in time. As a substitute, he had prepared his Go Pro Cameras.

Now they all sat in Eric's dorm room watching YouTube videos and getting psyched up for the evening ahead. Kimiko had set up her projector and the videos were being shown on the room's wall. The group huddled together, watching in rapt fascination as ghost hunters inched down a hall, their EMF detectors flashing red, as their thermometers measured drastic drops in room temperature, when the sepulchral silence in the dorm room was shattered by a blood-curdling scream.

Everyone in the room jumped, a few of them screamed as well, but all looked around the room for its source, until they realized that the sound of a murder in progress had come from Eric's phone. It was his new ringtone, selected especially for this evening. Bella was not amused.

"Damn you," she scolded, swatting his arm playfully.

Eric laughed as he picked up his phone and looked at the display, then tapped the screen. "Hey, bro. How's your date going?"

"It ended early," replied Chance.

"What happened? Did you grope her again?"

"Yeah, this time I got two big handfuls," dead-panned Chance.

"That's my boy," said Eric equally deadpan.

"So, anyway," continued Chance, "When are you guys leaving?"

"We can go now. We were waiting on you."

"OK, I'll head out to the lake and get a fire going. I'll meet you there."

"Sounds good. We're rollin' out now."

"One more thing," added Chance. "Could you bring me something to eat? I'm starving."

"No problemo, bro. We'll see you in a bit," said Eric, hanging up.

Chance pocketed his phone and started his bike. He checked his pockets to make sure everything was buttoned up, then pulled on his gloves.

He was ready to put his bike in gear when for no particular reason, he turned to look back over his shoulder at the hospital. There, standing in a third-floor window behind a security screen, he could see the silhouette of a person. After a second the silhouette raised its hand and waved, and he knew it was Marina.

He was relieved to see that she was OK. Smiling, he waved back. He felt bad leaving her behind, but consoled himself with the thought that he would see her again soon.

Putting his bike into gear, he rolled down the long driveway of the Haven-hurst hospital as twilight filled the valley.

Chance trudged out of the tree line and through the sand, his arms full of collected wood which he stacked on top of the pile of unused wood from the party on Friday. It was much more than they would need that evening, but he reasoned that this would not be the last time they would want a warm fire on the beach.

Using a discarded oar he had found, he dug a fire pit, and formed parapets around it that would protect the group from the wind. Lastly, he laid the fire.

The fire came to life quickly, and Chance, still a bit chilled by his ride from the hospital, was grateful for its warmth. Kneeling as he tended the fire, Chance became entranced by the twisting flames as they lapped at the wood, and danced over the pulsing embers. He sniffed the air as sap bubbled out of the wood's pores and ignited, filling the air with a pleasant pine scent.

The hypnotic effect of the fire relaxed Chance and gave him time to reflect on his visit with Marina. While it had ended with no small amount of tension, Chance's final glimpse of Marina as she stood in the window, had afforded him with some small measure of peace. Still, his feelings for this girl – who he had only just met – were baffling to him. He had hoped that his visit with her that evening would provide him with some answers, but instead, it had only raised more questions.

Turning his attention back to the fire, Chance tried to put the events of the last three days out of his mind. The fire had matured so he threw a large drift-wood log into the flames. Sitting back, he admired the subtle colors created as the mineral-saturated wood burned.

As he waited for his friends, his eyes were drawn to the old house brooding in the shadows cast by the firelight. Standing, he walked over to it and took in its sad condition. He noticed a large official looking sticker on its door, and went up on the porch to look at it. It was a notice of a tax lien auction and he realized that the neglected little house would soon have a new owner.

Chance peered through the windows and saw that the house was mostly empty. Only a few pieces of broken furniture remained. Trying the door, he found it to be locked.

Walking back out onto the sand, Chance turned and took it all in. The rising moon peeked out from behind the accumulating clouds, its light emphasizing the house's imperfections.

Even in its state of advanced deterioration, the similarities to Marina's drawing were obvious. Curious, he decided he would conduct a public records search to find out who owned it.

A moment later, Chance's attention was drawn to the nearby parking lot by the flash of headlights. Recognizing Conor's truck, he gave the house a final glance, then turned and jogged up the beach to meet his friends. When he got there, the group was already pulling supplies and equipment from the truck's bed.

"Hey, guys," said Chance as he arrived. They all greeted him and began hauling their stuff down the beach.

"Is that our fire?" asked Eric indicating the glow near the house.

"Yep," confirmed Chance.

Chance noticed Kimiko carrying a cooler and jogged over to help.

"Here, let me take that," he said, lifting it from her arms.

As he did, he grunted, surprised to find the cooler much heavier than he had anticipated. Kimiko looked at him with a smirk as she blew a strand of hair from her face.

"Hey, Kimiko, are you and me OK?" asked Chance.

Kimiko smiled sweetly. "Yeah, I was just embarrassed," she said.

"I'm sorry," he said sincerely.

"No, it was funny. I just needed some time to realize it."

Bella, who was struggling under her own burden, looked at Chance then cast a sideways look at Eric.

"Wow, Chance is such a gentleman, helping a lady carry a heavy load," she said, louder than necessary.

"Yeah, he starts out all gentlemanly," scoffed Eric, "then the next thing you know, he's going for your boobs."

"I'll try to remember that," said Bella, giving Chance a wink.

Eric laughed while at the same time taking the blankets from Bella, a sheepish expression on his face.

As the group set up camp around the fire, they began to check their equipment and chatter about the ghost hunt. Their work soon complete, the friends settled back to relax and wait for the right moment, not exactly sure when 'the right moment' would be.

For Kimiko and Bella, the right moment for smores was already upon them, so with obvious delight, they began to lay out the ingredients.

"We brought the smores stuff we didn't get to eat on Friday," said Bella, when she saw Chance looking at her.

"Did you guys bring me something to eat?" said Chance, almost pleadingly.

"You don't like smores?" asked Bella innocently.

Chance looked at her, disappointment creasing his face. But as his eyes moved to Eric, anger poked at him causing his face to twitch like a damn getting ready to burst. Either out of pity, or self-preservation, Eric relented.

"Enhance your calm, bro. There's a roast beef sandwich for you in the food keeper."

"Oh, thank God," said Chance hurrying to the food keeper.

"You're welcome," dead-panned Eric.

Inside the house, from behind the broken glass and deteriorating curtains, it watched, looking down on the group as they talked and ate. It studied them, curious and fascinated.

Chance opened the food keeper and found his sandwich nestled with a bottle of iced tea. Sitting back down he unwrapped his dinner, his stomach growling in anticipation. But as he peeled back the paper wrapper, an abomination was revealed to his eyes.

There, about two inches down the side, right where the roast beef was thick, was a perfect bite-shaped hole. It loomed there. If a hole could be smug, this hole was.

Chance calculated in his mind who could have, would have committed such an atrocity. After only a moment's contemplation, his eyes slowly shifted to Conor.

"What...the hell...is this?" said Chance coldly as he pointed at his disfigured meal.

"Oh my god," said Conor, feigning shock. "That's... just horrible."

Chance stared at Conor, and Conor stared right back at him, maintaining with obvious effort, his expression of complete innocence.

"Now that I think about it," interjected Eric in an over-the-top Monty Python character's voice, "that chap in the sandwich shop did appear a raw bit peckish."

"You know what?" said Chance with a sudden matter-of-fact tone, "I don't care."

At this he tore off a big bite, moaning with pleasure. Conor smiled as he watched his friend wolf down his dinner.

Kimiko finished assembling two smores and turned to Conor, who extended his arm, holding his blanket open like a great cape. Kimiko stepped in, snuggling under his arm as he wrapped her up, then sat with her, leaning back with a groan of satisfaction.

Bella sat with her head on Eric's shoulder as she impaled a marshmallow, then extended it into the fire. Chance sat alone, poking the fire with a stick as he finished his sandwich. Wadding the paper wrapper he tossed it into the flames, and watched as it was consumed.

Placing another log on the fire, his mind wandered back to Marina. It surprised him how much she possessed his thoughts. He had very much enjoyed her company, the music of her laughter, and the charm of her conversation. He was also more than a little intrigued by her insistence that they had known each other in what she referred to as 'the before time', and he looked forward to exploring that during future visits.

While Chance was sure he had never met Marina before, he could not deny the feeling of comfort and familiarity that gripped him when he was with her. He hoped she was sleeping peacefully. Her fear, as she had realized that the orderlies were going to take her away, had pierced him, and now he struggled with his feelings of helplessness at that moment of her distress.

"Uh-oh," said Bella breaking his thoughts.

Chance looked over at her in time to see her wipe off her forehead as she looked into the sky. Looking up he saw that a layer of clouds had blown in, and the full moon behind them had turned the sky to silver and soot.

"I think we're jinxed," said Bella.

"At least we're not getting our tires slashed," quipped Conor.

Conor was just trying to be funny, but his comment unintentionally triggered an anger in Eric that had been building since Saturday.

"Fuck Martin Wellington..." he said forcefully.

"Shush, not with the mouth I kiss," said Bella, placing her fingertips on his lips. "It's not a night to be angry."

Eric instantly mellowed as Bella began feeding him smores.

Chance and Conor looked at each other, impressed by Bella's ability to pacify Eric. While he had grown up in Boston's high society, Eric was a stereotypical Boston street brawler, and once he got angry, it normally took a while for him to calm down.

———

From the darkness, it voyeuristically observed the group. Two couples nuzzled one another, occasionally kissing sensuously, but one sat alone. It was this one that it found most fascinating. The increasing wind funneled through the house, whipping the remnants of the once beautiful curtains. Annoyed, the watcher moved to another window, where the offending treatments had long since wasted away.

———

Chance wasn't looking directly at the house, but his eyes were drawn by movement in an upstairs window. Without turning his head, he slowly shifted his eyes, and as he did a chill ran over his body when he saw two blue glowing dots staring down at him.

"Guys," he said in a conversational tone, but nobody responded.

Chance reached into his backpack and pulled out a monocular. Rising to his feet he walked over to where Eric and Bella were giggling and feeding each other smores.

Sitting down, Chance used the two distracted lovers to shield him from the glowing eyes.

"Guys!" he said again more forcefully, as he put the monocular to his eye and peered around the blanket-covered couple. "Something is watching us."

All conversation stopped as what Chance had said sank in. Conor and Kimiko stared across the fire as Eric and Bella's chocolate smeared faces peeked out from around their blanket, eyes wide and searching.

"Don't look, just get your stuff ready," said Chance.

As the others got their gear in hand and operational, Chance used his monocular to scan the upstairs windows, but now he saw nothing.

"Is it still there?" asked Bella, sitting motionless as Chance used her as a blind.

"No, I don't see it now."

"Kimiko pulled her digital camera out of her bag and connected the microphone, as Conor put on a headband with a go-pro camera mounted on it. Tightening the strap, he looked at Eric who looked back amused.

"What?" said Conor self-consciously.

"How are you not still a virgin?" said Eric, shaking his head.

Kimiko began recording Chance as he sat searching the house's windows. His image appeared, then refocused, on her monitor as she made adjustments. Slipping a pair of headphones on, she tapped on the mic and nodded her approval. Everything checked out. She was ready, but then a look of confusion creased her face.

At first, she thought she had lost audio. Reaching out she snapped her fingers in front of her camera, but discovered that everything was working properly. Pulling her headphones down around her neck, she realized that the reason she had heard nothing through her equipment was because a heavy and oppressive silence had fallen over their camp and the beach around them, the only ambient sound being the occasional pop from the fire.

The wind had stopped, as if a great being had suddenly inhaled and held its breath, causing a surreal stillness to envelop them. The leaves on the trees were motionless, and the formerly chopping lake now lay flat and thick like a pool of oil.

Chance felt it as well. For the first time since taking position next to Eric and Bella, he took his eye away from his monocular. He looked around confused, opening and closing his mouth in exaggerated yawns in an effort to equalize his ears. Even Eric and Bella were holding their noses as they tried to counteract the unexplained change in pressure.

Raising his scope back to his eye, Chance once again observed the upstairs windows. In the still air the formerly fluttering window dressings hung motionless, like slabs of meat in a butcher's freezer.

"What did you see?" asked Eric, feeling compelled by the viscous silence to whisper.

"It looked like the eyes in Kimiko's photo," said Chance, not taking his eye from the scope.

"Maybe it was a raccoon," offered Bella almost hopefully.

"Maybe," said Chance.

"There must be somebody in there," insisted Conor. "A bum or something."

"A bum?" challenged Kimiko. "A bum with eyes that glow?"

"What do we want to do, people?" pressed Chance. "We need a plan."

Conor took point. "I say we rush the house and find out who's in there."

"A paranormal frontal assault?" laughed Eric. "That's your plan?"

"You got a better one?"

Eric had to admit that he didn't, so he said nothing.

"Ok," began Conor, taking a breath, "We have to move fast and get in there before whoever's inside can react."

"The door is locked," said Chance, "and I don't know how sturdy it is, so whoever goes through first better hit it hard."

As Chance watched the windows of the upstairs room where he had first seen 'the ghost', the lifeless curtains surged once again.

"The curtains moved," whispered Chance. "Someone has got to be in there."

"OK, when I say 'go', we rush the place," said Conor, stepping into his accustomed role as team captain.

"Got it," replied Chance, "but wait until I see it again."

Eric nodded as Conor continued, "Kimiko, when we go, you hang back a few seconds, then follow, recording on the run. If something happens, we don't want to miss it."

"Kay," said Kimiko, her eyes sparkling with excitement.

When Conor said nothing else, Bella looked at him questioningly. "What am I supposed to do?"

Eric put his arm around her and pulled her close. "Your job is to be the sexy coed that gets chopped up in the basement."

"You are such an ass," said Bella, punching Eric's shoulder hard. Her anger more the result of fear than anything else.

Kimiko got up and moved next to Bella, as much to support her friend as to get a better filming angle on the house. Surreptitiously, she pointed her camera and began to record, moving her objective over its weathered facade.

Panning across the building, she started with the second floor, then lowering her frame, she swept slowly across the downstairs. At first what she saw didn't register as noteworthy. She saw broken windows and motionless tattered curtains, then panned across the black void of the front door which stood ajar, but stopped when she remembered what Chance had said.

"Chance, I thought you said the door was locked," she said.

"It is," he insisted, still fixated on the window where he had seen the eyes.

"Well, it's open now," said Kimiko, who then gasped. "Oh my God, I see it."

Chance quickly trained his monocular on the front door. Just as Kimiko had said, it stood partially open. Increasing the magnification of his scope, he looked deeper into the dark doorway. Instantly he felt every hair on his body stand up as he stared into a pair of glowing eyes that crawled with blue electric arcs like an intense lightning storm floating unblinkingly in the velvety blackness.

"I see it," he croaked. "It's just standing there, looking at us."

Chance, Eric and Conor all looked at each other, tensing. Kimiko's eyes searched their faces, waiting for the cue.

It came.

NINETEEN

"**Go, go**, go, go!" yelled Conor as he sprang to his feet.

Eric, and Chance moved instantly and all three boys launched themselves toward the house. In the tradition of all great charges throughout history, as they went over the top, they did so screaming battle cries from terrified faces, their shouts eliciting a startled scream from Bella.

Kimiko, on the other hand, was in the zone. Rising, she pointed her camera at the boys as they sprinted toward the house, silvery spouts of sand kicking up behind them. She waited a few seconds then charged after them, her primal war cry coming from a deep ancestral place.

Bella, now standing alone by the fire, her blanket still draped over her head like a shroud, was in a state of panic. "What did you see? What did you see?" she screamed as Kimiko sprinted away.

But Kimiko was gone and Bella realized that she was now alone. Every slasher horror film she had ever seen immediately flashed through her mind; the gruesome acts of slaughter inflicted upon the screaming girls that fell behind. With courage driven by fear, she dropped her blanket and ran after Kimiko, screaming as she did, but it wasn't a war cry.

As the paranormal assault team closed on the house, whoever – or whatever – was inside, slammed the door shut. Conor, determined not to let their quarry escape, began to give orders.

"Eric, go around back and make sure no one gets out!"

"On it," said Eric, peeling off and heading around the side of the house.

As Chance ran up onto the porch, he braced himself just before he slammed into the house's door, causing it to fly open violently as he disappeared through the threshold. Conor followed close behind, and he too charged into the dark house as Kimiko came running up behind him.

"Damn you Kimiko, wait for me!" screamed Bella.

"But Kimiko would not be stopped, and she stormed through the door and into the black room beyond without hesitation, her camera held out before her like a sword.

Bella ran onto the porch but stopped at the door. Realizing she was alone, she cursed under her breath and swore to herself that if she got chopped up in some basement, she would come back and make Eric Easton's life a living hell.

Inside the house there was at first a lot of shouting. Then, as flashlights came on, it became a confusion of light beams that frantically swept the dark space.

"Anybody see anything?" yelled Conor, but before anyone could respond, a scream cut through the room.

All of the light beams converged on Kimiko, who was bending down to pick up her camera from the floor.

"Miko, are you alright?" called out a frightened Bella from the doorway.

"I saw a face," replied Kimiko as she inspected her camera and mumbled a curse.

A that moment the sound of a crashing door made them all jump. Conor who was closest to the sound, let out a shrill yelp as Eric came through the back door holding his laser thermometer out in front of himself like a weapon, the red beam slashing through the dust in the air.

"Are you guys OK? Where's Bella?" shouted Eric.

Bella ran to Eric and held him tightly. Her relief was obvious as her fear quickly passed.

"I saw a face," repeated Kimiko, forcefully.

"Over here," said Chance.

All lights, and Kimiko's camera, followed his voice as Chance held up a child's doll.

"It's just a doll," said Chance, as he sat the doll on the window sill.

A nervous laughter broke out in the room as a sense of relief rippled through the group.

"Maybe those are the eyes you saw," suggested Bella hopefully.

"No, I saw the eyes upstairs as well."

"Maybe the doll..."

"What?" interrupted Chance. "Maybe the doll walked down the stairs and opened the locked door?"

Bella turned and placed her head on Eric's chest. As he held her, he looked at Chance, silently mouthing, "What the hell is wrong with you?"

Chance immediately felt bad. He could tell that Bella was frightened and was grasping for any explanation that would make her feel better. Everyone wanted an explanation. But Chance was looking for real answers. Answers that ran much deeper than a fun little ghost hunt would provide.

"Did you see anyone out back?" asked Chance.

Eric, still holding Bella just shook his head.

Reaching into his pocket, Chance took out the Electromagnetic Field Detector and took a reading.

"Whoa," he said, his eyebrows arching.

"What do you see?" asked Kimiko, coming over to look.

"E.M.F. levels are almost twice baseline," he said, slowly turning 360 degrees, holding the device out in front of him.

"Bad electrical wiring?" offered Kimiko.

Conor walked over to a switch on the wall and flipped it. "I don't think the power has been on in this place for a long time."

"Record the E.M.F. data," said Kimiko, "I'll upload it to the analysis program latter."

"Already done," said Chance.

Bella had recovered. She was more embarrassed by her reaction than upset with Chance. She hated that she had become 'That Girl'. The screamer that needs hugs. She swore to herself that from now on she was going to, 'Cowboy up', as Conor would often say and stop all this frail princess crap.

Closing her eyes, she took a deep breath and resolved herself. When she opened her eyes, for no reason, she looked up the dark stairwell. At the top of the stairs, squatting down behind the wooden balustrades, was a shadowy figure with glowing blue eyes. And it was staring directly at her.

Her scream was long and piercing.

Eric looked up and saw the creature regarding him, studying him, then turning it ran down the upstairs hall, the sound of its footfalls thudding on the wooden floor as it fled.

"It's up there!" yelled Eric, pulling Bella back.

Kimiko did not wait for direction. Holding her camera out in front of her, she stormed up the stairs, taking them two at a time, Chance and Conor fast on her heels.

Eric took Bella's hand and ran after the others, pulling her along with him. Trailing along behind him she looked around nervously, keenly aware that she was, once again, in the bringing up the rear, 'Sacrificial Lamb' position.

Reaching the top of the stairs, Kimiko peered around the banister and down the dark, empty, hallway. The doors to the rooms along the hall all stood open but for one at the furthest end.

The group of friends slowly filed into the passageway, their flashlight beams moving erratically over its walls, as the floorboards of the aging home creaked beneath their feet. Creeping toward the conspicuously closed door, Chance held out his E.M.F. detector.

Kimiko moved up next to him. Shoulder to shoulder they advanced, when the E.M.F. detector's display, which had been a fluctuating between green and amber, suddenly spiked to solid red.

But no one noticed the maxed out E.M.F. display. It was made superfluous by the blinding light that emanated in a violent flash from the gaps around the closed door. It was stunning, as if a brilliant blueish supernova had exploded inside the room.

The shock of light disoriented them, like a punch in the face. They flinched away as it lashed out at them, swirling loose leaves and accumulated trash from the floor around them in a preternatural, windless, tornado. Then, as quickly as it had come, the light withdrew, seemingly drawing the air with it an ethereal vacuum that pulled the loose detritus that filled the air, tight against the door's voids.

And then, it was gone. The darkness returned, and the door which had been closed, swung slowly open, its rusted hinges screeching.

The ensuing silence cut into Chance. He became anxious that whoever, or whatever, had caused these bizarre events, that had stared back at him with the same unearthly glowing eyes as the dark hooded figure from his dream, was making good its escape.

Advancing, Chance, with Kimiko a few steps behind, burst into the now dark room. The rest of the group quickly followed. Fanning out into the obviously empty room, they were filled with both relief and disappointment to find nothing there but an old wooden chair. Chance went to the closet, but again found nothing.

"The windows are locked," reported Conor.

"So, what was in here?" asked Bella, excitedly. "I saw it looking at me. We all heard the footsteps."

"I saw it too," said Eric, going to her.

"And what was that light?" added Conor, asking the question they were all thinking.

Looking at his E.M.F. detector, Chance reported that the ambient energy readings were now normal. He held up the device to show the others that the display now read minimal levels.

As the others talked amongst themselves, Bella's attention was drawn to one of the room's walls. She let Eric's hand slip from hers as she pointed her flashlight up at it.

"Whoa, check this out," she said as she stood transfixed.

As her flashlight beam washed over the soiled surface of the wall, and was joined by the others, a massive and intricate mural, rendered entirely in what looked like crayon, was revealed. It filled the entire wall, from floor to ceiling. The drawings on the far left were obviously the oldest, their colors faded by time and accumulated dust.

Bella was fascinated, and at the same time horrified, by the story the colorful etchings told. A family, loving and happy, torn to pieces in the sand not more than a few steps away from where she and the others had been eating smores. The realization sickened her. For Bella at least, Lakefront Beach would never be the same.

The story went on to show that one had survived the vicious attack, only to be sequestered in painful solitude. It was almost more than Bella could tolerate.

"Such loneliness," she said softly as she placed her fingertips gently on the wall.

Stepping up to the wall, Conor scratched some of the color from one of the more vibrant drawings on the far right of the mural. "It's still soft," he said, his forehead wrinkling as he sniffed the waxy smear on his fingers. "I think this was done recently."

Chance stepped up closer as thunder rolled in the skies above, and rain began to dot what was left of the broken window panes. An uneasy feeling crawled through him as he looked at the wall art. He recognized the story, and he recognized the style, but the conclusion it forced him to was impossible.

Kimiko dutifully scanned the group and room with her camera, recording everyone's reactions. When she centered her frame on Chance once again, she panned down to his hand in which he held the E.M.F. detector. The display screen was visible so she zoomed in on it, and her eyes grew wide. Taking her eyes off her monitor she looked at the E.M.F. detector directly. The display was solid red.

"Chance, look," she said urgently.

Chance looked at her questioningly, as she frantically pointed down at his hand. Finally understanding, he looked down. When he saw the maxed-out display, he immediately began to slowly spin, holding the detector out in front of him.

"What's causing..." he began, but stopped, as he looked out of the bedroom door, and down the dark hallway. A hallway that was no longer dark, because of an intensely bright light that was shining up through the stairwell from the first floor below.

Chance's jaw clinched, "It's downstairs!" he yelled as he bolted out of the room and down the hall.

Conor was with him, Kimiko right behind. Excited, Eric kissed Bella on the cheek, then charged after the others

Bella glanced around the room. Realizing that she was once again alone, she muttered another curse then stormed out the door.

"Eric, I swear I'm going to kill you!" she roared.

Chance bounded down the stairs, his flashlight beam whipping wildly. Behind him thundered the sound of running feet.

Conor followed closely, with Kimiko right behind recording Chance as he charged toward the bright light in the room below, but just as he jumped down to the last landing, the light withdrew with the same vacuumous implosion as they had experienced upstairs. By the time Chance ran into the downstairs room, it was as it was before, dark and empty. Conor, Kimiko, and Eric arrived a few heartbeats later. Looking around they saw only Chance, standing alone in the center of the room.

"Did you see it?" asked Conor excitedly, but Chance said nothing.

"Where's Bella?" asked Eric, when he saw that she had not arrived with everyone else.

Everyone turned to look up the stairwell just in time to see Bella descending the steps like a queen coming to court. Holding her hands folded primly in front of her, she positively floated into the room, and crossed to the door. Pausing there, she watched the rain fall outside, then turned and regarded Eric with cold eyes,

"You abandoned me," she accused.

As if on cue, a bolt of lightning ripped the night sky behind her, shaking the house.

Eric opened his mouth to respond, but Bella raised her hand, "I wish to return to Wellington," she said.

"Yeah, we should go," said Conor. "We've already been here longer than we should have."

Conor walked up to Chance and put his hand on his friend's shoulder, "We can put your bike in the back of my truck."

"Thanks, bro," said Chance.

Kimiko recorded a last quick 360 of the room before shutting off her camera. Conor came over to her and wrapped it in his coat. Looking up he saw Eric and Bella push out into the rain, Bella letting out a squeal as the cold rain soaked her.

The camera protected, Kimiko and Conor sprinted out the door and across the sand to their camp to collect their things, their fire now just a pile of soggy coals beneath a smoldering column of steam.

Chance surveyed the room one last time. All was still, and quiet. He checked his E.M.F. detector hoping for something – anything – but there was nothing, the display barely reading green.

He swept his flashlight a final time across the room, its beam visible on a universe of swirling dust motes. Still, he felt something drawing him in.

Chance could hear Conor yelling for him to hustle up. Taking one final look, he closed the door and ran to help the others break camp.

"Oh...my...God," gasped Bella, staring at the glowing monitor in open-mouthed astonishment

The others sat around her in a pile. They had watched and waited patiently as Kimiko tweaked the final edit of the video, now they shared the fruits of their little adventure.

The disheveled group of friends had hurried back to campus with their raw footage and data, Eric begging Bella's forgiveness the entire trip. As the others had changed into dry cloths, Kimiko had been busy downloading the video footage from her camera and Conor's Go-Pro.

She had also captured the data from the electromagnetic field detector and washed it through the analysis program she had acquired. Lastly, she had edited it all together. Now they huddled around in their sweats and t-shirts, Kimiko in her "Harley Quin" footie jammies, as she burned copies onto flash drives.

"Play it again," said Conor.

Kimiko moved the cursor across the screen and clicked play. Since she had synced both cameras, the display was a split screen. At the bottom of the screen was a bar that showed green, amber, and red, levels of the E.M.F. detector. Next to that was a sound wave analysis display. When the video ended, they all sat in silence staring at the frozen image of the final frame. It was Eric that spoke first.

"We gotta post this online," he said in an almost breathless whisper.

"If I wasn't there, I'd swear this was complete bullshit," said Conor.

"Look at the E.M.F. levels when that bright light came," said Eric, pointing at the screen.

"1420 megahertz," said Chance.

"The harmonic resonance of the universe," said Bella, unexpectedly, causing every eye to turn and look at her.

"What?" said Eric.

Realizing that she had suddenly become the center of attention, Bella straightened and cleared her throat. "I learned about it in my astronomy class. It has to do with the harmonics of hydrogen and how it has a unique resonance."

"So, you're saying this is a space ghost?" said Eric smiling.

"I'm just telling you what 1420 megahertz is," said Bella, reaching out and touching the tip of Eric's nose.

Chance turned back to the computer, thinking, but clearly not about what he had just heard. Something in the video was poking at him, but he couldn't put his finger on it. He stared at the screen, chewing on his lip.

"Play it again please," he said at last, but as the video started to run, a thought came to him.

"Wait, fast-forward to where you screamed," he said.

"Which time?" quipped Eric.

"Ha-ha," dead-panned Kimiko.

"Oh, that's right," Eric corrected. "One of those screams came from Conor."

"That wasn't me," protested Conor lamely.

Chance ignored the exchange, his attention fixed on the screen. "Run it from where you dropped the camera."

Kimiko dragged the slider to the right until the haunting face of the doll appeared, then clicked play.

A startled scream came from the speaker.

"Mute it," he said without breaking concentration.

Kimiko did as he asked, and Chance let the video run until the moment he saw himself place the doll on the window sill.

"OK, now fast forward to when we came back downstairs."

Kimiko complied, then clicked play.

Chance watched intensely as it progressed to the point the camera panned around the room during Kimiko's final 360.

"Pause there," he said, a wide shot of the front door leading out to the lake filling the screen.

"What do you see, Chance?" asked Bella.

"The doll," he said, turning to the others, "it's gone."

Everyone turned back to the screen as they contemplated Chance's words, and the meaning of the empty window sill.

"Is that the same window?" asked Conor.

"Yes," confirmed Kimiko, pointing at the screen. "That's the window next to the door."

"So where did it go?" said Chance, to no one in particular.

"Someone must have come in while we were upstairs and taken it," suggested Conor.

"Really?" replied Eric, "You think someone walked in from the beach while we were upstairs, just to steal a worthless doll? Do you actually hear the shit you say?"

"Well, it didn't just get up and walk out of there on its own," snapped Conor.

"Ooh, maybe it was possessed, like Chucky or Annabelle," said Kimiko, but her words had little impact, as the group had fallen silent, straining to find any explanation that could fit the evidence before their eyes.

"Hey, guys, we're all tired, and more than a little freaked out," said Eric. "Maybe we should call it a night and get some sleep."

"I'm sure I won't be able to sleep for the next week," said Bella rising.

"Yeah, I'm pretty wired myself," said Conor.

As Kimiko began to break down her equipment, Eric crossed over to Conor. "Sorry, bro," said Eric. "I didn't mean to jump on you like that."

"I had it coming," said Conor, chuckling. "A doll burglar. What a dumb ass thing to say."

Conor clapped Eric on the back, then headed toward the door.

"OK, I'll see you guys in the morning," he said as he walked out into the hallway holding Kimiko's hand.

Bella took that moment to step in front of Eric. She smiled coyly as she smoothed his pajamas.

"You look very sexy in your new PJs," she purred.

Bella had purchased the black silk pajamas for his birthday the week before, and this was the first time she had seen him wearing them.

"Thank you," he said smiling. "They feel so wonderful against my skin."

"I know, don't they?" she said, winking conspiratorially.

"How would you know?" he asked.

"If you don't think I wore them to bed at least once before giving them to you, then you don't know me at all."

"I thought that was you," he said, holding the lapel to his nose, "but sadly, your scent is fading. Since, as you say, you won't be sleeping for a week, perhaps you could stay here and put them on...for a few hours? Refresh them so to speak."

She smiled sweetly as she took hold of his lapels. Pulling him down she kissed him softly. "Ciao, mi armor."

"Ciao, Bella," he replied with a sigh.

Eric watched her go, then closed the door. Turning to Chance, he let out an exhausted breath.

"Wow, what a night," he said, plopping down on his bed, but Chance didn't hear him.

Chance had put on headphones and was studying the video intensely. When the partially open front door of the beach house came into frame, he paused the video. Zooming in, he focused on the bright, glowing, electric-blue eyes as they stared out of the screen, and into his soul.

TWENTY

Travis parked his car in front of his dormitory, then took out his phone and tried once again to call Martin. Listening for a moment he waited, but upon hearing Martin's voicemail pick up, he disconnected the call in frustration.

Travis had been trying to reach Martin ever since leaving Havenhurst. He knew Martin would be angry that he hadn't scored. He had hoped to let him know over the phone, so that the volatile Martin would have a chance to calm down before he came face to face with him. Finally, he had sent a text saying only that he hadn't been able to find what Martin 'wanted at the store'.

But Travis' failure to score was the least of his worries. The inventories Dr. Tallman was conducting were like an axe falling in slow motion toward his neck. He was fairly sure that they would eventually reveal his activities, and when they did, that would trigger a D.E.A. investigation.

At the very least it would result in tougher security and that meant telling Martin that Havenhurst was no longer a supply point, a bit of news that Travis was sure Martin would not take well.

Travis wasn't stupid. He realized that his only real value to Martin was as a supplier for their little enterprise providing Adderall to Wellington's overachievers, and Oxy to those with more dangerous tastes. Once he was no longer of any value to Martin...well.

Stepping out of his car, he looked up at the old four-story building, its red bricks mostly covered by newly sprouted ivy. He was surprised to see that the blinds in his room had been closed, but the lights in the room were on. He could just see their glow leaking out through the slats of the louvers, neither condition being how he had left them. Locking his car, he hurried to his room.

Arriving at his door slightly out of breath, he approached slowly, watching as the light shining beneath it was intermittently interrupted by a crossing shadow. As he stood listening, he could hear movement inside, as drawers were opened, and their contents dumped on the floor.

Placing his hand on the door's lever, he gently pressed down, but found the door locked. Reaching into his pocket, he took out his room key and slid it into the lock.

He turned the key slowly, but despite his efforts at stealth, as the tumblers pulled out of the lock's cylinder, the lock clicked loudly. Instantly, the sounds of the frantic search inside stopped, and the room went dark.

Pushing the door slowly open, Travis peered into the room. All he could see was the mess from the search he had interrupted, lying strewn about. Stepping over the debris, he entered cautiously.

He didn't see the figure that lunged out of his closet, but he felt it, as he was rocked by a violent blow that drove him to the floor. Flailing in an effort to fend off the attack, Travis rolled over and raised his arms defensively, but froze in motionless terror as a blade flashed up, and pressed firmly against his throat.

Looking up at the figure looming over him, Travis was both relieved and terrified to find that his attacker was Martin Wellington. But any relief he may have felt was wiped away, as he looked into Martin's crazed eyes.

They were wild and red, as though the boy had not slept in days. His face was pale as death and slick with sweat. His lips curled back, exposed a gnashing and horrific snarl. Martin was a grotesque presence and Travis knew why.

When Travis' business arrangement with Martin had started, it wasn't long before Martin was getting high on his own supply. Martin's drug of choice was Oxycontin. In the beginning he just took the pills, but later he started grinding the tablets up and snorting them. Recently, he had begun cooking and injecting it. That's when the hook went in deep. Now when Martin ran out, he became a complete psychopath, unable to even mimic civilized behavior.

For Travis however, it was not Martin's withdrawal-crazed expression that worried him most. What was of much greater concern, was the knife Martin held to his throat.

Large and gleaming, it was the same intimidating weapon that Travis had last seen – or at least thought he had seen – buried to its hilt in Chance Jordan's chest. Now it was pressing against his throat, where its razor-sharp edge had already drawn blood, the pain reminding Travis that with only a flick of Martin's wrist, the last thing he would see in this world would be his own blood, spraying in arterial spurts, across Martin's homicidal expression.

"Martin, come on, man. It's me," he pleaded.

"Shut up," said Martin, kicking the room's door closed.

Keeping his blade against Travis' throat, Martin reached over and dumped Travis' backpack on the floor, finding only an English Comp book and a laptop.

Martin frowned as he surveyed the contents. His fury building, he fixed Travis' eyes with his own.

"WHERE ARE THEY?!" he roared, pawing at Travis' pockets.

Finding nothing, he raged again, this time just inches away from Travis' face. His breath was hot and acrid, as spittle hung from his curled lips in long slimy strands. "Don't fuck with me! You said you'd get the shit tonight. Where is it!"

"I couldn't get to it," said Travis, his voice cracking with fear. "Dr. Tallman was there. I tried to call you."

"That's not my problem."

"It's both of our problem," said Travis, "He's doing an inventory. He's gonna find out about the missing stuff and when he does, it's a short step to me, then you, then prison."

Martin's eyes frantically searched Travis' as he processed this new information. "Bullshit, you're tryin' to cut me out," he said, coming to a conclusion.

Twisting the cruel looking blade so that its tip was pointed straight down at Travis' throat, Martin shifted his weight behind the tang. His body was shaking, and it caused the light from the street outside to flicker off the blade and across Travis' face.

Travis felt the blade's pressure slowly increasing against his throat. He was sure that he was about to die. He could feel that at any moment, his flesh would submit to the steel, that cold edge would slice through his arteries, and he would bleed out within seconds.

Most people who chase the opium dragon never catch it. After the ecstasy of that first high, they spend the rest of their drastically shortened lives trying to feel it again. But for Martin it hadn't worked that way. For him, the beast had circled back, sinking its teeth into him, and shaking him violently, and Travis knew he had to feed that beast, or it would take them both.

"Dude, if you're hurting, I have some Oxy here. I can fix you up," he said, his voice cracking with fear.

Martin relaxed, but only slightly. Paranoia gripped him as he looked at Travis coldly.

"You said you couldn't get any," said Martin suspiciously.

"I didn't, but I have my own stash. It's right over there," said Travis, pointing across the room.

"Where?" asked Martin, turning to look.

"Over there, in the leg of my bed."

Martin glanced at the bed, then back at Travis. "If you're lying...you're dead." he said.

"I swear, it's there."

Martin's grip eased as he slowly pulled the knife back. Standing he looked down at Travis, who held his hands up in submission.

"Get it," he said icily.

Travis slowly sat up, then rolled to his knees and scuttled across the floor to his bed. Lifting the end so that the bedposts came off the floor, he reached under it and pulled out a hard-shell guitar case, which he used to block the bedframe, so it remained elevated.

With his fingers, Travis probed a hole in the bottom of the bedpost. Extracting a zippered, leather, pencil bag, he held it out to Martin who snatched it out of his hand.

Martin opened the pencil carrier and pulled out a plastic baggie that contained some white pills. Dumping the contents onto Travis' desk, he selected a few of the tablets, then using the pommel of his knife, he crushed them into a fine powder.

Seeing this, Travis went to the door and turned the deadbolt, securing the room. He then started picking up the contents of his dresser drawers, which Martin had scattered about the floor during his frantic search.

Looking back at Martin, Travis saw him snorting a long line of powdered

Oxy through a rolled-up piece of writing paper. Leaning back in the chair, Martin took a deep breath and closed his eyes, his body slumping slightly as he relaxed.

"We need to talk about Dr. Tallman's inventory," said Travis, carefully.

"Who?" asked Martin without opening his eyes.

"Dr. Tallman," repeated Travis, "the pharmacist at Havenhurst."

Martin opened his eyes and looked at Travis, "Tell me everything that happened."

Travis detailed the events of that evening, Dr. Tallman's inventory and how Travis had returned a few times, but Tallman was still there, saying he would be working late.

Martin listened carefully, at one point crushing another tablet. When Travis was done, Martin spoke.

"Did Tallman say when the inventory would be completed?"

"He said he would be working on it for a few days. Why?"

Martin sat thinking as he used his school I.D. to chop up the crushed tablet, then scrape it into long neat lines that he vacuumed up his nose.

"Does anyone else know about this inventory?"

"I don't think so. My dad maybe, but I got the feeling he had just started."

"Then we still have time."

"Time? Time for what?"

"To finish the job," said Martin, sheathing his knife and stuffing the baggie of Oxy into his pocket.

"Finish?" said Travis, startled. "Are you crazy? Tallman knows. I can't go back in there."

"You're right," said Martin smoothly, a disquieting, evil grin cracking his face.

"To go back and skim a few more doses would be stupid." he said standing, which forced Travis to step back nervously. "That's why we're gonna take it all."

TWENTY-ONE

Dr. Tallman sat at his desk surrounded by stacks of purchase invoices and medication distribution records. He studiously compared them to the nurse's station computer records, and the more he looked, the bigger the problem got.

Invoices indicated ordering in excess of what the nurse stations had reported as dosages delivered. The implications were clear. Either the hospital had been shorted on the delivered narcotics, or dosages were being removed without being logged.

Tallman knew that determining whether or not the shortages he had found were actual, or just the result of paperwork errors, would require a physical count, and THAT would require another late night. Which, as far as Tallman was concerned, would have to wait until at least tomorrow.

It didn't matter when it was done really. The good doctor already had a fairly clear idea of what It would indicate, and it wasn't good. If he couldn't identify the problem, he was completely screwed.

Leaning back, he rubbed his eyes and looked at his watch. It was late. He shook his head when he realized how late, and that he had been at his desk for fourteen straight hours.

Standing, he stretched, then began to stuff his work into his briefcase. Exiting the Pharmacy, he locked the door before walking down the tiled hall toward the lobby, his footsteps echoing in the half lit vacant corridor.

At that time of night, the hospital was mostly deserted. Other than a small nursing staff that tended to hover around their nursing stations, and a roving security guard that tended to hover around the nurses, the only occupants were the patients who were locked in their rooms for the night.

Rounding the corner, Tallman walked across the lobby towards the front door, when a voice called out to him.

"Late night, Dr. Tallman?"

The voice was that of security guard Dick Dobos. He was working a double shift. One of many. Tallman suspected that Dobos wasn't as much interested in the overtime as he was reluctant to take off the uniform, which represented the only power he had in his otherwise pathetic life.

"Yes, Dick, it is late," said Tallman, using Dobos' first name intentionally.

Tallman didn't like Dobos. He knew that Dobos frequently went out of his way to make the lives of the patients more difficult than they needed to be. He also knew that the wanna' be cop required the patients to call him "Officer Dobos".

Tallman smirked slightly when he noticed that Dobos had winced slightly at being called by his Christian name. Without another word he turned and walked out of the hospital.

As the imposing door closed behind him with a heavy thud, Dr. Tallman stepped off the curb and pulled his coat tighter around him. The night seemed colder than it should have been, his breath expressing itself in misty puffs that floated in the night air.

As he walked across the parking lot, he noticed a black Cadillac Escalade parked at the curb. A young soldier in dress uniform leaned against its fender, manipulating a smart phone, the light from the device bathing his face in a cool light.

As Dr. Tallman walked toward him, the soldier glanced up. Pushing himself off the fender, he came to a position of quasi-attention.

"Good evening, sir," said the soldier.

"Good evening, young man. It's rather chilly out here tonight," said Tallman, pushing his free hand deeper into his coat pocket. "I hope you won't be out here much longer."

"You never know with Dr. Bains," the soldier said, smiling.

Tallman returned the smile and nodded.

"Well, good night," said Tallman.

"Good night, sir," replied the soldier.

Turning, Dr. Tallman continued to his car, a knowing smile on his face.

"Ah, the mysterious Dr. Bains," he mused under his breath.

Dr. Shelby tended to keep Dr. Sabine Bains under wraps whenever she visited the hospital. As a result, Tallman had only met her once, despite her having visited the hospital dozens of times before. Nevertheless, the effect she had on Dr. Shelby was obvious to everyone on his staff. He fawned over her, scurrying around to fulfill her every request, and it was widely whispered that Shelby and Bains often made use of the vacant exam rooms for activities... unprofessional.

Consequently, it was not uncommon for Bains' visits to last late into the night, the young soldier standing by outside, ever present, and infinitely patient.

Inside the hospital, Dobos turned his key, locking the front door. Giving it a tug to ensure it was secure, he turned and walked across the lobby to a nondescript door behind the receptionist's desk. Opening the door, he entered the hospital's security office.

Stepping into the security office was like traveling through time. If the hospital's lobby was a nineteenth century brothel, its security office was a twenty-fourth century starship.

The room was awash with the light of multiple monitors. They filled a whole wall of the office. Under them sat a futuristic control panel that controlled the hundreds of cameras throughout the hospital.

Taking a seat at the control panel, Dobos scanned the array of monitors. Tapping a pad, the large center screen changed to a view of one of the nurses' stations. Taking hold of a joy stick at the center of the panel, he began to manipulate the camera over that station.

As one of the nurses leaned over the desk making notes on a patient's chart, Dobos tried to zoom in down her cleavage with the high-resolution camera, but she moved away.

Disappointed, Dobos once again began to peruse the various monitors, when, as if jolted by an electric shock, he lurched forward and entered commands into the panel. Immediately the center screen switched to a woman doing yoga in the physical therapy room.

"Hello my dear," said Dobos leaning back to enjoy the view.

As she went through her routine, Dobos was riveted to the screen. So much so that he didn't notice Dr. Bains on another screen, pushing a girl in a wheelchair down a short hall and into an examination room.

⌐

Dr. Bains secured Velcro restraining straps around the wrists and ankles of a female subject on the examination table. The girl, mildly sedated, watched her helplessly, occasionally pulling weakly against her bonds, more confused than resistant.

"Who are you?" she asked, an edge to her delicate voice.

Bains ignored her. She rarely engaged with her subjects. Inserting an I.V. into the girl's arm, she tapped the screen of an E.K.G. monitor and made some notes on her pad computer.

Just then the door opened and Dr. Shelby entered. He was smiling until he saw the girl on the table, which caused his smile to fade to a much more grim expression. He carried with him the metal case that Dr. Bains had arrived with. Taking the case from him, Bains carried it to a table.

Shelby hovered over her shoulder as she flipped the latches and opened the case, intrigued by the heavy, white mist that billowed out and crept across the table. He moved closer, curious when he saw the futuristic looking syringe nestled inside along with a vial containing a fluorescent green liquid.

"What have we here?" he said, his fascination distracting him from the frightened girl on the table.

"A solution to the anomaly," said Bains as she lifted the vial and held it up to the light in obvious admiration.

TWENTY-TWO

A loud metal-on-metal clanking echoed through the darkened hallway as Dobos made his hourly rounds. The night nurse's yoga session had recently ended. Now he was amusing himself by banging his police Mag Light against the steel doors of the sleeping patients' rooms. Dobos did so love his petty torments.

He would stroll slowly along the corridor, flashlight in hand, dragging it along the wall until it hit a steel door jam, banged and slid across the door, then hit the door jam on the other side. Scrape-bang-scrape-bang, all the way down one side of the hall, and up the other.

Walking out into the main hall he approached one of the nurses' stations. Cinching up his pants, he leaned on the station's desk.

"You ladies doin' alright tonight?"

The two women exchanged glances, rolled their eyes, then invented duties that took them away to any place in the hospital where Dobos wasn't. Within a few seconds Dobos found himself alone, leaning awkwardly on the counter.

Dobos watched as the nurses left, "Alright then, I'll talk to you ladies later," he said. Then walking over to the elevator, he pressed the call button.

When the elevator car arrived, Dobos' finger hovered over the first-floor button, but at the last second, he inserted his pass key and selected the fourth-floor research level.

Stepping out onto the fourth floor, he pulled out his flashlight and directed the beam down the hallway. It was dark and deserted, only the red emergency exit signs at each end of the hall providing any light.

Dobos rarely came up to the fourth floor at night. Since access was controlled by a security keyed elevator, and the emergency stairwell was locked and alarmed, there was no real need for active security.

At five, the research staff would go home and security would clear the floor, double check the stairwell doors, then lock the elevator out of the floor. After that, the fourth floor became a ghost town.

Dobos dutifully checked each door to make sure they were locked, his rubber-soled tactical SWAT boots squeaking with every step on the freshly waxed floor.

He was about to cut his patrol short, and head back to the security office in hopes of catching another candid yoga show, when the faint sound of voices caused him to pull up motionless. Switching off his flashlight, he pressed himself silently into the shadow of a doorway and listened.

In the darkness he could see light leaking out from under the door of one of the exam rooms. Listening more closely he could hear the distinct murmurs of a male and female voice behind the door, and he smiled.

"Busted," he whispered softly.

Dobos had heard the gossip amongst the staff regarding the suspected after-hours interludes of doctors Bains and Shelby. Based on what he was hearing in the exam room this evening, it appeared the rumors were true.

Dobos wasn't stupid. He knew an opportunity when it fell in his lap, and he realized that if he could get a photo of Bains and Shelby together, his career would be set.

Moving with stealth, he crossed the hallway to the door of the observation room that serviced the exam room from which the voices were emanating. Quietly opening the door, he slipped inside.

Entering the observation room he peered around the frame of the large viewing window, then realized that that was silly since the window was a mirror on the other side. Standing up straight he looked into the exam room. He was not prepared for what he saw.

A girl was strapped to the table. She was visibly panicked and straining against her restraints. Her eyes were wide with fear as Dr. Bains stood over her, injecting what looked like radiator fluid into the girl's I.V. as Dr. Shelby stood back, arms crossed, watching as he chewed his thumbnail.

Dobos recognized the girl as a patient at the hospital. A paranoid schizophrenic named Nikki Van Pelt. She was known to cut herself then blame it on monsters that attacked her in the night, the scars of her many self-inflicted 'attacks' scoring her tattoo covered arms in shiny webs.

She claimed that these were the same monsters that had been responsible for killing her mother and stepfather. This gruesome double murder was the crime for which she was now committed to Havenhurst.

Dobos stood shocked, fascinated, and oddly aroused by the bizarre scene. He had always been attracted to the sexy, little goth girl. He found her long, black hair, heavy black eyeliner with matching lipstick that contrasted with her tattoo adorned ivory white skin, to be exotic and so very...dangerous. The fact that she was a convicted killer, just made her even hotter. She was Catwoman to his Batman. Seeing her now, bound and helpless, her gown falling open exposing her smooth ivory white legs, was almost more than he could bear.

Nikki's eyes were frantic as she watched the green fluid mix with the saline solution in her I.V., then slowly move toward her arm.

"What is that shit?" she said, both angry and frightened. "Dr. Shelby," she cried, "why are you doing this?" But Shelby did not respond.

Nikki turned once again to watch the mysterious green liquid as it inched toward the needle in her arm. When it at last entered her veins, she swooned. Her pupils dilated until her eyes looked like a pair of solar eclipses. They rolled back in her head as her body began to convulse in near erotic spasm, then she moaned, in what seemed to Dobos to be intense satisfaction, if not orgasm. That is if his hundreds of hours of downloaded porn were to be believed.

Bains circled the table, watching Nikki closely, smiling in approval.

"So fast," she cooed. "Much faster than the last formula."

Shelby stepped forward, now deeply engaged by the experiment.

"And now it appears to be stable in water," he said.

"At this point I will need this room to myself," said Bains.

Shelby was expecting this, while at the same time hoping that tonight would be the exception. Bains had made it very clear in the beginning, that the first trial of each new variant of the compound was to remain classified. Still his curiosity was killing him.

"I was hoping that perhaps this time..." pleaded Shelby, but Bains cut him off.

"We've been through this, Tom," she said firmly. "Now go downstairs, and wait for me in your office."

Shelby was crestfallen but quickly supplicated himself. He took one last look at Nikki, then walked out of the room.

Bains turned and walked to the instrument tray. Selecting a scalpel, she returned to the girl's side. Raising the blade, she cut the girl's gown down the middle until it fell open, exposing her naked body. A few more cuts, and the gown was gone.

Dobos was beside himself. He had seen some crazy shit during his time at Havenhurst, electro-stimulation, (they didn't like to call it 'electroshock' anymore), operant conditioning, hypnotherapy, even the use of hallucinogens. But things didn't get weird until Dr. Shelby had signed an agreement with the government to conduct psychological research. It was all very hush-hush, and that was when the enticing and mysterious Dr. Bains first showed up.

The first day that Dobos had seen her was memorable because it was the same day that the F.B.I. Behavioral Analysis Unit had brought in a serial killer for observation and evaluation. He was kept in a special cell on the fourth floor that Dobos liked to refer to as the 'Hannibal Lector suite'. If the stories he had heard were only half true, the reference wasn't far off.

Reportedly, their new guest had murdered his way across Europe, and three U.S. states, cutting his victim's hearts from their chests with surgical precision. The hearts were never found. Most believed he had eaten them.

The leading theory was that he was somehow connected to the Russian mob, or South American drug cartels, if for no other reason, the shear brutality of the murders, but also due to his stated motivation. When he was asked why he had killed all those people, the only thing he would say was, "They were witnesses."

Witnesses to what was never determined. The F.B.I. and Interpol had tried and failed to make even the most tenuous connection between the victims. Their only commonality was that they were all the same age and born within days of each other.

Unfortunately, it was the only thing he would say, in English, or any other language for that matter. Not that he was silent by any means. He was constantly mumbling something in a language that no one recognized.

Dobos watched, transfixed as Bains ran her fingertips gently over Nikki's milky white skin, her touch causing the girl to writhe and buck in what looked like spasms of desire. Bains smiled, nodding her approval.

She took a moment to admire the artwork inked onto Nikki's body, paying special attention to the image of a half human/half monster on her left shoulder. Then, having completed her inspection, she placed her hand on Nikki's arm. Giving the girl an approving pat, she stepped back against the window and spoke.

"Ahteh A'le bah rook."

Dobos' brow creased. He was fairly sure that the words Bains had just spoken, were the same words he had heard over and over again from the serial killer. But before he could give it another thought, he was stunned into disbelief, as the steel door to the exam room slowly frosted over in a thick mantle of ice.

Nikki stopped moving. Lifting her head she stared at the frozen door, the thick coating of ice sparkling like stars in a white sky. Her respiration increased, her exhaled breaths visible in the frosty air. Her body started to tremble, as the ice encrusted door began to sublimate, emitting a heavy fog that sank down its face, cascading like a waterfall that collected on the floor in a silvery pool.

Behind this white curtain something began to agitate the mist, as if someone, or something, was standing behind its veil, breathing through it. Then, as she watched, the nebulas vapor took on form, as a figure emerged from the fog shrouded ice.

Like stepping from behind a white silk curtain, it pressed out through the heavy rolling fume. While indistinct, its form was grotesque. Over seven feet tall, its face contorted, but without detail.

As it emerged, it was there, but not there, only the misty tendrils that clung to it hinting at any form. When at last it stepped through the vapor, the fog that had pooled on the floor splashed away, leaving a hideous void around a monstrous foot that could not be seen.

The preternatural beast moved into the room, wisps of vapor still clinging to it. It paused for a moment, then began to move slowly around the space.

Dobos was petrified, his hand sweating as he gripped his flashlight tighter and tighter. As the ice creature moved just beyond the observation window, he retreated a step when he saw the glass begin to frost over.

The smoking thing circled the examination table, as if stalking the prostrate girl bound there. To Dobos' surprise, Nikki was calm, looking at the creature closely, the way one looks at another person whom they think they may have met before.

The creature stopped at Nikki's feet and looked down at her. The swirling mist around it beginning to congeal and darken, as its mass solidified.

Smoke became scaled mottled flesh covering a grotesquely deformed frame. Its limbs were thick, like twisted steel, its body glistening with a viscus sheen. A gaping maw, filled with long dagger-like teeth, snapped impatiently, as a sickening snake-like tongue slithered out, flicking in the air as if tasting the fear of its offering.

Two thick, leathery wings protruded from its back. Bat-like, they hung like thick tapestries from misshapen appendages, fluttering occasionally in nauseatingly fleshy quivers.

Its massive chest surged with every breath, as eyes like burning embers darted between Bains and Nikki. The beast's thick, ape-like brow furrowed in consternation as it waited for permission yet ungiven.

The tension built up within the beast was palpable, even to Dobos watching from the next room. It wanted the girl. What it would do to her upon receiving approbation from Bains, Dobos could only imagine, and the fruit of his imagination both disturbed and aroused him. Thankfully, he didn't have to imagine for long.

The Fallen turned to Bains and let wail a thunderous roar. It was demanding, and impatient. Bains was unmoved by the protest, but as if taking pity on the beast, she spoke.

"El leq-ae mon Chuah."

As she spoke the creature spread its arms, and its body began to erupt in red electric fountains that spread in a web over its entire form. They intensified and grew until the beast was a mass of pulsing energy, its body burning with an iridescent radiance. When it could hold no more, it sprang at the defenseless girl.

When the electric maelstrom struck her, it wrapped around her body, drilling into every square inch of her flesh. Thousands of tiny red lightning bolts twisting and dancing on her skin as they burrowed into her.

Her face glowed intensely as if a fire were raging inside her skull. Her body lurched in violent painful spasms, as she screamed in agony.

After what felt like an eternity, the unearthly tempest passed within her, sinking into her flesh. Nikki fell limp and somnolent, her eyes rolling back in her head, as a sepulchral silence filled the room.

Dobos went numb with fear, his fight or flight response overridden by a horror induced paralysis. He wanted to be a hero. He wanted to spring into action, charge into that room and scoop up his beautiful goth Catwoman, but he just couldn't will himself to move. Instead, his bladder evacuated and a warm stream of urine ran down his legs, forming a pungent puddle around his feet.

Nikki's mouth worked silently, as if she were choking. Her eyes closed tightly, her body so slack that it seemed to be melting into the table. And then, she roared.

Blood vessels threatened to burst from her face and neck as she sounded a booming and angry ululation. It shook the room so hard that it startled the shock-frozen Dobos, causing his flashlight to slip from his grasp and fall to the floor with a loud clang.

Instantly, Bains' head spun 180 degrees on her shoulders, her burning ember eyes glowing hot, and staring through the glass. Her face distorted into that of the fallen she was, and she roared, driving her head through the glass pane.

Thousands of pebble-sized shards exploded at Dobos, cutting his face and driving him back, sprawling onto the floor. This time his bowels evacuated, and he screamed as he scrambled across the floor to the door. Throwing it open, he rolled into the dark, empty corridor and ran toward the emergency exit.

An audible alarm sounded as he burst through the door and into the emergency stairwell. Stumbling, falling, and screaming he rushed down the stairs and finally out into the night.

Private security guard Dick Dobos was later found by a sheriff's patrol unit, responding to a report of a security alarm activation at the Havenhurst Psychiatric Hospital. They reported that Dobos reeked of urine and feces, and was hysterically babbling about winged demons assaulting young girls.

Deputies recognized Dobos from his numerous ride-alongs, and as a member of the volunteer posse. As a favor to Dr. Shelby, they released him to Havenhurst on a 72-hour mental health observation. Cleaned up and dressed in a padded gown called a "Turtle Shell", Dobos was placed in a "safe room" with soft walls and no sharp edges.

Investigating detectives had visited Havenhurst and found no winged beasts or molested girls. They did however find a rather large collection of surreptitiously recorded video of patients and staff in various states of undress on a flash drive in Dobos' locker.

When questioned about this, Dobos would only curl up on the floor crying and muttering that Nikki had tried to kill him.

Dobos never recovered.

TWENTY-THREE

It was the pain that shocked Nikki the most. A white-hot, searing pain as if she had been ripped open, and molten iron poured into her. The acrid stench of sulfur choked her, filling her nose and throat with an unrelenting, raging fire.

Nikki clawed for breath, engulfed by a voluminous black cloud through which fingers of red lightening crawled, stabbing at her as they shredded the dark mass. With each spasm Nikki's throat closed tighter, her screams never able to vocalize above a deep muffled heaving.

And then...silence. A silence that came in a howling backward scream ending in a vacuum of nothingness. It wrapped around her, causing her ears to pop painfully, as if metal shivs had been forced deep into them.

She was sure she was dying, and she embraced it. As she lost consciousness, a peaceful smile spread across her face as she welcomed the tranquility of death.

As Nikki's eyes flittered open, she braced for the pain, but it didn't come. In fact, all she felt was...nothing. A startling lack of any sensation whatsoever. Looking around, she couldn't tell if her eyes were open or not, because all she could see was the deep velvet blackness that pressed in on her.

She could sense a floor beneath her, but couldn't see it. Holding out her hands, she was relieved when she saw they were visible. Looking down she saw her legs, her skin radiant and glowing like a body glows in a lighted swimming pool at night. Confused she looked around for the source of the light, but found none.

"Cool," she said, fascinated by her newly acquired luminosity.

Reaching out, Nikki probed into the darkness, but could feel nothing. Pursing her lips she puzzled, finally deciding to concentrate on the floor, since she could feel that.

The floor was not cold, nor was it warm. In fact, it was oddly neutral. The only evidence of its existence, was the pressure she felt against her body.

It occurred to her that perhaps she was still on the examination table, and for a moment she felt the cold grip of fear. But then she puzzled again, and her fear gave way to curiosity.

Sliding her fingers across the black, unseen surface she was seated on, she confirmed that whatever it was, it was not an exam table. Coming to her feet, she searched the space above her, feeling for a ceiling by extending her arms over her head, and standing on her toes, but again she felt nothing.

Now standing, she looked down at her feet, and realized for the first time she was naked. Nikki didn't mind being naked. In fact, she rather preferred it. It made her feel free. What did intrigue her, more than the fact that she was naked, was how exactly she came to be naked.

"Hmm,' she mused.

She thought back. She could remember a blade flashing, but if a blade had been involved, it wouldn't have been the first time. Her stepfather and his friends had forcibly raped her at knife point many times once she began to resist their advances at the age of thirteen.

"Oh, well, one thing at a time," she murmured.

Moving slowly, she groped her way through the inky black. Extending her arms, her fingertips searching for anything, as she slid her toes forward, feeling for a hidden precipice.

She was struck by how lonely the darkness felt. What she didn't know, was that she wasn't alone. From the darkness, glowing red eyes regarded her with fascination as she wandered in the murky void.

The Fallen was in complete possession of the girl's body. Now he peered into her mind, that place where all that she was, beyond the flesh of her earthly vessel, would reside as long as he remained within her.

He had taken humans before, listened to their cries for mercy. Sometimes he had even been moved by them. Some would try to play it cool, but he could always smell the stench of fear coming off them. But no matter how tough they thought they were, eventually it would all degenerate into pitiful pleading and bargaining. Oh, the bargaining.

But as he looked at this girl, he saw none of what he was accustomed to. Instead, she seemed fearless, inquisitive, and almost...amused.

Never before had this Fallen had more than a passing interest in a human. But this one...this girl, was different.

He was aware that many of his brothers and sisters had attempted to take her in the past, and she had resisted, fighting them off in sometimes bloody battles. He had watched her for many years, even protected her at times.

He had killed her stepfather on a snowy Christmas Eve as he came for her, drunk and naked. After sixteen long years of abuse, Nikki had determined that abuse would end. She vowed to fight him, to the death, if need be. So, she had brandished a large kitchen knife and was ready to use it.

"No more!" she had screamed. But this only seemed to enrage and arouse him all the more.

He had picked up a baseball bat, ready to beat her into submission. But when he raised it to strike, the Fallen had acted. Taking form, he opened the man's throat and belly, spilling his entrails onto the basement floor.

At that moment, Nikki's mother had entered the room, and the Fallen had disemboweled her as well. After all of her indifference to her daughter's continual rape, she had lost any sympathy the Fallen might of had, had it been in his nature to have any.

The last the Fallen had seen of Nikki, until her commitment to Havenhurst, had been her standing in her nightgown, covered in the blood of her parents, holding the knife she never had a chance to use.

Now he watched her again as she moved inside her mind. He took in her petit form, and her delicate features as she reconnoitered her new home, her curiosity and courage intriguing him.

He was fascinated by the ornate, and detailed, decorative markings on her skin. They were extensive, and most of them had not been there on the night he had set her free. Apparently, they had been acquired after going on the run that Christmas morning.

They covered her arms, and parts of her upper chest. On her back, starting just over the fronts of her shoulders, then flowing down her back along the contour of her hips, ending beneath her bottom on the backs of her thighs, were a huge set of wings. But the two sides of her back told the story of a soul in conflict.

On the right side of her back was a flowing depiction of the wing of an angel, its feathers soft and perfect. In contrast, on the left side was the leathery, misshapen wing of a Fallen, both rendered in exquisite detail. The fallen Creature of Light glanced over his shoulder at his own hideous winged appendages, pausing to contemplate them.

Looking back at the girl, his eyes pulsed as he took in the rest of her. His eyes tracing over her body were eventually drawn to the tattoo on her left shoulder. A flawless depiction of a Creature of Light, its beautiful flesh half torn away to reveal the horrific features of a Fallen beneath.

Surprised by it, he looked back to her face, and was startled to find her eyes fixed on his. She showed no fear, no surprise or revulsion, just a knowing.

For a long moment, he stared back at her, before closing the viewport, feeling somewhat unnerved by the experience.

TWENTY-FOUR

The light of the mid-afternoon sun shone through the windows of the massive stone turret at the west end of Wellington's student library. Their beveled glass cast a shower of geometric rainbows that danced across the stacks, and glistened off the polished oak table where Chance Jordan was sitting.

He was reading a collection of letters written by Confederate General George Pickett, of the Army of Northern Virginia. General Pickett had written these as his corps prepared for its assault on the Union center at Gettysburg.

The documents had been donated to the Wellington library because many of the officer cadre of Pickett's corps had been Wellington alumni. What struck Chance the most, was that many of these young officers were not much older than he was now when they died on that bloody day.

He found himself moved by their courage. He had been to Gettysburg, and had walked that historic ground. The idea of those boys drawing their swords and leading their men on that slow, one mile, advance into thousands of Union rifles, and cannons loaded with grapeshot, filled him with awe. He wondered if he were placed in a situation like that, where to do one's duty would very likely lead to his death, would he be able to draw his sword and charge into oblivion as they had.

Appraising his character, Chance leaned back, his wooden chair creaking under him. But his appraisal was cut short when he sensed a malevolent presence moving nearby. Peering up cautiously, the evil was confirmed.

Ms. Bertha Arroyo, the school's librarian, had sprung to her feet, and was moving across the room with the grace and determination of a charging rhinoceros. Chance knew what was coming. He had seen it many times in his four years at Wellington. Some unsuspecting, doe-eyed freshman had either by action, or omission of action, offended and enraged the over-developed sensibilities of the woman Wellington students referred to as "The Beast".

Arroyo was a bitter woman, with a sour disposition. She hated her life, and her life hated her right back. The only solace she could find was to use her position and authority to inflict as much distress as possible on any student that caught her attention. And she savored every opportunity that presented itself.

Sensible shoes squeaked furiously as The Beast waddled her five-foot, six inch, two-hundred and forty-pound frame aggressively across the room toward the unsuspecting student. Her face scowling, creased with senseless anger, hosted rage filled eyes that fixed on her next victim.

"Mr. Christie," she bellowed, "how dare you enter my library out of compliance."

Paul Christie, or "Pauli" as his friends called him, was the son of a powerful New Jersey family, with a long business and political history. Pauli was a down-to-earth kid that was well-liked by the other students. Despite his family's affluence, Pauli was brought up in an environment that had never abandoned the street edge that had made its political dynasty legendary. Consequently, he had a tendency to slip into his "Jersey Shore, Wise Guy" persona whenever confronted.

"What?" he asked, stunned by the intensity of the woman's rage.

"You know exactly what," she said, sticking out her barrel chest, that despite its size appeared to be distractingly devoid of breasts. It was as if she were wearing an umpire's protective chest pad under her too-small blouse and sweater.

"You received a student handbook upon enrollment," she puffed. "The dress code is there, and you are required to be in compliance at all times."

"How am I not in compliance?" asked Pauli, looking at himself bewildered.

"Your shirt collar is not buttoned," she said, pointing.

Pauli paused, looking The Beast in the eye. "You gotta be kiddin' me," he finally said.

Digging into his backpack he produced a booklet and began flipping through its pages, as Chance and a few others watched amused. Most freshmen would whither under Arroyo's abusive assaults, but Pauli seemed randy for a fight. Finding the page he was looking for, he turned to face The Beast with confidence.

"Look," he said boldly, "all it says here is that my tie must be firmly cinched around my neck."

Pointing to his tie, Pauli continued, "And if you will observe, the aforementioned accessory, is so configured."

Arroyo was incensed. Feeling her authority being challenged, she reacted as she always did, by spewing regulations like a cow's ass spews methane.

"Compliance order 704.3 states that uniforms shall be worn correctly with all buttons secured," she said, standing pompously, her arms folded across her chest as she glared at the boy through the glasses perched on the tip of her nose.

She threw her head back and snorted her contempt, which caused the overgrowth of hair in her nostrils to flutter. Pauli was not intimated.

"That's not what it says," he challenged. "You're making that up."

Chance watched Arroyo with anticipation. This was unprecedented, and he hunched his head into his shoulders as he waited for the explosion.

"It is in the unpublished compliance orders," said Arroyo, her body shaking in fury as she inched toward a total meltdown.

All she needed to completely lose her mind was a little push, and Paul Christie was all too willing to provide it.

"Unpublished compliance orders?" he said in mocking dismay. "You actually have secret rules that we're just supposed to know?"

Then, as if speaking to a complete idiot, Pauli put his hands on his hips and delivered the coup due grace. "What have you been smoking?"

Chance couldn't help himself. He let out a loud guffaw, which drew an icy stare from Arroyo, and giggles from students nearby.

Refocusing her fury on Pauli, she roared, "You are on report, now sit right there."

Indicating a chair, she pulled out a radio and called for security.

Pauli sat down and glanced over at Chance who was now standing as he stuffed his study materials into his bag. Chance gave the boy a supportive smile and wink. He was glad that Pauli was taking it all in stride. In fact, the boy even looked like he was having fun.

"Hang in there, Pauli," said Chance, shouldering his bag.

"Do you have a comment, Mr. Jordan?" barked Arroyo menacingly.

Chance let out an exasperated breath as he strolled toward the door. "A comment, Ms. Arroyo? More comments come to mind than I have time to offer."

When Chance reached the library door, he turned to find Arroyo still glaring holes in him. Flashing his winning grin, he reached up and loosened his tie, unbuttoned his top button, then spun on his heel, and walked away.

Pauli just smiled his wise-guy smile.

As Chance walked down the hall the final bell began to chime, and students flooded into the corridor in a chattering wave of youthful energy. Groups crowded together, looking at computers and phones, laughing as they watched Pauli's run in with The Beast on social media. The boy was quickly attaining hero status.

Checking the time, Chance hustled back to his dorm to change his clothes in preparation for his visit with Marina. As he packed the art supplies he had purchased for her, he smiled as he imagined her joy upon receiving them.

He paused for a moment and took stock of his feelings. He was surprised when he realized how excited he was to know he would soon be seeing her again.

TWENTY-FIVE

As Chance walked through the foyer of the Havenhurst Psychiatric Hospital, he smiled and waved to the receptionist at her desk. She smiled back broadly, wiggling her chubby fingers at him as she reached for the phone, waving him through as she did.

Walking to the elevator, he pressed the call button, then leaned against the wall as he waited. When the elevator doors finally opened, he was surprised to find Marina, Nurse Denali, and the huge orderly that had snatched Marina away on Saturday, standing inside.

At first Chance didn't recognize Denali, or the giant black man, whose name he later learned was Bo, as they were wearing street clothes, and Denali's hair was down, rather than in the tight bun she normally wore. But Chance didn't have much time to think about it as Marina came bounding out of the elevator and excitedly took his arm.

"I have a surprise for you," she gushed as she enthusiastically bounced at his side. "We're going on a field trip."

Chance looked at her, then Denali, confused. He had only been to the hospital a few times, but so far, his impression was that it was more like a prison than a hospital. Denali had used the term "field trip" once before, but the idea that he and Marina could ever visit with one another outside the hospital's walls, was a possibility he had not considered. Especially since the last time an outside activity had been mentioned, the evening had ended early, and not pleasantly.

"A field trip?" he croaked.

"There's a spring carnival near here," offered Denali as explanation. "I only found out about it a few hours ago, and Dr. Shelby agreed that such an experience could be very therapeutic for Marina."

When Chance hesitated, she added, "I realize it's short notice, but we hoped you wouldn't mind."

He didn't mind at all, but even if he had, one look at Marina's pleading eyes as she bit her lip in anticipation, would have melted his heart. Besides, he found himself enchanted by the prospect of an evening with Marina outside the sterile confines of the hospital.

"Of course, I don't mind," he said at last, eliciting a squeal from Marina.

"Excellent," said Denali. "We'll take the hospital's van."

The group piled into a van and after settling in, Chance presented Marina with her gift. Excited, she reached for it, but then hesitated, looking with slight trepidation at Denali. Realizing what was happening, Chance looked at the nurse who was now turned around in her seat, watching them.

"Dr. Shelby said it would be OK if I brought Marina some art supplies," he said.

Chance opened a small wooden box to show Denali that it contained an assortment of pastels and colored pencils, and chalks. Denali nodded her approval.

Marina was overjoyed. Taking the box, she examined her new options and contemplated the possibilities.

"Thank you so much," she said sincerely, then leaning over she kissed Chance on the cheek.

Denali and the orderly, Bo, looked at each other, shocked. In the course of four days, Marina had gone from thinking all boys had cooties, to kissing one on the cheek. It was a stunning progression.

Setting the box on the seat between her and Chance, Marina dug into her backpack and pulled out her sketch pad along with a small drawing board. Peeling off a sheet of paper, she gave it, and the board, to Chance.

"Here, we can draw together," she said, smiling broadly.

Marina positively bubbled as she excitedly dove into her art, delighted with her new medium. Chance watched, caught up in her elation. Her joy was infectious, and it moved him deeply. As he watched he was surprised to discover that his eyes had become damp with emotion.

He quickly wiped them dry, looking around to see if anyone had noticed. That was when he saw Denali smiling at him in the reflection of her vanity mirror. She regarded him with a thoughtful expression, then raised the sun visor as if to give him some privacy. Embarrassed, he wiped his eyes again and tried to draw.

Marina worked with intensity, concentrating on her own art when not stealing peeks at Chance's. She covered her mouth, trying to stifle her giggles over his misshapen stick figures.

"Hey, I thought we agreed, no laughing," said Chance, scolding her with a smile.

They both laughed and returned to their drawings, but Marina was distracted. She kept looking at Chance as if in disbelief that he was actually sitting there beside her. In her mind this wasn't just any boy, he was Sari'El, and it was as real to her as the sun in the sky. Just as she was sure that they had once loved one another, in a time long before this one. She knew these things to be true. She felt them as part of her being.

But it was only her love for him that she could remember. Nothing else could fight its way through the fugue. Her memories were only flashes of images mere pulses of emotion that were, at times, overwhelming.

The strange part for Marina was that he did not remember her, and she couldn't understand why. Unless, she pondered, that what she had been told about her memories, for the last eleven years was true, that they were all delusions created in her mind. Delusions like the dogs with hellish, disfigured faces, that had torn her family apart.

Marina had learned to keep those memories to herself, suppressed deep inside, lest Dr. Shelby's "treatments" once again become necessary. That was a potential that frightened her as much as the memories themselves.

Since arriving at Havenhurst, Marina had been medicated and manipulated

– even tortured – to accept, if not truly believe, that the nightmarish visions she had of the night her family was killed, were in fact only manifestations of her mind. Mental fictions, nothing more.

Despite these professional 'opinions', Marina didn't know what to believe. She did know, however, that insisting something was real, that a therapist had decided was a delusion, never went well for a patient at Havenhurst.

Therapists were a big part of Marina's daily routine. She participated in group therapy sessions several days a week, and while these sessions were supposed to be a place of safe disclosure, they were more often a minefield-like confessional, where what was said was weaponized to be used against the patients. Marina had learned it was best to be careful about what she shared.

Marina's friend Nikki, had been slow to learn this lesson. Nikki was a stubborn, and independent girl that never backed down, no matter how many times she had ended up in the treatment room.

Anytime Nikki would insist that the winged creature that had gutted her mother and stepfather was not only real, but her savior, the treatments would commence. Marina had watched, horrified at times, as Nikki was administered – often forcefully – medication and treatment that reduced the petite girl to a nearly comatose state.

"You know what they want to hear," Marina would say.

"And you know what they want to see," Nikki would retort. "So, you better start making happy art, or you'll end up like me."

Marina knew that Nikki was right. It was why she had stopped depicting the death of her family, and instead began to draw happy little houses, under happy little rainbows. Dr. Shelby didn't recommend treatments for that.

Now with Sari'El by her side, or Chance as he called himself now, she found herself confused. The flashes of a past with him were happy and perfect, and she tried desperately to capture it in her art. She knew she was risking more treatment, but she hoped, that if she provided the right detail, he would remember her as well.

"May I see it yet?" asked Chance, leaning over.

"Not yet," said Marina earnestly, as she playfully nudged him away.

"Okay, okay," laughed Chance, raising his hands in surrender. "I didn't know you were such an artiste."

"Yes, you did," she replied without looking up. "You just don't remember."

Marina immediately bit her lip, having forgotten that nurse Denali was nearby. Peeking up through her hair she was relieved to see that Denali was engaged in an animated conversation with Bo and was paying her little mind.

Looking over at Chance she let out a sigh. Happy to be with him, she went back to her drawing.

As Travis activated his turn signal, he observed the hospital's van turning out of the driveway. He recognized the van's driver as Bo, one of the orderlies, but he couldn't make out the two people in the back seat before the van pulled out onto the road and drove off. It didn't matter, he had more important things to worry about.

Travis drove up the hospital's carriageway and through the main parking lot to a side lot where he knew there were few security cameras. Selecting a parking space against a dense tree line, he backed in slowly until his rear tires bumped against the concrete curb.

Only a few windows looked out onto this small parking lot, and Travis scanned them, looking for any curious faces. Satisfied that he was unobserved, he pressed a button on his console, opening the car's trunk. Looking in his mirror he saw the lid rise, obscuring his view.

Almost immediately the car shook momentarily as if someone had jumped on its bumper. When Travis looked in his side view mirror it was just in time to see Martin disappearing into the forest.

Scanning the building once again, Travis got out of his car and walked back to the open trunk. Reaching in, he pulled out a large gym bag, then lowered the lid until the powered trunk latch grasped it and seated it snugly.

He glanced into the tree line but Martin was nowhere to be seen. The only hint of his passing was the swaying of a singular branch in the still air of the coming twilight. After a few moments, even that movement dissipated into nothing, returning the forest to the stillness of a painting.

Travis knew Martin was out there. He could feel his malevolence reaching out from the oppressive silence, and it caused a chill to sweep over him. Staring into the darkening forest, he was startled when his phone rang. Pulling it out he answered it.

"Hello? OK...yeah, I'm going. Just stay out of sight until its dark. I'll come out to the dumpster when it's all clear. It could be a while so be patient."

Nervous, Travis tapped his phone and put it back in his pocket. Giving the dense forest one last look, he turned and walked toward the hospital.

From the concealment of the forest's undergrowth, Martin watched Travis cross the parking lot and disappear around the corner of the building. Sitting down, he leaned against a tree to wait.

The Oxy he had taken from Travis was long since gone, and the dragon beckoned as withdrawal gripped him hard. Everything irritated him, the musty smell of the damp forest, along with the incessant buzzing of crepuscular insects darting about the forest canopy, all combined to make his skin crawl.

His lifelong fear of any insect crawling on him only made the situation worse. Even something as benign as a housefly lighting on his hand was enough to send him into panic-fueled flailing.

Panic and rage took turns pressing out from his head, threatening to fracture his skull. He needed his fix.

Unconsciously, he tapped the constellation of injection scars along the crook of his arm, and a phantom rush of serotonin made his eyes roll back as his body was tricked into thinking the needle was near.

Yes, he would wait, but not patiently.

TWENTY-SIX

Nikki grinned. He was back. He kept coming back and every time he did, Nikki could feel his eyes on her, looking her over like a malevolent doorman sizing her up through the peephole in the door of some mob-run gin joint.

She had tried to look directly into those eyes, but every time she did, the peephole, which seemed to float in the nothingness, would wink out of existence. She had once even jumped up and charged, screaming, at those floating eyes. They had vanished before she could get to them, but their obvious startled surprise at her audacity had caused her to double over in a deep belly laugh.

Sitting down she pulled her heels up under her bottom and rested, leaning on one arm. Turning her head, she balanced her chin on her shoulder and searched for him. He was there, just as she expected, watching from the edge of her periphery, floating like a shadow in the darkness.

Exploring her new environment had become a bore. She was surrounded by an endless nothing that she found mind numbing.

"Maybe this is hell," she mused.

It would have been a perfect hell for Nikki. She shuddered to imagine an eternity with no stimulation. Death by boredom. The only respite from her hell being the continual visits of her mysterious voyeur, whose attention she found oddly comforting.

Pausing, she took an assessment of herself and the current situation. She was still naked, but that didn't bother her. She assumed it was one of the reasons her captor kept coming back to look in on her.

It had become clear to her since the age of thirteen that men enjoyed looking at her body. Petite, yet round in all the right places, she had learned early that men lusted after her, and that she could use their lust as a weapon. Nikki had become quite adept at manipulating men to get what she wanted.

So, if whoever was on the other inside of that peephole wanted to look at her, let 'em look. All that meant to Nikki was that sooner than later the balance of power would shift in her favor, and she would make him her bitch.

She laughed at that, then coughed as her dry throat burned. She longed for something cold to drink.

Closing her eyes, she imagined how satisfying an ice-cold beer would taste. Almost instantly, a sweating glass of amber liquid appeared from nothing next to her hand. Her brow rose in amazement.

Without moving her head, she confirmed that her voyeur was still there. 'Can he read my mind?' she wondered.

Dipping her finger into the liquid, she examined it. Rolling it between her fingertips she tested its viscosity. It felt like beer. Lifting the glass, she examined the tiny bubbles rising through it, then sniffed it. Finally satisfied, she took a sip. It was beer.

She drank deeply, giving a satisfied sigh as she finished off half of the glass. Raising the glass to her lips once again, she had a momentary thought. It was more of a preference, than a desire. Quite simply, she thought that she should have asked for a Cola-Weissen.

It was an uncommon drink in the United States. She had been introduced to it by a German man she had lived with while on the run in Hollywood. He would often mix Hefeweissen beer, half and half with Coke-a-Cola. Nikki found the concoction rather refreshing.

Just as this thought bounced into her head, the color and taste of her beverage changed to the sweet banded flavor of a Cola-Weissen. Even the glass changed to the tall sloping glass that her German lover had always used.

"Curiouser and curiouser," she whispered. Drinking deeply, she regarded her captor. "Thank you," she said, looking into the red burning eyes as she lifted her glass.

This time he did not vanish immediately. Instead, their eyes held each other's for a long moment. Finally, the peephole slowly slid shut.

"He'll be back," she whispered as she lay down stretching like a cat. "He'll be back."

The floor, or whatever it was she was lying on, was getting uncomfortable, and Nikki's mind wandered to an image of a feather bed she had seen in a Vogue magazine. Stretching again, she imagined how wonderful that bed would feel, when the fingers of her outstretched hands touched something.

Startled, her eyes flew open as she sprang to her feet, ready to fight. A reaction that had become all too automatic as a result of her time living on the streets, and more recently while incarcerated at Havenhurst.

Nikki quickly realized that what she had touched was not a potential rapist, or Dobos looking to cop a feel, but rather the skirt of a giant bed. And not just any bed, but the exact bed she had seen in Vogue. Right down to the Egyptian cotton sheets, and overstuffed pillows.

She stared in disbelief, reaching out to confirm it was really there. It was solid, its brass head and footboards glistening from unseen light sources. Nikki crawled up onto it and sprawled across its expanse, its softness nearly swallowing her whole.

Nikki lay quietly as she tried to make sense of it. Relaxing, she stared up into the nothing and closed her eyes. When she opened them again, she was greeted by a galaxy of stars.

Then, as if in a storm of revelation, she understood. She, was in control of this place. She could have anything, and all she had to do, was desire.

Biting her lip, she smiled mischievously.

"Curiouser and curiouser."

TWENTY-SEVEN

Chance and Marina strolled together along the midway of the Spring Carnival sharing a cotton candy. From time to time their arms would brush together, and Chance could feel Marina press harder against him when they did.

As Carnival barkers shouted their challenges at the passing crowd, Chance could see that Marina was becoming more and more intrigued by them. He couldn't help but smile as he watched her. Her face was filled with wonder as she reacted to the myriad of lights and sounds of the various rides and attractions.

The crowd was larger than Chance had expected for a weeknight. Still, it wasn't so crowded that he and Marina couldn't walk together, comfortably distracted by each other's company.

He would occasionally glance over his shoulder to make sure that Nurse Denali and Bo were still there. Each time he did, Denali would smile and give him a dismissive wave, as if to say, 'don't worry about us, you two just have fun'.

As they strolled past the food court, Chance saw that Marina was looking closely at the various exotic foods available.

"Would you like to share a chocolate malt?" he asked.

Marina turned to look at him, the lights of the midway sparkling in her eyes. "I don't think I've ever tried one before."

Chance stopped in his tracks. "You have never tasted a chocolate malt?"

Marina just shook her head.

"Come on," said Chance directing her to a food concession.

As Denali and Bo sat down chatting at one of the nearby picnic tables, Chance stepped up to the concession's window. "One large chocolate malt and two straws please," said Chance to the old man behind the counter.

"Would you like whipped cream with that?" asked the old man.

"Yes please. That sounds great."

After a minute or so, the old man was back with the malt. Topping it off with a small mountain of whipped cream, then added some chocolate sprinkles. Finally, he stuck two straws into the sweet dessert.

"Here you go," he said, pushing the drink out of the window.

"Thank you, sir," said Chance as he took the malt and presented it to Marina. "Give it a taste," he said.

Marina tentatively sipped on the straw, and when the dark brown liquid made it to her lips, her eyes grew wide.

"Oh my God, that is so good. I had no idea." she said, now pulling on the straw in earnest.

Chance smiled broadly, then looked up at the old man who was now watching with growing interest.

"It's her first malt," he explained.

"You gotta be kiddin' me," said the old man. "How's somethin' like that happen?"

"It's a long story," said Chance, as he dug out his wallet to pay for the drink, but the old man waved his hands.

"No, that one's on the house," he said, smiling. "That was fun to watch."

"Thank you, sir. That's very kind of you."

"My pleasure," said the old man with a pleasant smile as he handed Chance some napkins. "Your girlfriend's a cutie. A real keeper. I wouldn't let her get too far away."

"Oh, she's not..." started Chance, but then just smiled at the kindly ancient and added, "I'll be careful, sir. Thank you again."

Chance turned, a huge grin spreading across his face as he did.

"Did you hear that?" he said, but his question fell flat, and his stomach jumped up into his throat, as he realized that Marina was gone.

Frantically his eyes searched the crowd, but she was nowhere to be seen.

Panicking, he looked at last to Denali. Both she and Bo sat looking back at him with amused expressions.

Denali let Chance roast on the spit a few seconds longer before taking pity on the boy and extending her finger, pointing across the midway. Chance followed the gesture, and relief washed over him as he saw Marina standing at a game booth, looking up at an enormous stuffed white tiger. Waving sheepishly at Denali, Chance walked across the midway to join Marina.

"Hey, what ya lookin' at?" he asked as he joined her.

"Isn't he beautiful?" she said, unable to take her eyes off the plush animal.

Chance had to admit, the huge tiger was impressive. He had never seen anything like it. It was extremely well made and looked almost alive, posed as if it were lounging in the shade of a tree, its golden-brown eyes ever watchful.

Chance could see how much she wanted it, and he shook his head when he realized how much he wanted to experience her joy at taking it home with her.

The carney looked at Marina. He was smiling a nearly toothless grin, as he leaned against the counter, casually tossing a softball in the air.

"One dollar gets you three balls," he challenged. "Knock all three bottles down on the first ball, and he's all yours."

Marina looked at Chance, anxiety prickling her skin, as she handed him the malt and began digging in her pocket. After a second, she pulled out a crumpled one-dollar bill and handed it to the carney, who presented her with three softballs, then stepped back, leaning against the side counter.

Marina's eyes traveled from Chance, to Denali, then to Bo, who had by then joined them. Turning back to the game, she set two of the balls on the counter and concentrated on her target, as Chance sipped on the malt, looking on in interest.

Marina took a breath then wound up and hurled the ball with all her might at the three stacked metal bottles. She missed. The second ball missed as well. The third ball knocked the top bottle off the stack, but nothing more.

The carney smiled his one tooth smile and handed Marina a key chain with a small penguin attached. She wrinkled her nose in disappointment, then took the chocolate malt from Chance, and tried to drown her sorrow in its sweetness.

"Let me give it a shot," said Bo, his voice low and booming.

Marina bounced with delight as the mountainous man stepped forward, dollar bill in hand. It was a comical scene as the scrawny carney, whose weight topped no more than one-hundred and thirty-pounds – and that only after a heavy meal – stood looking up at the hulking, three-hundred-pound, black man.

The carney took Bo's money, then handed him a softball. As the big man's hand closed around it, Chance mused to himself that the softball in Bo's hand looked like a baseball in his own.

As Bo stepped up to the counter and addressed his target, the carney stepped back.

"Bo's gonna smash those bottles," Marina whispered, as she clutched Chance's arm in nervous anticipation.

Chance smiled and nodded, but he wasn't watching Bo. Instead, his eyes were on the carney, as the odd-looking man leaned against the side counter and surreptitiously ran his fingers under its edge as if searching for something.

Bo's throw was forceful. His tree limb-sized arm arced in a broad parabola that sent the ball screaming toward the stacked bottles in a blur of fluorescent yellow. His throw was perfect, his aim flawless. So, it was shocking to all when Bo's ball struck the two bottles at the base of the stack, but only one of them rocketed away along with the bottle that had been stacked on top. The third and final bottle stood motionless, but for the slightest, nearly imperceptible, momentary wobble.

Bo was incredulous.

"That's a bunch of shit!" he roared threateningly, his eyes fixed on the carney. "This game is rigged."

Marina covered her mouth and gasped.

"Bo!" said Denali sternly.

"I'm sorry, Barbara, but something's wrong here. There's just no way that bottle should still be standing."

"Hey, I run a clean game," protested the carney. "Watch."

He reset the bottles on the pedestal, then picked up a softball, wound up, and delivered a straight, if unimpressive, strike, causing all three bottles to fly off the pedestal and rattle to the floor.

"See?" said the carney. "You just have to know what you're doin'." Then realizing what he had said, he looked at the agitated giant, and was relieved to see the woman still had a from grip on his arm.

"Let me give it a shot," said Chance, stepping forward. "I'm pretty sure I know what I'm doing."

Chance held the carney in a cold stare, but the carney's attention was divided between Chance's eyes, and the array of awards and insignia that decorated the letterman's jacket he was wearing. They attested, undeniably, to his quality and accomplishments as an athlete. Chance tossed a dollar bill on the counter and picked up two softballs, one in each hand.

"Let's do this," said Chance.

"You get three..." started the carney.

"This is all I need."

"You gotta knock all three down with the first ball," said the carney, confused.

Chance looked at him but said nothing. Unnerved, the carney retreated to reset the bottles.

Chance handed the softballs to Marina, then removed his jacket and hung it over her shoulders. She looked up at him, her eyes alive with excitement.

"Take care of this for me," he said, holding her eyes in his.

Taking the softballs from her, he turned to regard the carney, who once again stood leaning on the side counter, his fingers curled under its edge. Chance pursed his lips knowingly, then turned his attention to his target.

He tossed the ball up and down, casually, in his right hand, getting a feel for its weight. In his left hand he rolled the second ball on his fingertips, manipulating it gently. When he made his move, it was fluid and shockingly fast.

Tossing the ball in his left hand in a lazy lob directly at the carney's face, Chance waited, knowing the man would instinctively raise his hands to protect himself. As he did, Chance fired a wicked side arm strike with the ball in his right hand. When the ball struck the bottles, the tiny pyramid exploded in a cacophony of clanking metal.

Marina let out a squeal of delight, and threw her arms around Chance.

"I knew you would do it," she bubbled.

Marina then turned to the carney to receive her prize, her face bright with joy. But that brightness faded as she looked up at the carney who stood, arms folded, shaking his head.

"Nope," he said, with a sadistic smirk on his face, "the rules say you can only throw one ball at a time. Your boyfriend threw two. So, you get nothing."

Marina's eyes filled with tears. She turned to Chance, disappointment verging on anguish heavy on her face. Chance felt rage surge up inside him, but it was Denali that reacted first.

"You crooked little son-of-a-bitch!" she yelled as she lunged at the man. But now it was Bo who was restraining HER.

"Take it easy, Babs," said Bo, gently.

"OK, I'm calling security, y'all are outta here," said the carney, picking up a radio as a crowd began to form.

Denali charged forward again, her feet coming off the ground as Bo pulled her back. Startled, the carney lifted his radio, but as he did, Chance spoke in an ominous tone.

"I wouldn't do that if I were you," was all he said.

Everyone turned and looked at Chance, but he just stood there scrolling through his phone.

"Oh? And why's that?" asked the carney warily.

Without looking up from his phone, Chance replied, "Because if you do, you will end up in jail, and she'll go home with that tiger."

"Bullshit."

"Then by all means, call security, so we can have a chat about that button under the counter that you press whenever you think someone's going to beat your game."

The carney blanched, and looked nervously at the counter under which the button was hidden.

"Yeah, that button," said Chance, now looking at the carney as he held up his phone.

"That's just a security call button."

"So, press it, and let's get this party started. Then I'll press mine, and speak to the state Attorney General, who happens to be my dad's poker buddy. He'll get the police down here, and then we can find out what that little button of yours really does."

The dentally challenged man glared at Chance with disdain, but that disdain melted into fear, then finally submission.

"Look, I don't want any trouble, so just take the tiger, and we'll call it even," he said at last.

"You gonna need any help getting that tiger down?" asked Bo, leaning on the counter.

Bo didn't wait for an answer. Instead, he reached up and plucked the tiger down from the display and gave it to Marina.

Marina was beside herself with joy. She hugged Bo, then took the tiger, squeezing it to her chest. Then her eyes searched for Chance. Running to him she embraced him tightly.

"Thank you, thank you, thank you. I'll never let him go," she vowed.

Bo patted Chance on the shoulder, "Pretty impressive. So, you know the Attorney General, huh?"

"Nope. I don't even know his name."

"Obviously, since the Attorney General is a woman," said Bo laughing.

"Good thing HE didn't know that either," said Chance smirking.

Nurse Denali smiled broadly as she watched Marina dance with her tiger to the music of the midway. Chance watched as well. He couldn't take his eyes off her. Everything about her overwhelmed him. The light in her eyes, the beauty of her smile, and the music of her laughter. He marveled at the perfection of her slightly upturned nose, and how her hair created a copper halo around her face as the multi-colored lights of the carnival flickered around her.

He could feel his emotions spinning out of control. Gloriously out of control. She made him feel alive, and his heart full as if ready to explode. He couldn't explain it, but then realized that he didn't need, or want to.

The rest of the evening was magical. Chance and Marina visited the entire carnival, Marina holding her champion closely as he carried her tiger across his shoulders. But far too quickly, the evening was at its end.

"It's almost time to go, guys," said Denali, looking at her watch.

"Do we have time for one last ride?" asked Marina hopefully.

"One more," agreed Denali.

"Then let's make that one our last ride," said Marina pointing.

Chance followed her finger to the Ferris Wheel.

"I think that would be perfect," he said.

Chance sat in the glow of the van's dome light, a satisfied expression on his face. He watched Marina, his eyes caressing her as she sat putting the finishing touches on the drawing she had been working on since leaving Havenhurst, her white tiger lounging in the back seat, observing them.

As Marina worked, she slipped her hand under the jackets piled on the seat and held Chance's hand. Their fingers intertwined, and he unconsciously stoked her skin in soft lambent circles.

Chance replayed the evening in his head, the cotton candy stroll, the chocolate malt that came with an old man's admonition to not let Marina, "get away", and the joy on Marina's face as she danced with her tiger. But while these memories were beautiful, by far the most treasured image in Chance's mind was that of the ten minutes they had spent together on the Ferris Wheel.

Marina had placed her tiger at one end of the bench, thereby 'forcing' herself to sit close to Chance. Her hip touched his, and he could feel her warmth. He had made room for her by putting his arm across the back of the seat, inviting her to snuggle up against him, and she did, reaching up to hold his hand as it draped over her shoulder.

Pressing his face into her hair he had breathed her in, and the scent of fresh air and wild flowers greeting him. Now, as he sat next her in the van, he found himself longing to breathe in her essence once again.

Turning his head, he looked out of the van's window and into the tenebrous night. Off in a distant meadow, he could see the vespertine twinkle of fireflies, and he marveled at their beauty.

He looked back at Marina with the intention of calling her attention to the luminescent display, only to find that she was already watching it in wide-eyed wonderment. When his eyes met hers, he fell into them, stunned silent, as a soothing warmth washed over him.

Marina looked back at him, love flooding her face. Chance's chest tightened, and he found it difficult to breathe as every nerve in his body seemed to catch on fire.

TWENTY-EIGHT

Dr. Shelby stood at the sink in the private bath of his office, his eyes watering as he plucked deviant hairs from his nostrils. He was awaiting the arrival of Dr. Bains and so, from time to time, would perk up and rush to the window, looking out with the giddy anticipation of a teenaged girl waiting for her prom date, only to be disappointed by the empty parking lot below.

Once he was sufficiently plucked, he put on a fresh shirt and reapplied his cologne. Next, he went about fussing over a table for two he had set beside the window. Nervously looking at his watch, he walked to his desk to check his email, but when the lights of a vehicle shone from outside, he ran excitedly to the window once again.

He got to the window in time to see a black S.U.V. park, and the young soldier who drove Sabine Bains get out and hurry around to open the rear passenger door. Shelby's heart skipped as the soldier offered his hand to Dr. Bains. He watched as she placed her hand delicately in the soldier's, then swung her legs out and stepped down.

Seeing her touching the handsome young soldier in his Army dress blue uniform, caused a momentary jolt of jealousy to burn through him. But he quickly pulled himself together, and went to work lighting an array of candles around the room.

When he had finished, he stood back and looked at his work. Satisfied that his romantic stage had been properly set, he gave himself one last check in the mirror, inhaled a quick blast of breath freshener, then hurried out of his office to greet his Sabine.

Travis stepped out from the janitor's closet dressed in his green overalls. He was, once again, "The Janitor". Pushing his cart from door to door, he went about his job unnoticed, overtly collecting bags of trash, while covertly making mental notes of who was working, and where.

His biggest concern was the facility's cameras. His coming and going was not an issue. Getting Martin in and out, on the other hand, would be more problematic. But Travis had a plan. To set it in motion, however, would require him to be inside the security office.

Travis guided his cart through the lobby. The receptionist had already gone home, along with the rest of the day shift, so the building was mostly vacant. As he parked his cart in front of the security office, the door opened and George Squire, the night shift guard, came out and hurried across the lobby fumbling with his keys as he walked.

Selecting a key, George quickly inserted it into the lock and pulled the heavy door open just in time for Dr. Bains, and her driver, to step through. Bains entered and handed a small metal case to the soldier, then removed her coat and laid it over his extended arm. The soldier held out the metal case, and Bains took it back from him, giving him a dazzling smile as she did.

Travis couldn't hear what was being said, but he could tell that George was totally stupid over Bains. The guard just stood there, looking at her with a goofy grin on his face, and an obvious erection tenting the front of his pants.

Bains leaned over and said something to the soldier. He listened carefully, then nodding, the soldier turned and walked out the door, just as Dr. Shelby entered the lobby looking quite pleased with himself.

Travis watched with disdain as his father fawned over Bains. Though he had never met the woman personally, he despised her. Yeah, she was an attractive woman, and there was something about her that could be overwhelming, as evidenced by George's reaction. But what bothered Travis the most, was that his dad was banging her. At least he was pretty sure he was banging her.

He understood his father's motivation toward infidelity, sort of. He knew his mom could be a bitch, and that she spent most of her days strung out on

Valium. Still, she was his mom, and it pissed him off that his dad was fucking around on her.

Pulling on some latex gloves, he selected some cleaning supplies and entered the security office. The room was awash in the cool blue light of the various monitors. Closing the door behind him, Travis moved quickly to the system's CPU. He was examining it when the door opened and George walked in looking flushed.

"Hey, Travis," said George as he took a utility belt down off a hook on the wall and began to put it on.

"Hey, George," said Travis, quickly beginning to wipe down the control desk. "I'll be done here in just a bit."

George slipped a flashlight into a ring on his belt, then pushed a radio into a pouch.

"Did you hear about Dobos?" asked George.

"Yeah, what a trip, huh?" replied Travis.

Travis had learned all about what had happened to Dobos via the hospital's gossip line. Apparently, Dobos had flipped out, and was now on suicide watch.

Travis had seen people on suicide watch before, and he knew it wasn't a pleasant place to be. Stripped naked, the patient was dressed in a thick padded suit that looked like a tortoise shell, then locked in a cell with no music, TV, or reading material, just a hole in the floor for bodily functions. The lights were kept bright, twenty-four hours a day, and it was impossible to sleep due to the screaming of the patients in the other rooms. It was Travis' opinion that if a person didn't want to kill themselves before being placed on "suicide watch", it was a sure-fire way to make any sane person consider it.

"I heard he said that Nikki VanPelt was a monster that had attacked him," said Travis.

"Yeah," confirmed George, "he said that Nikki was some kind of hideous creature with wings, or some shit like that."

"I always thought Nikki was kinda cute," said Travis, shaking his head.

"I know, right?" said George, taking a clipboard off the wall. "He must've been trippin' on something."

"If he was, I want some."

They both laughed.

"OK, I gotta hit my rounds," said George, opening the office door. "I'll catch you later."

"Later," said Travis as the door clicked shut.

Travis blew out a breath as he looked up at the monitor and watched George walk across the lobby and down the hall. Sitting down at the control panel, he smiled at his good fortune. Dobos' little meltdown meant that "Super Cop" wasn't manning the cameras, and that was a relief. George was not anywhere near as obsessive.

Pulling out a flash drive, he inserted it in a USB port and an icon appeared on the screen for a program called "Frame by Frame". He clicked it, and a progress bar appeared below a flashing notification.

"Searching for active video feeds."

After a few seconds another window opened.

"120 active video feeds detected. Select feeds you wish to loop."

Travis selected the feeds for the pharmacy and various hall cameras.

"Input length of video loop."

Travis looked at the monitors, thought for a moment, then typed "one second," and clicked enter.

"Duration of program?"

He typed "one hour", then pressed enter again.

"Auto program purge at termination?"

Travis clicked, "yes."

"Program running."

Travis closed the window and unplugged the flash drive. Collecting his cleaning supplies, he walked out of the security office.

The wheels of the janitor's cart squeaked rhythmically as he pushed it along, now laden with trash bags. Without further delay, he moved down the hall toward the hospital's side door. Taking out his phone, he tapped the screen. Martin answered, agitated.

"What the fuck's taking you so long?"

"Relax," said Travis, "I'm bringing you in now. Meet me at the dumpsters in five minutes."

Travis hung up before Martin could respond. Pocketing his phone, he proceeded to the side door. His life was spinning out of control, and he loved the sensation.

The door to the outer office opened and Sabine Bains swept through with her customary fluid grace. She was immediately followed by Thomas Shelby, who was positively beaming.

"Please come this way," he said, opening the door to his office and stepping aside.

Bains hesitated. She was impatient to get to work on the issue that had brought her there. The young girl who was resistant to the catalyst, the anomaly.

She hated that her work could be compromised by a child, and she was in no mood for Shelby's sophomoric, and fumble fingered attempts at romance. Reluctantly, she entered his office.

The room was bathed in the light of numerous candles, and as Shelby entered, he closed the door and stood in nervous anticipation. His heart was beating rapidly, his hands clasped before him sweating profusely as he waited for her approval.

"Would you like a drink?" he asked as he moved to a silver champagne bucket that glistened from the condensation beading on its surface.

Bains turned and regarded Shelby with emotionless eyes.

"Where is the anomaly?" she said coldly.

Shelby was crushed. He knew Bains' mood could be unpredictable, but he had hoped for a private, more intimate, interlude with this woman who filled his every thought.

"She is away on a field trip, but should be returning shortly."

Bains' eyes shifted to the small table for two that Shelby had prepared. Shelby, sensing the ice around her cracking, pressed.

"The lab is prepped," he continued. "The anomaly, will be returning after lights out. Even if she were here now, we couldn't begin before then anyway."

There was nothing more that could be done. Though pathetic, Shelby was an extremely valuable asset, so with a sigh, Bains relented. Her expression softened and Shelby smiled in relief.

"This will have to be put in cold storage," she said, holding out the metal case.

"I will see to it personally," said Shelby, struggling to contain his excitement.

Taking the case from her with a slight bow, he pulled out a chair, and offered her a seat at the table. As she sat down, he inhaled her essence, and his head began to swim in an ocean of lust.

Travis used his security pass key to open the side door and disable the alarm. This was a normal nightly procedure as he prepared to take the trash out to the dumpster. Pushing the door open he carried out two large trash bags and proceeded across the parking lot. As he approached the dumpster he scanned the dense tree line for Martin, but saw nothing.

"You there?" he whispered into the darkness.

"Here," came Martin's voice.

Even though Travis was expecting him, the sight of Martin's expressionless face and lifeless eyes, half hidden by shadows, startled him. Reaching into his overalls, he pulled out another set, along with a cap, and tossed them to Martin.

"Put these on, then walk to the door. Take the cart and go to the end of the hall and turn right. Go to the janitor's closet and wait inside. I'll text you when I'm in the pharmacy."

Martin quickly pulled on the coveralls and put on the cap. Then crossing the parking lot, he disappeared through the door. Travis waited a few seconds, then followed.

In the security office an "open door" warning light went on, and George looked up at his monitors. On the screen he saw Travis taking bags of trash out the door. He quickly dismissed it, going back to his Sudoku, unconcerned. Why should he be concerned, after all? It was only the janitor.

TWENTY-NINE

It had been another long day for Dr. Gregory Tallman, and that long day had turned into another late night. His self-proscribed inventory had revealed some startling deficiencies. Numerous dosages of Oxycontin, Adderall, and Valium were unaccounted for.

The proscription charts, pharmacist logs, and distribution records all lined up, which meant the missing drugs had been removed from storage. Tallman had his suspicions, but he knew he better have more than that before making any accusations. One thing he did know for sure, he wasn't going to take the fall for this.

As he paged through the documents, his desk lamp flickered. Reaching over he tapped it with his finger, and the bulb arced brightly, then died.

With a muttered curse, Tallman pushed the button on the lamp's base repeatedly to no effect. Reaching up to unscrew the lightbulb, he yanked his hand away as the hot bulb burned his fingers. Pulling out a handkerchief from his pocket, he tried again, and finally extracted the failed device.

Rising from his chair, he examined the burned-out bulb as he exited his office and walked down the hall to the storage room. He hoped he could find a replacement. If he couldn't, he would have to call it a night, and get a new bulb in the morning. He hoped it wouldn't come to that. He wanted to get this done.

The sound of a key sliding into the lock of the pharmacy's outer door was almost imperceptible. As the door slowly opened, Travis peered inside.

The room was dark as usual with the exception of the widely spaced security lights. Listening for a moment he heard nothing, and so pushed the door open wider and eased his cart through the doorway.

Leaving the door ajar, he shouldered a large black sports bag and walked back into the pharmacy's storage area. When he reached the rear isle where the administrative offices were located, he cautiously peeked around the corner and was relieved to see that all the offices were dark and unoccupied, including Dr. Tallman's.

Stepping across the walkway, Travis tried the door of the Schedule II drug storage room but, of course, it was locked. Taking out his phone he sent a text to let Martin know the coast was clear.

Travis stood looking at the door. The moment had arrived, the point of no return. Making his choice he backed up a step and listened. All remained quiet and still. Taking a deep breath, he drew up his strength and resolve, then with all the force he could muster, he kicked in the door. The door jamb exploded inward in a shower of shattered wood, and in that moment the rush he had felt on the night he believed he had helped kill Chance Jordan returned like a wildfire.

Inside the room were locked metal cabinets that lined the walls of the ten-foot by ten-foot space. The only light in the room came from the glow of a refrigerator, its glass door made opaque by frost.

Reaching into his sports bag Travis pulled out a crowbar and wedged it into the gap between the cabinet doors. Gripping it tightly he leaned into it, but the door held firm. Readjusting the tool's bite, he leaned on it again, this time bouncing against it.

With a creaking groan, the metal door began to warp. Without warning the crowbar broke free, sending the boy face first into the steel door, smashing his fingers then bouncing back, hitting Travis in the mouth before falling to the carpeted floor with a muffled clang.

"Shit," he muttered, touching his bleeding lip.

Frustrated, Travis picked up the crowbar and violently forced it into the gap he had made. Leaning on it once more he pushed hard with all he had, and with a loud crack the locker door burst open.

With a sense of satisfaction, Travis surveyed the bounty of narcotics before him. He had been there before, but his time was different. This time he wasn't sneaking in to skim a few pills. This time he was acting boldly, aggressively. He was there to take it all.

"Fuck it," he said under his breath as he grabbed the sports bag and held it open in front of the locker.

Reaching in, he swept the contents of one shelf into the bag. It was easy, and going so smoothly, just as Martin had laid it out. And then, the lights in the room came on.

"Travis? What are you doing?"

Travis jerked around toward the voice, dropping the sports bag, its contents spilling around his feet. Squinting in the harsh light, Travis looked at the doorway and saw Dr. Tallman standing there, his hand still on the light switch. Tallman's eyes moved accusingly from the assortment of drugs on the floor, to Travis' face.

"You don't move," said Tallman reaching for his cell phone. "I'm calling your father."

"No, please Dr. Tallman. It's not what it looks like," said Travis panicking.

"It's exactly what it looks like," said Tallman tapping his phone, "and I'm not losing my career, and my family, just so some overindulged snotnosed brat can get high."

Dr. Shelby sat sipping champagne, lost in the moment. He was so deeply entranced by Bains that he almost didn't notice when his phone began to vibrate. Unwilling to allow anything to intrude on his special moment, he turned off his phone without looking at the screen.

Dr. Tallman looked at Travis, his eyes hot with anger and contempt, as he held his phone to his ear.

"God damn it," he spat, aggravated when he heard Dr. Shelby's voice mail message start.

Travis stood dumbly, not sure what to do or say. "Please, Dr. Tallman," was all he could squeak out.

The sound of the crunch was sickening, and the shock and surprise that replaced the anger on Tallman's face was total. His hand slacked, and his phone slipped from his grasp. His body jerked, and the doctor reached behind his back, clawing as if trying to scratch an itch that was just out of reach.

A second crunch sounded, and again Tallman's body shook. His breath was driven from him in a rasping wheeze, as blood and spittle sprayed from his mouth, flecking Travis' startled face.

The stunned boy stood frozen, his mind trying to catch up with the horror before his eyes. He looked at Tallman, watching the doctor's life flicker between confusion and the black void of death. Finally, the doctor's body grew slack, and crumpled to the floor, revealing Martin Wellington standing behind him, a bloody knife in his bloody hand.

Travis looked down at the dead body of the former pharmacy director, then back up at Martin, stunned. "What the hell did you do that for?" he said, finally finding his voice.

Martin did not respond. Instead, he bent down and wiped his blade clean on Tallman's shirt, the two wounds he had inflicted gaping from the dead man's back.

Travis dropped to his knees and rolled Tallman's body over. He checked him for a pulse and listened for a breath, but detected none. His face filled with horror, as he looked up at Martin.

"He's dead," said Travis, still trying to grasp what was happening. "You killed him. Why'd you have to kill him?"

"He was a problem. Problem solved," said Martin sliding his knife into a scabbard under his coveralls.

Stepping over the body, Martin picked up the sports bag, then went to the open locker and began sweeping the contents of the shelves into it. After a few seconds he turned and looked at Travis.

"Go get the cart. I'll finish up here."

But Travis was in shock. He kept muttering as panic set in, "Oh my God, oh my God."

Without warning, Martin violently snatched Travis up off the floor. Slamming him up against a locker; Martin drew his knife once again and held it to the frightened boy's throat.

"Are you going to be a problem?" said Martin, in a smooth even voice that seemed devoid of all emotion.

Travis immediately calmed, despite the knife that was held so tightly to his throat that it cut him each time he swallowed. He looked down at the body of Dr. Tallman, the last 'problem' Martin had solved, and shook his head.

"Good," said Martin, pulling the knife back and releasing him. "Now, go get the cart, while I finish up here."

Travis nodded his understanding, as blood trickled down his throat and stained the collar of his T-shirt. Giving Tallman's body a wide berth, he left the room as Martin went to work prying open the remaining lockers.

When Travis returned with the janitor's cart, he and Martin lifted Tallman's body and stuffed it into the cart's trash bin. When the corpse didn't fit, Martin solved that problem by breaking Tallman's legs, the sound of the cracking bones giving Travis the dry heaves.

As Travis covered the body with trash, Martin poured a large bottle of codeine cough syrup onto the blood-stained carpet, it's deep crimson color completely concealing the blood pool.

As Travis began to muscle the now awkwardly heavy cart out of the door, Martin crossed the room and peered through the frosted glass of the refrigerator.

"Now what do we have here?" he asked.

THIRTY

The Fallen Creature of Light was captivated by his new vessel. He had taken humans many times before. Short lived and disposable, he would discard their rotted corpses as soon as he was finished with them. But this girl, Nikki, she was different.

As he had entered her body, and spread out within her form, he had felt a completeness, a sense of calm that he had never experienced. Now he considered the possibility, dared to contemplate the unthinkable, that this Taking could be a bonding.

He had heard the legends, rumors really, of such bondings. Celestial beings who had found peace living in a bizarre symbiosis with a human vessel. He secretly longed for such a thing. He had been at war for so long he had almost forgotten what the simplicity of peace felt like.

But for a child of light, Fallen or Celestial, to be coupled with a human as a companion, to exist as equals within the vessel, was nothing less than blasphemy. Creatures of Light and humans were not equals. The purpose of humans was not to be companions. Nevertheless, the temptation for some, could be overpowering.

Those that gave in to that temptation were called Rephaim. They became outcasts of both the Triad, and the Legion of the Morning Star. Considered traitors and deviants, they were relentlessly hunted down and destroyed.

Forced into the shadows, they had no choice but to live their lives in seclusion, hidden from view for eternity, their only consolation being that they would spend that eternity, together.

No one knew for sure how many Rephaim there were. Many Creatures of Light had vanished in the fog of the war. After the defeat, and casting out, of the Legion, thousands of years before, the reports of celestials breaking away from both the Triad, and the Legion, to bond with human vessels, had increased. He That is Three, and The Son of the Morning Star denied it of course, neither willing to admit to discontent amongst their ranks.

The symbiosis of a bonding was simple. The Creature of Light would gain the pleasures of the flesh, sensations they would never know as celestial beings. The close bond with their human vessel would also allow them access to the unique flavor of the vessel's human emotions. The combined experience being like a drug that once tasted, became an addictive need.

As for the human, they gained a life as a quasi immortal. Quasi because the flesh vessel would still need to eat, drink and sleep, though much, much less. Their bodies, normally fragile, became nearly indestructible. Anything short of catastrophic dismemberment would quickly heal.

The vessel also gained access to the Celestial's near infinite mind. Within that mind anything, and everything, was possible. It was a playground of lucid dreams, whose only limitation was imagination.

For the vessel, however, the price could be difficult to...stomach. What made the symbiotic relationship complete was the method required for the flesh vessel to maintain, and nourish, the resident Rephaim. It was, to say the least, a macabre procedure.

The Fallen knew that to even postulate such things as a bonding was forbidden, even treasonous. And yet, the possibility of an eternity in such a state of balanced bliss was so tempting – regardless of the cost, a temptation that, for him, was strong with this girl.

He had been watching her since she was a child. Intrigued by her resilience and tenacity, he had developed an odd connection with her that had kept him close.

On the night he had slaughtered Nikki's mother, and more satisfyingly her stepfather, it had been a selfish impulse. He shouldn't have cared if the girl had lived or died, but he did. He just didn't want to lose contact with this particular human.

Thinking about Nikki made him long to look in on her again. It was another selfish impulse, but he couldn't help it. In his eyes she was perfect, even in her flaws, which, in the most private depths of her psyche, she amplified to sometimes grotesque proportions.

With each glimpse of that psyche, he learned more. Under normal circumstances he would simply sift through the detritus of a vessel's mind and, as if paging through a photo album of its life experiences, search for those thoughts he deemed expedient to his goals. Once finding the emotions that he needed, he could control and manipulate the vessel.

Inside the vessel's mind, he would control what they saw and felt. He often drew on the vessel's concept of the afterlife, placing them in their own personal "Hell", but it was always what he decided it should be. So that is why it was with profound surprise that he began to hear the dulcet and soothing sounds of a piano coming from beyond the locked door of Nikki's mind.

Confused, he stared at the door. Except for the drink he had provided, he had given her nothing but darkness. But that darkness had been somehow compromised. Along with the haunting music, he saw a flickering of light leaking out in a glowing aura.

Manifesting the peephole, he reached for it but froze motionless as the sound of singing now touched his ears. Languid and beautiful, but with a rasping edge, it drifted through, then filled, the voids of his war weary soul like warm honey.

Hesitating, he slid the peephole open, unsure of what he would find. What he did see made his eyes grow wide in wonder. Somehow, he had lost control of his vessel's mind. A situation that should have been impossible, had become reality.

Somehow Nikki was directing and manipulating the environment in which they would interact. And truth be told, he didn't mind, but he was not prepared for what he saw.

Nikki was sitting at the foot of a luxurious feather bed, singing as she played a massive white, grand piano. Black candles covered the instrument's lid, and filled what looked like millions of candelabra that stretched out in every direction to an infinite horizon. Rivers of molten wax flowed over a travertine floor around her, growing in size as they merged, until pouring over the edge of a great stone precipice in a thick black fall.

He took in the scene, dazzled by its presentation, and frightened by its implication. It was overwhelming, but in spite of this awesome beauty, his eyes were drawn back to Nikki.

She was still naked, and he wondered why? It occurred to him, that if she was, it was because she wanted to be, and this pleased him.

Sitting perched on an antique piano bench, her back was to him, her bare feet crossed at the ankles as her bottom spread out invitingly on the seat's cushion. Her alabaster skin still luminescent, was warmed by the soft yellow glow of the candlelight.

Nikki could feel his eyes on her, and her skin tingled in excitement when she heard the door of her mind creak open, and the sound of heavy footfalls walking up behind her. Her delicate fingers fell motionless on the keyboard as he moved in close, the silence so complete that she was sure she could hear the candles burning around her.

"Please, don't stop," said the Fallen, his voice a deep pleasant rumble. His eyes moved to a polished silver goblet on the piano top. In its reflection he could see that Nikki was looking at him, and was surprised when she moved over to make room for him on the small bench. As he sat down next to her, his naked hip touched hers, and the ornate bench creaked under his bulk.

An unfamiliar sense of trepidation filled him as he sat looking down at the piano keys. Now it was his turn to feel her eyes upon him, and it made him uncomfortably aware of his frightening visage.

But Nikki was not frightened, and she did not look away. Instead, she turned and looked directly at him. Disconcerted, he tried to avoid her gaze.

"You shouldn't look at me," he warned.

"I'm not afraid of you," she said softly. "I find you too beautiful to be afraid of you."

"You don't know what I am," he said grimly.

"I know exactly what you are," she said looking him in the eyes, "and I know who you are."

Her comment startled him, and he looked at her confused. Reaching up she took the silver goblet and held it before him. His face was clearly visible in its polished surface, and his reflection stunned him.

His countenance had changed, and as he raised his right hand to touch his face, he realized his hand had changed as well. Gone was the grotesquely mottled flesh of a Fallen. His long clawed fingers, now elegantly human, touched his face and confirmed that human flesh now covered what moments before, was a nightmare.

Nikki's fingertips joined the Fallen's on his face, and he startled at her touch.

"It's OK," she whispered.

As she marveled at his beauty, she caressed his soft flawless skin and chiseled features. Long light blond hair, that fell in ringlets, caught the flickering candlelight. Placing her hands on both sides of his face, she turned him to look at her, and as she did the true nature of his transformation became clear.

The right half of his face, indeed the entire right half of his body, was now flesh, invitingly soft and human, but the left was something else entirely. It retained the vicious and vindictive penalty inflicted by He That is Three on the soldiers of the Legion, and any who dared turn away from the Triad.

Nikki's eyes held his, then looked down at her shoulder where the incongruous tattoo of the half Fallen, half human, decorated her flesh. It was obvious that she had altered his appearance to match that of her skin art, but at the same time he was struck by how accurately she had remembered, and then rendered his misshapen face.

His image had been burned into her memory, and from her memory, she had drawn him, and from her drawing had committed his image to her flesh. Now, at long last, he sat beside her, and it brought her an uncharacteristic sense of calm.

She remembered the night he had come and killed her mother and stepfather. She recalled how, as he had appeared, her room had become deathly cold. So cold that when he had disemboweled her parents, their bodies were almost completely obscured by the steam rising from their piled entrails

Nikki gazed up at him, her eyes glistening with emotion. Almost afraid that if she blinked, he might vanish. For so long she had dreamed of meeting, face to face, the creature that had set her free.

"It is you, isn't it?" she asked.

"So, it would seem."

"Am I dreaming?"

"No."

"Am I dead?"

At this the Fallen paused. "No, but in time you may wish to be," he said ominously.

Nikki puzzled at this, then looked at him earnestly. "Will you stay with me?"

"Yes, if that is your wish."

"Forever?"

Now it was his turn to puzzle. The answer to her question had so many conditions, and the result she was requesting would exact a terrible price on both of them. She looked at him with pleading eyes, but he could see that she did not fully understand the reality of their union.

"Is forever what you want?" he asked.

Nikki only nodded.

"This will not be easy...for either of us," he said, stroking her cheek with the back of his human hand. "Forever has a price."

"I'll do whatever I have to," she said, leaning her face against his hand. "I just want to stay here with you."

He took a deep breath and steeled himself. "The only way we will be able to stay together forever is if you feed us."

She looked at him quizzically, but said nothing.

"To nourish us," he continued, "will require you to feed on the essence, the life force, of other living creatures."

"The essence?" she questioned.

"Blood," he explained. "In the waking world you will need to keep the true nature of yourself concealed, as you hunt blood to sustain us."

Nikki looked at him wordlessly as she slowly put the pieces of what she had just heard, together.

"You want me to become a vampire? Are you serious?"

The Fallen was taken aback by her response.

"No, you will not be a 'vampire'. At least not as described in the tales of your storytellers."

"So, I'm not gonna sparkle?" she asked dryly.

"What?" he said, confused.

"I'll explain it to you later."

"Nikki, this is serious. You...we, will become outcasts. Feared by mortals, and despised, even hunted by the Legion as well as the Triad."

"The Legion and the Triad?" asked Nikki.

"To them we are an embarrassment, an abomination that must be destroyed."

Nikki could see how serious this was for him, even if she didn't fully understand everything he was saying. Pausing she took his hands in hers. She marveled at the different textures, rough scale and silky skin.

"I understand," she said at last, looking up at him, "and I will do what I have to do."

"Very well," he said as he traced the symbol for infinity on the palm of her hand, "forever shall it be."

Kissing her palm to seal his oath, he placed her hand on his heart, then laid it upon the piano.

"Now play for me."

Her fingers began to move and her haunting music once again filled the infinite space around them. Nikki let out a satisfied sigh, and the Fallen allowed himself a moment of peace, pushing the consequences of their choice from his mind. His human hand began to trace languid circles over the tattoos on the small of Nikki's back. Then as Nikki rested her head against his arm, she began to sing.

THIRTY-ONE

Chance was shaken back into the moment by the slowing of the van as Bo prepared to turn into the Havenhurst driveway. He had been watching Marina as she put the finishing touches on her drawing, and as she toiled, he had become lost in her. Reluctantly intruding, he squeezed her hand and she looked up at him.

"We're almost at the hospital," he said, sorrow obvious on his face.

Marina looked up and saw the massive sandstone building looming on the hill ahead. Turning to look at Chance, she bit her lip, and pulled her hand away from his as she began packing up her belongings. Chance immediately felt the loss.

Bo drove the van up to the front of the hospital and parked. Nurse Denali jumped out and walked to the hospital's front door, as Chance opened the van's side door and climbed out. Reaching in, he took Marina's tiger, then helped her step down.

As Bo pulled away to take the van to the garage, Chance and Marina found themselves alone for the first time since they had known each other. Standing there they just looked at one another, a strained silence overcoming them. The kind of silence that tends to precede a first kiss, or an uncomfortably awkward moment. It was the awkward moment that won out, as nurse Denali called for them to come inside.

Self-consciously, Chance stepped back and gave the stuffed tiger to Marina. Turning, they walked in silence toward the now open hospital door, the only sound being the crunch of the driveway's gravel under their feet.

In Thomas Shelby's mind, the evening had gone wonderfully. After a slow start, Sabine Bains had, for the most part, been very attentive and receptive to his romantic overtures.

The drug trial experiment scheduled for that night was prepped and ready. All that was left to do was wait for Marina to return and the swing shift to go home.

It had not been a pleasant evening for Dr. Bains, however. Throughout the evening she had experienced moments of what she could only describe as extreme anxiety caused by a disturbance in the energy field known as "The Veil".

The Veil had periodically rippled and, as it had washed over her, then through her, it had made her nauseous. It had been very directional, like ultralow bass frequencies pounding on her from the distance. It had the quality of both harmony and discord, and carried an undeniable power.

As the phone on Dr. Shelby's desk began to ring, another massive pulse pounded through her. Excusing himself, Dr. Shelby went to the phone.

"Dr. Shelby...oh, excellent. Thank you, George." Hanging up he turned to Bains. "Marina has returned from the carnival," he announced. But before Bains could respond, he noticed the look of distress on her face.

"Are you feeling okay, my dear?" he asked.

"Yes, I'm fine," she replied, annoyed that she had shown weakness. "Get the anomaly into the procedure room. I want to get this over with."

Moments later, Shelby and Bains walked into the foyer as George stood smiling, looking out through the open front door of the hospital. He had been joined by a few of the nurses, and all were in bubbling anticipation of the field trip party's return. As Denali, Marina and Chance entered the foyer, the room exploded with laughter and chatter.

"And who is this?" asked George, indicating the enormous stuffed tiger that Marina was holding.

"His name is Sam," said Marina proudly. "Chance won him for me."

In excited breaths, as she clung to Chance's arm, Marina recounted the story of how he had won the great beast, and how proud she was of him.

The nurses who had spent the last several years watching Marina age, but not mature, within her stagnated emotional and psychological shell, now glanced at each other with shocked expressions and raised eyebrows. The girl that they had cared for, for so many years, was blossoming into a woman right before their eyes. As Shelby joined the group, one of the nurses took his arm and smiled up at him.

"Our little girl is growing up," she said softly.

Shelby just smiled and nodded, caught up in the moment. Bains, on the other hand, was much more tacit.

Staying back, she watched intently as Marina and Chance interacted. She sensed something in the boy. Something powerful, powerful and dangerous.

Chance noticed the woman standing at the other end of the room. He could feel the intensity of her stare crawling all over him like tentacles, but his attention was quickly pulled back to Marina as the clamor in the room began to subside.

"Marina, it's time to say good night to Chance," said Denali.

The group quieted down as it moved a few feet away from the young couple to give them some privacy. The excitement in Marina's demeanor faded as the reality of the night's end loomed. Clutching her tiger, she looked up at Chance with mournful eyes.

"Thank you for a wonderful evening," she finally said.

"It WAS wonderful. Thank you for inviting me."

"And thank you for winning Sam for me," she said, hugging her tiger.

"Take good care of him," said Chance, reaching out and patting the tiger's head.

"I will," she said, gazing up at him. "Will I see you tomorrow?"

"I have baseball practice and some homework to do, but I can come see you after dinner."

Marina smiled, then hesitating she glanced over her shoulder at Denali and the others who were trying hard to look like they weren't looking. Summoning her courage, she stepped up to Chance, rose up on her toes and kissed his lips.

Her kiss was gentile and soft. Not more than a feather's weight. If her kiss had landed upon still water, not a ripple would have been seen. Yet it rocked Chance to his core.

Bains was rocked as well. As Marina's lips had touched Chance's, Bains was overcome by a pulse of energy that assaulted her senses. Instantly nauseous, she was forced to steady herself against the wall.

As Marina stepped back, both she and Chance became acutely aware that all of the conversation in the room had ceased, and the hospital's foyer had become as quiet as a tomb. They both turned to look at the assembled group only to find that all of them, including Dr. Shelby, had given up all pretense of disinterest, and instead stood in slack-jawed stupefaction at what they had just witnessed.

It was Denali that came to her senses first.

"Marina, we should get you to bed. It's late."

Marina, a bit weak-kneed, turned and joined nurse Denali as she walked toward the elevator, but before she got there, Marina suddenly turned and called out.

"Sari'El, you forgot your present," she said as she held up the drawing she had been working on so feverishly.

Chance quickly crossed the short distance and took the drawing.

"Look at it later," she whispered, "and I'll see you tomorrow." Throwing her arms around him she hugged him tightly.

"Tomorrow," he said as he rolled the drawing and placed it inside his jacket.

Chance saw that Denali was looking at him. She reached out and touched Chance's shoulder, giving him a soft smile and look of approval. With an affectionate pat on his arm, she turned away toward the elevator. As she did, Chance was sure he saw a tear in the eye of the hard-as-nails head nurse.

As Chance waved goodbye to the beaming Marina, Dr. Shelby stepped up beside him.

"Hello, Chance," said Shelby, "It's nice to see you again."

"Good evening, Dr. Shelby. It's good to see you again as well."

"Did I hear correctly, that you plan to return again tomorrow evening?"

"Yes sir," said Chance with mild trepidation. "I hope I didn't overstep my bounds."

"No, not at all," assured Shelby. "Your visits with Marina are a source of great joy for the entire staff."

Chance watched as Marina and Denali stepped onto the elevator. Marina, holding her tiger, waved one last time as the elevator's door closed.

"She sure has changed since the day I first met her," commented Chance.

"Yes, we have noticed that as well. She seems to be maturing at an exponential rate. Meeting you has been life changing for her.

"I can't say that meeting her hasn't changed me as well."

"It has affected us all, son," said Shelby, smiling. "You go get some rest, and we'll see you tomorrow."

"Yes sir. Thank you, sir. Goodnight," said Chance turning and walking to the front door where George was waiting.

"Quite a night," said George as Chance approached.

"You don't know the half of it," replied Chance, smiling. "Hey," he continued, "Do you think it would be okay if I used the restroom before I go? It's a long ride back to Wellington."

"Sure, but make it quick," said George looking at his watch. "I'm already late for my rounds."

"I'll be quick, thanks," said Chance as he took off jogging toward the restrooms.

The lights in the hallway were dimmed, but there was enough light provided by the security and night lights for Chance to find his way. The staff had gone back to their stations and so the halls were empty. So it was with great surprise that as Chance rounded a corner, he was barely able to avoid two unexpected janitors struggling to push a large trash cart.

"Excuse me," said Chance politely.

But the janitors said nothing. They just stared, first at him, then each other.

Chance was not sure what the problem was, and so he finally actually looked at the two men, then looked again, and finally recognized them as Travis Shelby and Martin Wellington. Chance now took in the scene before him in its entirety.

Both boys were dressed in janitor's coveralls, but where Travis' fit him properly, Martin's were too long in the leg, and too tight in the middle. Each had a large black hockey bag strapped across his back, and Martin was holding a metal case.

Several questions raced through Chance's mind: When did Martin start working at Havenhurst? What were the hockey bags for? And why was that cart so heavy?

But those questions became secondary as Chance looked into Martin's cold eyes, and sensed the ruthless calculus taking place there. Before Martin could reach any conclusions, Chance decided that the call of nature could wait, and so backing away, he returned to the foyer.

After bidding Chance goodnight, Shelby had turned expecting to see Sabine Bains, but she was gone. Curious, he walked down the hall looking for her.

As he entered his office, he found Bains standing at the window staring out into the darkness. Her hands were clasped in front of her, clenched so tightly that they had lost all color. Shelby approached her slowly.

"Is there a problem my dear?"

"She called him Sari'El," said Bains evenly.

"Yes, that is a name Marina has given to him since they met," said Shelby, confused by her reaction.

"Why didn't you mention this?" said Bains, her anger now apparent.

Shelby was caught off guard by the intensity of her anger over what, to him, seemed to be an unimportant detail.

"I'm sorry, it just didn't seem relevant," he croaked.

Bains looked at him, clearly on the verge of implosion. "He is not to be permitted near the anomaly again," she said through clenched teeth. "He is dangerous. Do you understand me?"

Shelby stood dumbly, unable to speak.

"DO-YOU-UNDERSTAND-ME?" she repeated, each word a thrusting dagger.

"Yes, I understand," he said at last.

"We can waste no more time. Get the catalyst and meet me in the procedure room," she ordered in a dark emotionless tone that frightened him.

Shelby quickly left, and as the office door closed the sound of a motorcycle starting in the parking lot drew her attention back to the window. Looking out through the blinds, Bains saw Chance standing beside his idling bike. She looked at him, appraising him, trying to see some obvious sign of what she now suspected.

"Are you Sari'El?" she whispered.

Chance stood beside his motorcycle as he strapped his backpack to the rear seat and prepared for the long cold ride back to Wellington. A short distance away a uniformed soldier occupied himself with his phone.

Chance's unnerving encounter with Martin and Travis had been pushed aside by his memories of his magical evening with Marina. His emotions were so muddled. He had only known her for four days, and yet he felt a connection to her which ran so much deeper. She consumed him, and even though he had said good night to her only moments before, he already missed her.

Reaching into his jacket he pulled out Marina's drawing. As he unrolled it, he became immediately self-conscious, reflexively looking over his shoulder.

The drawing was similar to one of Marina's earlier works, the idealized nude images of himself and Marina, walking together. But in this drawing, his arms were wrapped around her from behind, her hair flowing back over his shoulder as he held her, resting his cheek against her.

The biggest, most notable difference, however, was not the subject matter, but rather the artistic realism and quality. Marina's first pieces were done in crayon, and while detailed, they were not overtly so.

This new drawing, produced in colored pencils and pastels, was shockingly realistic and idealized. As Chance looked at the drawing, he was sure he could see her hair flowing in the breeze, the trembling pout of her lips, even the halting rise and fall of her breasts. It was breathtaking.

Suddenly he pressed the drawing against him, paranoid that someone might see it, even though the only other person in the parking lot was the soldier, who barely gave Chance more than a passing notice.

Chance noticed a light come on in a window above and looked up at the cold stone edifice of the hospital. There in a window was Marina's unmistakable silhouette. Raising her hand she waved sweetly, and his heart ached in his chest as he returned her farewell.

Rolling up the drawing, he put it back into his jacket, then throwing his leg over, he mounted his machine. As he pulled on his gloves, his eyes were drawn to movement in a first-floor window. He looked but saw nothing, but at the same time a wave of cold washed over him causing a shiver to momentarily wrack his body.

Tightening his jacket, he dropped his bike into gear and began to roll down the hospital's long driveway. As he reached the highway, Chance stopped and activated his left turn signal. The road was devoid of traffic, but Chance sat unmoving, his bike idling beneath him.

Marina's drawing poked at his mind. It was as if it were whispering to him, trying to tell him something that he couldn't understand. Reaching into his jacket, he took it out and looked at it once again, though he didn't know what he was looking for.

Looking over his shoulder, he saw that Marina was still standing in her window. Making a decision he put the drawing back in his jacket and activated his right turn signal. Stomping on the gear shift lever, he brought his engine up to a full throaty roar and aggressively accelerated out onto the empty highway and in the direction of the lakes.

Glancing one last time over his shoulder, he saw that Marina's window was now dark. Pulling back on his throttle, the painted lines on the road merged into one, as the hobgoblins that vexed him once again began to fall away.

Travis Shelby jogged across the Havenhurst parking lot to his car. As he opened the door, he was shocked to see Martin sitting with his head back, an empty syringe still inserted in his arm, hanging limply in his flesh as it bobbed with every beat of his heart.

"He's not going back to campus. He turned toward the lake," said Travis regaining his composure.

"Excellent," said Martin in a sleepy voice. "Follow him."

THIRTY-TWO

Bains hung a saline bag next to an examination table, then placed E.K.G. patches and leads on a procedure tray. Surveying the room, she let out the satisfied sigh of a hostess ready for her first guest. Almost immediately, her first guest arrived, and with a look of horror on his face.

"It's gone," blurted Shelby, his face a ghastly ashen white.

Bains and Shelby entered the pharmacy to find the night security guard shining his flashlight at the shattered door of the schedule II drug storage room. Inside, the lockers stood pried open and empty. In the center of the room lay an empty bottle of codeine cough syrup, its contents spilled out and soaking into the carpeted floor.

More important to Bains though, was the smashed refrigerator. Her eyes surveyed the pebbles of broken glass covering the floor, then fell on the empty shelf inside where the catalyst had been stored.

"When did this happen?" inquired Bains coldly.

"The pharmacy staff left at five, so some time after that," speculated Shelby.

"Was there anyone here after five?" she asked.

"George?" said Shelby, looking at the guard.

"Dr. Tallman has been working late the last few nights," said the guard. "I don't think he has left yet. His car is still in the parking lot."

"Will you please see if you can locate him?"

"Yes, sir," said George, turning to leave.

"And George, please notify the Sheriff's Department."

"Yes, sir."

Bains stood thinking. The audacity of the act implied confidence, and the volume of what was taken required preparation. Only an intimate knowledge of the pharmacy's layout, and the hospital's security, would provide that.

"Who else was in this facility tonight?"

"Other than facility staff, only Chance Jordan, but he was here for just a few minutes," said Shelby.

Bains took out her phone and tapped the screen.

"Hello?" came a male's voice.

"Jeremy?"

"Yes, Sabine. What can I do for you?"

Shelby squirmed, not liking Jeremy's familiar tone with his Sabine.

"Has anyone left the hospital grounds since we arrived?" she asked.

"In the last thirty minutes, a boy on a motorcycle..."

"That would be Chance Jordan," said Shelby, trying to be helpful.

"Shortly after," continued Jeremy, "two other boys in a silver car."

"A silver car?" questioned Shelby, gasping.

"Moving quickly down the hall to one of the offices, he looked out the window. His heart sank when he saw that Travis' car was gone.

"Travis, what have you done?" he whispered.

Turning from the window he was surprised to find himself face to face with Sabine Bains, her eyes intensely fixed on him.

"Who is Travis?" she asked coldly.

THIRTY-THREE

Chance couldn't explain why he felt drawn to the old abandoned lake house. He didn't know what he would do when he arrived, or what he expected to find for that matter, only that he needed to be there.

The air was cool, and he could smell the water of the lake in the air as he pulled into the house's long dirt driveway. As he approached the house, moonlight filtered down through the forest's canopy, and combined with the bluish hue of his headlight to produce ghostly shadows that darted among the trees dotting the property.

Parking his bike near the house, he took in the neglected structure. Even as beat up as it was, he could see it still had good bones, and with a little love it could be brought back to life.

Chance noticed that the door, which Eric had broken down, had been boarded shut, so he walked around to the lake side door. The peacefulness of the place was calming, the only detectable sounds being those of waves lapping at the beach, and the rustle of the soft breeze in the trees.

Stepping up onto the house's rear porch he peered through the window, though it was too dark to see inside. Trying the door he felt the knob turn, but the door didn't move. Turning the knob again, he put his shoulder into it, and this time it gave way. The hinges screeched as it opened, like a door in an old black and white horror film, and he stood in the threshold waiting for something to happen, but nothing did. Using his cell phone as a flashlight he scanned the room.

The house was just as he remembered it – musty, dusty, and empty. The only stick of furniture was a heavy oak dining table that had collapsed, two of its legs folded beneath it.

Glancing over at the window, he couldn't resist a quick look for the missing doll that had vanished from the sill. It wasn't there.

Moving slowly, he headed up the stairs, the boards creaking as he climbed. Reaching the top, he paused when he heard a sound, but quickly dismissed it as the wind tussling tree limbs against the house.

At the end of the hallway, the door to the room where the mysterious voyeur with the glowing eyes had vanished, stood open. As Chance walked into the room, he directed his light at the wall, and the colorful crayon mural came to life again. He paused for a moment, taking a breath as the emotions which had threatened to overwhelm him the first time he had seen it, began to tug at him again.

Stepping forward he placed his hand gently on the images, the waxy texture feeling slightly sticky in the damp mountain air. Again, he felt a connection to the story. Whoever had drawn them had suffered a catastrophic loss, and their pain still permeated their creation. Chance could empathize. Even after the passage of eleven years, he still felt a hole in his soul from the loss of his mother.

"What am I doing here?" he said to himself.

The story these drawings told was Marina's. It was an inescapable conclusion. But Chance knew there was no way she could have drawn these. The stories he had heard were...crazy. Even if they were only partly true, they were a level of fantastic more suitable to a Dean Koontz novel than a child's memory.

So, if not Marina, then who? The variables began to flood Chance's mind. Who could possibly know Marina's story so intimately, then come here, into this room, and render it from the perspective of an eyewitness, in such a childlike manner? In crayon no less.

"Craziness," he muttered.

Frustrated he turned to leave, but as he did a flash of color caught his eye. Stepping back, he held up his light, and a portion of the mural he had not seen before peeked out from behind the room's door, which had been pushed back against the wall.

Reaching out, Chance moved a chair out of the way, and pulled the door away from the wall, then stood back in stunned silence. There before him, was an exquisite pastel and colored pencil replica of the drawing Marina had given him just that evening.

It was massive, starting at the ceiling the unfinished life-sized mural stretched a third of the way down the wall. In disbelief, Chance pulled Marina's gift from his jacket and held it up for comparison.

While the drawing on the wall was only partially complete, what was there was stroke for stroke, and line for line, identical to what he held in his hand. The implications were more than Chance could accept. For Marina to have been the creator of the wall art before him, she would have had to have been in the room. Tonight.

But that was impossible. When he left the hospital, he had seen Marina standing at her window. There was no earthly way she could have beaten him to the lake with enough time to complete the work of art that now vexed him from the wall.

Stuffing Marina's drawing back into his jacket, Chance moved quickly out the door. He could not explain what was happening, or even what he was doing. All he knew for sure was that the only person who could help him begin to make sense of this was Marina, and he felt compelled to see her, even if he had no idea how he would be able to make that happen.

Running down the hall he reached the stairwell, then descended it in leaps, but as he reached the last step he was rocked by a violent blow to the head. The attack came out of the darkness. Heavy and crushing, it knocked Chance into a barely conscious stupor. Stumbling, he fell away from his attacker. He would have fallen to the floor had it not been for the wall.

Another crushing blow, so hard it made his ears ring, buckled his knees and drove him to the floor. He threw his arms up over his head in hopes of deflecting the devastating attack, only to feel white hot pain as his forearm was shattered.

Peering up through the crook of his arm, Chance dared a look at his assailants. There were two of them, but with the moon shining brightly at their backs, all he could see were their black silhouettes as they ruthlessly kicked him, whooping and laughing as they did.

Chance was fading. He knew he was teetering on the verge of unconsciousness, so in a last-ditch effort, he lunged out, wrapping his good arm around the legs of the nearest shadow as it pummeled him.

It worked. The faceless assailant stumbled and fell back, dropping the heavy club it was holding, the wooden cudgel ringing as it landed on the hardwood floor.

Rolling over onto his back, Chance's eyes searched frantically for the second attacker. He found him, advancing with his arm raised, the unmistakable glint of polished steel in his hand. As his attacker lunged, Chance kicked up, driving his heel hard into his attacker's solar plexus.

The shadowy figure dropped to the floor with a groan as air left his lungs. Wasting no time, Chance rolled to his knees and gained his feet just long enough to stumble out the door, only to collapse again in the sand outside.

Still borderline senseless, Chance crawled across the sand. He tried to regain his feet, but quickly fell back to his knees.

The feel of the cool sand and the brisk air of the lake, slightly revived him. For a moment he dared to hope that his attackers might break off their assault and let him escape. That hope, however, was dashed by the sound of a familiar voice mocking him from behind.

"Where ya goin', Jordan?"

Chance turned, looking back in the direction of the voice to see Martin Wellington stepping down from the porch, clutching a monstrous blade. Behind him was a smiling Travis Shelby, emerging from the house's dark doorway.

Martin's eyes fixed on Chance as he stalked slowly toward his prey. Seeing his advance, Chance frantically scrambled across the sand on his knees, and one good arm, in a vain effort to escape.

"I'm gonna gut you, Jordan," taunted Martin, "and I'm gonna gut you slow."

Martin walked up next to Chance, looking down on him with a sinister grin. Then without warning he violently kicked the helpless boy in the ribs, causing him to flop over on his back, groaning in pain.

Holding out his knife, Martin stood over Chance. "I'm gonna enjoy this jock," he said wickedly. "I'm gonna cut you up into little pieces. By morning you'll be nothing but fish shit."

"My, how charming," dead-panned a woman's voice from the shadows.

Martin spun around, crouching defensively as Sabine Bains stepped out into the moonlight. Stunned, Travis took a step back, on the verge of flight as he saw his father's mistress holding the metal case he had last seen when Martin had tossed it into the trunk next to the lifeless body of Dr. Tallman.

"Now," began Bains, "which one of you is Travis?"

Her eyes moved slowly over Martin, then shifted to Travis. "Ah, you," she said, pulling her coat a little tighter around her, she stepped closer to him. "You have your father's eyes."

As Travis looked on, a spark flickered, then grew in intensity until it covered Bains' irises with the glow of burning embers over which crawled arcs of red electric energy. When the whites of her eyes turned to an oily onyx black, Travis let out a frightened, choked scream. Backing away, he stumbled and fell to the sand, unable to move.

"You know this bitch?" shouted Martin, agitated.

Bains turned to Martin, her eyes blazing. In a smooth gesture she raised her hand in Martin's direction and clenched her fist tightly.

Martin gagged. Dropping his knife, he began to claw at his throat as if trying to pry loose the hands of some phantom. Fighting for each breath, his eyes began to bulge, and turn red from petechial hemorrhaging. As he struggled, he felt the crushing pressure on his throat intensify, then his feet lost purchase with the earth as he began to rise into the air.

Travis sat in shock. Immobilized by fear, he watched Martin rise and hover six feet off the ground, his feet kicking like a condemned man dancing at the end of the hangman's rope.

Like Travis, Chance sat staring in disbelief, his attempts at escape temporarily halted by the unbelievable scene before him. With each passing minute, his head was clearing from the vicious beating he had received. His strength slowly returning, he glanced at the nearby tree line hoping that it might offer him cover to escape. But his attention was drawn skyward by the familiar sound of heavy wings pounding the air above the tree tops.

Martin, even in his state of strangulation, heard it. The air around him became frigid, and feeling the heavy beating of the wings, turned his blood-stained eyes up in search of its source. When he saw what was descending upon him, his eyes bulged even further.

Broad leathery wings momentarily eclipsed the moon as the misshapen creature descended, lighting gracefully in front of him, its burning eyes looking at him with such intensity that his face glowed. Its mottled and scaled skin shimmered in the light of the moon. Thick bands of muscle twisted around its sturdy frame, as its great barreled chest heaved with every breath.

And then it roared. A deep thunderous roar that reached back from primordial time, and reeked of the stench of sulphur.

Without warning, the choking force at Martin's throat released, and he fell to the ground, gasping. Rolling over onto his back he looked up at the winged monster just as its massive, taloned foot, came down violently on his chest, pinning him to the ground.

The pressure on his chest was so heavy it felt like a truck was parked there. The pain was excruciating as his ribs cracked, then snapped, driving his breath from him as the jagged bone punctured his lungs. Martin struggled to breathe, pink foam frothing from his mouth and nose as his lungs collapsed.

Bains walked up next to the Beast and looked down at Martin. The creature's burning eyes regarded her, but it did nothing else until she spoke.

"El leq-ae mon Chuah."

The Fallen roared as red electrical charges began to emerge from its skin, erupting from every pore. The brilliant web of energy grew in intensity until it completely obscured the creature in a cocoon of sizzling arcs. Then, in a deafening thunderclap, as though every lightning bolt from a hurricane had flashed at a single moment, the Fallen's shroud of electricity shot across the short distance and wrapped around Martin's body.

The arcs drilled into Martin's flesh, stabbing and twisting like glowing daggers. His body shook, convulsing like a man in an electric chair. His eyes and the hallows of his face glowed red, as if his head were filled with a fire, giving him the appearance of some demented jack-o-lantern.

Finally, the electric arcs began to subside. As the maelstrom sank into Martin's flesh, he was left motionless on the ground.

Travis, fighting horror induced shock, watched in anticipation, of what he did not know. Sure that Martin was dead, he considered running, but couldn't tear his eyes from the horrifying scene. Instead, he waited for what might happen next.

Then, Martin's body twitched. Only slightly at first, but it nevertheless startled Travis. And then, Martin stood up as if nothing had happened at all.

Travis' hopes blossomed as Martin casually bent down and plucked his knife from the sand and looked at Bains with the cold, lifeless, killer's stare that Travis had seen so many times before.

"Yeah, kill the bitch," screamed Travis jumping to his feet.

But Martin made no such move. Instead, he and Bains turned and looked at Travis, both now with eyes that burned on pools of glistening blackness.

Travis began screaming in high pitched, panicked yelps.

"Deal with that," commanded Bains.

Martin strode aggressively toward Travis, and within a few steps was upon him. As Travis screamed, Martin's knife swung out in a deadly arc that cut through Travis' throat, severing his head almost completely. It flopped back and hung down, dangling on his back like a used-up rag doll. His scream turned to gurgling spurts as his blood, black like used motor oil in the moonlight, shot up creating a macabre Greek fountain, his headless corpse wobbling then crumpling to the ground in a heap.

Adrenaline surged through Martin, an overwhelming sensation for a Fallen in its first vessel. The world was instantly so much more intense than he ever thought possible. He could feel the cool breeze on his skin as it came off the water, and he reveled in the sticky viscosity of Travis' blood on his hands, its sweet metallic copper smell filling his nostrils.

Lifting his blood smeared blade to his mouth, he tasted it with the tip of his tongue. Savoring it, as he ran his tongue along its length.

"Glorious," he said, taking a deep breath.

Turning, he looked at Bains, a joyous insanity in his glowing eyes. The slaughter of the human had unleashed an insatiable passion to kill. A passion that he craved to satisfy once again. His burning eyes searched for his next victim, but where he expected to find the wounded Chance Jordan, he found only sand.

Roaring in anger, he frantically searched the tree line for the human, but saw only a glimmer at the foot of a tree. Walking briskly to it, he found a crumpled letterman's jacket which he quickly discarded. Coiling to launch into pursuit, he was stopped cold by the voice of Sabine Bains.

"Wait!" she bellowed, the fire in her eyes turning blood red. "Bring him to me, alive."

"Alive? Why?" he said clearly annoyed.

She looked at him for a moment, deciding whether or not to punish him for his impudent tone.

"Yes, Baka'El," he said, bowing his head.

"Alive," she emphasized. "Now go."

As Martin bolted into the forest, he sounded another Jurassic roar that shook the night. Starlings burst from their nests and into flight, circling overhead in an undulating organic cloud.

Bains walked casually to the discarded letterman's jacket. Picking it up she held it to her face and inhaled deeply, swooning as she did.

As her intoxication subsided, she noticed a rolled sheet of paper in the jacket's inside pocket and plucked it out. Unrolling it, she gazed at the drawing, a slight approving smirk on her face.

"Hello, Sari'El. Is that you?" she whispered almost lovingly, but when her gaze shifted to the female image, she frowned. "But you, my dear, who might you be?"

A distant roar shattered the night once again. Bains lifted her head and looked in the direction of the sound. Discarding the jacket she rerolled the drawing, and slipped it inside her coat, before casually strolling into the forest.

THIRTY-FOUR

Chance Jordan ran, stumbling through the forest, trying to put as much distance between himself and the nightmare he had just witnessed as he possibly could. As he pushed through the undergrowth, a bestial roar, of a kind he had never heard before, shook the forest around him.

Pausing for a moment, he listened. In the distance he could hear the sound of a powerful, and unstoppable force, bulldozing its way through the thicket. Then the forest shook again.

"Jordan!" came a booming vociferation.

The sound of Martin's menacing voice was unmistakable, and yet very different. A powerful element of evil now permeated it, amplifying its malevolence, and it chilled Chance to his core.

Even though blinded by the heavy stream of blood from the huge gash on his forehead, that streamed down his face and into his eyes, Chance forced his feet to move. His lungs burned with every rasping breath, and his legs, on the verge of collapse, felt like sacks of wet sand.

"I will kill you, Jordan!" taunted Martin in the distance.

Chance knew he was fading, and that Martin was gaining on him. As he fled, he stumbled forward like a drunk, falling from tree to tree, until unexpectedly, he broke out of the brambles and into a clearing. Surprised by the sudden space, he reached for the support of a tree that wasn't there and fell, face down, onto the soft grass.

"Jordan! I know you can hear me. I can smell your fear."

Chance WAS afraid, but he had reached the limit of his endurance. Taking a deep breath, a fatalistic calm washed over him.

The smell of the fresh spring grass filled his nose, as the cool evening dew revived him slightly. Touching his forehead, he felt the gaping wound there, and the moment took on a surreal quality as he watched his blood dripping in long elastic strands onto the grass beneath him.

He was pretty sure he was concussed. His head was throbbing, and he had to fight back the impulse to vomit. Looking down at his arm he became fascinated by the sight of his ulna protruding from the flesh of his right forearm, the bone jagged and surprisingly white in the moonlight.

Rolling over onto his back, he looked up at the clear night sky. Searching his mind for options, he found none, and came to the inescapable conclusion that he was done.

The sound of crashing tree limbs, and underbrush, grew closer as the thing that was once Martin Wellington bore down on him. Chance readied himself, for what he did not know, when a blinding flash lit up the small clearing in several rapid-fire arcs.

Rolling back over, Chance searched for the source of the light and was awed by what he saw. Floating about a foot off the ground, some fifty feet away, was what appeared to be a shimmering pool of black water. Tilted up vertically, like a standing mirror its surface crackled with blue electric arcs that extended to its edges.

The vertical pool quivered and rippled. Black as oil, it was filled with tiny points of light that sparkled as they bent and twisted into a vortex, spiraling inward until they vanished at the pool's center

The dark pool began to pulse, the frequency distorting its surface into changing geometric shapes. The electric arcs intensified and then from the midst of this maelstrom, a human form emerged. Electricity crawling over its body, it stepped from the shimmering surface.

The mysterious being stood, looking at Chance. Dressed in black jeans and wearing a black hoodie pulled up over its head, its only discernable features were its eyes, pulsing and glowing with the same blue electric arcs that had crawled over its emerging form.

"Jordan!" came Martin's voice.

The thundering vocalization snapped Chance out of his fatalistic fog and back into the moment. He looked clearly now at the dark figure, but the entity only stared back at him with its eerie, blue, electric eyes. Then surprisingly it raised its hand and motioned for him to follow. Turning, it stepped back into the sparkling membrane, electric webs crawling over its body, and was enveloped by the black pool, before vanishing.

Chance wanted to follow, but his body just wouldn't move. He had been both comforted and terrified by the appearance of the black hooded figure from his dreams. Comforted by its familiarity, yet terrified by the fact that its presence always seemed to accompany death.

As he lay bleeding and broken in the grass, he began a bizarre calculation. In his mind he weighed the known threat of that which was converging on him through the forest, against that of an electrified pool of vertical water, within which his personal harbinger of death awaited him.

His calculations ended as a tree at the edge of the clearing crashed to the ground, and Martin burst into view, his face still spattered with the blood of Travis Shelby. But Martin pulled up short, seemingly startled by the presence of the pulsing, glistening pool hovering there.

Having made his decision, Chance willed himself to move. Tapping his last cache of strength, he struggled to his feet and ran, half falling toward the enigma of an electrified pool of vertical black water.

Martin, shaking off his surprise, and realizing that Chance was attempting to get to the glowing black hole, charged with a roar. With a final lunge, Chance dove head first into the pool just as Martin launched himself at the boy. But as Chance's body passed through the black membrane, it collapsed in a brilliant flash.

Martin sailed through the empty space where Chance had once been, crashing to the forest floor with a thud, temporarily blinded. Springing to his feet he let out a roar of anger just as Bains stepped out of the trees and into the tiny meadow, her eyes surveying the scene.

"The human escaped through an Ingwaz," explained Martin.

"An Ingwaz? Are you sure?" said Bains, surprised.

"I saw him pass through it with my own eyes."

Bains strolled to the center of the clearing. Arms crossed, she tapped her finger on her chin as she pondered this development.

If this boy, Chance Jordan, were indeed the Light Warrior, Sari'El, on earth in a human vessel, why did he not defend himself? Sari'El could have vaporized both the human vessel, and discharged the energy of the Fallen possessing it, but instead he fled.

It made no sense, Unless Sari'El was not here in a vessel, but was in fact birthed as a human. She had heard of this. In his ever-growing paranoia, He That Is Three had sent, countless members of his inner circle to earth as mortal births as a test of their loyalty, a test he calls, "The Time of Temptation".

If that were true, however, how was it that he could open an Ingwaz? The answer was that he couldn't and that left only one possibility.

"He must have a physical guardian," she said at last.

"A physical guardian?" asked Martin confused.

"They are rare," said Bains as she squatted to pick a sample of grass. Sniffing it she continued, her voice taking on an almost romantic quality. "They are assigned only to the most important Children of Light during the Time of Temptation. Their purpose is to protect, but also to inform the Triad of potential disloyalty."

"Who was this Chance Jordan in the before time that he would be given such a thing?"

"I have reason to believe that he is Sari'El."

"Sari'El? The Triad's High War Bringer?" said Martin, panic clear in his voice. "He must be destroyed!"

"No, not yet," responded Bains in an almost sing-song voice.

"What?" exclaimed Martin, now incredulous. "His destruction would shift the balance of power. We must kill him!"

Bains' face distorted into the hideous visage of a Fallen as she spun to confront Martin. Drilling into him with her eyes, she let out a roar that made Martin's earlier vocalizations seem like the mewling of kittens by comparison.

"Silence!" she bellowed, forcing Martin to avert his eyes. "He is in a Time of Temptation, you fool. He can be turned, and if I can turn him, he will no longer be a War Bringer of He That is Three. He will be mine."

Martin paused, his panic turning into ruthless ambition. He realized that if Bains gained control of Sari'El, a Warrior of Light, and the Triad's War Bringer Prime, she would become a force within the Legion of the Fallen. And he would be at her side.

"Forgive me Baka'El" he said, lowering his head. "How do you wish to proceed?"

Pacified, Bains' face returned to its former beauty. Retrieving a small mirror from her coat, she vainly checked her appearance. Satisfied, she put it away.

"I will use the girl," she said after a pause. "Sari'El seems quite taken with her."

"Girl? What girl?"

"At Havenhurst," she said smiling, as the pieces began to fall into place. "An anomaly that somehow knows Chance Jordan as Sari'El. Their emotions, their...love, it ripples the veil. She is his weakness. He will come willingly for her."

"What of the Guardian?"

"The Guardian's primary function is to protect, observe and then report to the Triad. It cannot interfere with any choice, but to be sure we will use this," she said, indicating the metal case she still held. "The Catalyst will make Sari'El willing, and, if we are lucky, confuse the Guardian long enough for Sari'El to be turned. If it can't be done, I will sample his essence and then destroy him."

Martin nodded. "But how can we introduce the Catalyst without alerting his guardian?" he asked.

Bains thought for a moment, then remembering Chance's letterman's jacket, asked, "Wellington, does it have a private well?"

"Indeed it does," said Martin.

"That will work nicely for our purposes, as well as for a test," said Bains.

THIRTY-FIVE

Eric Easton checked his watch. Wearing a worried expression, he bounded up the stairs of his dormitory building with an obvious urgency. He was worried about Chance. He knew Chance had left directly after practice to go visit Marina, but he should have been back by ten o'clock. It was now quickly approaching eleven, and if Chance missed bed check, it would trigger a whole new list of problems.

Reaching the third floor, Eric ran across the hallway to his room's door. As he bolted through the door, he experienced a momentary wave of relief when he saw what he at first believed to be Chance, sitting in his easy chair, paging through an old issue of Playboy magazine.

"Thank God, you're..." he blurted, but stopped in mid-sentence as he realized that the person sitting in his chair wasn't Chance, but was in fact Conor Jackson.

"Oh, it's you," Eric finished.

"Up yours, too," said Conor without lifting his eyes from his 'reading'.

Eric didn't react as he crossed the room to the window. "What are you doing here anyway?" he asked as he took out his phone and called Chance for the tenth time, but as before, it went directly to voicemail. Tapping the screen, he sent a text.

"Researching colleges," said Conor, holding up the magazine. On its cover was a stunning coed in a letterman's sweater, open to the waist, the words "Girls of the S.E.C." strategically placed to barely cover her ample breasts.

"I'm leaning toward L.S.U," he said with a smile.

"I wouldn't rule out Florida State," said Eric still peering out the window.

Conor turned the page and groaned, "Oh yeah, Florida State has definite potential."

"Dude, where did you get these?" asked Conor as an afterthought.

"My dad has tubs of them in the basement."

"Do you realize what these are?" asked Conor.

"Porn," said Eric matter-of-factly.

"These," said Conor, holding up the magazine, "are history."

"History," snorted Eric, dubious.

"History," insisted Conor.

Eric turned from the window and regarded Conor with a 'This better be good' expression as he folded his arms in mock interest. "Do tell."

Conor cleared his throat and sat up straight, "Around 2016, Playboy, an internationally recognized men's magazine, made the decision, some would say ill-advised, to eliminate nude models from its pages. Overnight the 'Centerfold', the iconic locker liner, and inspiration for heterosexual males and lipstick lesbians around the world, vanished, becoming nothing but a cherished memory."

Conor now stood for effect. "That makes this," he said as he snapped the magazine open, causing the centerfold to unfurl dramatically, "a historical artifact of a lost culture." Conor reverently folded the centerfold back into the magazine. "Thankfully, due to public backlash, Playboy came to its senses, not long after and the centerfold returned, but the incident remains a reminder of how precarious our beloved institutions can be. They should teach a class on this subject," he added.

"YOU should teach a class on this subject," said Eric smiling, but genuinely impressed with his friend's historical knowledge.

"Yes, I should," said Conor.

"I'd take that class."

"You bet your ass you would," said Conor smirking, as he sat down to return to his 'college research.'

Eric turned back to the window, a smile on his face, but his smile quickly faded as he scanned the parking lot and saw that Chance's Harley was still not there.

"Chance still isn't back," said Eric, worried, "and it's almost time for bed check."

"Oh, shit," said Conor, jumping up. "What time is it?"

"He's got three minutes."

"Who's on duty tonight?"

"Arroyo, I think."

"Ooh, the Beast," said Conor with an expression like he had just thrown up in his own mouth.

"We gotta do something," said Eric. "Slow her down. Give him some time."

"Time ain't gonna help him if he doesn't make it back. No, I have a better idea."

Conor held up his copy of Playboy. On the page was a photo of two coeds. Twins, identical in every way.

"Brilliant," said Eric, smiling.

"OK, the Beast will check my room first," said Conor, walking to the door. "Keep your door open, I'll be coming back fast."

Conor ran from Eric's room and flew down the stairs, sliding down the banister to the second floor. Below him he heard the first-floor stairwell door slam, followed by the heavy footfalls and squeaking leather shoes as Arroyo attempted to charge up the stairs, never achieving more than a labored waddle.

Conor sprinted down the second-floor hallway, dodging a handful of stragglers scurrying to their rooms. As he reached his door, he was thankful to see that his roommate, Rheinhard, had left it open in anticipation of Conor's need for a rapid ingress. Running through the door, Conor flipped the door closed behind him then launched himself onto his bed.

Arroyo, hearing the activity on the second floor, trudged up the stairs as fast as her stubby legs would carry her. When she reached the second-floor landing, she heard a door slam and vowed to punish the culprit who had not been in their room on time.

Arroyo loved writing students up for being out of place. After years of taking her personal issues out on them, she felt she had at long last found her purpose in life. She believed it was her duty to make the students suffer as much as she had suffered throughout her own pathetic life. She rationalized her behavior by seeing herself as the victim. It helped her justify her sadistic nature.

As she entered the second-floor hallway, Arroyo paused a moment, attempting to triangulate on the door that had slammed. After a few seconds her eyes fixed on the most likely suspect.

Though the intrusion was expected, both boys nevertheless jumped as Arroyo pounded on their door like a cop with a warrant.

"Bed check," she said in her gruff monotone as her key hit the lock and the door swung open in one smooth motion.

As Arroyo entered the room, Conor, in a last second decision, grabbed a book off the night stand and opened it, pretending to read. Almost instantly he realized that the book was upside down. Flipping it over smoothly, he tried to look nonchalant.

Arroyo's eyes pierced them, first one then the other, roasting them on the spit of her many issues. Clearly suspicious, but unable to determine why, she frowned and checked off her roster, then backed out the door, slamming it unnecessarily hard.

When the door closed Conor jumped up and ran to the bathroom where he turned on the shower. Running back into the room he went to the window and opened it.

"What's going on?" asked Rheinhard in his thick German accent which had gained him the sobriquet of "The Terminator"- though his accent was not the only reason for it.

The German was massive. Six foot five, and three hundred pounds, he carried himself with a stereotypical Prussian sternness, made even more imposing by his military style haircut, chiseled features, white blond hair and sky-blue eyes.

In the eyes of his teammates and his opponents, he was simply a machine. He had earned letters in baseball, and track, but his prowess at football had earned him a full ride scholarship to the University of Southern California. He had received many such offers, but the idea that as a USC Trojan he would be playing his home games in an arena called "The Coliseum", was too much to resist.

The truth of Rheinhard von Steiger, however, was that despite his hard and intimidating exterior, once a person got to know him, it became obvious that he was a big teddy bear. A gentile giant who loved to play with his friends and make bad jokes.

"We gotta save Chance's ass," said Conor.

"What happened?"

"Chance isn't back on campus yet."

"Scheise."

"Exactly, now gimme a hand," said Conor sitting on the window sill.

Rheinhard jumped up and came to the window. Taking Conor's hand, the big German lowered his friend down the side of the building until his feet were only eight feet from the ground, then let him go.

Conor landed lightly, then waved to Rheinhard. "I'll be back."

"That's my line," said Rheinhard, smiling.

Conor ran to the end of the building where he quickly climbed up the fire escape to the second floor. Looking through the fire escape door's window, he could see Arroyo moving from dorm room to dorm room down the hallway.

Climbing over the railing and onto the building's decorative ledge, he inched his way around the corner of the building to the stairwell's window. Using his school I.D., he slipped the latch and pushed it open.

Jumping down onto the landing inside, he moved smoothly up the stairs to the third floor where he stopped and peeked around the corner. When he saw Arroyo was just two doors away, he quickly ducked back.

He heard Arroyo pound on a door. "Bed check!" she bellowed as she stepped into the room.

In that moment Conor darted across the hall and through the door of Eric and Chance's room. Closing the door, he ran into the bathroom and stripped down to his underwear.

"She's two rooms away," he said, turning on the faucet and dabbing shaving cream in his face, just as Arroyo pounded on the door.

"Bed check!" came Arroyo's grating voice.

Eric sat at his desk and turned to look at Arroyo, as Conor leaned out of the bathroom.

"Good evening, Ms. Arroyo," said Eric, his voice more cheerful than the circumstances would dictate. "It is always such a joy to see you."

Arroyo harrumphed, then left, making sure to slam the door as she did. Standing in the hallway, she heard laughter erupt from inside the room. Scowling at the door, she turned and waddled away.

THIRTY-SIX

Chance's mind swam in a series of bizarre disconnected images: Martin Wellington holding a knife, a woman with eyes of fire, the black hooded figure from his dreams, and Marina waving from her window. But these images existed only in his periphery. When he tried to look directly at any one of them, they would dissolve into mist.

A pool of water, calm and smooth, now formed before him and he peered into it. There he saw his reflection, battered and bleeding, floating at its center. As blood dripped from the wide gaping wound on his forehead, it fell into the pool, disrupting his reflection. But each time his reflection dissolved, it would slowly return as before.

As he watched this cycle repeat, over and over, a pinpoint of light began to pierce his reflection at its very center. The point of light grew in intensity until it formed a fissure of luminosity that cut across his face.

Brighter and brighter it grew, until it stung his eyes. Again, his reflection shattered, the stinging in his eyes becoming too much to bear. Squeezing his eyes shut, he waited. When he opened them again, the pool of water was gone, and he found himself lying face down in the sand, the nascent sunrise peeking over the horizon.

A curious raven stood a few feet away, watching as it tried to decide if the boy was edible. When Chance lifted his head from the sand and coughed, the bird flew off, crying a startled complaint.

Blurry-eyed and disoriented, he rose from the ground, sand still clinging to his face. He was confused. He remembered coming to the lake, but everything after seeing the new artwork in the upstairs bedroom of the lake house was mired in a fog, if not missing completely. Groggy, he looked at his watch.

"Oh, shit," he blurted as he saw the time and realized that if he left immediately, he would barely be able to make it back to campus before his morning weight room session.

On unsteady legs he made his way to his motorcycle. Finding it parked where he had left it, he walked up to it, catching a glimpse of his face in one of the mirrors. His reflection conjured in his mind an image of his face, bloody from a gaping wound, staring back at him from a pool of water.

Leaning in close, he inspected his face in the mirror. No blood, no wound, not a scratch to be seen. As he reached out to adjust his mirror, he looked at his arm. It looked normal, and for some unknown reason he found that surprising. Standing up straight he pulled his arm in close to his chest and cradled it as if it were broken, absentmindedly running his hand over its unblemished skin.

Shaking off his disquiet, he reached to turn on his bike's electronics, only then realizing that he didn't know where his keys were. Patting his pockets, he didn't feel them, so he stuffed his hands into every pocket he had in a frantic search, a sense of dread poking at him mercilessly as his search came up empty.

And then he remembered. His keys were in the pocket of Conor's letterman's jacket, but for the life of him he couldn't remember where, or even when, he had taken it off.

Looking around quickly, he didn't see the jacket anywhere nearby, so he began to slowly walk around the house to the lake side, searching as he went. As he walked into the clearing behind the house, a flash of red along the tree line caught his attention.

Shading his eyes from the sun, he looked more closely. There, laying crumpled by a tree, was Conor's jacket, its red leather sleeves ablaze in the early morning light. Jogging over he picked it up, quickly searching its pockets. His sense of relief was overwhelming as his fingers touched his keys and phone.

Shaking the jacket out he checked it for damage. Other than being covered with sand, it looked fine, but as he held it up, he noticed what looked like blood on the inside lining.

Instantly, images of dark, faceless figures, laughing as they pummeled him, flashed through his mind. His right forearm began to ache again, and he looked down at it as he shook it, trying to dislodge the phantom pain. Taking a deep breath, he tried to clear his head of the disturbing images, and his body of those uncomfortable sensations. Swinging the jacket around him, he slipped it on in one fluid motion as he started jogging back to his bike.

He had only taken a few steps when he was halted by the sound of a woman singing. At first, he wasn't sure if he was truly hearing it, so faint was the voice that at times it became lost in the sound of the wind in the trees.

Chance turned his head, trying to locate the voice's source. Initially he thought that it might be a local resident taking an early morning walk, but dismissed this when he realized that the beautiful voice was coming from inside the old lake house. Intrigued, he forgot entirely that any delay could put him squarely in the cross hairs of coach McCune, and went in search of the source of the singing.

As he drew closer, the now haunting voice pulled at him. It fueled a multitude of questions, not the least of which was whether or not the source of the enchanting voice was the mysterious artist whose work covered the wall of the upstairs room.

Entering the house he moved quietly, but froze in place when the singing abruptly stopped. He waited for a moment, then proceeded, moving through the small room to the stairwell.

Nearby, he noticed one of the heavy oak legs from the old broken table laying on the floor. He stopped and looked at it, and a faint vision of a shadowy figure, bringing it down on him like an axe flittered in, then out, of his consciousness. This mental fragment was quickly displaced, however, as the beautiful voice started singing again.

Silently he climbed the stairs, his heart pounding a hole in his chest. Reaching the top he peeked around the railing, but only saw the same empty hallway he had seen before, this time illuminated by the rising sun.

Listening, he was certain the singing was coming from the room at the end of the hall. With great caution and stealth, Chance crept toward the room, determined to catch the singing artist in the act. More so, he was determined to not let whoever it was, pull another vanishing act, should the artist, and the glowing-eyed specter from Saturday night turn out to be one in the same.

Stepping up to the door Chance paused and took a breath. The door was only half open, so turning himself sideways he slipped into the room and, as he came around the door, his jaw dropped.

"Marina?" he sputtered, shocked.

Marina, caught in mid artistic stroke, spun around completely surprised and screamed, her box of pastels and colored pencils falling to the floor. Terrified she backed into the corner, her hands pressed tightly to her face.

Coming to his senses, Chance became horrified by the fear he had induced in her. Reaching out, he took her hands.

"Hey...Marina, it's OK," he said in a consoling tone. "It's me, Chance."

But Marina's panic did not abate, and Chance was now afraid that this could possibly push her to some kind of breaking point. Thinking quickly, he decided to take a calculated risk.

"Marina, it's Sari'El."

At the sound of the name Marina calmed, her terror-induced shaking subsiding. Unsure, she peered up from behind her still-trembling hands as if to confirm it was really him. When she saw his face, she went to him, wrapping her arms tightly around his neck. Chance held her closely, as her body quaked against him.

"Shh-shh-shh," he whispered, calming her.

Stroking her hair, he kissed her forehead, "You're safe. Nothing's going to happen to you."

Marina looked up at him, her eyes brimming with tears. "You won't tell on me?" she asked, her voice shaking.

"No, of course not," he reassured her.

As he held her, he looked at the bedroom wall where Marina had been working. The unfinished mural he had seen the night before was now mostly complete. A life-sized masterpiece which, even in this strange situation, he couldn't help but be impressed by.

Chance leaned back from their embrace and looked at her. Placing his finger under her chin he lifted her face and pushed a few strands of loose hair away, tucking them behind her ears. His heart fluttered a bit as he looked at her.

"Are you okay?" he asked, smiling.

Marina nodded meekly.

Chance took a deep breath, "Marina, what are you doing here?"

She looked at him with a hint of trepidation, then looked down, fidgeting.

"I come here to draw," she said softly.

Chance looked up at the mural on the wall.

"You must come here a lot," he said with an amused expression.

"Marina looked at him and smiled. "Yeah, I guess I do."

"Do Dr. Shelby and Nurse Denali know you're here?"

"No," she said, looking down and shaking her head slightly.

"How did you get here without them knowing?"

At this question, Marina's trepidation returned. Looking at her hands, she nervously picked at her fingernails. Chance could see that the question had made her uncomfortable, so he dropped it.

"Never mind," he said, pulling her close again. "It doesn't matter."

At this he felt her relax. For a few seconds they just held each other, saying nothing.

"What are YOU doing here?" she finally asked, breaking the silence.

"I..." began Chance, but then he paused as if his thought had escaped him.

When he didn't finish his sentence, Marina pulled back and looked up at him, curious.

"Well?" she podded.

"I don't really know for sure why," he finally said as he looked down into her eyes. "I just wanted to I guess."

"Well, I'm glad you came," she said, nuzzling into his chest.

Chance held her, content to rock her in his arms, his face resting against her hair. Marina pulled back to look at him, and he gazed back while reaching up and lovingly stroking her cheek.

He longed to kiss her, and as if sensing his longing, Marina rose up onto her toes to reach his lips with her own. But just as their lips touched ever so slightly, just as their building passion threatened to erase all inhibition, Chance's phone rang with a ring tone of the live concert version of Rod Stewart's, *If you think I'm sexy*.

Marina burst out laughing.

Chance knew immediately that the caller was Eric Easton. Not because Chance had selected that song as a designated ringtone for Eric, but precisely because he hadn't.

Ever since Chance and Eric had been friends, Eric had amused himself by surreptitiously taking Chance's phone and changing the designated ringtone that would play whenever he called. Eric would turn off the vibration function, set the volume to maximum, and then wait until he knew Chance was in the library, or in class, on a date, or any other serious moment, and then call.

In the past Eric had intruded upon one of Chance's English finals with Sir Mixalot's, *Baby got back*. But without a doubt, Eric's most legendary punk was when he disrupted a speech by former U.S. President Bill Clinton with 2 Live Crew's, *Me so horny*.

Chance, his jaw clenched, dug his phone out of his pocket.

"Hello, Eric," he said, clearly annoyed.

"Dude, where are you?" said Eric urgently. "Morning conditioning starts in an hour."

Chance looked at his watch. "Shit. OK, listen. Bring my workout stuff to the weight room. I'll meet you there."

"Will do," said Eric. "But, bro, where were you last night?"

Chance ended the call without responding.

"I'm sorry," he said, turning back to Marina. "I have to go."

Upon hearing this, Marina's mood went from contented joy, to restrained sadness. Squatting down, she began to collect her scattered pencils. Chance watched her for a moment, then joined her on the floor.

Marina didn't look at him as they silently went about their work. She couldn't. She knew that if she did, she would start to cry, and she didn't want to do that. So, she kept her head down.

As Chance helped collect the scattered art supplies, he glanced at Marina. Her hair hung down around her face, obscuring it, reminding him of the first day he had seen her, and it bothered him. She had made so much progress in the last few days. The idea of her taking a step back was something he found horrifying to think about.

Soon all of Marina's things were back in their box, and he took her hand and helped her to her feet. He stood there looking at her, but she still would not dare to meet his gaze, and an idea came to him.

"You know," he began, "just because I have to go, doesn't mean we can't be together a little longer."

Marina looked up at him with questions, but more importantly hope, in her eyes. Chance smiled back reassuringly and took her hand.

"Come on," he said, pulling her with him.

Walking out of the room, Chance led Marina down the hall and together they descended the stairs. Reaching the bottom, Chance once again looked at the solitary table leg laying on the floor and scowled slightly. He couldn't explain why it bothered him so.

Putting it out of his mind he led Marina through the living room to the open door. But as Marina approached the threshold, she wrenched her hand from his and stopped, frozen with fear.

Surprised, Chance turned to her and was shocked by the fear he saw in her face.

"I can't go out there," she said softly, but urgently.

"Why? What's out there?

"They're out there," she said, peering out the door.

Chance looked around confused.

"Marina, no one's out here but me," he said in a reassuring voice. "Besides, do you think I would allow anything to happen to you?"

The look on Marina's face was one of having been slapped by reason. Collecting herself, she took a deep breath, then boldly stepped through the doorway, keeping her eyes fixed on Chance. As she cleared the doorway, Marina flew into Chance's arms.

"No," she said holding him tightly. "Of course, nothing can happen to me when I'm with you."

Clinging to each other, Chance guided Marina around the house to the driveway where his bike was parked. Unlocking the yoke, he flipped on the ignition and started the engine.

Marina stood back and watched, fascinated, as Chance prepared his machine. She looked at the Spartan crest emblazoned on the back of his jacket and her head filled with romanticized images of heroic knights and their ladies. As Chance stood next to his bike, slipping on his gloves, Marina imagined that he was her warrior.

His preparations complete, Chance turned back to Marina and was greeted with a vision he found quite captivating. Marina was standing with her back to the sun as it rose over the lake, its early morning rays blazing through her hair, creating a swirling copper halo around her angelic face.

Chance hadn't noticed until that very moment that Marina was wearing the same white sundress that she had worn during his first visit on Monday. Now, as she stood looking at him, the light of the morning sun shining through her dress, made it translucent, and offered a vision of her form not dissimilar to that of the portrait she had rendered inside the house.

As a last thought his eyes trailed down her body, and he smiled as he noticed that she was barefoot. He was captivated by the smallness of her feet and the perfect curve of her toes as they wiggled in the sand. He wondered if this observation meant he had a foot fetish. 'Conor will be so proud,' he mused to himself.

The engine of Chance's motorcycle suddenly idled down to deep melodic lope, indicating that the machine was warm and ready to ride. Chance unlocked his helmet from the frame and hooked it on one of his mirrors. Swinging his leg over the bike, he settled in and stood it up center, then with a flick of his foot he retracted the kickstand. Extending his hand to Marina, he grinned.

"Come on. Let's get you home."

When Marina finally realized what Chance intended, her sweet lovesick expression faded, and she took a step back.

"No," she stammered. "I must stay here."

"Marina, there is no way I can just leave you here," he said matter-of-factly. "I got to go right by the hospital. I can drop you off."

"No," she repeated emphatically as she backed up another step.

"OK, OK," he said, raising his hands in surrender. "I guess I'll just have to stay here with you."

Shutting his engine off he put his kickstand back down and dismounted, hanging his helmet on his mirror. Tugging off his gloves one finger at time, he walked toward Marina, who stood clutching her pencil box.

Standing in front of her, he finished taking off his gloves. Stuffing them into his jacket pocket. Taking a deep breath, he looked out at the lake.

"Of course," he continued, "I will miss my classes, so they will most likely kick me out of school."

Chance paused for dramatic effect. Marina was listening intently, and he could see that she was considering this information.

"If I do get expelled," he continued, "I'll have to go live with my dad. That's kinda far away, but I might be able to come see you every few months or so."

"No!" Marina exclaimed, her voice filled with panic. "I don't want you to move away."

"Marina, there are only two choices. We both stay here, or you let me take you back to the hospital, Cuz there is no way I'm going to just leave you here."

Marina thought for a moment, once again looking down at her hands.

"OK," she said at last, "I'll go with you."

Chance smiled and took off his jacket as he stepped closer to her. He felt a bit guilty about having so blatantly manipulated Marina, but he truly would not have been able to drive away, and leave her there alone.

"Here, put this on," he said, holding it open for her. "It might be a little chilly on the road."

Slipping on the jacket, Marina couldn't help swooning as she pulled it tight around her as if in an embrace. Her reaction was not lost on Chance, an odd sense of jealousy momentarily gripping him when it occurred to him that Marina was cuddling Conor's jacket and not his own.

Chance remounted and started his bike, then motioned for Marina to join him. Marina took a step toward him, but then stopped.

"Just a sec," she said, placing her pencil box on the ground. "I need to get something."

Marina bolted around the side other side of the house and ran to a small patch of wildflowers. Stooping down she selected one. Picking the flower, she smelled it and smiled.

As she did, a fly landed on her nose and she swatted it away, but it was quickly replaced by another. Swatting again, she stood up and became aware of an incessant buzzing of hundreds of flies. Unable to swat them all she retreated, running back to Chance.

For a moment the roar of Chance's Harley-Davidson drowned out the sound of the swarm. But as Chance and Marina sped away, the heavy droning of thousands of wings once again dominated the still morning air.

As the sun rose in the sky, its light streaked over the glassy water of the lake and fell upon the swarm as they crawled over a patch of rust-stained wet sand. It was the beginning of a good day for the flies.

THIRTY-SEVEN

Marina stood beside Chance's idling motorcycle as she took off his letter-man's jacket and held it out to him. It had indeed been a chilly ride from the lake, but she had not noticed it much. Cuddled up close to Chance, her arms wrapped around him, she had felt almost toasty.

Chance, still seated on his bike, took the jacket and laid it over his gas tank. As he did, he reached for Marina's hand and pulled her closer.

They looked at each other wordlessly, their hearts beating like drums. At last their lips touched, softly, tenderly at first, but quickly the passions they had repressed all morning burst into flame. Their lips crushed together hungrily, and Marina's body, so soft and inviting, pressed against him. Far too soon for either of them, they broke their embrace.

"I don't want to go," said Chance, his breath rasping.

"I don't want you to go," said Marina, sadly, "but you have to, or you might have to move away."

Chance nodded as he took a deep breath. He knew she was right, and that his emotions and desires, were pushing him dangerously close to making fool-ish choices.

"Are you sure you're going to be okay here?" he asked, looking around at the surrounding forest.

Marina had directed Chance to drop her off about a quarter mile from the hospital. Following her instructions, Chance had parked on a forest service road directly off the highway. While the location seemed safe enough, the idea of leaving her there alone did not sit well with him.

"I'll be fine," she assured him. "I know where I am now. Please, you have to go."

"Chance smiled weakly as he slipped on his jacket. He noticed that it smelled of her, and he breathed her scent in deeply as he zipped it closed.

Dropping his bike into gear he looked at her. "I'll try to come see you tonight."

Marina smiled, and stepped back, waving an unhappy farewell as Chance let out his clutch and pulled away.

Chance had only traveled a short distance, when, hoping for a last glimpse of her, he looked into his mirror. When he didn't see her, he stopped his bike and looked back over his shoulder. A cloud of dust hovered over the dirt forest road, and as it dissipated, he realized that Marina was nowhere to be seen.

It didn't seem possible that she could have moved that quickly through the forest, especially barefoot. He scanned through the trees but didn't see even a hint of her.

Letting the clutch out once again he continued to the highway. As he reached it, he saw that the road was devoid of traffic, so pulling out into the lane, he accelerated aggressively toward Wellington Academy.

Within seconds he was passing Havenhurst. Looking over he saw that the lights in Marina's room were on and worried a bit that her absence had been discovered. Hoping that wasn't the case, and realizing there was nothing he could do if it were, Chance leaned on his throttle as his mind filled with memories of his time with her.

Their ride from the lake had been one of the most perfect moments Chance had ever experienced. Marina had clung to him, her softness and warmth so enticing against his back. As she held him, her hands touching his chest, her body seemed to fit to every contour, and he found himself longing to feel her warmth once more to see her sparkling eyes in his mirror as they peeked over his shoulder.

Shaking off his lovesick daze, he turned his attention to the ribbon of asphalt that twisted in front of him. Pulling back on the throttle, his machine began to scream as he bore down on an insane, high-speed sprint for Wellington Academy.

"Mister Jordan! What is your major malfunction?" bellowed McCune, his voice reverberating through the cavernous weight room.

Chance had made it back to campus with literally seconds to spare. He had driven directly to the sports complex and, as he had run down the hall past Coach McCune's office, he had dared a glance in through the coach's open door. McCune had greeted him with an icy stare from over his coffee mug as he raised his arm to look disapprovingly at his watch.

Thankfully, Eric had brought Chance's gym bag, and Chance quickly changed into his workout clothes. He had been tying his shoe when the coach had made his entrance.

"No problem, sir," said Chance, standing up. "I just misplaced my keys."

McCune looked him over for a few seconds as he sipped his coffee. "Get to work," he finally barked as he turned and began to patrol his kingdom.

Coach McCune had been in too surly a mood to risk his overhearing any casual conversation about missing bed check and staying out all night. So rather than invite his wrath, Eric and Conor had decided to postpone their interrogation of Chance until after the morning workout. As the boys emerged from the locker room, they headed toward the dining hall for breakfast.

"Thanks for bringing my stuff," said Chance.

"No problem," replied Eric.

"And thanks for thinking of this," added Chance, indicating the fresh Wellington uniform he was wearing.

"Again, no problem," said Eric, a smirk curling his lips. "I've had a few all-nighters. I know how hard it can be to take the walk of shame and still smell fresh."

"Ah geez, here it comes," muttered Chance.

Eric chuckled and clapped his hands together. He had been waiting for several hours for this moment.

"So... what happened last night?" he said.

Chance didn't respond immediately. Instead, he walked silently, hands in pockets, as Eric and Conor flanked him, intent on his answer.

"What happened," he finally said, "was I missed bed check and I'm probably going to get written up."

"Nope," said Conor simply.

"What do you mean, 'nope,'" asked Chance.

"What I mean," explained Conor, "is that you have no idea how close you came to getting busted, but didn't."

Chance looked at Conor, then Eric, confused and searching for an explanation.

"No shit," said Eric earnestly. "Conor pulled off a total Mission Impossible and saved your ass."

Chance looked at Eric dumbfounded, then turned to Conor for confirmation.

Conor nodded, "It was a beautiful thing. We had the Beast running around in circles, and she never had a clue."

"So... I'm good?" asked Chance, disbelievingly.

"No, I'M good, you're lucky," said Conor as Eric nodded agreement.

A wave of relief washed over Chance as he threw his arm over Conor's shoulders.

"I owe you big time, bro," said Chance sincerely.

"You're a trust fund baby," replied Conor. "You can afford it."

Chance laughed, heaving his gym bag over his shoulder. As he did, Conor looked at the bag and noticed the red leather sleeve of a letterman's jacket inside the open zipper.

"Hey, is that my jacket?" asked Conor, reaching into the bag and pulling it out. As he did, sand flaked off and into his face.

"Dude, this thing is full of sand," he said, shaking the jacket sharply. "What did you do, roll around on the beach in it?"

"He may very well have," said Eric, fingering the sandy material.

Conor shook it again. This time giving it a hard vertical snap.

"Hey, take it easy. My phone's in the pocket," said Chance.

Conor reached into one of the jacket's pockets, and when he did, consternation registered on his face. Withdrawing his hand from the pocket, he produced a beautiful, if slightly mangled flower. Chance knew immediately who had put it there.

Looking slowly over at Chance, Conor held up the flower, pinched between his thumb and forefinger, as if he had just found a rancid jock strap.

"You got some splainin' to do, Lucy," said Conor, recalling the classic catch phrase from his 'History of American Television' class.

Chance was thrown by the reference.

"What? Who's Lucy?" he sputtered.

"Oh-My-God," said Eric, as he reached out and took the flower from Conor. "You weren't alone last night."

It was an accusation, not a question. Eric stepped forward, his hands clasping the lapels of his blazer as he slipped effortlessly into his Sherlock Holmes persona. "Based on the sand particulates left on your jacket--"

"MY jacket," Conor corrected.

"My apologies. Mr. Jackson's jacket," said Eric bowing slightly in Conor's direction. Conor returned the gesture.

"You must have been on or near a beach. And this..." he said, holding up the flower and sniffing it, "is a species of local wildflower that I have personally observed growing exclusively near the beach off Lakefront Road. More commonly referred to as Haunted Beach."

Chance grabbed at the flower but Eric pulled it away.

"So..." continued Eric, relishing the role of detective, "what are the facts? One: you were out all night and not answering your phone or responding to text messages. This is not typical behavior for you, so you must have had something... better to do. Two: based on the sand trace detected, and the species of flower found on your person, you were obviously at Lakeside Beach. Three: Judging by the condition of Mr. Jackson's jacket, you were clearly in full body contact with said beach. Most likely in... shall we say... a horizontal position."

Eric took a few steps away, tapping his chin with his finger as he walked. "Now, I have known you for several years. So, I know that it is highly unlikely that you would lie horizontal on the sand alone. So, the only question that remains is, with whom were you horizontal?"

Spinning on his heel, he looked at Chance as he considered the evidence. Chance stood silently, his hands on his hips, rolling his eyes, hoping that his friend was finished. He wasn't.

"It most likely was not anyone from this institution of learning, or we, your closest friends, would at the very least, be aware of a potential for intimate relations. So, who do we know outside of these hallowed halls that might be willing to end up...horizontal with one Chance Jordan?"

"It's no big deal," interrupted Chance. "After I got done at the hospital, I decided to go to the lake to clear my head, and... well... I'm not really sure what happened after that. I guess I fell asleep, because I woke up on the beach this morning. Alone."

"That's it?" said Conor, incredulous. "You fell asleep? We went through all that crap to save your ass because you were sleepy?"

Eric leaned over so he could look Chance in the eyes, "Sleepy? Is that what the cool kids are calling it now?"

Chance rolled his eyes. Turning, he walked briskly down the sidewalk.

Eric and Conor watched him go. Looking at one another, they smiled, then chased after him.

"Does little miss sleepy have a name?" asked Eric as they caught up with him.

Chance was not upset by their grilling. In fact, he was amused by the efforts of his friends to pry information out of him. But, as he began to respond, he stopped when he saw several sheriff's patrol cars parked in front of the school's main entrance. His face took on a scowl of concern that forced Eric and Conor to pause their inquisition and look to see what had caused it.

"What the hell is going on here?" said Chance.

"Maybe little miss sleepy filed charges," quipped Eric. "How many times do I have to tell you? 'No' means 'no.'"

Conor laughed. "Hell, sometimes even 'yes' means 'no'. It's gettin' to where you need a notarized contract just to get to third base anymore."

Eric turned and looked at Conor as if his friend had just grown a toe from his forehead. "Third base? Did you seriously just say 'Third base'? What are you, twelve?"

Laughing, the boys continued on their way to breakfast. Chance held out his hand and Eric returned the wilting wild flower.

"Probably should put that in some water," he said smirking.

"Conor," said Chance, "Let me take your jacket to be dry cleaned. I'm really sorry I messed it up."

"No big deal," said Conor, tossing it to him. "Thanks."

Chance stuffed the jacket back into his bag as the trio entered the main building and looked around the Grand Foyer. The student body was abuzz from all of the police activity, and Chance got the definite feeling that more than a few of the collected groups of students had turned to look at him, but he dismissed it as paranoia.

"What's with all the cops?" Chance heard Eric ask.

Turning, he saw that the question had been directed at Bella and Kimiko, who had joined them.

"Word is they are looking for you," said Bella, looking at Chance. "They are in your dorm room right now."

"Me? Why?"

"I'm not sure," she said, "but I think it has something to do with Martin and Travis missing bed check. I hear they are still missing."

"So, what if it they are missing? What does that have to do with me?" said Chance.

The girls shrugged in unison.

"They're probably off getting stoned," said Conor.

"Mr. Jordan," came an unexpected woman's voice.

Every head turned to see Head Mistress Kristen Rasmussen accompanied by two uniformed deputies. Chance recognized one of them as Lieutenant Redinger from the night of the beach party.

"Young man," said Rasmussen, looking at Chance, "you need to come with us."

Redinger stepped forward and took Chance by the arm, at the same time relieving him of his gym bag.

"Please come with me, son," said Redinger gently.

"I don't understand," protested Chance without resisting. "What is this all about?"

"We have some questions," explained Redinger as he smoothly handed the gym bag to another deputy. "We are going to transport you to the station so we can talk."

With a firm grip Redinger directed Chance out of the school's front doors and to the patrol cars beyond, a crowd of curious students following behind. Reaching his car, Redinger opened the rear passenger door and held it open as Chance got in. After closing the door, he put Chance's bag in the trunk, then got in and started the engine.

Chance looked out the window at the quickly gathering crowd, and found Eric and Conor, both with concerned expressions. As Redinger put the car in gear and began to pull away, Chance looked at Eric and held up his hand to his ear, mimicking a phone while mouthing the words, 'call my dad'.

Eric nodded his understanding and began tapping the screen of his phone as he spun and walked away from the assembled crowd. Chance took a deep breath as he saw Eric talking into his phone. After a moment Eric looked up at him and held up his thumb.

Chance let the breath out and sat back. Relaxing a bit, he consoled himself with the knowledge that the cavalry would soon be on its way.

THIRTY-EIGHT

Marina had arrived back in her room, safe and undetected. Turning on her room light, she paused for a moment as she saw herself in the reflection of her mirror. She felt...different, and as she looked at herself, she wondered if the difference might be evident there, but she puzzled when she saw that her reflection was unchanged. Deciding to take a shower, she undressed.

As her sundress dropped in a crumpled pile at her feet, she looked at herself again. Twisting her lips in thought, she reached behind her back and unhooked her bra, then slipped off her underwear.

Standing up again she took in her naked form. At first her eyes looked only into her own, but soon they traveled down her body.

Until that moment Marina had only acknowledged the shape of her body in her drawings because she drew what she saw. Now, as she looked into the mirror, she saw something else entirely.

Pulling her hair down over her shoulders, she let it fall loose, cascading down her chest. Running her fingers through her wavy mane, she pushed it aside and gently cupped her breasts, fascinated by their weight and roundness.

Letting them fall, she watched them sway, and come to rest, deciding this pleased her. Continuing her moment of discovery, she traced her fingers along the contours of her body. As they reached the curves of her hips, her path turned inward and she began to lightly stroke her tummy in slow lazy circles.

Marina tried to put a label on the feelings that her time with Chance seemed to have awakened in her, but before she could give it much thought, she heard a door slam in the corridor outside her room. Interrupting her exploration, she quickly put on her robe as an orderly came down the hall unlocking the doors of those patients with open movement privileges. Gathering up her toiletries, Marina slipped into her shower shoes, and grabbed her towel as she left her room.

Walking into the shower room, she found it to be empty. This was not unusual since other than herself, only two other women on her ward had open movement privileges: Ellena Hursh, a paranoid schizophrenic, convinced that all men were manipulative perverts that only wanted her for her body and Marina's close friend Nikki van Pelt, who tended to sleep late.

This suited Marina just fine. She had come to enjoy turning on all four showers at the same time so as to fill the small shower room with billowing clouds of steam. Hanging up her robe, she set about doing just that.

Once all of the showers were running, Marina turned off the lights making the room semi-dark, and busied herself laying out her soap, shampoo and conditioner. When all was ready, she stepped under the spray of hot water.

As it began to wash over her face, Marina looked down at her feet just in time to see the last few grains of sand, that had been trapped between her toes, wash away. She made a mental note to sweep her room when she got back, just in case some sand might have fallen there. "Beach sand in her room would be difficult to explain," she mused.

As Marina turned her face into the water, her mind wandered back over the events of that morning. Chance discovering her at the house had been an unexpected joy, and the ride back to the hospital an indescribable thrill, that had stirred her deep into her core.

She pictured him in her mind, his eyes so green they looked like forests she could get lost in. His chest, which she had explored with her hands as she clung to him, so hard and chiseled, yet inviting to the touch. And when he had touched her, his strength had such tenderness that it had sent waves of pleasure through her body.

Pouring some soap into her palm, she closed her eyes and began to lather her body, as she reminisced on their motorcycle ride. She sighed softly as she pictured herself, holding him between her legs as the vibrations from his machine translated up into her.

While it was her hands that slid over her body, in her mind it was Chance's hands that caressed her. Folding her arms around herself, Marina imagined Chance's arms, strong like twisted bands of steel, encircling her.

Her fantasies began to make her head spin, and then without realizing it, her hand traveled down her body. Moments later she was rocked by an unexpected wave of overwhelming pleasure. Her knees began to buckle and she reached up to grip the shower head, letting out a low throaty groan.

Breathing heavily, she slowly regained her composure, not sure what had just happened to her. Straightening up she placed her hands on the tiled wall, and let the hot water wash over her face.

As her head cleared, she was shocked into alertness by the shape of a person standing in the heavy folds of steam. At first she was afraid, but her fear quickly subsided when she realized that the unknown intruder was her friend Nikki, standing naked under one of the other showers.

"Well, you seem to be having a good morning," said Nikki smiling. "Am I interrupting something?"

Marina was immediately embarrassed. Wondering to herself how long Nikki had been there, she suddenly felt compelled to cover her nakedness, even though she had taken showers with Nikki many times before.

"No," said Marina timidly.

With a smirk on her lips, Nikki sauntered across the shower room floor, her eyes fixed on Marina. But Marina's eyes wandered, traveling over Nikki's body, curious.

Marina was fascinated by how different Nikki's body was from her own. She puzzled as to why she had never noticed it before, but it was becoming clear to her that she was beginning to notice many things she hadn't noticed before.

Nikki was small, her features a beautiful mixture of delicate and hard. Her breasts while not large, jutted out from her chest like halves of grapefruits on a cutting board. Her hips, not as round as Marina's, were narrow, almost boyish. Nevertheless, her femininity was striking and undeniably powerful. As Marina looked at her, she found herself awed by Nikki's Gothic beauty in a way she had never been.

Nikki smiled, under Marina's gaze. As Nikki drew closer, Marina reflexively took a timid step back until she was stopped by the cool tile wall. Marina was not afraid of her friend, but as Nikki advanced, she had an intensity that Marina had never seen before.

Marina watched, transfixed as Nikki stepped through the flowing shower stream, parting it like a veil of glass beads. She moved in, closer and closer, stopping only as their bodies ever so lightly touched.

Nikki stood there, gazing into Marina's eyes. Reaching out she touched Marina's face, then with the lightest touch began to trace her fingertips over her body. Leaning up, Nikki kissed her. When, Marina took a shuddering breath, Nikki embraced her.

"I envy you," said Nikki, holding Marina tightly. "You have so many things to look forward to, so many new experiences, and some of them are so gonna rock your world."

"Like what?" asked Marina, gently returning her friend's embrace.

"So many things," sighed Nikki, "your first love, your first lover. And you're gonna do it right. You're going to be in love with someone who loves you. Not like what happened to me."

Marina's eyes teared. Nikki had shared with her stories of the abuse she had suffered growing up, and she hugged Nikki even tighter. She had never seen Nikki so emotional, so vulnerable, and she found it a little frightening.

"Are you okay?" asked Marina.

"I'm fine," said Nikki. "It's just, that I know you're gonna be out of here soon. You're gonna get a chance to live your life, and I want you to live it like you stole it."

Marina looked at Nikki confused, not understanding the reference. Nikki tried to explain.

"Live, Marina. Live big. Take chances and be crazy every once in a while. Moderation is for monks."

"Chances?" asked Marina.

"Like...don't ever stop singing. You have an amazing voice. Do something with it. Promise me."

"I promise," said Marina, still a bit confused by their conversation. "I've always loved singing with you."

"And one more thing," said Nikki nearly swooning. "At least once, you gotta ride on the back of a Harley, with your legs wrapped around some hot guy. If that don't get it done for you, it'll get you close."

Upon hearing this Marina tensed and Nikki felt it. Leaning back, Nikki looked deeply into Marina's very guilty eyes, and they told her the whole truth. Now it was Nikki's turn to be confused. How and when could Marina have possibly experienced the sensual joys of the backseat of a Harley-Davidson? Only one possibility came to mind.

"Hey," said Nikki looking closely at Marina, "doesn't that boy, who's been coming to see you ride a Harley? Did Denali let you...?"

Marina just looked at Nikki with a deer-in-the-headlight expression. She might as well have signed a confession.

"Well, I guess we have some catchin' up to do, don't we?"

Marina nodded weakly but with a subdued smile on her lips. Nikki smiled back then leaned forward and softly kissed Marina's lips.

"We'll talk soon," she said.

Turning, Nikki walked to her robe with an obvious lightness in her step. Marina watched her go, captivated by her tattoos that moved seductively with each footfall.

Throwing her robe around herself, Nikki strolled toward the shower room door. Turning she smiled as she appraised Marina one last time.

"You've changed, girlfriend," said Nikki, with a seductive wink, "and I kinda like it."

Then, trailing eddies of steam, Nikki was gone.

Marina let out a long breath. She wasn't even sure she had been breathing at all during what had just happened.

Stepping back into the shower's stream, Marina let the water wash over her face. She thought about what Nikki had said, that she had changed. Marina decided that yes, she WAS changing. The world around her was coming to life, and Chance was at its center, and she wanted more.

THIRTY-NINE

"Why did you stop?"

"Because she is my friend. She's my only friend."

"That has never stopped you in the past."

"Marina is different."

"How so?"

"Marina is good. She deserves for her first lover to be someone she loves."

"You are a paradox."

"I hope you don't mind."

"Of course not. In fact, I find your unpredictability quite charming."

"I love you, my immortal."

"As I do you."

FORTY

Chance was tired, hungry, and pissed off. He had been in the interrogation room for over five hours and, except for a restroom break, had been under the constant harangue of a tag-team of detectives. He couldn't remember the name of one of them, but the other one, Detective Ruth Wheeler, he swore he'd never forget.

Detective Wheeler was a severe looking, middle-aged woman with short-cropped hair and a permanent scowl. Tall, and athletically muscular, she was an imposing figure. Her physical appearance seemed to drive her interrogative style: aggressive, in-your-face, and relentlessly intimidating.

Wheeler had her reasons. Growing up the only girl in a house with four brothers, she had always had to fight for her place in the pecking order. Her home life had instilled in her an individual fighting spirit and independence that now shaped all of her interpersonal interactions.

As a cop she excelled. She had graduated top of her class from the police academy, and made detective faster than anyone in the history of her department. Despite her success, she nevertheless felt that she had to be twice as good to be taken seriously.

Consequently, Ruth Wheeler operated with a permanent chip on her shoulder. To her colleagues this came off as over exuberance, even arrogance, so they often referred to her as "Super-Cop", among other things.

Chance had other names for her as well. In their short time together,

Chance had come to the impression that Wheeler had grown up watching Dirty Harry movies, as well as reruns of *Chicago P.D.*, and *Law and Order*, because almost everything that came out of her mouth was an old cop cliche.

"Look, Chance, save us all some time. Level with me and I'll tell the D.A. that you cooperated. I can't help you if you don't talk to me."

Chance rolled his eyes. "I don't think 'helping me' is in your nature, Ruth."

Angered, Wheeler slammed her hand down on the table. Chance was expecting it and didn't jump, which seemed to annoy Wheeler all the more.

"I have leveled with you," continued Chance, "but you refuse to believe me. Instead, you continue to imply that I am somehow involved in the disappearance of Martin and Travis, when the reality is that they are both probably off drunk somewhere and will stumble back on campus in time for lunch. So, Ruth, if you really want to 'help' me, how about getting me something to eat? I mean, you are a public servant, right?"

Wheeler looked as though her head were going to pop as she glared at Chance like she wanted to choke the living shit out of him. Chance just glared right back at her. Fortunately for both of them, the tension was broken by a knock on the mirrored window that took up one whole wall of the interrogation room.

Exasperated, Wheeler turned her glare to the window before spinning and walking out of the room. As she did, Chance was sure he could smell pizza, and it made his stomach growl.

"That kid knows something," said Wheeler as she entered the observation room. Walking over to a coffee maker, she poured herself a cup, grumbling.

"How about letting me talk to him?" suggested Redinger as he looked at Chance through the window. When Wheeler didn't respond, he turned to look at her and found her leaning against the coffee service, looking back at him, a doubtful expression on her face.

"I've dealt with him before. He knows me, and he knows I played baseball at Wellington. He might open up for me."

After a moment's contemplation, Wheeler nodded her approval. Redinger walked over to a small refrigerator and took out two Cokes, then put a slice of pizza on a paper plate and walked into the interrogation room with Chance.

When Redinger entered, Chance's head was down, resting on his forearms. Chance didn't move, so Redinger put one of the sodas and the pizza, on the table near Chance's head. Sitting down, he leaned back and popped the tab on his own soda and took a sip.

When Chance heard the sound, it took a few seconds to register. Peeking up over his forearm he was greeted by a sweating can of coke and a large slice of Canadian bacon and pineapple pizza. Sitting up he looked at the food but didn't make a move. Instead, he looked at Redinger, suspicious.

Redinger smiled and lifted his drink as if toasting Chance.

"I swear it's not poisoned," he said before taking a long drink.

"Just making sure I'm not gonna choke on any strings attached," said Chance.

Redinger chuckled, "You have my word as a Spartan, the only thing stringy about that pizza is the cheese."

Chance reached for the pizza, folding a slice in half as he bit off a huge bite, opening his soda, with one hand. Still chewing, he drank deeply. Letting out a sigh of relief, he sat back and looked at Redinger.

"At last, the good cop," he said, taking another bite. "I was getting a bit tired of bad cop."

"Detective Wheeler's not so bad once you get to know her," said Redinger in a calm, philosophical tone.

"Well," said Chance, taking another long drink, "she sure can be a bitch until you do."

Redinger smiled broadly as he looked over at the two-way mirror. Wheeler stood on the other side watching.

"You haven't seen bitch yet, you entitled little prick, but she's comin'," she muttered.

Redinger sat forward and leaned on the table, his expression becoming serious. "Chance, I'm not going to lie to you, the circumstances don't look good here."

Chance threw his hands up exasperated, "I don't know what else I can tell you. I went to Havenhurst to visit Marina. That was around five p.m. We went directly to that carnival, then returned around nine-thirty. I went to Lakeside

Beach where I fell asleep. I awoke this morning and returned to school in time for morning workout."

The door opened and Detective Wheeler walked back in. Leaning against the wall she folded her arms and listened.

Redinger opened a file folder, then spoke, "Chance, let me lay out the situation the way we see it. We are missing three people: Travis Shelby, Martin Wellington, and Dr. Gregory Tallman. There has also been a burglary of the Havenhurst pharmacy where Dr. Tallman was the pharmacist. C.S.I. found blood trace in the drug storage room. A lot of blood. Enough to make it look like someone may have died there."

Chance's brow furrowed as he leaned forward, fascinated by these new details.

"Now here is where it gets dicey for you," continued Redinger. "You admit to spending the night at Lakeside Beach. We've had forensic teams out there for the last few hours and they report more blood. One detective said it looked like a slaughter house. So everywhere you've been, it looks like someone has died."

Redinger took a sheet of paper from the file and read it. Chance watched as his face took on an expression of confirmation.

"So naturally, our next question is 'Why?' Based on our interviews with some of your classmates, we know you had a few heated exchanges with Martin and Travis, a shoving match in a chemistry class, and a near fight in the dining hall."

Redinger watched as that sank in, waiting a few beats before proceeding.

"Then there's the party Friday night, at which most of the team's cars had their tires slashed. Word around campus is that you, and the rest of the team, believe that it was Martin and Travis that did it."

"Us bad cops call that motive," said Wheeler.

"For murder? Are you nuts? said Chance.

"Perhaps," interrupted Redinger, "but it doesn't explain why when you say you spent the night at the lake, the Wellington bed check roster says you were on campus at eleven p.m. Somebody's lying."

Redinger leaned back thoughtfully, as he studied Chance. The boy had some pretty damning circumstantial evidence stacked up against him, but Redinger didn't get the impression that Chance was twisting to get off the hook, but rather was trying to make sense of it all.

"When was the last time you saw either of them?" asked Redinger.

"Last night, at the hospital," said Chance, annoyance building in his voice.

"You mean you saw Travis Shelby at the hospital?" clarified Wheeler. "When was the last time you saw Martin Wellington?"

"No, I saw both of them there," said Chance as if speaking to a small child. "I figured Martin had gotten a job there, too. They were both dressed like janitors."

"Where exactly did you see them?" asked Wheeler, walking over to the table.

"In the hall," replied Chance. "I was on my way to the restroom."

Redinger's eyes met Wheeler's. "The restrooms are across the hall from the pharmacy," he said.

"Were they carrying anything?" pressed Wheeler.

"They were pushing a trash cart," said Chance as he thought back, "and they both had big hockey bags. I thought that was strange."

Redinger and Wheeler looked at each other, a new array of scenarios playing out in their minds. But their process was interrupted by a heavy knock on the door. Before they could react, the door opened abruptly.

The man that entered dominated the room, tall with dark hair that was frosted silver at the temples, his broad shoulders and a barrel chest gave him the presence of a nightclub bouncer.

Stepping into the room he took in the scene before him like a general surveying a battlefield, but rather than a uniform, he wore a six-thousand-dollar Ralph Lauren, Purple Label suit, and instead of medals, he flashed a business card, from diamond adorned fingers that were perfectly manicured.

Chance recognized him immediately. The cavalry had arrived.

"My name is Daniel J. Raynak," he began in a slow and disarming southern drawl, "and I will be representing Mr. Jordan in this matter."

Smiling, he extended his card to Wheeler, having correctly surmised that she was the alpha in the room.

"I don't care who you are," said Wheeler, snatching the card from his hand. "I'm conducting an investigation, and I'm not finished with this suspect."

"Suspect?" said Raynak, keying in on the word. "Suspect you say? Quite to the contrary, Mr. Jordan is here as a courtesy and a cooperating witness. But if your investigation has now focused upon him as a suspect, may I assume that he has been properly mirandized? And if so, would you please provide me with a copy of his signed waiver of rights form?"

Wheeler just looked at him blankly.

"No?" said Raynak, placing his hand on Chance's shoulder as he watched the defensive lines of local law enforcement begin to crumble. "Then this interview is over. Charge my client, or we will be leaving."

Chance leaned back in his chair. Folding his arms, he smiled at Wheeler smugly.

"I will give you a few minutes to decide your fate," said Raynak, putting his briefcase on the table. Touching the chair that Redinger was seated in he looked at the Lieutenant, "May I have this chair, sir?" he asked politely.

"Please, be my guest," said Redinger, springing up, which caused Wheeler to scowl at him as if he had just committed treason.

"Thank you," said Raynak, taking the seat. "Now, if you would not mind, may we please have some privacy so that I may consult with my client?"

"Of course," said Redinger, stepping toward the door. "May I send in some refreshments?"

"Why, that would be awfully kind of you," said Raynak, smiling. "I would like some coffee, light and sweet, and Mr. Jordan here will have another Coke-a-Cola."

Raynak looked at Chance for approval. Chance just smiled and nodded.

"Oh, and perhaps some pastries?" said Raynak, now in complete control. "This is a police station after all. I'm sure you can scare up some donuts."

At this Wheeler stormed out of the room, her anger hanging in the air like flatulence. Raynak's eyes followed her departure, gleaming with amusement.

"My, my," he said, "I do hope that Detective Wheeler is not feeling cross."

"Please don't worry yourself about Detective Wheeler," said Redinger as he prepared to leave. "When she is on a case, she can sometimes lose her sense of humor."

"And her manners as well, it would seem."

"At times," conceded Redinger.

"You, on the other hand, appear to be rather well-versed in the art of etiquette," observed Raynak.

"Lieutenant Redinger is a Wellington alumnus," explained Chance.

"Ah," sounded Raynak as if finally understanding. "Then the intrepid detective Wheeler must be a product of public schools."

There was a hint of pity in Raynak's voice that forced a tight-lipped smile on Redinger's face as he turned for the door.

"I'll be back with your refreshments shortly," he said, opening the door.

"We thank you ever so much," replied Raynak as the door closed.

Just as the door clicked shut, Redinger found himself having to restrain an enraged Wheeler.

"I'll show that arrogant bastard some public school etiquette," she said through clenched teeth, while brandishing a can of pepper spray.

"Ruth, that would be an extraordinarily bad idea," said Redinger.

Wheeler looked at Redinger and quickly calmed, just as detective Rich Leoni entered the room and pulled up short, seeing Wheeler and Redinger in what looked like an awkward embrace. Opening the file he was carrying, he bowed his head as if reading and cleared his throat.

Wheeler and Redinger jumped apart as if they had been electrified. Leoni began talking as if nothing were out of the ordinary.

"Ruth, you need to see this," said Leoni, holding out the file.

Comporting herself, Wheeler reached out and took the folder and began to read.

"What is it?" asked Redinger.

"Preliminary forensic report," said Wheeler. "They found so much blood trace at the Lakeside house they are sure we are looking for a body."

"We're already looking for a body."

"This would be a different body."

"What?" exclaimed Redinger, surprised.

"The blood at the beach doesn't match the blood from Havenhurst," said Wheeler as she handed him the file. "Read it for yourself."

Leoni finally spoke, "Ruth, if Chance Jordan is good for this, he would most likely have blood all over him. At least on his clothes from last night."

"Nope," said Redinger, reading. "They went over his clothes, his motorcy-cle, dorm room and locker. All clean."

"I saw blood on the inside of his letterman's jacket," protested Leoni.

"Yep, they saw that too, and it's his blood."

"It was a lot of blood," said Leoni, doubtful.

"Still his."

Leoni was struck silent. He walked over next to Wheeler as she stood leaning on the sill of the observation room window looking at Chance and his attorney in the next room.

"Hmmm," sounded Redinger still reading.

"What now?" said Wheeler sounding tired.

"C.S.I. found a wooden table leg at the lake house. They say it has a lot of blood trace and embedded hair. Looks like it was used to beat the shit out of somebody."

"Do they know who?" asked Wheeler.

"You're not going to believe this," said Redinger, an astonished chuckle rumbling in his throat.

"Who?" asked Wheeler, turning to look at him.

Redinger's eyes flittered over as he jerked his head toward Chance.

"How is that possible? There's not a mark on him," said Leoni, stunned.

At that moment Wheeler's phone chirped. Pulling it out she held it to her ear. "Wheeler." As she listened, her brow furrowed.

"Where?" she asked at last. "Hold on. I'm putting you on speaker."

Wheeler touched her phone then spoke again, "OK, Danny, taken it from the top."

"As I was saying, we located Travis Shelby's car hidden in the forest about a mile from Wellington Academy. We just got a telephonic warrant, but wanted to wait for you."

"How'd you get a warrant so fast?"

"Here let me show you why," said the voice on the phone.

Wheeler's phone chirped again as a slightly shaky face time session started. "Here, look at this," said detective Danny Maxwell as he pointed his phone at a silver car.

The car looked undamaged and unremarkable, except for one thing. There were two perfect, bloody handprints on its trunk lid.

"Has C.S.I. processed those prints?" asked Wheeler.

"Yes, and they said they're so pristine, they could use them to teach a class," replied Maxwell.

"Then go ahead and open it up," said Wheeler.

"Pop it!" shouted Maxwell to someone off screen, and immediately a uniformed deputy with a Halligan tool stepped up to the car and jammed the long heavy steel bar under the lip of the trunk lid. After a few manipulations the lid popped open. When it did, the deputy with the tool leaned over to the side and threw up.

Detective Maxwell brought his camera in closer. "You seeing this?" he asked.

"Oh my God," was Wheeler's only response.

The video feed showed two bodies, stuffed at odd angles into the car's trunk. One had been decapitated, its head sitting on its lap, its mouth open as its eyes rolled grotesquely back into its head.

"I'm pretty sure the head belongs to Travis Shelby," said Redinger, swallowing hard as the C.S.I. tech leaned in to search for I.D.'s.

"It's Tallman and Shelby. C.O.D. seems obvious," said Maxwell reading the I.D.'s

"Keep me informed," said Wheeler, but before she could end the call, Maxwell spoke again.

"We have an I.D. on those bloody handprints," he said looking at a computer. "They belong to Martin Wellington."

Wheeler turned and looked at Chance. "Cut him loose. Before we can find out if he's involved, we have to find Martin Wellington."

FORTY-ONE

Marina sat quietly next to Dr. Shelby as they drove along a winding, forested road through the Virginia mountains. It was an unplanned, and unexpected, outing.

Dr. Shelby had come to her in the day room around midmorning and asked her to get dressed for a field trip. Marina had been very excited as she got ready. She was sure that she would soon be seeing Chance, and so she had brushed out her hair, put on some makeup, then put on a pair of black Levis and a white cotton tank top that had been gifts from Nikki.

Looking in the mirror, she wrinkled her nose. Nikki's top was small on her, but that wasn't the problem. The problem was that her white institutional bra, which was showing through the thin material, looked like a lumpy medieval torture device. Deciding to discard it she stripped down and removed it. Then slipping the tank top back on, she looked at herself again.

"Much better," she said, smiling.

Pulling on a white hooded jacket she headed back to the day room where she found Dr. Shelby waiting.

Following Dr. Shelby out of the hospital, Marina looked for Bo and Nurse Denali in the van, but did not see them. So, when Dr. Shelby walked her to his private vehicle, and opened the door, she balked. She asked where they were going, but all Shelby would say was that it was a "surprise".

"Will anyone be coming with us?" she asked, hoping Chance might be joining them.

"No," said Shelby. "This surprise is just for you."

After that short exchange the rest of the drive was silent. Marina didn't mind. All she could think about was Chance and their time together anyway. The carnival, and their unexpected meeting at the house had been a joy, but what occupied her thoughts the most was their all-to-brief motorcycle ride.

Holding Chance, smelling him, her arms wrapped around him as she squeezed his body tightly against hers, had ignited a slow burning fire deep within her. It had grown in intensity, fogging her mind until she had accidentally – and so wonderfully– quenched it in the shower. Nikki had been right. So very, very right.

Realizing where her mind had wandered, Marina glanced self-consciously at Dr. Shelby as if he might somehow know what she was thinking. But if he did, he did not show it.

Turning back to her window, Marina continued to watch the scenery go by, losing track of time. After a while, she felt the car slowing. Sitting up she looked around, confused by where they were going.

Dr. Shelby turned onto an unmarked, paved road that led back into the forest. After about a hundred meters Marina saw a plain sign that read "U.S. Army Research Facility, White Mountain, Access Restricted".

"Is this where we are going for the field trip?" asked Marina, her voice sounding unsure.

But Shelby said nothing as he stopped at a security gate manned by soldiers dressed in black.

After showing his I.D. to the soldier, Shelby was directed through the gate, and he drove to the main building and parked. The cold appearance of the facility made Marina uneasy – the ten-foot-high fences festooned with razor wire, the featureless concrete building with windows too small for even a child to squeeze through.

And then there were the soldiers, aggressive and frightening looking men, with angry faces. They were all dressed in black uniforms and carried vicious looking weapons. They moved along the fence and around the building, some even perched on top. Still more of them patrolled the dense forest outside the fence using A.T.V.s.

When Marina got out of the car she could see, and even feel, the soldiers looking at her as she walked with Dr. Shelby, and though she didn't want to, their stares forced her to cling to his arm. She silently wished Chance were there. She knew she would feel safe if he were holding her.

Inside the door they were met by another soldier, his weapon slung at an angle across his chest.

"I.D. please," he said.

Dr. Shelby handed him a photo I.D. and the soldier examined the card, and Shelby's face. Satisfied, he inserted the card into a slot beside the door. Instantly a green light lit up the slot and the door buzzed open.

The soldier returned Shelby's I.D. as he pulled open the door, and smiled at Marina, causing her to cling to Shelby's arm even tighter. Once inside they were met by Bains and a lab tech in scrubs.

"Hello, Sabine," said Shelby, shaking off Marina and crossing to Bains.

"Hello, Thomas," replied Bains who then turned to Marina. "And hello to you, Marina. Do you remember me?"

Marina only nodded.

"Marina, this nurse is going to take you to an examination room where we will run a few tests," said Bains, in a strained sweet voice.

The lab technician reached out to take Marina, but Marina took a quick step back, half hiding behind Shelby.

"It's OK, Marina," said Shelby, stepping aside and placing his hand on her back. "I will be here the whole time."

The lab tech stepped forward again and this time took Marina by the arm and led her down the hall. Just before they turned a corner, Marina looked back at Shelby, hoping for a smile of support, but he was engrossed in conversation with Dr. Bains.

Suddenly Marina felt alone – very, very alone.

FORTY-TWO

Martin was in a state of bliss. He clearly remembered his fear while looking up at the winged beast that had stood over him, and the sensation of his rib cage crushing as the monster had ground him under its massive foot.

And then there was the searing hot pain as the creature had taken him, his blood beginning to boil as his body seemed to fill with fire. Then suddenly, the pain was gone, his fear was gone, and he felt invincible like he had taken a massive hit from a crack pipe, and then multiplied it by a thousand.

There was something else, however. As good as his body felt, he realized that he was no longer in control of it. He could feel everything, smell everything, but it was as if his life had become a video game that someone else was playing. The odd thing was that he really didn't mind. Whatever this thing was that was in control of him, it made him feel more powerful than he ever had before.

He thought back to the moment he had watched, fascinated, as Travis had been decapitated, and how he had become caught up in the Fallen's elation. He remembered the rush he had experienced as his once un-athletic body had charged like a raging bull through the forest in pursuit of Chance Jordan. How he found the strong smell of Jordan's fear, and the anticipation of his blood, warm and sticky, spilling from his body and steaming in the cool night air, to be so intoxicating.

Now Martin watched through the windows of his own eyes, as his possessor sat concealed in the tree line observing Wellington Academy. He had hidden the car in the forest, then moved with stealth, reconnoitering as much of the school as possible.

Earlier that morning he had watched as several police cars had arrived, then left the campus. Unfortunately, all of that activity had taken place on the opposite side of the school from his perch, so he was unsure as to what it had all been about.

Ultimately, Martin had found a well-concealed position near the academy's pump house. Inside this twenty-by-twenty-foot outbuilding was the pump and purification system that pulled water from a deep aquifer, then stored it in an underground cistern that supplied the campus.

Martin had been ordered to introduce the Catalyst into the water supply at three o' clock. He was then to locate Chance Jordan and observe him, and the student body, for signs that it had taken effect.

It had been explained to him that the effects would resemble an intense reaction to MDMA, the drug humans referred to as 'Ecstasy'. The Martin vessel had a useful knowledge of that drug's characteristics. All inhibitions would break down as the student body gave in to even the slightest suggestion. Agency, without morality. An entire school campus stripped of its inhibitions. All social and moral boundaries obliterated. It would be utter mayhem.

Looking at his phone, he saw that it was time. Rising from his hiding place, he jogged across the lawn to the pump house.

Reaching the door, he saw that it was locked with a heavy padlock. Grasping it, he twisted it hard, snapping it from the hasp. Then, kicking the door open he walked in. The windowless room was dimly lit in a soft purple haze emanating from the ultraviolet disinfecting chamber that purified the water before sending it to the cistern.

As Martin walked around behind the pumping equipment, his skin tingled from the electromagnetic field emitted by the U.V. lights. Made uncomfortable by the sensation, he looked down at his hands and saw that the lights had caused his skin to look white, the veins beneath forming a deep black web.

Refocusing on his mission, he quickly found the access cap in the pipe that led to the storage tank. Twisting the heavy iron cap with one hand, it screeched and ground, having been cemented in place by decades of rust. When at last it broke free, Martin tossed it aside effortlessly and it landed on the concrete floor with a loud metal clang, like a dumbbell discarded by a weight lifter.

From his pocket he produced a small metal case. When he opened it, a thick white vapor flowed from it. The tendrils reached down like ghostly fingers searching for the floor, only to dissipate before finding it.

Reaching into the billowing cloud, Martin extracted a glass vial nested inside a gleaming metal framework, sparkling with frost. Inside the vial was a fluorescent green liquid that glowed intensely in the ultraviolet light.

Grasping the vial at one end, he twisted a thin corrugated ring. As it turned, a spout popped up with a solid click, gas hissing as it escaped under pressure. With a satisfied smile, Martin poured the contents of the vial into the open pipe.

As the last drop hung from the lip of the spout, Martin reached out with his finger and collected it. Spreading the stolen droplet across his teeth like high grade cocaine, he smacked his lips, then ran his tongue over his teeth.

"Not bad," he murmured impressed. "Not bad at all."

                                                           —

Bertha Arroyo was in a good mood. All the police activity at the school that morning had really fired her up. And getting to see Chance Jordan stuffed into a police car was a bonus that had put an uncommon pep into her step.

She had been disappointed however, to see that the boy had not been taken away in handcuffs, but the pitiful expression on his face, as the patrol car had pulled away, had been extremely satisfying.

After that delicious bit of morning drama, Arroyo had been inspired to duty, and so retired to her lair to don her, "security outfit". It consisted of a black windbreaker with a reflective patch on the back that read, of course, 'security'. On the front was pinned a security officer's badge which she kept polished to a high sheen. When the badge wasn't hanging on her jacket, she kept it in a leather badge case that she could flip open in the face of any student foolish enough to question her authority.

She also had purchased a black leather, basket weave, police utility belt, from which she hung her radio and a matching leather key hook. On the back she had a handcuff case containing a set of Smith and Wessen handcuffs and a pepper spray pouch. The school had nixed the pepper spray, however.

"Damn bleeding-heart administration only coddles these little snobs," she often complained.

Arroyo's last piece of equipment was a five-inch tactical flashlight that she kept on a lanyard tightly cinched around her wrist. She wanted to keep it close and ready for action, just in case.

The flashlight had six modes. They ranged from narrow to broad beam, plus a strobe feature that, according to the infomercial Arroyo had been watching when she purchased it, would disorient even the most persistent attacker. She had absolute confidence in its effectiveness, and was convinced that without it, she most certainly would have been ravaged by now.

That same infomercial had bolstered Arroyo's confidence in other ways as well. While she had watched amazed as the flashlight was dropped from a helicopter, and run over by a Humvee and remained undamaged, what sold her was that it was the same tactical flashlight used by the Navy Seals. Now that she had one, she felt that kind of made her a Navy Seal too.

Arroyo had patrolled the campus for the rest of the day, but was disappointed that it had not been more eventful. She was about to call it a day when she spotted Martin Wellington running out of the forest and disappearing behind one of the maintenance buildings.

She was excited. Martin had been missing since bed check last night, and now, here he was. His little sidekick, Travis Shelby, probably wasn't far behind. Arroyo decided she would snatch them both up. It would be the perfect ending to an excellent day.

Peering around the corner she didn't see him, but she did notice that the door to the pump house was open. There were about twenty meters of open lawn between her and the pump house, and she realized that she needed to cover it undetected, and as quickly as possible.

She considered low crawling. It was something she had seen Navy Seals do on the Discovery Channel. But she was wearing new slacks, and wasn't at all sure that if she were to lie down on the ground, that she would be able to get back up again.

Gripping her tactical Seal flashlight she took a deep breath, then bolted toward the pump house. Her feet moved furiously as she waddled, her squeaking, sensible shoes honking like arguing geese with every step.

Reaching the pump house, she flattened herself against its wall, so out of breath she thought she might pass out. Regaining her composure she listened intently, but could only hear the humming of the pumping equipment.

"He's probably smoking the refer," she thought to herself as she sniffed the air for evidence.

Deciding that action was the best course, she prepared to enter the pump house. Fumbling excitedly with her tactical flashlight, she selected a mode appropriate for the mission at hand, then inched closer to the open door.

In her mind she saw herself kicking in the door and storming the room, but since the door was already open, that lovely bit of melodrama was not possible. She considered leaning in and closing the door so she could then kick it in, but decided against it.

At last, she was ready. Holding her U.S. Navy Seal flashlight up beside her face as if it were the barrel of a handgun, she took a breath and stormed into the pump house.

"Martin Wellington, what are you doing in here?" she shouted as she swept the dim room with the beam of her flashlight. Martin did not respond, he just stood there, staring at Arroyo from over the pump equipment. "You come out here this instant! You're on report!" she commanded shining her bright light on his face as she pulled out her notebook. "Did you know the police are looking for you?"

"I thought they might be," said Martin as he slowly walked around the pump. His eyes fixed on hers as an evil smile spread across his face.

"Where is Travis Shelby?" asked Arroyo, scanning the room once again.

"I think you might find the answer to that question rather disturbing," said Martin inching closer.

"You don't scare me, young man," said Arroyo, advancing on Martin. "It would take more than the likes of you..."

The terrified scream that emanated from the pump house was quickly drowned out by preternatural snarls and the sounds of tearing flesh. Then... silence, as Arroyo's prized tactical flashlight rolled into the open doorway, its high intensity L.E.D.s strobing frantically as the pump house door slammed shut.

FORTY-THREE

As Chance walked out of the Sheriff's station there was a town car waiting to take him back to school. In a nearby field sat a helicopter, its jet turbine engines whining in an increasing pitch as its rotor began to spin.

Next to the town car, its driver stood holding the door open as Chance climbed in. Looking up, Chance saw Daniel Raynak exit the sheriff's station. The attorney smiled and gave Chance a crisp salute as he walked purposefully to his waiting aircraft. Chance waved and smiled as he remembered his first meeting with Raynak in his Richmond office.

During that meeting, Chance had learned that Raynak was a graduate of Virginia Tech, had been a commissioned officer and helicopter pilot, serving in the U.S. Army's First Air Cavalry Division. In his office there were several photos of the attorney in uniform with his men sitting in and around various military helicopters, a testament to his pride over that period of time in his personal history.

Chance also recalled that Raynak had a large collection of civil war relics on display. Inside a glass case were two antique pistols, a cavalry sabre, and a Confederate general officer's uniform. Above the case hung an oil painting of Confederate cavalry general J.E.B. Stewart.

As Chance had stood looking at the artifacts, Raynak explained what each piece was, and its historical significance. But it was Raynak's parting words to Chance, as he shook his hand, that had stayed with him.

"Always remember, son," Raynak had said earnestly, "if you ever get in a tight spot, dig in and hold on, because with one phone call, the cavalry will be on its way."

Chance leaned back into the plush seats of the town car and let out a sigh of relief. He watched Raynak's helicopter lift off, then nose down as it gained speed and altitude before vanishing over the horizon. The only thing that would have made it more perfect would have been if it had flown into the sunset.

The long ride back to campus had given Chance time to reflect, and in his reflection his thoughts mostly dwelled on Marina. But he was also troubled by what had happened at the beach – or at least what he vaguely remembered happening. It was all so confusing. Looking up he saw that his car was driving through the gates of Wellington Academy, so he forced himself to focus on the present.

The baseball team was already on the field as the car pulled up to the sports complex. Thanking the driver, Chance jumped out of the car and jogged into the building. Alone in the locker room, he quickly changed into his practice uniform, then grabbing his equipment bag, he walked down the tunnel to the dugout.

Chance was tired. He felt as if he had been up all night, and the tumultuous events of the morning had only added to his fatigue, leaving him feeling wrung out.

Even so, he found himself craving the physical grind of baseball practice. He needed the sense of normalcy that he knew being with his team would bring. Especially after a morning that was anything but normal.

He knew he would not be in any trouble for being late. If Coach McCune was anything, he was fair. But what does one say in situations like this?

"Hey, coach, sorry I'm late, but I got hung up at the police station because they think I murdered somebody," seemed like an awkward way to start a conversation.

Reaching the dugout, he dropped his bag on the bench and took out his mitt. Taking a deep breath, he pulled his cap down tight, and trotted up the steps and onto the field.

As he came up out of the dugout, he saw coach McCune standing across the diamond, his arms folded as he watched the infield work from the first base coach's box. McCune saw him immediately.

"Nice of you to finally join us, Mr. Jordan!" bellowed McCune, teasingly.

Chance waved then began jogging around the baseline toward him.

"Oh, no, don't hurry, Mr. Jordan," continued McCune, " Take your time. If you're feeling tired, take a break, enroute."

The players on the field and in the batting cages began to clap and whistle as Chance jogged down the third base line. Cat calls were even coming from the bleachers behind the dugout.

"Yeah, hustle up, ya bum," came one voice.

"Damn prima donnas are ruining the game," said another.

Chance turned to find that the source of these derogatory comments was Kimiko and Bella. The girls had become a fixture at practices, often lounging in the sun directly behind the home team dugout.

Chance tipped his cap to the ladies and smiled. They smiled back, waving. Chance also noticed Jäger in the stands, a few rows further up. Chance couldn't explain it but seeing the odd boy sitting there, his piercing blue eyes watching, was for some reason comforting.

As Chance came to a halt in front of McCune, the gruff field marshal appraised him with a stern expression.

"Sorry I'm late coach," said Chance, but McCune waved it off.

"How ya feelin', son?"

"It's good to be home, sir."

McCune considered this for a moment, then nodded his understanding.

"Very well, Mr. Jordan. Shortstop, if you please."

"Yes, sir," said Chance, smiling as he ran out onto the diamond.

Conor stood on the pitcher's mound, grinning. He looked at Chance and ran his finger along the bill of his cap in salute. Chance returned the gesture.

As Chance arrived at his shortstop position, Eric came over from his position at second and shook Chance's hand.

"Wanna play some ball?" he said, handing Chance the baseball.

"Yeah," said Chance, tossing the ball in his hand. "I really do."

FORTY-FOUR

Marina had been poked, tested, and sampled for the better part of the day. While no one had been rude to her, no one had been particularly friendly either and the feeling of anxiety, she had felt ever since seeing the facility's building, had not diminished. She had been moved from lab to lab, and at the moment was sitting in a frightening looking room that was flooded with harsh light. Though the room was warm, she felt cold.

The lab was black from top to bottom, and dominated by two tables with human forms molded into their shining metal tops. They looked as if bodies had been pressed into them. Above each table was an array of hoses and tubes that were connected to clear human-shaped plastic shrouds that hung suspended in the air. Marina shuddered, a chill running through her body as she tried to imagine their use, and prayed they would not put her in one.

For the time being, Marina sat on a gurney alone. Looking up she saw a large window to a room high above the floor. On the other side of the glass, she could see Dr. Shelby and Dr. Bains talking. Shelby looked at Marina and smiled weakly.

"Have your tests provided any explanation as to why she is resistant to your compound?" asked Shelby, as he looked down into the lab.

"I don't believe it is resistant any longer," said Bains.

Shelby turned from the window, a look of confusion on his face. "What leads you to that conclusion?" he asked.

"I have been looking at the anomaly's test results, in particular it's brain scans. They show increased activity in its frontal cortex, a physical sign of emotional maturity that was absent from its scans six months ago."

"Yes," said Shelby, suddenly excited, "Marina has shown a marked change in her emotional maturity ever since she first met..."

"Exactly," said Bains. "Ever since meeting the boy it calls, Sari'El."

"What are you going to do?" asked Shelby apprehensively.

"I am going to inject the anomaly with the Catalyst, directly."

"What dosage do you plan to use?"

".02ccs of 1ppb diluted solution."

"So much?" said Shelby, visibly startled. "Won't that be dangerous?"

"The anomaly will succumb, and while it is vulnerable, I will lure Sari'El to me."

Just then a technician carrying a tray entered the lab where Marina nervously waited. The tech set the tray down next to Marina and wordlessly began to open several small packages, extracting small square patches from which hung wires.

Marina watched the woman as she peeled off the covering from the adhesive back of the electrodes and uncoiled lead wires, but when she attempted to attach the electrodes to Marina's temples, Marina swatted them away.

Seeing this, Shelby began to search the control panel with his eyes.

"How do I turn on the intercom?" he asked, then seeing what he was looking for, reached for the panel. "Oh, here it is."

Shelby pressed a button marked 'intercom' and it lit up as he began to speak.

"Marina, just relax," said Shelby, soothingly. "It's only an electroencephalogram. You've done these before."

Marina looked at Shelby and then the technician. Finally, she relaxed and allowed the electrodes to be attached to her. When she was done, the technician collected her tray and left as silently as she had entered.

Seeing that Marina had calmed, Dr. Shelby turned his back to the window and leaned back against the control panel with his arms folded as he spoke.

"I must admit, I am more than a little concerned. If Chance Jordan – or Sari'El as you and Marina prefer to call him – is as dangerous as you say, why on earth would you wish to provoke him, then 'lure' him here?"

"Sari'El is not your concern," said Bains flatly. "He will soon be under the influence of the Catalyst, and once he is, he will no longer be a threat."

"Then why do you need Marina?"

"If he is Sari'El, he will not reveal himself unless provoked, and he is far too disciplined to be easily provoked, but his devotion to the girl, will draw him out. Then, once I have him under my control, I will turn him, or at the very least, harvest his essence."

"You sound very confident."

"It has been done before."

"And if you can't...control him, as you put it?"

"Then Sari'El will have to be destroyed," said Bains with the same nonchalance that one might order weeds be plucked from a garden.

Shelby looked at Bains, surprised by her callousness, but as he looked at her, the control room was flooded by an intense blueish flash of light.

Startled, Shelby jumped away from the window as Bains sprang forward and looked down into the lab. What she saw stunned her.

Marina was standing in the center of the lab, her arm raised in front of her. Her index finger was extended and touching the center of a shimmering black vertical pool filled with thousands of sparkling stars that swirled out of a growing vortex.

Just then the lab door opened and the technician returned, this time carrying a tray with a saline I.V. When the tech saw Marina standing before an Ingwaz, she startled, dropping the tray.

Inside Bains' head, panic and rage battled for control as she reached for the intercom button. When she saw that the intercom button was already lit, rage jumped to the forefront as she realized that her conversation with Shelby had been broadcast into the lab where Marina had been listening.

"Stop her you fool!" Bains screamed into the intercom.

The startled tech ran toward Marina, but she had already stepped into the Ingwaz and vanished, the electric portal collapsing in a blinding flash.

Sabine Bains roared, her beautiful face distorting hideously as she pounded her fists on the control panel, smashing it. Horrified, Shelby backed away and pressed against the wall. Turning, Bains' burning eyes fixed on the terrified man as she stalked toward him.

On the lab floor the tech stood frozen as she listened to the preternatural howling and snarling, intermixed with the pleading, then screams of Dr. Shelby coming from the control room.

Then, all fell silent, and the control room window exploded as Dr. Thomas Shelby's broken body was flung through it. With a sickening wet thud, the mangled, blood-soaked corpse landed limply on the laboratory floor, his jaws torn open into a grotesquely frozen scream.

In a remote corner of the Wellington Academy grounds an innocuous breeze rustled the loose forest detritus that was accumulated along the edge of the well-manicured lawn. Within this seemingly meaningless disturbance a small pinpoint of light winked into existence. Hovering and pulsating a few feet above the ground, its luminosity increased until, in an explosion of light, it expanded into a shimmering black-liquid Ingwaz, fingers of electricity crawling like incandescent spiders over its surface. Within seconds Marina emerged, encased in an iridescent web of energy that quickly dissipated as the Ingwaz collapsed behind her.

Taking a moment to get her bearings, Marina surveyed the area. In the distance, across a vast lawn, she could see the academy's campus. She recognized the buildings from the photos Sari'El had shown her during their visits, and was grateful that the 'Looking glass', the name she used when referring to an Ingwaz, had deposited her in the exact location from where the photo had been taken.

At one end of the campus, she saw the distinctive stadium lights rising up above the large building in which Sari'El had said he spent most of his time. Deciding that would be the best place to start looking for him, she set off purposefully across the lawn. Her heart beat heavy in her chest and she picked up the pace, hoping she was not too late.

FORTY-FIVE

Martin crouched just beyond the tree line, watching the Wellington baseball team practice. After a thorough reconnoiter of the campus, he had come to the conclusion that Chance Jordan was not there. He had found Eric Easton and Conor Jackson easily enough, and deduced that if Chance Jordan were on campus, he would be with them. So, he had found a hiding place where he could keep them under surveillance, confident that if Jordan did show up, it would be here.

Not long after settling in, Martin's attention was drawn to the sound of shouting from the ball field. Looking up, the Fallen smiled as what could very well be the great War Bringer Prime, Sari'El, emerged from the dugout. Moments later Martin's phone buzzed.

"Yes, Baka'El," said Martin, his eyes fixed on Chance.

"The situation has changed," said Bains in a cool authoritative voice. "I have identified the Guardian. It is the girl."

"The girl from the hospital?" clarified Martin.

"Yes, I'm sending you a photograph now."

"What are your instructions?"

"The guardian is most likely on her way to the school, if not there already," said Bains. "Continue to observe. You will soon begin to see the effects of the Catalyst on the student body."

"Yes, Baka'El."

"Have you located the human, Chance Jordan?"

"I am observing him as we speak."

"Stay with him. The Guardian will attempt to make contact soon," said Bains sternly. "You must not alert them to your presence. If one or both come under the influence of the Catalyst, notify me immediately, I will be standing by with capture teams."

"It will be done Baka'El."

The line clicked off and Martin dropped his phone into his pocket. Sitting back, he began to scan the stadium for the Guardian of Sari'El.

"I'm going to go get something to drink," said Kimiko, standing. "You want something?"

"I'll come with you," replied Bella, rising.

Both girls collected their things and waved goodbye to the boys on the field as they walked out to the stadium's breezeway. Stopping in front of a bank of vending machines, they made their selections. As Kimiko twisted off the cap of her ginger ale, Bella selected a bottle of cold water.

"Looks like somebody is lost," said Kimiko.

Bella stood up, snapping the cap off her water and taking a sip as she looked at Kimiko, confused by her comment.

With her eyes, Kimiko gestured down the breezeway. Turning, Bella found what had caught Kimiko's attention. A girl, with long auburn hair tied back in a pony tail. She was wearing a plain white hooded sweat jacket and jeans, and was taking tentative steps along the breezeway, peering into doors as if looking for someone.

"New student?" asked Bella speculatively.

"So late in the school year?" replied Kimiko.

Without further discussion the two girls decided simultaneously that the situation warranted further investigation, and so they casually approached the pretty lostling. Marina noticed the two of them drawing nearer and regarded them warily.

"Can we help you?" asked Bella, smiling.

"I must find Sari..." but Marina silenced herself. "He said he would be here."

The girls looked at Marina with blank expressions.

"Do you know his last name?" asked Bella.

Marina paused, confused. To the best of her memory Sari'El had no other name. But her memory of him was becoming foggy, like a curtain of haze descending around a dream. Fighting the fog, a name came to her mind.

"Jordan," she said at last.

Kimiko and Bella looked at each other then back at Marina. "Do you mean Chance Jordan?" asked Kimiko.

"Yes, that's it. Chance Jordan, he is called Chance Jordan now," said Marina, excitement rising in her voice.

The girls puzzled over Marina's comment. Their brows furrowed as they tried to make sense of it, but decided to let it go.

"Chance is at baseball practice," explained Bella, moving past Marina's odd comment.

"I must talk to him," said Marina, her voice taking on a tone of urgency.

"Who are you?" asked Bella.

"My name is Marina."

Kimiko and Bella looked at each other again, this time their faces registering surprise.

"Marina?" asked Kimiko. "You mean like, from Havenhurst Marina?"

Marina was startled to discover that these two girls knew who she was, and became suddenly fearful. Bella sensed it and raised her hands.

"Hey, it's okay. Chance is our friend too," she said.

"I must speak to Chance," said Marina dropping her voice, "he is in danger."

"Danger?" said Bella deciding the girl from Havenhurst was perhaps being delusional. "Believe me, he will be in even more danger if you go out on that field and try to talk to him."

"Oh yeah," agreed Kimiko, "Coach McCune would kill him for sure."

Marina's eyes widened upon hearing this.

Bella saw Marina's expression and laughed nervously. "She's just kidding around," assured Bella as she punched Kimiko in the arm. "Coach McCune wouldn't actually kill Chance."

Marina seemed to relax. Bella turned to look at Kimiko, a strained smile on her face as she spoke through clinched teeth.

"What's wrong with you?" she said under her breath. "You can't say stuff like that to Havenhurst people."

"Oops," mouthed Kimiko.

"Look," said Bella, turning back to Marina, "Chance won't be done with practice for another half hour."

"I will wait for him here, then," said Marina.

"That is not a good idea," said Kimiko, looking at Marina. "Arroyo is on a tear today. If she comes through here and sees her without a guest pass..."

Kimiko let the consequences hang in the air. Bella looked at her then at Marina, confirming what Kimiko had already noticed.

"Crap," said Bella.

"I have an idea," said Kimiko, turning to Marina. "We're meeting up with Chance and some friends after practice for a pizza party. You can come with us and meet Chance there."

"You want to sneak her into the dorm?" said Bella smiling.

"Can you imagine the look on Chance's face?" said Kimiko. Then turning again to Marina, she added, "We're going to take you to Chance's room so you can surprise him there."

Marina smiled broadly at this. Stepping up beside her, Kimiko and Bella interlaced their arms with hers, and the trio headed toward the dormitory, chatting animatedly.

───

For Chance, baseball practice had been exactly the cathartic experience he had hoped it would be. Slipping back into his competitive, elite athlete mindset, he had been able to easily discard the thoughts from a day best forgotten.

The relief he had felt had been almost complete. But now, as the team came together in the infield for McCune's daily sermon on the mound, he couldn't help but feel somewhat disheartened that reality was about to impose itself on him once again. If there was one silver lining, it was that he would soon be on his way to see Marina.

As McCune's sermon ended and the team left the field, Chance lingered within the pack of his brother Spartans, finding their presence soothing. Making his way through the raucous locker room, Chance sat down and took off his cleats as he prepared to take a shower. He was placing his shoes in his locker when without warning, two very big, and very strong hands came from behind and took hold of him by the shoulders.

Wincing, he tried to rise, but was forced back down onto the bench as a deep resonating voice spoke into his ear. "You are coming to my party, ja?"

Chance didn't have to look. The thick German accent told him everything.

"What party?" Chance croaked through the pain.

"You expect me to believe that you don't know what I'm talking about?" said Rheinhard, squeezing harder, forcing a pained yelp out of Chance.

"I swear, I don't know about any party."

As Chance grimaced, Eric and Conor sat down next to him.

"Rheinhard," said Eric calmly.

"Ja?"

"We never had an opportunity to tell Chance about your party."

"Oh," said the German, leaning down next to Chance's ear, "would you like to come to my party?"

"Yes, I would, very much," whimpered Chance.

"Excellent. I will see you there," said the giant German, releasing Chance, then tussling his hair before walking away.

"What the hell?" said Chance as he waited for the blood to return to his upper body.

"Rheinhard is having a party," said Eric, smiling.

"No shit," said Chance.

"Come on," said Conor, patting his back. "Let's change at the dorm so we don't have to get dressed twice."

Eric agreed, so the three friends grabbed their bags and headed for the locker room door. As the sound of running showers and shouting players was muted by the closing doors, the boys were greeted by Bella and Kimiko.

"Hi, Chance," said the girls in harmonious unison.

"Hey," replied Chance, suspicious of their demeanor.

"How'd things go with the police?" asked Kimiko.

"My attorney advised me not to talk about it," said Chance with a serious voice, but a smirk on his face.

Hearing this, Bella walked over and cuddled up to Chance's arm. "You can't even talk to me?" she said, batting her eyelashes theatrically.

"Especially you. He even mentioned you by name."

"That's OK, Kimiko and I have a secret, too," retorted Bella.

"I'm sure you have lots of them," said Chance.

Eric pulled Bella away. "As your attorney, my dear, I advise you to remain silent as well," he quipped.

"Well, we won't have to remain silent for much longer," said Kimiko, giggling.

"And why is that?" asked Eric.

"Because we stashed our secret in your dorm room," said Bella.

"What'd you put in my room?" asked Chance, sounding annoyed. "I've had a really bad day, and I'm in no mood for any bullshit surprises."

"Easy, tough guy," said Kimiko, poking her finger into Chance's chest. "I'm pretty sure our surprise will be a soothing balm to your crappy day."

Reaching up she tapped Chance's nose. "Just-you-wait-and-see," she said.

"Come on Chance," said Conor, pulling Kimiko to his side. "Let's go eat some pizza before my girlfriend decides to kick your ass."

The group laughed and headed out across the Commons toward the dorms. As they did, Jäger stepped out of the breezeway, watching them go. Walking over to a drinking fountain, he took a drink of water and immediately jerked his head back. The water tasted strange.

Touching his lips, he examined the liquid that dripped from them. Something was wrong. Something was very, very wrong.

FORTY-SIX

The walk back to the dormitory had been pleasant. The group of friends fell into its usual playful banter, and everyone seemed to relax. Chance, at last, detailed the story of his long interrogation by detective Wheeler, and how Daniel Raynak had arrived, guns blazing.

"Raynak was amazing," gushed Chance. "From the moment he walked in, he owned the place. By the time we left, he had them serving us donuts and coffee."

Chance put his arm over Eric's shoulders. "Thanks for your help today," he said.

"You know I got your back, bro, but it was your dad that was all over it."

"Where was he?"

"Hong Kong. He's probably on his way home now."

"No," said Chance casually, "he has most likely already spoken to Raynak, knows the situation is under control, and that it does not require the presence of the Great and Powerful Nelson Jordan."

Eric studied Chance's face. "You okay bro?" he asked concerned. Eric was very aware of the strained relationship Chance had with his father.

"Hey, I'm great," said Chance in mock exuberance. "I'm an American man about to enjoy an Italian pizza, as the guest of a shaved German ape. What more could I want?"

Again, the group laughed, but Kimiko and Bella only giggled as they whispered secrets to one another.

"Oh, I think you might add something to your list once you see what's in your room," said Bella in a sing-song voice.

"Well, it's my room, too you know," complained Eric.

"The surprise is for Chance," said Bella coldly. "If you touch it, perhaps even if you look at it too fondly, you will find the consequences to be unbearable."

"Don't threaten me with a good time," said Eric, grinning.

"It doesn't matter," interjected Kimiko. "I'm sure Chance won't want to share."

The girls locked arms in solidarity and giggled once more as they pulled open the doors to the dormitory and walked inside. The boys all glanced at each other with amused expressions and followed the girls in.

When the group reached Chance and Eric's dorm room, they waited as Chance searched his sports bag for his keys. A commotion down the hall drew Conor's attention.

As he watched, he saw several students milling about the hallway seemingly disoriented. Conor recognized one of them as a teammate from the football team.

The boy staggered, and as he reached for a door, lost his balance and fell face first into the door jamb. Almost immediately the door opened and the prostrate boy was dragged inside.

"Wow, they're starting the weekend early," muttered Conor.

Kimiko turned to see what Conor was talking about, but by then the incapacitated footballer and his inebriated entourage were gone.

Chance finally found his keys and unlocked the door. As it swung open, he and Eric peered into their living space apprehensively. It was an anticlimactic moment.

The room was empty of anything unusual, and looked just as Eric had left it. Looking at each other there was a palpable disappointment. Entering the room cautiously they scanned the area, waiting for someone or something to spring out at them.

"Watch out for trip wires," said Conor from the open doorway.

Eric and Chance froze mid-step, looking down around their feet, then immediately felt stupid for doing so.

"Shut up," said Eric, looking back at Conor.

Standing up straight, Eric regarded the girls at the door. "So where is this big surprise?"

Before either girl could respond, the bathroom door opened and Marina stepped out into the room, steam billowing around her. Her hair was wet as if she had just stepped out of the shower, and beads of water ran down her face collecting on her lips. Dressed only in her tight white tank top, that had become mostly transparent as it clung to her damp body, and a pair of white French cut panties, another gift from Nikki, Marina's eyes fixed on Chance with intensity.

Wordlessly, Marina crossed the room. Stalking up to a flabbergasted Chance, she kissed him with a passion that stunned him. Her hands ran freely over his body, until sliding up his back she pulled him tightly to her, pressing her damp body against his.

"Holy shit," said Conor from the door. "Who the hell is that?"

Kimiko was impressed. As a self-described 'Femme fatale' she was rather proud of her ability to seduce and manipulate men. Even so, she had to give this girl some respect.

"Nice move Havenhurst," she said as she watched Marina clinging to Chance.

"Havenhurst?" questioned Eric, the name growing in significance within the context of the situation. Looking at the half naked girl cleaved to his best friend, Eric finally stammered, "That's Marina? From the loony-bin Marina?"

"Eric!" exclaimed Bella as she went to his wardrobe and pulled out a pair of jeans and a shirt. Grabbing him by the arm she pulled the shocked teenager to the door.

"That's the girl Chance has been going to visit?" said Conor, at last finding his words. "That's not possible. She's...hot."

Kimiko turned and looked at Conor, her eyes narrowing with annoyance. "You are so going to pay for that," she said coldly.

Bella finally got Eric to the door, and shoved him into the hall. "Come on, let's give them some privacy," she said.

"But I want...details," complained Eric as Bella began to pull the door closed. "Details, bro... details," he shouted as the door clicked shut.

Chance had heard none of this. From the moment Marina had walked into the room, she had become the only thing he was conscious of. Calm and at peace he became lost in her. Holding her in his arms, he felt complete again as he experienced the same satisfied serenity that had filled him that morning at the lake.

As Marina's lips crushed passionately against his, he felt his head begin to spin, an odd sensation of near drunkenness overcoming him. His lips burned, as if he had been sipping Corn Whiskey, and everywhere his skin touched hers, he felt the same heat penetrating his flesh.

Reality for him had taken on a dreamlike state, like watching the world through a hazy, Vaseline-covered lens. Breaking their kiss, Chance looked around the room, only then realizing that they were alone, and could not remotely remember when his friends had left.

Marina was not so distracted. Unbuttoning Chance's shirt, she slipped it off his shoulders, then in one easy motion removed her tank top. Embracing him again she reached up with her lips, as he felt his skin tingling and warming intensely.

Feeling overwhelmed, Chance gave in to the strange intoxication. Sweeping Marina up in his arms he carried her to his bed.

Martin Wellington clung like a spider to the outside wall of the dormitory building. Nestled among the freshly sprouted ivy that covered the building's facade, he was nearly invisible to anyone that was not looking directly at him.

As he peered through the window, watching Chance and Marina, his eyes glowed like burning embers. Reluctantly, He pulled back and took out his phone.

"Baka'El, the Guardian appears to have been exposed, and is under the influence of the Catalyst," he reported.

"And what of Sari'El?" asked Bains.

"It is difficult to say, but it is highly likely that he has been exposed through physical contact with the Guardian. To what extent I cannot be sure."

"We can wait no longer; we will have to risk it. Continue to observe. The capture teams are coming in."

The screen went dark. Pocketing the phone, Martin crept back to the window where he found the two lovers, still in passionate embrace.

Three black S.U.V.s roared through the gates of Wellington Academy just as night fell over the campus. Speeding along the narrow streets, the dark convoy dodged students that wandered the grounds in a daze, seemingly oblivious to their surroundings. Some were fighting drunken, mindless brawls, others had discarded their clothes and were dancing to unheard music. In the distance, bands of students and staff marched together holding Molotov Cocktails, the burning fuses creating a surreal procession of merry arsonists.

Watching all of this through the window of the lead vehicle, Bains smiled. She was pleased to see that the mass delivery of the Catalyst via the school's water supply had worked to perfection.

With a jolt, the convoy jumped the curb and skidded to a stop in front of the dormitory where Martin was waiting. Bains quickly exited her vehicle as Martin approached.

"Where is he?" she asked, looking around at the growing chaos.

"Both he and the Guardian are in a room on the third floor," said Martin pointing at the room's window.

"Are they alerted to our presence?"

"I doubt it," said Martin.

"How can you be so sure?" questioned Bains.

"Because they lie together."

Bains was visibly surprised, even impressed, by this news. Not that physical intimacy between a Guardian and its ward was expressly forbidden. It was just never talked about, as it was considered to be...taboo.

"Sari'El is full of surprises," said Bains, looking up at the dorm building.

"That they are both compromised by the Catalyst is the only explanation," said Martin.

"Not the only one," said Bains with a slight smile of approval. "But, we must proceed with caution. Even compromised, together they are extremely powerful, and potentially dangerous."

"Perhaps some additional leverage would be helpful?"

"What do you have in mind?" asked Bains, intrigued.

"A group of Chance Jordan's closest friends are at this moment in a single room in this very building," said Martin pointing at the dormitory. "If we take them with us, it could cause Sari'El to hesitate."

"Excellent," said Bains. "Take half of the men and seize them. I will take Sari'El."

Chance lay stroking Marina's hair as she held him closely, her arm across his chest. As he gazed, still feeling the half-drunk sensation that he could not explain, he noticed a golden light flickering on her face. Looking around, he realized that the light also filled his room, and its source appeared to be coming from outside his window.

Pushing up on his hands, he peeked over the window sill and saw that the library was burning. Around it danced the silhouettes of his classmates, making it look like some kind of Pagan ritual, but then remembering the burning of the Library of Alexandria, he admitted that the burning of books wasn't an exclusively "Pagan" activity.

Chance smiled at the mayhem, then thought that an odd reaction as he rather liked the library. He considered running out there and defending it, but that thought vanished from his mind as Marina pulled him back down into her arms, kissing him softly.

Exploring her body with his fingertips, he traced her contours, touching her lightly, as if with a feather. Marina purred her approval, snuggling closer. But their enchanted moment was abruptly shattered by the sound of a gunshot in the hallway.

Startled into semi-sobriety, Chance and Marina sat up in bed as screams filled the building around them. More gunfire rang out, and Chance got out of bed, quickly sliding on a pair of jeans as Marina covered herself with a blanket.

Moving cautiously toward the door, Chance listened as the screaming was joined by the thunder of heavy footfalls stampeding up the stairwells and through the narrow halls. As he listened, he tried to figure out where the sound was coming from, but then he realized that whatever was out there, had stopped outside his door.

Backing away, he furrowed his brow in confusion, just as his door exploded inward. Soldiers dressed in black tactical armor flooded into the breach. His drug addled mind made him at first think it was all a dream, and he found himself watching, fascinated.

Then a loud pop sounded, and he felt his whole body begin to convulse as electric current coursed through him, every muscle in his body cramping simultaneously. As he fell to the floor, he heard another pop and saw Marina being dragged naked from his bed.

The last thing Chance heard, as a needle was jammed into his neck and darkness closed in around him, was the sound of Marina screaming his name.

Then, silence.

FORTY-SEVEN

Nikki lay poolside on a chaise lounge, sunning herself, as a deliciously textured feminine voice, accompanied by a ukulele, sang in the background. Her Fallen sat next to her, gently running his hands over her body as he lovingly applied coconut scented oil to her skin. As he traced her tattooed wings, an easy smile showed on his contented face.

In their time together, Nikki had learned that her immortal's name was ReyRa'El, but she found that name rather ostentatious and too "Bibley," so instead she called him simply "Ray-Ray". He found her irreverence charming.

Turning, the Fallen regarded the young musician that floated in the pool. She drifted upon an enormous inflatable swan, singing as she dipped her feet in the water.

"Who is she?" he asked.

"That," said Nikki, turning her head to look at the girl, "is Grace Vanderwaal."

"Is she a friend of yours?"

"No, we have never met, but I love her music," said Nikki wistfully.

"Does she inspire you?"

"She inspires many people."

"It is you that inspires me," he said, leaning over and lightly kissing Nikki's oiled bottom.

"Not in front of Grace," she scolded, swatting him away.

Ray-Ray laughed, but Nikki did not laugh with him. Instead, she looked at his face, concerned. He looked tired; a greyish hue having come over his skin as a strange frailness gripped him.

"Are you feeling OK? she asked.

"I am fading," he said, taking a breath.

Instantly the pool and the adorable young vocalist vanished. Now Nikki and Ray-Ray sat in the center of the big white feather bed, as before, surrounded by the endless sea of flickering candles. Taking his hand she looked into his eyes, worried.

"Is there anything I can do?" she asked with a hint of panic in her voice.

"Yes," he said solemnly. "I need you to feed."

Ray-Ray had explained the price of their symbiotic relationship, and the sanguine ritual required to maintain it, how she would be required to draw the life force of mortal humans from them by drinking their blood. Nikki had been anticipating this moment, but up until now, the enormity of this reality had not been completely real to her. It had just become, very real.

Malevolent Fallen did not concern themselves with whether or not their vessels fed. If they wished to maintain the vessel, they would feed. If not, the Fallen would feed directly off the life force of its vessel until its flesh rotted from its bones, its internal organs becoming jelly and failing. At that time the vessel would be discarded, and left for dead.

Either way, malevolent or benevolent, the Celestial required the life force found in the blood of the living to sustain itself, and Nikki would do anything for her Immortal.

"What must I do?" she asked.

"Close your eyes," instructed Ray-Ray. "It is here."

Nikki closed her eyes, and immediately there was a knock at the door. Her eyes flew open at the unexpected sound, shocked to find herself sitting on her bed in her room at Havenhurst.

Startled, she called out, "Ray-Ray?"

"I'm here," came his voice, soothing and reassuring from inside her mind. "Don't be afraid."

"I'm not," she unconvincingly lied.

Looking up at the window in her door, Nikki saw the smiling face of Ethan Horner, the day orderly. Ethan was a kind man, and unlike most of the others that would peek into showers, or cop the occasional grope, Ethan had always been a gentleman. Opening the door, Ethan poked his head in.

"You OK, Nikki? I heard you yell something."

"I'm fine," said Nikki, trying to look normal. "It was just a dream."

Ethan lingered, sensing she had more to say.

"Could I talk to you a minute?" said Nikki nervously.

"Sure," said Ethan, stepping into the room. "What's on your mind?"

As Ethan drew closer Nikki felt her body tense, coiling like a rattlesnake. She didn't do it intentionally; it was more of a reflex. She could hear his heartbeat, and shivered in involuntary excitement at the thought of his blood pulsing just beneath his thin layer of skin, as her canine teeth extended, sharp like icepicks.

In her mind she was conflicted. As a young girl she had often fantasized about becoming a "vampire". And while she wasn't a vampire, at least not like what she had always imagined them to be, she was now faced with the reality that she would have to kill this kind man just to drink his blood.

"Do I have to kill him?" she asked Ray-Ray.

"You can take as much, or as little as you wish," came his reply. "But the less you drink, the more often you will need to."

"But, if I let him live, he will tell others," thought Nikki as she looked at Ethan, the smiling orderly unaware that the possibility of his death was being debated.

"No," came the Fallen's reply, "as you drink, force your saliva in through the wound. It is a venom that will make your prey highly suggestible. Command him to forget, and he will find himself later, wondering where the time went."

"But the wound."

"Lick the wound. It will heal in seconds, without a trace."

Reassured, Nikki rose and took a step toward the man. Ethan took a halting step back.

He couldn't explain why he did that. His rational mind told him this was Nikki, a sweet, if strange girl that he felt unthreatened by. Sure, her gothic appearance gave her a bit of a scary presentation, but since he had gotten to know her, he had discovered that she was rather kind, and even gentle. Still, she had an edge, and at this moment his instincts told him that he was face to face with a predator.

His instinct for self-preservation told him to run screaming from the room. But his reason told him that this girl was no threat, and so he hesitated, and in that moment, Nikki was upon him.

In the following hours, Ethan Horner, the day shift orderly, went down to the basement and brought Nikki Van Pelt's personal property up to her room, along with a suitcase filled with clothes. Later that afternoon, he sat in the break room sipping tea as he absentmindedly rubbed a sore spot on his neck.

He couldn't recall having injured himself, and when he looked at the spot in the mirror, he couldn't see anything to explain it, so it slipped from his mind. Looking at his watch, his brow furrowed.

"Where did the time go?" he wondered.

FORTY-EIGHT

When Chance awakened, he was blinded by a bright, focused light. Foggy and disoriented, he tried to lift his hand to shade his eyes, but found that his arm was restrained. Pulling with his other hand, confirmed that it was bound as well.

He tried to sit up, but couldn't due to a restraint around his throat. He was, however, able to move his head. Looking down his body he saw that he had been stripped naked, and his feet were secured to the table with heavy, thick straps.

"Confusing, isn't it?" came a voice.

Squinting, Chance tried to locate the source of the disembodied female voice that seemed to lurk beyond the bright light. Then, as he searched, a woman's face moved over his, shading his eyes.

"Is that better?" she asked, smiling.

Chance looked at the face above him. Even in the harsh light, and deep shadow, he recognized her.

"I know you," said Chance, his senses slowly returning. "I saw you at Havenhurst."

"I'm flattered that you noticed me," said Bains.

"Where am I, and why am I tied up?"

But as the miasma lifted, flashes of memory surged forward through the fog: a door exploding, black-uniformed soldiers swarming in, every muscle in his body convulsing violently. Then, the last image stormed to the front.

"Marina! Where is Marina?!" said Chance threateningly.

"Calm yourself, Sari'El. Your Guardian is safe."

"My what?" said Chance, confused.

Bains ignored the question as a medical technician stepped in and forced a blood-draw needle into Chance's arm, causing him to wince.

"I apologize for your discomfort," said Bains, stroking his forehead. But I promise that in a few minutes it will all seem quite inconsequential to you."

"Where is Marina?" said Chance again, his anger growing.

"As I said, the girl is safe, and will remain so as long as you cooperate," said Bains.

Chance strained and thrashed against his restraints, but to no avail. His anger and frustration showed on his face, as Bains watched him, intrigued. Turning she studied an array of monitors that displayed his vital organ and brain function.

"Elevated heart rate, increased respiration and blood pressure, massive activity in the prefrontal cortex and hippocampus," said Bains, reading the data aloud. "Sari'El, I think this relationship with your Guardian may not only be unethical, but unhealthy."

Chance was once again confused by Bains' use of the name Sari'El, and her odd reference to a relationship with some guardian that he did not understand. "Look lady, my name is Chance Jordan, not Sari'El. The only person who calls me that is Marina."

"Yes...she does," said Bains, looking deep into his eyes, "and I find that very interesting."

"It's just a made-up name. It doesn't mean anything."

"No, I can assure you it is not a made-up name," said Bains as she walked around to the other side of the table, "and if she calls you that, it most definitely means something."

Bains pondered him. "So, what does it mean, Sari'El, that you are here?"

Moving closer, she placed her hand on his chest, pressing down gently until from under her palm a purplish light came to life. Growing in intensity, the light radiated out from between her fingers and the edges of her palm, as though she were holding down a tiny sun that threatened to burst from his chest. When she took her hand away, the light vanished, and she stepped back, looking at Chance, perplexed.

"You don't remember," she said, disbelievingly. "You don't know."

"Remember what?" said Chance, both bewildered and frightened. "What did you just do to me?"

Bains reached up and turned off the large parabolic operating room light over the table upon which Chance was bound. Again she studied him; her arms folded across her chest.

With the light off, Chance could see more of the room around him, the most unnerving aspect being a large body-shaped clear plastic shroud hanging ten feet above him. Across the room was another table, identical to the one he was on, but that table was unoccupied. High on the wall was a large window to a room that overlooked the lab below. Chance noticed that the center pane was broken out.

"Kahn'Ra!" shouted Bains.

Chance did not know what the word meant, but he looked to Bains nonetheless, and was instantly horror-stricken when Martin stepped up beside her.

"Yes, Baka'El," said Martin, his eyes filled with hate as he glared unblinkingly at Chance.

"Summon the Seer," ordered Bains.

Martin stared for a moment longer, then with a slight smirk, he turned and walked out of the lab. As he left, Bains stepped closer to Chance, her eyes moving hungrily over his body.

"I had hoped to avoid this," said Bains sincerely as she ran her finger across Chance's chest, then lifted it to her lips, savoring its taste. "You are, after all, so very pretty."

Chance wanted to ask what she intended to do, but instead found himself fighting back an unexplained attraction to the woman. It caused him to stir, if ever so slightly, and Bains noticed that stirring.

Looking back to his eyes, she smiled innocently. "Did I do that?"

Bending down she kissed his cheek, causing him to look away, his face red with embarrassment. At that moment, the lab's large doors swung open violently and Martin walked back into the room with Mrs. Ross following close behind.

"Hello, Mama," said Bains, smiling.

"Hello, sweetie," said Mrs. Ross, walking up beside Bains, who bent down and kissed the kindly woman on each cheek.

Mrs. Ross took a moment to look Chance over.

"Oh, my," she said, sounding impressed, "I can see why you are so interested in this one."

Her eyes lingered on Chance for a moment before she walked over to a table where she put down her purse and opened it.

"Would you like a Butterscotch?" she asked as she rummaged through it.

"No, thank you, Mama," said Bains with a pleasant, patient expression.

"Anyone?" asked Mrs. Ross as she looked around the room at the various techs, while holding out a golden-wrapped hard candy in her gloved hand.

All politely declined.

"No?" said Mrs. Ross, obviously disappointed. "Very well, more for me then."

Snapping her purse closed, Mrs. Ross straightened her skirt, then regarded Bains with a smile. "Now, sweetie, what can I do for you?" she asked.

"Mama," began Bains, gesturing toward Chance, "I believe this human may be Sari'El."

"Really?" said Mrs. Ross looking him up and down. "The War Bringer Prime? Well, if nothing else, he certainly looks the part."

"Look lady, I told you my name is Chance Jordan. I'm not this Sari'El person you think I am."

"See what I'm dealing with, Mama?" said Bains, exasperated.

"Did you look into his Light?"

"Moments ago."

"And what did you see?"

"That he does not know he is Sari'El."

"Perhaps he is not the great warrior," said Mrs. Ross looking at Bains, but Bains said nothing.

"Nonetheless, you believe that he is."

Bains only nodded.

Mrs. Ross took a deep breath. "Very well," she said, looking at Chance as she walked around the table to a position directly behind his head.

"What are you gonna do?" asked Chance, straining to look back at her.

"Shh...shh...shh, be calm, young man," cooed Mrs. Ross. "This won't hurt a bit."

Reaching out, she spread the fingers of her gloved hands over Chance's face. She did not touch him. Instead, she held her hands hovering just an inch from his skin.

Chance's eyes almost immediately rolled back in his head. His shoulders slumped, and his eyelids fluttered, as his body twitched in irregular spasms.

The ancient Seer closed her eyes as she began to tilt her head, ever so slightly from side to side, as if she were listening to distant voices. Then her brow furrowed, as if she were confused by what she heard. After several seconds, she withdrew her hands and stepped back, taking a deep breath.

"What is it Mama? What did you see?"

"He has been sealed with a powerful Celestial warding," said Mrs. Ross, both surprised and impressed. "I have only seen a warding of this magnitude once before."

She circled the table, looking at Chance with a new found respect. Still groggy, Chance tried to follow her with his eyes, but his head lolled as if he were drunk.

"Is he Sari'El?" asked Bains anxiously.

"I could not see. That truth is behind the seal, but make no mistake, even if he is not Sari'El, this young man is no ordinary Creature of Light," said Mrs. Ross with a grave expression on her face. "This child was placed on earth in the flesh for a purpose. A purpose that He That Is Three intended to keep a secret. Even from him. And this is no Taking. He was born in the flesh, severed from his Celestial past, and that past hides behind the seal."

"That would explain why he is accompanied by a Guardian," said Bains, thinking out loud.

Mrs. Ross turned and stared at Bains shocked. "He has a Guardian?"

"Relax Mama, I have secured the Guardian in a holding cell," said Bains, "she is no longer a threat."

Mrs. Ross now looked horrified. "His Guardian is here?"

"It is sedated," explained Bains.

"It must be HEAVILY sedated," said Mrs. Ross, panic tainting her voice. "If it gains even a moment of clarity, and senses that its ward is in distress, it will come, laying waste to everything and every one of us."

"It is heavily sedated. I have taken every precaution," said Bains, her voice losing some of its patience. "Now...can you break the seal?"

In her panic, Mrs. Ross had almost completely forgotten about Chance. Now her attention re-engaged, as she turned to look upon him once again. Smoothing her skirt and giving the bottom of her blazer a tug, she composed herself.

"I can try," she said, sounding doubtful, "but if I force open the seal, the warded memories could possibly evaporate, leaving only an empty, mindless vessel. Your prize would be lost."

"Good," said Martin. "Let Sari'El die."

Bains shot Martin a look that drove his eyes to the floor.

"I had hoped to turn him," she said, looking back to Mrs. Ross.

"Even if you did turn him, the seal would remain. He does not control it," said Mrs. Ross, then she paused for a moment, thinking.

"What is it, Mama?"

"The Guardian. Perhaps the Guardian controls it. But it would be too dangerous to wake it enough to try."

"Is it possible to break the seal without destroying him?" asked Bains hopefully.

Mrs. Ross looked at Chance and sighed, "Yes, it is possible, but highly unlikely."

"I will have to risk it. I need to find out what the Triad is up to."

"Please turn down the lights," said Mrs. Ross, walking back to the head of the table, tugging on the fingers of her gloves as she did.

The lights in the lab dimmed until the room was nearly dark, the only light being a soft beam that illuminated Chance's body and Mrs. Ross' face.

As Mrs. Ross pulled her gloves off, Chance's eyes widened in horror. The woman's hands, which had appeared normal while in her gloves, became gnarled and disfigured as they pulled free. Their skin was black with age, as if they had been mummified thousands of years before, the blackened skin stretched thin over boney fingers that were twisted like corkscrews.

"This time, it may sting a bit," she said to Chance.

Reaching out, she once again placed her hands at the sides of Chance's head. Closing her eyes, she began to whisper a chant in an ancient melodic language, long lost to time.

Chance felt a calming warmth wash over him, an intoxicating peacefulness that left his body limp. But that sense of well-being was short lived.

Looking up at the old woman, Chance saw her begin to quake as if electrified. Her fingers began to elongate, growing out in undulating coils until they were at least twelve inches long. Then their tips split open, forming the mouths of vipers that hissed and snapped, striking out and latching onto Chance's face.

Chance cried out in pain as their fangs sank into his flesh, their venom burning a straight line down to the center of his skull. Convulsing, his eyes wild with pain, he looked up at the old woman pleadingly, but his face turned ashen as her eyes met his.

The old woman's kindly appearance was gone, replaced by a dark weathered skin stretched like crepe paper over her skull. Her lips, dry and shrunken, had curled back in a snarl, revealing brown and rotted teeth. Her eyes, a sickening jaundiced yellow, stared back into his, as the veins in his face and neck bulged, and his mouth opened in a scream of agony.

FORTY-NINE

A medical technician, dressed in surgical scrubs, walked along the stark hallway of the detention wing of the White Mountain Research Facility. Following behind was a soldier in black tactical armor, carrying an assault weapon.

The facility had been placed on high alert since the capture teams had returned from Wellington, and that was not unusual. What was highly unusual, in the opinion of the trained operators that had taken part in the capture, were the security measures put in place around one of the girls they had brought back.

Specifically, they read: No one was to have contact with the prisoner without an armed escort. Only medical staff were authorized to enter the holding cell, and only for the periodic welfare checks that were to take place every thirty minutes.

That particular aspect of the security procedures wasn't the problem. It was what followed that raised eyebrows.

The armed escort was to remain outside the room with their weapon locked, loaded and trained on the prisoner. If the prisoner were to show even the slightest sign of consciousness, the security personnel were authorized to fire, expending one full magazine into the prisoner. An eighteen-year-old girl.

In an addendum to those orders, and unknown to the medical staff, security personnel had been instructed that if the need to fire presented itself, and the medical technician was in the line of fire, the med tech was expendable.

As they reached the door of detention room two, the soldier took up position and raised his weapon. Flipping its selector switch to "full auto", he nodded to the med tech indicating that he was ready.

He watched as the tech punched the code for the door's electronic lock into its keypad. When the door opened, he took a deep breath as he aimed his weapon at the unconscious girl on the bed.

The med tech entered the room and checked the girl's I.V.s, then pried her eyelids open while shining a pen light into her widely dilated pupils. There was no reaction. Finishing quickly, the med tech hurried out of the room, closing the steel door with a heavy mechanical clunk as the lock re-engaged. When the soldier heard the door lock, he relaxed, taking his finger off the trigger guard, and lowering his weapon.

Without a word, the medical technician turned and walked away, but the soldier lingered. Stepping up to the detention cell door, he stood looking through its thick glass window at the unconscious girl.

In his time as a special operator in the U.S. Army, participating in operations in Afghanistan, Syria, and several lesser known African and South American countries, he had been given some rather bizarre orders, and seen some really screwed up situations. But now, as he stood on American soil, looking at this girl in the cell, and the over-the top security measures in place around her, he couldn't help but feel this mission had gone sideways.

He had been on the capture team that had taken her and the boy. She had put up no resistance as she was pulled naked from the bed, screaming. Her eyes had only registered fear and confusion, right up to the moment she was tasered, and Dr. Bains had injected her with a sedative. It made it difficult for him to reconcile this beautiful, and seemingly harmless young woman with the national security threat he and his teammates had been told she was.

"Who are you?" he said, thinking out loud.

"Her name is Marina," came a voice from behind him.

Startled, he spun around and found himself staring into the eyes of a beautiful Japanese girl, who was looking at him through the window of the detention cell across the hall.

The girl stepped back, startled by his intense expression, and for some reason he could not explain, it bothered him that he had frightened her so. The situation cut him.

He was a warrior. Driven by duty and honor to volunteer for Special Forces training. He was one of the 'Good Guys' that defended the weak and helpless. Now he found himself kidnapping high school students, and frightening pretty girls. His sense of honor was being stretched to the breaking point.

Disconcerted and conflicted, he turned and walked down the hall. He tried to soothe the discomfort of his challenged principles with the balm of his devotion to duty, but as he looked back over his shoulder, and saw that the girl was still looking at him, his principles poked at him once again.

Kimiko watched the soldier as he walked away. A few moments before, as she had looked into his eyes, she had seen a killer, but now as she watched him go, she was not so sure. Just before the soldier had passed from view, he had looked back at her, and in that moment, she had seen empathy, even sorrow, in his troubled eyes.

Kimiko's attention turned back to Marina. She could see the girl lying on her bed, and she had been watching as the nurses periodically came and went, examining her. But what she found shocking, was how the guards would point their guns at Marina whenever they would open the door, and how despite all the poking and prodding, Marina remained still. As Kimiko watched, Bella stepped up beside her.

"How is she?" asked Bella, peering out through the window.

"It's hard to say," said Kimiko, her face etched with concern. "She hasn't moved."

"Why are they doing this to her, and not us?" wondered Bella aloud.

"You feelin' left out baby?" came Eric's voice from behind them.

"Don't worry," said Rheinhard. "They will get around to us."

"We gotta get out of here," said Conor sounding anxious.

"What?" laughed Rheinhard. "You don't want to stick around and get probed?"

"Probed?" said Conor, startled.

"Ja, probed," confirmed Rheinhard. "They have those big metal probes they stick up your ass. Makes you talk. That is, if you can stop screaming."

"Shut up, Rheinhard," said Kimiko, dismissively.

"Maybe we can pick the lock," suggested Conor.

"Dude, what lock?" said Eric, pointing at the door which was devoid of any visible locking mechanism. "Unless you've been doing summer internships with Chris Angel, we're not going through this door unless someone comes and opens it."

Kimiko walked across the room and sat down next to Conor, leaning into him as she pulled his arm around her. "We'll get out of here, lover," she said soothingly.

Bella stayed by the door, watching Marina with a look of concern. She felt an inexplicable protective inclination with regard to this strange girl that she had only just met, and seemed to have Chance all twisted in knots.

"Are you okay? asked Eric, placing his hands on Bella's shoulders.

Turning she embraced him. "I'll be fine," she said.

Looking one last time at Marina, Bella saw that she remained quiet and still on her bed. Holding Eric tightly, she buried her face into his chest.

But Marina wasn't completely motionless. Beneath her closed eyelids, her eyes darted frantically, as if she were dreaming, but it was no dream. In her mind's eye she could see Chance screaming, his eyes wide in agony, as what looked like snakes bit into his face. She could see a hideous ghostly creature floating in the air at the head of a table where Chance lay bound. She could see now that the serpents that were tearing at Chance's face were the twisted fingers of the creature's gnarled hands.

Marina's body began to violently convulse, as if it were she that was under attack, her thrashing causing the I.V. in her arm to be ripped out. Suddenly she fell motionless except for her lips that quivered as she whispered, "Sari'El."

Chance's screams shook the lab. Straining against his restraints, his torso arched off the harvesting table as pain forced his body to violently convulse.

The Seer floated above him, hovering, as if held aloft by an ethereal wind. Her long white hair whipped, unbound, around her in tangled strands, as electricity arced through it like a lightning storm in a monsoon's cloud, reaching out and crawling over the walls and ceiling of the lab.

Chance could feel the Seer inside his mind, poking at him with a dagger, red hot, as if drawn from a forge. Blood ran from the wounds on his face, in crimson streams, as the serpents tore at him.

Chance felt himself breaking, and just as he was on the verge of collapse, a distant and familiar voice touched his mind.

"Sari'El."

Instantly Chance's eyes softened. His mind flittered momentarily away from the pain, as he searched for the source of the faint voice.

This fleeting distraction enraged the Seer. Feeling her grip on the boy slip, ever so slightly, she bore down, pressing harder into Chance's mind, and once again the boy's eyes locked on hers.

But the distant voice came to him again. This time clearer. This time, closer. "Sari'El."

"Marina," whispered Chance, as his body relaxed, falling back to the harvesting table.

"What did he say?" asked Martin.

"He calls the name of the Guardian," said Bains, anxiously stepping forward. "Are you sure it is secure?"

"Yes, Baka'El it was..."

But before Martin could finish his sentence, Chance's body began to rise slowly, his eyes closed, his body languid and relaxed, but still secured to the table. The Seer was confused. The boy should have been writhing in anguish from his mind being pried open, but as she looked at him, she saw a face that was almost...peaceful.

"Marina," said Chance again, his eyes opening, but not looking at the Seer. Instead, they looked through her, to a point a million miles away.

⌒

Bella leaned against Eric as a feeling of sudden cold caused a shiver to wrack her body. The conversation in the cell had died down, and the group of friends sat in silence, contemplating their fate.

Thinking once again on Marina, Bella kissed Eric on the cheek then got up and walked to the door to check on her. Stepping up to the window, she looked across the hall. What she saw made her jaw drop open.

Marina was floating in the air a few feet above her bed. Laid back, and apparently unconscious, her flaccid body was suspended, limp like a marionette hanging from its last string. Her only movement was an almost imperceptible quiver of her lips, as if she were whispering to some unseen person in the room with her.

Bella took a sudden deep breath. She wanted to calmly call Eric. She didn't want to scream. She had promised herself that she would not be the screaming girl. But when she opened her mouth, she screamed.

Everyone in the room startled, then jumped to their feet and ran to Bella, who stood with both her hands over her mouth, trying desperately to hold in the scream that had already escaped. Crowding around the small window the group stood in silent, wide-eyed horror.

"What's happening to her?" asked Bella, both worried and frightened.

"Is she alive?" asked Kimiko, crowding in next to her friend.

"It looks like she is talking to somebody," said Rheinhard.

"Marina!" yelled Bella, but there was no reaction.

"Marina!" she yelled again.

This time Marina's eyelids flew open, revealing eyes that looked like pools of black oil. At their center were irises of blue electric arcs that crackled and crawled like webs over their shining black surfaces.

The group gasped in unison.

Bella, against every effort, screamed.

Chaos reigned in the lab as the Seer fought to regain control of Chance's mind. The electrical field around her intensified as she screamed in rage.

Thick, crackling bolts of electricity shot out from her like tentacles. They scorched the walls and ceiling, carving molten trails into their surfaces, or exploding in a cascade of sparks as they came in contact with the light fixtures and equipment around the room.

The medical technicians, that had not fled from the lab in terror, had taken cover under the various desks and tables. Only Martin and Bains stood watching, seemingly unconcerned about the electrical maelstrom around them.

As they watched, Chance began to murmur. Unintelligible at first, his nascent soliloquy grew stronger and clearer, until Bains' eyebrows rose in recognition.

"He is speaking First Tongue," she said, astonished. "He must be Sari'El."

At that moment, Chance's eyes fluttered, then slowly opened. To the shock of all, his eyes were black and filled with crackling celestial energy.

"He awakens!" yelled Martin, his eyes wide in terror, as if he had just opened a gift, only to find a coiled cobra inside. Drawing a pistol from his waistband, he chambered a round and pointed it at Chance's head. "We must kill him now."

"No, you fool," said Bains, reaching out and ripping the weapon from Martin's hand. "Look."

Martin's eyes followed her outstretched hand to the needle that had been inserted into Chance's arm. The tube that had, until that moment, been filled with the deep crimson of human blood, was now glowing with a bright luminosity.

"That," said Bains, "is the pure Celestial essence of a War Bringer Prime of the Triad. A wearer of the War Hammer, and I must have it."

Looking around the darkened room, Bains' eyes fell upon a technician cowering under a table.

"You," she commanded, pointing at the terrified man, "change the collection vial."

The tech looked at her but didn't move. Unwilling to step out into the electrical tempest raging through the lab, for fear of being vaporized. Instead, he moved further back under the table.

"Do it now!" roared Bains, her eyes now pulsing with fire.

Becoming more fearful of Bains, than of being incinerated by an errant bolt of lightning, the tech darted to the harvesting table. Crouching as if under fire, he quickly attached a fresh collection vial to the blood draw tube, just as an electric charge struck the E.K.G. machine next to him, causing it to explode in a shower of sparks and bits of shrapnel.

His task completed, he dropped to the floor and scurried back to the relative safety of the of the equipment table, as white-hot torches of electricity melted crevices into the black rubberized floor around him.

Bains watched in fascinated excitement as the test-tube sized collection vial began to fill with Chance's glowing blood. Even the wounds in his face leaked light as his essence ran in luminescent rivers.

Most of the lights in the lab had been destroyed. Only the faint glow of a lone red emergency 'Exit' sign provided any visibility beyond the erratic blinding flashes strobing around the room. Consequently, Martin did not notice the dark figure in the black hooded sweatshirt and jeans that stepped up beside him. He did, however, sense its presence. An uncomfortable presence that pricked at his skin.

His attention on Bains and Chance momentarily broken, his eyes shifted, and he immediately realized that someone was standing beside him. Turning, Martin saw the black hooded figure. It seemed to be watching as the Seer bored into Chance's mind.

Martin was at first confused, not sure who the dark figure was, and so did not immediately react. Then the figure turned to regard him, and Martin found himself staring into eyes that glowed with electric blue arcs. But, just as Martin's face registered understanding, and his hand moved ever so slightly toward the pistol in his waistband, the dark figure raised its hand and a specular shockwave issued from its open palm, throwing Martin across the room.

Turning quickly, the shadowy figure unleashed another shockwave from its outstretched hand. The pulse drove both Bains and the Seer away from Chance, and slammed them against the wall, causing the Seer's frightening visage to instantly return to that of the motherly Mrs. Ross, as her contact with Chance was broken.

Chance now lay unmoving. Falling back, unconscious, onto the harvesting table's contoured surface, his eyes returning to normal as they closed.

The dark figure walked slowly to Chance's side and gently removed his restraints. Scooping up his limp body, the mysterious intruder turned away from the table, holding Chance in its arms.

One of the medical personnel, watching from beneath a table was moved by the tender, almost loving way the black hooded figure cradled the frail, seemingly lifeless boy. Walking barefoot, it proceeded across the laboratory floor, unperturbed by the thousands of glass shards that covered it.

As it walked, it raised its hand, and an Ingwaz exploded into existence. Stepping into the black pool, the dark figure and the boy vanished in a flash of light.

A sepulchral silence fell thick over the lab. The only sound, the intermittent crackle of damaged light fixtures as they shorted and sparked.

Off to one side, a large table that lay mangled against the wall moved slightly. It flew into the air, crashing to the floor, as Martin stood up from where the shock wave had flung and buried him.

"He's gone!" yelled Bains angrily. "How?"

"It was his Guardian," said Martin.

"No, that is not possible," said Bains, stunned.

"I saw the Guardian with my own eyes. It was the same Astri Celestial that saved Sari'El in the forest."

Bains ran to the harvesting table and saw that the glowing vial of blood was still there. Reaching down she plucked it from its holder. Holding it up, she gazed at it, dazzled. Then her eyes narrowed in anger.

"I want to know how the Guardian escaped!" she roared.

⌐

The group of captives all crowded around the door of their tiny cell, transfixed by the preternatural scene playing out in the cell across the hall. Marina, a girl they had only heard of before today, lie limp and unflinching while floating a few feet above her bed. Her head was back, and her eyes open revealing eyes of a nightmare. Intense and blue, they looked like tiny plasma globes. Then, without an apparent reason, they returned to normal, and she fell back to her bed, unconscious.

"What happened? Is she okay?" asked Bella, her voice filled with concern.

"I don't know what she is," murmured Eric pensively.

Further discourse was cut off by the sound of a door lock buzzing down the hall, followed by heavy, thundering footfalls running toward them. Bella strained to see what was happening, pressing her face against the glass, but she jumped back as a group of soldiers darted into view, their weapons raised. Two of the soldiers pointed their rifles at the group through the window, another two directed their weapons at Marina.

"Step back away from the door!" commanded one of the soldiers threateningly, his hand flexing on the pistol grip of his assault rifle.

The frightened teens moved quickly to the far side of the cell, clinging to one another. One of the soldiers looked in at them, then crossed to Marina's cell and peered in through the window. Touching his earpiece, he began to speak.

"The girl is here, and unresponsive," he said calmly, in contrast to the aggressive, ready to fight posture his team had assumed. But his transmission was met with an uneasy silence.

"Copy last?" he finally asked.

"Are you sure?" came Bains' voice over the ear pieces of each team member. The question made them look at one another baffled.

"Yes, ma'am. I'm looking at her now."

Another long silence ensued.

"Bring her to me," said Bains at last. "Bring all the prisoners to me."

FIFTY

When Chance awoke, he was disoriented. The room he was in flickered with firelight, and as he looked up, he could see shadows undulating over a massive expanse of natural rock. Realizing he was on a bed, he sat up and took in his surroundings.

The room was filled with enormous stalactites that hung from the ceiling, and equally massive stalagmites jutting up from the floor. The cavern made him feel as though he were in the maw of a giant beast, the light of torches dancing off its shining fangs.

Looking at himself he discovered that he was dressed in blue jeans that were not his. Swinging his legs out of the bed, he sat up, touching his feet to the cold stone floor of the cave. On the foot of the bed lay a white shirt. Taking it, he slipped it around his shoulders.

Holding his head in his hands, he tried to push away the fugues. He wondered if it all had been a dream? He wondered if he were dreaming still?

As he sat in his fog, movement caught his eye. When he looked up, he saw a girl enter the room carrying a tray upon which sat a large steaming cup.

He watched as the girl cautiously approached, and upon seeing that he was looking at her, she cast her eyes down. Stopping in front of him, she held out the tray tentatively, as though she, and the contents of the tray might be deemed somehow unworthy.

Chance couldn't help but stare. The girl had a strange, ageless beauty, and though he tried to guess her years, he could not. As soon as he came to a tentative conclusion, a shadow would cross her face, and his opinion would change.

Her skin was pale, so pale it seemed to glow. Her hair, a breathtaking cascade of white, flowed to her waist and floated on the air as she moved.

Chance reached out and took the mug. Sniffing it, he discovered that it was some kind of broth. Holding the warm vessel in both hands, he drank and immediately felt his energy return as the hot broth spread out through his body.

"Thank you," he said, but the girl did not look at him.

Tipping his head, he tried to look into her eyes, but she only bowed her head further.

"What's your name?" he asked, gently.

Without explanation, the girl began to shake. She was terrified by his question. Her hands gripped the tray as if it were the only thing keeping her upright.

Chance's empathy panged. He could not understand why this girl was so afraid of him, but felt terrible that she was.

Reaching out he placed his hand on hers, hoping to reassure her that she was safe, but the gesture had the opposite effect. As his fingers touched her hand, she recoiled, dropping her serving tray as though she had been burned. Stepping back, her terrified eyes at last rose to meet his.

Now it was Chance who felt the cold hand of terror gripping his heart. He looked into the girl's ghostly eyes, her irises as snow white as her hair, and recoiled in shock. Startled, he dropped his cup of broth, and it shattered at his feet.

The girl cowered, seemingly torn between a desire to flee, or beg for mercy. Her obvious confusion snapped Chance out of his shock at her appearance, and he attempted to console her.

"Don't be afraid. I'm not going to hurt you," he said almost pleadingly. "You have no reason to fear me."

"She has every reason to fear you," came a voice from the shadows. "She knows what you are, and she knows who you are."

Chance's head jerked around in the direction of the voice. Shading his eyes, he searched the shadows beyond the burning torches for its source.

As his eyes adjusted, he saw a dark shape perched on a boulder. It was wearing black jeans and a hoodie that was pulled up over its head. It sat with its knees pulled up to its chest, its arms wrapped around them as it rested its head on its forearms. Chance immediately recognized the dark figure from his dreams.

"Vielen dank, Claudia. Das ist alles," said the dark figure.

The girl squatted down and collected the shards of broken cup, placing them on her tray. Rising, and still obviously trembling, she quickly bowed to Chance and the dark figure before retreating.

Chance's eyes followed the girl as she scurried to the chamber's door. As she passed through it, he noticed a woman standing in the passageway.

She was stunningly beautiful. Tall and elegant with pale skin, dressed in a flowing white lace gown that buttoned up the front with black pearls. The cuffs of its long sleeves, and its standing collar were adorned with delicate silver embroidery. Around her neck she wore a golden chain upon which hung a red, heart shaped stone, that provided a shock of color.

She stood watching, her white eyes fixed on Chance, as her snow-white hair, billowed around her in wisping strands, as if spun from clouds. The ghostly woman studied Chance for a moment, a look of interest and fascination on her flawless face. Then turning on her heel, she was gone.

Chance's attention now turned back to the dark figure. Standing, he pointed at the doorway where the girl had fled.

"Why was she so afraid of me?" he asked seriously. "Who does she think I am?"

"The answer to both of those questions is the same. You are Sari'El."

The statement struck Chance like a hammer.

"They know you from nineteen years ago," continued the dark figure, "and from thousands of years before that, when as the Tyr of the Triad, you hunted them down and slaughtered them on sight, as abominations and traitors."

Chance's mind was spinning as he tried to process the insanity of these words. Words that he knew in his heart, were true.

"Who are you?" he asked.

"I am, as you require," came the cryptic reply.

But Chance was in no mood for cryptic. "OK, smart ass. I 'require' you to take off that hood, and tell me who the hell you are," he said.

At this, the dark figure slid off the rock and approached Chance, which made Chance take a small step back. As it stepped up to Chance, it stopped, pulling its hood back. Chance drew a surprised breath.

"Jäger?" said Chance. "What are you doing here?"

"I am here because you needed me to be here. I had to protect your mission."

"My mission? What mission?"

"I can say no more."

For some reason, Chance understood that. "Where am I?" he asked, looking around at the cavern.

"You are in the lair of the Weisse Frau. Deep in the Thüringen Mountains," replied Jäger.

"The lair of the what?"

"The White Lady," translated Jäger.

"And, why did you bring me here?"

"You were in danger. A Seer was attempting to expose your soul, and I needed someplace where you could not be found. I was able to convince the White Lady to allow me to bring you here."

Chance was stunned. His mind raced through the images in his mind. "All that shit...really happened?" he said, looking at Jäger with startled, and frightened eyes.

Jäger said nothing.

Chance sat back down on the bed as he began to sort through those images. Realizing that they were not nightmares, but memories, terrified him – a witch with snakes for fingers, the searing pain, Bains, Martin...

"Marina!" he exclaimed at last. "She is still there. They have her. I have to go back!"

"There is nothing you can do," said Jäger.

"You got me out. Get her out."

"No, she is not essential."

"Essential?" said Chance, flabbergasted as he rose from the bed to confront Jäger. "What the fuck are you talking about?!"

"She is not essential to our mission," clarified Jäger in a calm, collected voice.

"She's essential to me," said Chance, taking a threatening step toward Jäger, but the diminutive boy was unimpressed.

Anger and frustration surged through Chance. He wanted to lash out, to somehow force Jäger to help him rescue Marina, but he could not bring himself to raise a hand against him. For reasons he could not explain, Chance felt not only a companionship with the boy, but a deep abiding respect for an authority he perceived around him.

Chance's panic and rage grew, then without warning, he wailed in agony, clutching his head as white-hot knives burned through his mind. Falling to his knees, Chance strained, writhing in anguish, as visions of Marina strapped to the same table upon which he had been bound and tortured filled his consciousness. He saw the witch, her serpent hands tearing into Marina as she screamed.

"No!" he roared, striking the cave floor with both fists.

His eyes locked on Jäger, and a spark danced across them, then another, and another. A blackness began to flood his eyes, as if up-welling through his pupils until both were filled with what looked like glistening oil. His irises sparked to life, in a ring of blueish electric arcs, that grew more and more intense.

Jäger's normally quiescent expression gave way to dismay, then his own eyes filled with celestial energy. He watched as Chance rose to his feet. For a moment the two Creatures of Light stood silently, staring at one another, the tension in the room heavy, and palpable.

"Hello, Sari'El," said Jäger calmly. "It has been a long time."

"Indeed, it has my friend," said Chance.

"You know this meeting should not have been possible," said Jäger, regaining his composure. "How is it that you are able to pierce the veil?"

"I do not know. But how it has come to pass is unimportant. All that matters now is Zisa," said Chance using Marina's celestial name. "Why is she here?"

Chance's eyes demanded an explanation, but Jäger hesitated.

"Why?" insisted Chance.

"It was necessary. But you were not written to meet her. That you did has terminated many important timelines, and opened other possible outcomes. Outcomes that were not intended, or accounted for," said Jäger.

"I must go to her, now," said Chance

"No," said Jäger forcefully, "To do so would put you at risk, and you are vital to the last viable timeline. Your mission can still be accomplished."

"I will not allow Zisa to perish at the hands of a Fallen," said Chance through clenched teeth.

Jäger's face creased, as if not believing what he had just heard.

"Sari'El, what is wrong with you? Your priorities have been torn asunder. You yourself wrote the parameters of this mission. We all agreed, even Zisa. All of us understood the risks."

"I cannot permit her light to be extinguished due to my doing nothing."

"Many will die before this is over. Many will be lost, but a deviation now could cost thousands to have their energy scattered needlessly."

"Not her, not if I can prevent it," said Chance determinedly. " She was not supposed to be here. You placing her here has already altered the timeline. Now it is in flux."

"Your love for Zisa, is overriding your reason," said Jäger.

"That may very well be, but it changes nothing," said Chance. "A Seer is at this moment attempting to crack Zisa's Warding."

"It will be fruitless," said Jäger, confidently. "Zisa will implode her mind before she would allow that."

"Exactly, and that is why I must go for her."

Extending his arm, Chance pointed his finger and immediately a universe of stars in a shimmering black pool began to expand from its tip in a swirling vortex of light and color. Then, just as quickly as it had begun, the Ingwaz collapsed into nothing.

Chance looked around, confused, until he realized that he had been encapsulated in a sphere of swirling red smoke. Jäger stood on the outside, looking in as Chance walked up to the wall of the sphere and touched it with his open hand. Radiating from his hand, the smoke solidified, growing brighter, as a corona of red energy outlined his fingers.

Chance looked at Jäger as he stepped back from the wall.

"A Blutsphäre? Really?" said Chance, both annoyed and amused.

"I'm sorry, Sari'El," said Jäger, his expression softening, "but I cannot let you go."

"Remove this now," said Chance forcefully.

"I will not," said Jäger, with equal force.

Chance raised his hand, and as he did, a shining black orb appeared, hovering just above his palm. It pulsed with celestial power, blue electric arcs slithering over its glassy surface. Then, with incredible power, he hurled the orb directly at Jäger.

When the orb struck the surface of the swirling energy field, it exploded in a brilliant flash of light, its energy discharging into the smoke like lightening crawling through a burning thunderstorm as it dissipated.

The cavern quaked violently, causing Jäger to stumble back as a giant stalactite crashed to the cave floor a few meters away. Regaining his balance, Jäger squared up on Chance.

"This is not helping our mission," said Jäger, angered and clearly restraining himself.

"Then to hell with the mission!" shouted Chance.

At this Jäger stood shocked, the anger he had been restraining braking free. "You have been too long in the flesh, Sari'El."

"And you have been too long without a soul," retorted Chance as he launched another orb at his prison's wall.

The cavern shook again, and as the walls trembled, the woman in white ran into the room, a look of concern on her face. Seeing her expression, Jäger held out his hand in reassurance that all was well.

"You know this can't hold me for much longer."

"True," agreed Jäger, fully aware that under the hammer of a War Bringer, his Blutsphäre would soon crack like an egg. "But, it will hold you long enough for fate to take its course."

Chance understood what Jäger was saying. Eventually he would destroy the Blutsphäre, but it would take time, more time than Marina had. Realizing he only had one card to play, he played it.

"I declare the right of agency," he said calmly.

Jäger stared at Chance stunned. Agency, the right of choice and self-determination, was the highest law of the Astri. Especially those in the flesh. Chance's invoking of it changed everything. A Creature of Light declaring agency, was free to make any choice, and thereby suffer any consequence. But there were rules.

"As your Guardian, I have the right to counsel you," said Jäger.

"And what counsel could you bring, that would convince me to abandon someone I love to such a fate?"

Jäger looked down thinking. When he looked back up at Chance, his eyes had returned to normal, and the swirling sphere of smoke was gone.

"I will need you for this, my old warrior," said Chance, walking up to Jäger, one of his most trusted lieutenants, and placing his hand his shoulder. "When this battle lays on, I will need you to get Marina and the others free of it, and to safety."

"I will do this on one condition," said Jäger. "When the battle is done, you will allow me to purge your mind. You will return to cover, and there wait for the moment your mission calls you forth."

Chance considered this briefly, then nodded. "Agreed."

"And do not forget," continued Jäger gravely, "since you join this battle of your own free choosing, I will not be able to interfere with its outcome."

"I understand," said Chance.

"Keep in mind also, you cannot afford to underestimate your opponent, nor over estimate yourself. You are only just awakened from your seclusion, and recently addled by a powerful compound. You are weak, and more vulnerable now than you have ever been before."

Chance nodded his understanding.

"Very well," said Jäger, as he turned and walked toward the arched entrance of the cavern's room, where he joined the White Lady. Standing side by side they watched as Chance opened an Ingwaz and vanished in a brilliant flash of light.

"Sari'El has changed," said the White Lady.

Jäger took the woman's hand and rested his head against her arm. "He has found love," he said, wistfully, "and love changes us all."

The White Lady looked down at Jäger and smiled. Bending down she kissed the top of his head,

Yes, it does," she said with a sigh. "Yes, it does."

FIFTY-ONE

The laboratory was, once again, a chaotic maelstrom of random electrical charges, but this time it was Marina's anguished cries that echoed through the room. Hovering over her was the Seer, its serpent fingers biting into her face.

Marina's dark red blood flowed through a clear blood draw tube to collection vials, and watching the process closely, was Bains. She waited for any sign that the girl's celestial being was surfacing. If it did, and the girl's blood turned to light, Bains was ready.

Bains was nearly shaking with anticipation. She already possessed the blood essence of a War Bringer, but now with this girl she believed she had something else. What, however, she did not know.

She no longer believed that Marina was a Guardian. That disastrous error having played itself out when the actual Guardian had appeared and claimed Sari'El. Still, this girl had opened and passed through an Ingwaz, which meant she could draw on energy from beyond the veil, something only a Celestial being of considerable power should be capable of.

Adding to the mystery, the Seer had discovered that the girl was as strongly warded as Sari'El had been, and just as the boy, this girl had no idea of the secrets locked deep within her. Bains did not know what Marina was, or what her purpose for being on earth in the flesh might be, but if she had to tear the girl's soul apart to find out, she would.

The other captives sat terrified, their hands and feet bound with zip-tie handcuffs, as they huddled in the corner of the lab. The strobing of electric discharges emphasized their horror-stricken faces, as Martin stood over them, his eyes glowing like burning embers, as he menaced the group with a pistol.

The strain of suppressing his desire to kill was showing on his face. He was wet with sweat, and his body shook like a junkie in need of a fix. Worse than that, his flesh looked like it was beginning to rot, as large sores had opened up, from which fetid pus oozed.

Martin was indifferent to his condition. He was instead, fascinated by the varied reactions of his victims to the threat of an impending violent death. As the muzzle of his weapon moved from one face to the next, he studied them. Some looked away, as if not seeing the gun somehow made them safer. Others looked down the barrel with terror-stricken expressions, waiting for the bullet to emerge that would shatter and end them. Eric Easton seemed defiant, but the reaction that got Martin's attention the most was that of the Japanese girl, Kimiko.

She seemed unimpressed by the threat he posed, and this annoyed him. She watched his eyes, emotionlessly. Then her expression changed, to one of befuddlement as the girl's attention was drawn away by something behind him.

Martin turned, following Kimiko's eyes, then stepped back in surprise when he saw an intensely bright flood of light building outside the door. It leaked in through the door's tiny windows, and from the gaps around its edges, as if a giant search light was coming to life in the hallway outside.

Martin raised his hands, shading his eyes. Just as he did, the door exploded inward, the blast knocking him to the floor, flinging furniture and lab equipment in all directions.

As the door disintegrated, light flooded into the room, causing Martin to wince from its lux. Then just as it had come, the light withdrew, and Chance Jordan stepped through the ruined threshold.

Chance surveyed the room until his eyes fell upon the Seer. It hovered over Marina, still attached to her face by its serpent fingers. When the Seer saw him, its eyes grew wide, like yellowed cue balls pressed into her mummified skull, and let out a shrieking, piercing wail.

Chance did not hesitate. His hand shot out sharply toward the Seer, and the shrieking stopped as the witch began to flail violently in the air as if being crushed by some unseen force that shook her like a doll. The snakes that were attached to Marina released, and began snapping at the pulverizing force that held the Seer aloft.

Chance's electric eyes bored into the panicking witch, his face creased and shaking with rage. Then he clenched his fist. The Seer let out a stifled scream and went limp, the sickening sound of its bones being crushed filling the air. When the Seer fell motionless, Chance released her, and the witch's broken corpse dropped to the floor in a heap.

Martin at last rose from where he had been thrown, and a cold terror ran through the body of his vessel, as he looked into the vengeful eyes of a War Bringer of the Triad. The Fallen assessed his situation. His flesh vessel was beginning to decompose as it burned up from the inside, the smell of rotting flesh strong in the air. He knew he would soon abandon it. Knowing he could not do single battle with a Warrior of Light, he chose retreat.

As Chance looked into the rotting human's eyes, he saw them change from the burning embers of a Fallen, back to normal. For a brief moment, Martin's eyes beheld Chance pleadingly.

"Help me," said the rotting boy.

But as the words left his mouth, his head spun three-hundred and sixty degrees, the bones in his neck snapping like a stalk of twisted celery. His head flopped, as his body fell limp to the floor.

Red electric arcs began crawling over Martin's lifeless corpse. Growing in intensity, they rose in vertical fingers that congealed into columns, that twisted into whirling flame devils of raw energy.

Spreading out, the flame devils began to take on shape until solidifying into the winged form of a Fallen. Its broad fleshy wings quivered, then flapped rhythmically as it rose into the air. Letting loose a shriek, it pounded its wings, launching itself upward dissolving as it passed through the ceiling and vanished.

Chance stood looking up at the ceiling through which the Fallen had fled, its surface covered in an incongruous mixture of scorch marks and ice crystals. The only sound in the room was Bella's frightened whimpering. As he looked at the group of teens still bound in the corner, he saw them look back at him in silence, unsure if he was friend or foe.

"What would you have me do?" asked Jäger, stepping up beside him.

"Please get them clear of this place," said Chance, pointing to his friends. "I will meet you outside."

Jäger wordlessly nodded, then turned and walked over to the group of teens. Kneeling down he touched their plastic restraints with the tip of his finger, and the zip-ties melted, snapping off.

Chance turned and went to Marina on the harvesting table, as Jäger opened an Ingwaz and motioned the stunned group of teens toward it. Tentatively they rose, looking awestruck. At times Jäger was forced to take them by the hands to reassure them that they were safe.

One by one they walked to the Ingwaz and stepped through, until only Eric remained. The boy paused, looking back at his best friend, trying to make sense out of all that he had seen.

As Chance removed Marina's restraints, he sensed Eric watching, and turned to regard him. He saw the questions in his friend's eyes, and his heart went out to him, but now was not the time.

"You should go," he said.

Eric paused for a moment, then nodded. Turning, he stepped into the shimmering membrane and was gone.

Returning his attention back to Marina, Chance realized that she was semiconscious, looking up at him with unfocused eyes. Leaning down he kissed her tenderly.

"Be still, I'm going to get you out of here."

Gently, he finished removing the last of her restraints, and pulled the blood draw needle from her arm. Lifting her limp body from the table, he turned and carried her to the Ingwaz where Jäger stood waiting.

Stepping up to him, Chance laid Marina into Jäger's arms. Despite Jäger's diminutive stature, it was as though Chance had given him a feather pillow.

"Please protect her," said Chance.

"It will be done," said Jäger.

Turning to leave, he stopped when Chance placed a hand on his shoulder.

"Thank you, Kerub'El," said Chance.

"Good luck, my friend," said Jäger, before stepping through the Ingwaz.

The lab was now silent, but Chance knew he was not alone.

"How charming," came Bains' voice, booming with a preternatural quality it had not possessed before as it reverberated in the cathedral-like laboratory.

Chance turned slowly; his electric eyes glowing as he scanned the debris.

"Hello Baka'El," said Chance.

"Who is she, Sari'El, this child you risk your life for?"

"I risk nothing."

"You risk more than you realize."

"From who? You?" said Chance, chuckling. "I find you overconfidence amusing."

"And I find your arrogance predictable," retorted Bains.

"You cannot stand against me. You are alone. Your minion has fled."

"I do not stand alone," said Bains as she stepped out from behind a pile of wreckage, her eyes pulsing intensely with the glow of burning embers, but at the same time crawling with the blue electric arcs of pure Celestial energy.

"You see, Sari'El," said Bains, holding up the glowing vial of his blood, "I have you, to stand with me."

Chance now saw that in her other hand she held a syringe. It glowed, slightly, with the residue of his Celestial blood, a droplet hanging like a tiny star from its tip, and on her arm, a glowing pinhole wound.

"You are an abomination," said Chance, his voice a mixture of anger and revulsion.

"Yeah," said Bains, rolling her eyes, amused, "I get that a lot."

Chance squared himself off with the Fallen. Opening his hand, a shining black orb appeared, floating above his palm. It crackled with blue electric arcs that floated over its surface, and intertwined with his fingers.

Bains let the syringe fall from her hand. Her eyes followed it until it stuck, like a dart in the lab's rubber floor. She looked back at Chance and held out her hand, as an orb formed over her open palm, pulsating with both the red energy of a Fallen, and the blue Celestial energy of a Warrior of Light. She smiled at his surprised expression.

"As you can see, Sari'El," said Bains in a smooth, seductive voice, "you are part of me now."

Chance was done talking. With a well-practiced agility, he hurled his orb, striking Bains, driving her back into a pile of metal tables and broken equipment, the glowing vial of Celestial blood falling from her grasp.

Silence fell over the room. Nevertheless, Chance stood tensed, a second orb already crackling in his hand.

Moving cautiously forward, Chance peered into the tangle of debris and saw Bains' body lying motionless. Relaxing, he allowed the orb in his hand to wink out as he turned and walked toward the lab's door, unaware that a shadow was slowly rising behind him.

When the first orb struck Chance, it stunned him, driving him to his knees. Then a second orb hit him, blowing him across the room and smashing him against the wall.

Straining to remain conscious, Chance rose to his feet. He watched as Bains rose into the air, her glowing eyes fixed on him as two more orbs formed in her hands.

Chance took a deep, calming breath, then locked his eyes on Bains as he rose into the air to meet her, lightening orbs crackling to life in both hands.

FIFTY-TWO

Confusion reigned as alarms sounded, and black-uniformed security personnel swarmed around the White Mountain Research Facility.

Unnoticed by any of them, a pinpoint of light winked into existence a few feet above the ground, just outside the perimeter fence. The pinpoint grew in intensity until finally exploding into a shimmering Ingwaz. Moments later, Conor came tumbling out of the portal followed by the others, all of them sprawling onto the damp grass. Once the last of them had come through, the Ingwaz collapsed.

Disoriented, the travelers looked around at each other, in silence. It was Bella who noticed that not everyone had arrived.

"Where is Marina?" she asked, worried.

"Chance was getting her," said Eric.

"Chance?" said Rheinhard, shocked. "Chance was in there?"

"Who do you think rescued us?"

"That thing was Chance?" said Conor, stunned.

Before Eric could respond, black-uniformed soldiers surged from the forest, their weapons leveled, as they shouted for the startled teens to lay face down on the ground. Those orders were lost, however, in a deafening explosion that knocked all of them to the ground.

The soldiers instinctively hunkered down, their heads on swivels as they assessed the threat around them. But soon the security team, as well as the group of teens, were staring uncomprehending, at the research facility.

As they watched, what looked like half of the building's roof exploded into the night sky in massive blocks of broken concrete. Brightly illuminated bolts of red and blue streaked out in all directions, causing the air to peal in thunderous screams. Then more explosions were heard, booming from within the quickly crumbling walls of the facility, and they shook the ground violently.

"Secure the prisoners to the fence," shouted one of the soldiers.

At this, the small unit of men jumped up and began dragging the frightened teens to the chain link fence, and handcuffing them to it. Some used metal handcuffs, others plastic zip-tie, flexi-cuffs.

"Keyros," shouted the soldier that seemed to be in charge.

"Sir," responded one of the men.

"Stay with the prisoners."

"Roger that," said the soldier.

"The rest of you are with me," said the team leader.

All but the soldier named Keyros took off at a jog down the fence line, their black fatigues melting into the night. Within seconds they were only partially visible as more glowing projectiles lit the night sky.

Every eye was riveted to the research building as more explosions rocked it. Colorful missiles punched holes through it at odd angles, as if the source of the bright projectiles was moving throughout the building's various floors, firing indiscriminately in every direction.

The result of this massive internal barrage was that the building was collapsing, like its walls were made from brittle clay. The heavy steel reenforced concrete structure was crumbling and falling in on itself, as if imploded by a demolitions team.

The handcuffed teens, and the lone soldier, covered themselves as more incoming missiles impacted all around them, each explosion taking out huge sections of fence, and shattering trees like stale pretzels.

Dirt and debris flew into the air as explosions thundered around them. Tree limbs and sections of fence rained down, partially burying them, as they took cover.

Inexplicably, the metal fence began to crawl with electric charges. Spreading out along its length they enveloped the young prisoners attached to it. Terrified, the teens began to scream, swatting at the spidery arcs in a vain effort to brush them away.

When the soldier, Keyros, pushed out from under the pile of broken tree limbs that had buried him, he looked at the panicking group and was momentarily stunned by the scene. Quickly regaining his composer, he leapt forward, pulling his handcuff key from his tactical vest.

Grabbing Kimiko's handcuffed wrist, he braced for the pain of an electric shock as the blue webs quickly crawled over his hand and up his arm, but to his relief and surprise, he felt nothing more than a pleasant tingling. Pulling Kimiko's wrist closer to him he stumbled, and almost fell, as the chain link fence gave way, its steel mesh shattering like glass.

The electric webs vanished instantly as contact with the fence was broken. Keyros stared perplexed, at the small hole he had torn in the fence. Reaching out, he swiped his hand at the steel mesh and watched, amazed, as a large portion of it exploded, falling to the ground in tiny shards. The discovery forced him into action.

Reaching down, Keyros took hold of Rheinhard and pulled him hard away from the fence, and again the steel links shattered. Then stepping over Rheinhard, Keyros repeated the action with Bella. Eric and Conor, seeing what the soldier had done, yanked hard at their bonds and were free, the electric webs that covered their bodies, quickly dissipating.

Keyros now returned to Kimiko. Taking hold of her handcuffed wrist yet again, he turned it so he could get to the keyhole, but was shocked when the steel Smith and Wesson handcuffs disintegrated in his hand.

Picking up a piece of broken metal, he looked at it, uncomprehending. The steel looked normal, but as he squeezed it in the palm of his gloved hand, it crumbled like a dry leaf, and even through his glove, he could feel it was cold as ice.

He did not, however, have time to ponder this mysterious discovery, as more explosive spheres impacted around their position, striking trees which splintered and fell in huge piles inside the tree line surrounding them, as they burst into bizarre, yet beautiful, blue flames.

"Everybody stay down! Keep you heads covered!" shouted Keyros over the booming explosions.

Looking around, Keyros assessed their position. The facility grounds were being pulverized. Escape into the forest was impossible due to the wall of preternatural blue flames engulfing it. He decided staying put was their best option.

Looking down, he saw Kimiko cringing with every blast. She looked at him, her dark almond-shaped eyes seemingly pleading with him to make it go away. It made him feel helpless. Unbuckling his chin strap, he removed his helmet and placed it on her head.

"Kevlar," he said, knocking on the helmet. "Nothing gets through that... you're gonna make it."

He gave her his best strained smile, and Kimiko nodded meekly, as tears rolled down her cheeks, creating tiny trails as they washed away the grime. She looked back at him, and took in his hard, yet compassionate face. It was then that she realized that he was the same soldier that she had seen outside the door of her holding cell, and she took an odd comfort in knowing he was there.

Eric lifted his head and looked around him. He saw Rheinhard face down with his arms covering his head, the giant German doing everything he could to be as small as possible. Off to the side, Kimiko and the soldier who had stayed to guard them, were lying facing one another, and Eric could see that the soldier was talking to her, and for some reason, she was now wearing his helmet.

Eric searched for Bella and found her convulsing with fear. Crawling over to her he wrapped his arms around her, and she immediately clung to him.

Resting his cheek on hers, he pulled her tightly against him. He was trying to be brave, but the fear he was feeling was overwhelming. He began to talk, speaking words of reassurance in Bella's ear, but when she took his hand and squeezed it, he was embarrassed to realize that he had been reassuring himself. Pulling Bella tighter against him, he closed his eyes and waited, morbidly wondering if it would hurt when the next explosion tore him apart.

And then...silence. A thick oppressive silence, so viscous that it seemed hard to breathe inside it. Lifting his head slowly, Eric dared a glimpse and saw his friends, and the soldier lying motionless, fires from the now burning facility building casting long shadows over their bodies.

"Is it over?" asked Bella, fear and hope mingling in her voice.

"I don't know," said Eric.

Half of him wanted to go to his friends, but the other half feared finding their broken bodies, turned inside out and mangled from the bombardment.

To his relief, one, then another, and another began to move, the thick layer of dirt that covered them, falling away as their bodies shifted. The only one that wasn't moving was Conor.

Crawling over to his friend, Eric found him unconscious, and bleeding from a gash in his forehead. After cleaning away the debris that covered him, Eric tried to wipe away the layer of loose dirt from Conor's face, but the blood only mixed with it and smeared into a macabre mask.

"Bella, come help Conor," yelled Eric, remembering that she had First Aid training.

Bella quickly came to Eric's side, and upon seeing Conor's wound, ripped a strip of cloth from the bottom of her shirt and carefully packed it. Looking over at the soldier, she called out to him.

"Do you have any water?" she asked.

The soldier and Kimiko came over, and Keyros pulled out a tube from his Camelback water pouch. Using it, Bella cleaned off Conor's wound and irrigated his eyes.

"Kimiko, hold this bandage," said Bella, taking Kimiko's hand and placing it on the blood-soaked piece of cloth covering Conor's wound. "But don't press too hard, he might have a skull fracture."

"You know what you're doing," said Keyros, impressed.

Reaching into his vest he pulled out a field dressing and tore it open.

"Here, use this," he said handing her the dressing.

Bella packed the new bandage onto the wound, and tied it to Conor's head. Next, she checked his arms and legs for other injuries.

"Is he going to be OK?" asked Kimiko.

"It's not as bad as it looks," said Keyros, "I'm sure he'll be fine."

Keyros stood and began to walk away when Kimiko spoke. "What is your name?" she asked.

Keyros looked at her a moment then answered, "My name's Chris," he said.

"Thank you, Chris," said Kimiko, taking off his helmet and handing it to him. Keyros smiled. Taking the helmet, he turned to survey the area around him.

The forest still burned with blue flames, but the trees that were either down or snapped at mid trunk, were not consumed by it. Huge sections of the perimeter fence had been obliterated, the once flat and green expanse between it and the facilities building, now a heavily cratered no man's land.

The formerly massive and imposing building was almost completely leveled, illuminated by scattered, isolated fires that had sprung up amongst its ruins. Numerous human bodies, limp and broken, lay strewn upon the ground, and amongst the twisted steel and shattered concrete. As Keyros looked on, Eric stepped up beside him.

"You OK, kid?" asked Keyros.

But Eric said nothing, and his silence made Keyros look over at him.

Eric's attention was directed skyward, and so Keyros followed his gaze. When he saw what the boy was looking at, it was his turn to stare.

There, hovering in the sky, about one hundred meters above the destroyed research facility, was the boy Chance Jordan. Around his body was a glowing energy field, that at first looked like wings. They pulsated in an almost living luminescence, made visible by the smoke from the fires below.

In each of the boy's hands were glowing spheres that were covered with electric webs, like those that had crawled over the soldier's hands moments before. And the boy was not alone.

Hovering some fifty yards away was Dr. Sabine Bains, glowing spheres clutched in both of her hands as well.

And she looked pissed.

FIFTY-THREE

Chance waited, observing Bains from across the short distance between them. As Sari'El, he had fought many battles for the Triad throughout time, but none like this.

In the past he had been one of the most dangerous celestial beings to take the field. But as he engaged in battle on this night, he knew he was a mere shadow of his former self.

As Jäger had pointed out, his awakening had left him in a sluggish, somnolent state. As he fought against the fog of his long slumber, and the effects of Bains' Catalyst, which was still pressing down upon him, he found every movement he made to require a supreme effort.

The battle he had been fighting against Bains had lasted much longer than it should have. By injecting herself with his pure Celestial essence, she had become powerful beyond design. Possessing the strength of a Warrior of Light, she had inflicted great damage on him. But Bains was also showing signs of a battle less one-sided than she had hoped for.

The smugness that had once dominated her face, had been wiped away. Nevertheless, she had reason to boast. The fact that she had been able to stand, one on one against the mighty Sari'El and still live, was unthinkable, and it filled her with hubris.

Despite her success thus far, Baka'El knew that she would not be able to defeat Sari'El unless she found a weakness to exploit before the effects of his essence within her faded, and she could already feel that happening.

Watching Sari'El closely, she searched his posture for signs he was wounded, and his face for signs of fatigue. Then she searched his eyes...yes, his eyes, they betrayed him.

For a flicker of a moment, that hung like an eternity, Sari'El had glanced down at the small group of humans huddled by the tree line and Baka'El had seen it. In that almost undetectable furtive glance, she knew she had found the weakness she had been looking for. Sari'El loved these mortal creatures, and that love would destroy him.

Streaking high into the night sky, Baka'El launched two, red glowing, spheres at the helpless group of humans below.

"Everybody down!" screamed Keyros as he saw the incoming orbs.

The group scattered, diving to the ground. Bella threw her body over Conor in an effort to protect him, and upon seeing this, Kimiko did the same.

Keyros braced for the explosion, but when the muffled sound of it only boomed in the air, he realized that the missiles had not impacted his position. Looking up, he understood why.

Hovering above him was the boy his team had snatched out of the dormitory at Wellington Academy and Keyros could not believe what he was seeing. The boy had taken up a position about fifty meters overhead, and was shielding the defenseless group from the incoming fire. As more orbs came in, Keyros watched as the boy was pummeled like a fighter pinned against a cage wall.

The attacks took their toll on Bains as well. With every Lightning Sphere she launched, Chance could see the energy field around her fade and flicker as she used the power of his stolen Celestial essence. But while he knew that the power his blood had bestowed upon her would eventually ware off, he also knew that he would not be able to endure the punishment of her continued attacks much longer.

Trying to draw her fire away from his friends, Chance darted out at angles, launching return salvos, but Baka'El was relentless. She knew the War Bringer's love for the humans would compel him to sacrifice himself, placing himself in the line of fire to protect them. Counting on this, she concentrated her attacks on the helpless group.

Gaining altitude, Bains could see the lights of local towns and cities glowing in the distance. In a further effort to distract Chance, she unleashed a barrage in their direction.

Chance was torn by the sickening choice Baka'El had given him, but it only served to strengthen his resolve to destroy her.

Eric saw that the forest around him had become impassable by the tangle of broken trees and an eerie wall of blue flame. In the other direction was a wide-open space, pockmarked with the craters of hundreds of explosions, with more detonating every second. But all of this was secondary to the reality of his best friend Chance, fighting a pitched ariel battle overhead.

The two combatants moved so fast, and changed directions so quickly, that at times they were no more than a sparkling knot of light in the sky. The glowing missiles they issued sizzled with a sibilant sound as they cut through the night air that had become as cold as winter.

Some missed their targets, impacting in the forest, adding to the destruction there. Others streaked across the sky and over the horizon. But those that found their mark, did so with terrible effect. If not deflected by the glowing energy fields around Chance and Bains, the orbs exploded on impact, jolting the recipient, as frighteningly aggressive arcs of electricity spread out over their shields, seemingly eating away at them.

Eric could see what was happening. Chance was sacrificing himself to protect those on the ground. He could not maneuver, and as long as they were exposed, they were his weakness.

Eric searched for a way to get the group away, to give Chance an opportunity to fight without having to worry about them. But the barrier of blue flame made that impossible. And that's why what he saw next was all the more unbelievable.

In the midst of the blue flames, a pinpoint of light expanded into a shimmering black hole through which Jäger emerged. He stepped into the clearing appearing calm, despite the violent chaos around him. His eyes crawled with blue electric arcs, set in black pools, as he advanced, holding out his hand before him.

The soldier, Keyros, was startled by Jäger's appearance through the Ingwaz. Coming up on one knee, he pointed his weapon at the alien looking boy. Jäger did not react to the soldier. All he did was raise his hand, and Keyros crumpled to the ground unmoving.

As Jäger walked to the terrified group, a winking pearl of light came to life in his palm. It grew brighter as he stopped at their center. Raising both hands above his head he clapped them together above his head, then spread them to the sky. Pearls of light now rested in both of his palms as he spoke.

"Helga Ve-Thetta ok hindra alla illska."

With these words, the pearls of light flashed brilliantly, like camera flashes. The light that exploded from them spread out, billowing like an opening parachute, then solidified into a chitinous dome that completely covered the group.

But Baka'El did not notice Jäger's dome as it flashed into existence behind Chance. Her eyes were fixed on the fading Warrior of Light. Her mind was consumed with dreams of the glory that would be hers for killing Sari'El, the mighty War Bringer.

Her continuous bombardment had bloodied and weakened him. His glowing Celestial essence ran in tiny rivers of light from his nose, mouth and ears, but as she had worn him down, so to had her own power waned.

In what she hoped would be the final effort of the battle, Baka'El released a massive salvo of Lightning Spheres. It was a salvo so intense that if Sari'El did not move, it would crack his energy field and obliterate him, discharging his energy into the universe.

And then, beyond all expectation, Sari'El moved, launching spheres as he did.

Startled, Baka'El turned to face the assault, so that the most powerful part of her energy field was between her and Sari'El. Drawing power away from her flanks, she reinforced her forward shield. But what she did not realize was that the orbs she had fired a few seconds before had struck Jäger's dome, and reflected back, directly at her.

When her own Lightning Spheres struck her flank, she was dazed, and instinctively turned to face this new and unexpected threat. It was the mistake Sari'El had been waiting for.

As Baka'El turned her shield to face her self-made assault, she exposed her almost completely unprotected flank to Sari'El. Without hesitation he sent a rapid-fire burst that hit the Fallen like a freight train.

The combined impact of both her own, and Sari'El's Lightning Spheres pounded her, causing her body to jerk and spasm with each explosion until finally the glow of her shield winked out. Bursting into flames, she fell from the sky, her burning body striking the ground with a sickening thud.

Sari'El descended, landing softly beside the broken Fallen. Once beautiful, she now lay shattered and bleeding, the luminosity of her blood fading as it leaked from her many burns and lacerations.

She gazed up at him, through him, with eyes that looked out into eternity. Her mouth was working as if trying to speak, but only produced blood and spittle that ran down both sides of her face. Squatting down next to her, Sari'El tried to hear her words.

"It's not over," she said defiantly as her eyes focused on him.

Sari'El stood up, a Lightning Sphere crackling to life in his hand.

"It is for you, my sister," he said solemnly. "It is for you."

Reaching out, he held the sphere over her prostrate form, then dropped it onto her chest. Her eyes grew wide as she stared at the sphere in horror. It sat, perched on her, as its lux increased in intensity until at last it began to slowly sink into her sternum.

Screaming, she flailed wildly, as if she had been dropped into a fire. Her previously dimming eyes suddenly burst with light, as though a sun had manifested inside her head. Fissures, tiny at first, began to split open in her skin, like ice dropped into hot water until they grew into a Kafkaesque road map covering her entire body.

As the fissures widened, light poured from the tears in her flesh. They grew brighter and brighter until the Fallen was completely consumed. When, at last, the light waned, nothing remained except for a perfect rendering of Baka'El's nude, winged form in what looked like dry ice.

The bizarre sculpture quickly sublimated. When the vapor finally dissipated, it left nothing behind but the winged silhouette of the Fallen in a fine white powder.

"Sari'El," came a voice from behind him.

Turning, he found Jäger standing there, his Guardian's eyes still glowing with Celestial energy. Near the tree line, he saw his friends and a soldier lying unmoving on the ground, and concern creased his brow. But before he could express it, Jäger's hand shot up to touch his forehead, and in a flash of light, Sari'El, the War Bringer of the Triad, fell to the ground unconscious.

Jäger surveyed the destruction around him. The research facility was completely destroyed, its walls torn open like a ruined doll house. The ground around him was churned over and pocked by hundreds of impact craters, so much so that it resembled more of a lunar surface than a forest clearing. The tree line around the complex was mangled as if a blind, drunken giant had tried to hack it down with a blunt sword.

In the distance Jäger could hear the lone siren of a first responder drawing closer. Raising his hand, he extended a finger and an Ingwaz opened before him. Looking down at Chance, he smiled. Then stepping into the specular opening, he was gone.

The first emergency vehicle to arrive at the White Mountain Research Facility was a park ranger from the Shenandoah National Park. The forest service had been alerted by a fire-watch tower that had observed a spectacular fireworks display in the distance.

Normally local law enforcement would have been dispatched, but in the last fifteen minutes, local 911 operators had been swamped by reports of explosions and missile attacks, even UFOs. Several local towns were in flames. There was even report of rioting and arson at a local college prep high school and widespread structure fires, including a psychiatric hospital. It was chaos.

When the ranger arrived on the scene, he searched the area with his spotlight and immediately found Chance and the others. As he began to render aid, he was relieved to discover that, other than being unresponsive, they all were alive and apparently unharmed. Although one boy was covered with what looked like blood, he had no injury that could account for it.

The group was mostly what looked like teenagers, but there was also a uniformed man among them. Well-equipped and armed with an M-4 assault rifle, he appeared to be a soldier of some kind, but bore no insignia.

Moving toward the destroyed building, the ranger found more victims, but these were less fortunate, their bodies torn open, their entrails steaming in the unnaturally cold air.

As he surveyed the grisly scene, he was startled by a loud crashing sound behind him. Drawing his weapon, he scanned the ruins for movement as he crept up on the source of the sound, and was stunned by what he saw.

Rummaging through the broken concrete and twisted steel was a winged monster, the likes of which he had never seen. The creature clawed through the debris, seemingly frantic as it threw large chunks of stone, and flung a mangled metal table aside as if they were made of paper.

Suddenly the creature stopped and stared down at its feet. Reaching down, it plucked a glowing vial from the rubble, holding it up as if it were the most precious object it had ever beheld.

Gripping its prize, the monster spread its wings and rose into the night sky, then with a Jurassic roar, it shot through the darkness and disappeared over the horizon.

The stunned ranger stood staring. He was in shock, so much so that he didn't notice the arrival of the three Black Hawk helicopters, or the soldiers that were fast roping down from them, then spreading out to secure the area.

FIFTY-FOUR

When Chance opened his eyes, all he could see was a dense white mass that glowed intensely at its center. Blinking, his vision cleared slightly and he realized that the white mass was in fact, white acoustic ceiling tiles surrounding a recessed fluorescent light fixture.

"Oh, you're awake," came a disembodied woman's voice as her face moved over his. "Hi, there," said the smiling face. "Welcome back. I'll go get the doctor."

The face disappeared and Chance once again tried to bring the acoustic ceiling tiles into focus, but found that the random pattern of variously sized pinholes in them wreaked havoc with his depth perception. As he tried to adjust to it, a bright light shined into his eyes.

"What's your name?" asked the doctor as she flashed her pen light from side to side.

"Chance...Chance Jordan."

"Do you know what day it is?"

Chance paused, thinking. "Um...Wednesday, I think," he offered tentatively.

The doctor smiled as she clicked off her pen light.

"Well, I guess that's a reasonable response," she said as she began to check his reflexes, "since you've been in a coma for the last eighteen hours. It's Thursday evening."

Chance pondered this, straining to remember the lost time.

"Where am I?" he asked.

"You are at the Bethesda Naval Hospital," said the doctor.

"Bethesda? Why?"

"You and your friends were found unconscious outside a federal research facility that had been destroyed in some kind of attack. "Do you recall anything about that?"

Once again Chance strained to remember, shaking his head. He could recall baseball practice, and he had an odd recollection of the Wellington library burning. For some reason he remembered soldiers, and even more strangely Marina.

"Marina. Is Marina here?" he asked.

He tried to sit up but the doctor effortlessly pressed his shoulders back to the bed.

"There were two female victims brought in with you, but we have identified them, and neither one is named Marina," said the doctor.

"Everyone is fine, son" came a familiar voice.

Chance looked toward the door and saw his father, Nelson Jordan, smiling as he walked up beside his bed. On his arm was his father's latest live-in solution to his mid-life crisis, Vonda.

"Mr. Jordan," said the doctor speaking to Chance, "you can't just jump out of bed. You have been in a coma for several hours, and we still don't know why."

"Relax, son," said Nelson. "I'm sure all your friends are going to be just fine."

Just then a nurse entered the room with a look of urgency.

"Doctor, the other coma patients have awakened," said the nurse breathlessly.

"Which ones?" asked the doctor.

"All of them."

"All of them?" said the doctor stunned

"Every single one."

"I'll be right there," said the doctor, turning to Chance as the nurse left the room.

"Let me go take care of your friends," she said, taking his hand, "I'll be back to check on you soon."

Chance nodded as the doctor quickly left the room, and another nurse entered to take her place.

"How are you feeling, son?" asked Nelson once the doctor was gone.

"A bit dizzy," said Chance, but he wasn't looking at his father. Instead, his attention had been drawn to a large man in a dark suit that had stopped the doctor in the hall and flashed some kind of badge in her face.

The doctor, seemingly unimpressed, and more than a little annoyed, had shaken her head 'no', then walked away. Now the hulking ape in a necktie was staring at Chance intensely through the room's window.

"And a little weak," added Chance.

"I'll get you something to eat," said the nurse.

After the nurse had left, Nelson placed his hand on his son's shoulder. "You get some rest. I'll come back and check on you in the morning," said Nelson sincerely.

"Dad, please find out what's going on with my friends," pleaded Chance, his worry obvious.

"You bet," said Nelson, patting Chance's shoulder, before turning for the door.

Vonda bent down and kissed Chance on the cheek.

"You get well soon, handsome," said the buxom blond. Turning, she followed Nelson out of the door, stopping to look back at Chance to give him a playful wink before leaving.

Finally alone, Chance relaxed a bit. Closing his eyes, he drifted off to sleep.

The next morning, Chance was getting dressed as he and his father watched in stunned silence, the television news coverage of the devastation in Virginia. The screen was filled with images of burning and collapsed buildings, fallen bridges, and first responders fighting in the aftermath of what was now being called a meteor shower. The governor had declared the affected regions disaster areas, and invoked martial law. National Guard troops were deploying in the streets, and police in combat dress were patrolling four to a car.

Chance was buttoning his shirt when the doctor walked into the room to speak with his father. When she saw Chance dressing in street clothes, she looked at him quizzically.

"You wished to see me, Mr. Jordan?" she asked, her eyes moving from Chance to regard Nelson.

"Yes. Let's talk in the hall," he said. Then looking at Chance, "You finish getting dressed, son. I'll be back in a minute."

Walking out into the hallway, Nelson turned to address the doctor, but she spoke first.

"Mr. Jordan, why is Chance getting dressed?"

"Because, Dr. Webster, it is my intention to take my son home where he can be cared for in safety."

"May I remind you that we still don't know what caused your son's coma? It could be dangerous to take him out of the hospital."

"How are the other kids doing? asked Nelson.

"They are all awake and alert," she said, a bit thrown by his shift in focus.

"So, other than observation, no testing or treatment is occurring?"

"That would be correct."

"Then continue to observe the others. I will observe my son at home."

"Mr. Jordan, I must inform you that if you discharge your son, it will be against medical advice."

"I understand," said Nelson, taking out his phone. "My attorney will sign any release documents you require."

"Very well. I will bring the forms."

"Thank you."

The doctor turned and walked up the hall to the nurses' station where she picked up the phone. Nelson watched her, and noticed a large man in a dark suit stop and speak to her, all the time glancing down the hall at him.

"Gotta be a cop," muttered Nelson as he went about sending a text message to his attorney regarding Chance's discharge paperwork. When he finished, he looked up and was startled to find the big man was standing next to him.

"Mr. Jordan," said the big man, his voice deep and resonating as he held up a badge and credentials, "I'm special agent Jonathan Rush, FBI. I need to speak with your son."

"Is my son under arrest?" asked Nelson, his tone clearly confrontational.

"No, sir. I just have a few questions."

A nurse arrived with a wheelchair for Chance and passed the two alpha males squaring off in the hallway. Trying to avoid eye contact, he entered the room.

"Then you can wait until my son's attorney is present," said Nelson, producing a business card. "If you call my assistant, she will give you his number and help set up a meeting."

"Do you think your son needs an attorney?" asked Rush, taking the card with visible annoyance.

"Are you a cop?" asked Nelson in a matter-of-fact tone that positively dripped with sarcasm. "Do you lie to people to get them to say things you can twist into a reason to arrest them? Yes? Then without a doubt, my son needs to have an attorney present."

At that moment the nurse wheeled Chance out into the hall and Nelson immediately placed himself between the FBI agent and his son.

"Good night, agent Rush," said Nelson as he turned away, not waiting for a reply.

Chance had been torn over leaving his friends behind at the hospital, but Nelson Jordan did not easily accept no for an answer, especially from his son. Chance did, however, get a moment to visit with his friends, and while he may have been conflicted about leaving, they all had strongly urged him to take the opportunity to go home.

It made sense. Conor had developed a bad headache, and while there was no visible reason, the doctor had placed him on a concussion protocol, so he had another twenty-four hours to go. Besides that, Kimiko was there and he didn't want to leave her. Eric didn't mind sticking around since Bella was there. And Rheinhard, being sixteen, couldn't leave until his parents arrived from Germany.

The only thing that could have kept Chance at the Bethesda Naval Hospital would have been if Marina had been there, but she wasn't. In fact, she was nowhere to be found.

Everyone but Rheinhard had at least some memory of Marina having been with them, but no one could agree on where and when. Consequently, their collective fugues made it so that no one could agree on, at what point exactly they had lost track of her, if she had in fact been there at all.

Ultimately, Chance had said his goodbyes and was escorted to the hospital's rooftop helipad where a helicopter waited to fly them home. During the flight, Chance's mind was filled with worry for Marina, especially as they flew over some of the destruction wrought by the meteor shower.

The flight was soon over, and Chance was home. Wasting no time, he sat down at his computer and spent the rest of the day online, and on the phone, trying to find Marina. A few clicks later, he was horrified to learn that Haven-hurst had taken a direct hit, and been completely destroyed.

There was nothing left. According to news reports every patient, along with the night shift staff, had been killed in the explosion and fire. The once impressive building was now nothing more than a pile of smoldering wreckage being picked through by firefighters and cadaver dogs.

Chance was becoming more and more distraught as each hour passed. He strained to stay positive and hopeful, but as he watched the body count from Havenhurst and Wellington rise, the ever-increasing possibility that Marina might be in one of those tiny black body bags, made him feel nauseous.

There was only one reason he had for any hope at all. That was the uncertain and fractured recollections of his friends that claimed to remember seeing Marina, outside the walls of Havenhurst. The odd thing was that none of them could describe her.

At the hospital, Bella, had been fairly sure that Marina had been in a jail cell with them. Kimiko didn't remember that, but she did have a faint recollection of seeing Marina at Wellington. At the baseball field, specifically. When she said this, Bella began to question her own memory, pointing at Kimiko with a confused expression.

"Yeah...," said Bella tentatively, "she was at the stadium."

Conor had a completely different recollection. He remembered seeing Marina in Chance's dorm room, but he quickly dismissed that. "She's gotta be at Havenhurst," he had said. Now as Chance watched the various news feeds, Conor's conclusion rang ominous.

In one last hope, Chance had called the sheriff's department and asked them to check the house at Lakeside Beach. It had taken several hours, but they finally called back and confirmed that it was empty.

As the day came to an end, Eric had called and he brought Chance up to speed on the rest of his friends. Rheinhard had been discharged to his parents, and was safely on his way home. Kimiko and Bella had convinced their parents to let them stay in the U.S. for the summer, and were planning on renting a car for a road trip.

Eric, being Eric, had left the hospital and moved into the Presidential suite of the Charlottesville Hilton, and had taken Conor with him. They had also driven out to Wellington to get their belongings from their dorm rooms.

Chance had learned that despite all of the mayhem at the school, it had not been completely destroyed. The library had burned down, as well as half of the classrooms, but the dorms were undamaged. It was also, with a sense of relief, that he learned that the Grand Foyer had survived as well. Eric had also told him that they had picked up his Harley, which Chance had completely forgotten about, and said they were planning to bring it out to him the next day.

Lastly, Eric informed Chance that several members of the baseball team, who had been injured during the riot, had been admitted to Charlottesville General Hospital. He said that he and Conor were planning to go visit them, and wanted to know if Chance wanted to come along. Of course Chance had said yes, and immediately felt like a total ass because, in his frantic search for Marina, he had forgotten about his brother Spartans.

Hanging up, Chance stared at his computer's screen and yawned, as fatigue jumped on his back like a bear from a tree. He couldn't explain why he felt so beat up. His body felt like it always did the morning after a particularly tough football game.

His worry for Marina consuming him, he shut down his computer and made one last check of his phone for messages. There was one. It was from Eric.

"Go to bed. You sound stupid tired. See you around 10:00 a.m," was all it said.

Chance undressed, and as he crawled into the familiar softness of his own bed, he took a deep breath, and quickly passed out from fatigue.

FIFTY-FIVE

The next morning Chance awoke completely refreshed and hungry. Slipping on some jeans, and a Wellington Baseball polo, he went in search of food. As he jogged down the steps, his nose filled with the delicious aromas of an active kitchen wafting up the stairwell. His single-minded goal was interrupted, however, by the sound of his father's voice calling out to him as he reached the bottom.

"Chance, you're up. Good," said Nelson, cheerfully. Chance turned to see his father inspecting his golf bag, and dressed for the game. "How ya feelin'? asked Nelson.

"I'm feeling pretty good," said Chance.

"Good enough for eighteen holes?" asked Nelson hopefully. Over the years Chance had picked up the game. It was one of the few things he and his father shared, and ultimately Chance had grown to enjoy it.

"Sorry, Dad; Eric and Conor are coming over. We're going to Charlottesville to visit the guys in the hospital."

"That sounds like a good use of a day," said Nelson nodding. "If you're hungry, Monique has made breakfast."

"I'm starving," said Chance.

"Good, because she was very excited to cook for you again, and she went a little nuts in there," said Nelson, grinning as he nodded toward the kitchen.

Monique was Nelson's maid. His French maid. Sometimes Chance still choked on the cliche', but Monique really was French.

Nelson had hired Monique to help Chance's mother shortly after he was born. Of course, Nelson had made a play for her, but Monique would have none of that. In very short order Monique and Chance's mother had become close friends, and Chance had grown up knowing her as a trusted member of the family.

"I'm gonna get a couple rounds in. I'll be back before dinner," said Nelson, shouldering his bag and walking up to his son. "It's good to have you home."

Nelson playfully punched Chance in the shoulder, then spun around and headed for the garage as Monique walked out of the kitchen.

"Bon jour, Monique," said Chance embracing the woman, and kissing her on both cheeks.

"Bon jour, Monsieur Chance. Welcome home," said Monique in her thick French accent. Smiling pleasantly, she added, "Would you like to take your breakfast in the Winter Garden? It is such a beautiful morning."

"Yes," replied Chance, returning her smile. "That sounds wonderful."

"Go have a seat," she said, pushing him toward the large glass enclosed patio. "I will bring it out to you."

As Monique disappeared into the kitchen, Chance walked out into the Winter Garden and sat down with a satisfied grunt on one of the white wicker sofas. Outside the glass, a slight breeze pushed a leaf across the surface of the pool, and Chance found himself craving a swim. But that thought was interrupted by a sing-song voice from the doorway.

"I hope you're hungry."

Chance turned to see Vonda, his dads latest, standing in the threshold of the patio's French door, holding a silver serving tray piled high with Belgian waffles, eggs, and bacon. But despite his hunger, Chance had trouble noticing the food, because what Vonda was presenting along with it, was distractingly delicious as well.

Vonda stood there wearing a clinging silk robe that hung open, revealing matching panties and a bra that strained to contain her massive bosom. Chance had to admit, she was a stunning vision.

Vonda was not tall, but her shape was full and curvaceous in every way a man could find inviting. So perfectly proportioned, yet perfectly excessive. With her huge breasts, wasp waist, and wide hips, Chance often thought she looked like a pornographic cartoon from a Japanese Manga.

His father had found her working in a "Gentlemen's Club" in Ontario, and had taken a liking to her immediately. Chance understood his father's attraction. He felt it as well. Vonda was one of the most incredible visuals a man could conjure. The only problem was that this particular visual was banging his dad, and that was a line Chance just couldn't cross.

It wasn't out of any sense of loyalty to his father. It was just that the idea of sharing a woman with his dad, just grossed him out.

At that moment Monique entered the Winter Garden, looking Vonda up and down with obvious disapproval.

"Monsieur Chance," said Monique, regaining her bearing, "your friends are here."

Vonda was visibly annoyed by this interruption, and stomped her foot in agitation, which only served to emphasize that her bra was two sizes too small.

Rising to his feet, Chance walked out to the foyer giving the disgruntled Vonda a wink and a smile as he walked by, which seemed to console her a bit.

"There he is," said Eric as Chance walked in.

"Dude, this life of luxury you're living sure seems to agree with you," said Conor, chiming in. "You look good."

The friends embraced, clasping hands as they did, but as Conor stepped back, Chance held onto his hand as if inspecting it.

"A manicure? Really?" said Chance dryly.

"And a pedicure, too," admitted Conor proudly, admiring his hands.

"What have you done to this boy?" said Chance, chuckling as he looked over at Eric. But Eric's attention had shifted to something over Chance's shoulder.

"Holy shit," muttered Conor, his eyes fixed on the same point as Eric's. "Who is that?"

Chance turned to see that Vonda had entered the foyer carrying the breakfast tray, and still dressed like a Victoria's Secret model.

"You boys hungry for something?" asked Vonda, mixing the obvious with the implied.

"Famished," said Eric, smiling back.

"Totally," added Conor as both boys stepped around Chance and approached Vonda like a pack of wolves.

"Help yourselves," said Vonda, giddy from all the attention. "It's all scrumptious."

"No one would dare say otherwise," said Eric, his well-polished charm now fully engaged.

Conor, on the other hand, had been reduced to a tongue-tied idiot.

Vonda bent down and placed the tray on the table, making a show of it as the boys ogled her while grabbing waffles and rolling them up with eggs and bacon as filling.

"Don't forget the whipped cream," said Vonda, giggling.

"Ah, yes, the whipped cream," said Eric smoothly, his eyes moving languidly from Vonda's eyes to her deep cleavage and back. "It seems to make everything you put in your mouth so much more...delicious. Wouldn't you agree?"

Eric dipped his waffle in the bowl of whipped cream, then took a bite, leaving a smear of cream on his lip. Reaching out with her finger, Vonda scooped up the errant blob, and seductively placed it in her own mouth.

"I do indeed," she purred.

Having finally had enough of the spectacle, Chance walked up and made himself a Belgian breakfast taco. Dipping it in the whipped cream, he began pushing his friends toward the door, both of them groaning in protest.

"Guys, how 'bout we get to the hospital and visit our brothers?" said Chance.

"But...crap," said Eric, giving in.

"Feel free to drop in any time," said Vonda, pouting. "There's always plenty of fresh whipped cream in the fridge."

"Eric tugged against Chance in one last weak effort to stay for more "waffles", but as Chance pushed him out of the house, Eric could only return Vonda's goodbye with a groan of uncomfortable desire.

FIFTY-SIX

The visit at the hospital went well. Chance, Eric and Conor had made the rounds, and all of the Spartans were in high spirits, despite the loss of a teammate.

That teammate was outfielder Bryan Varne. Bryan's body had been found in the dormitory, dead from a gunshot wound to the chest. He was one of three Wellington students to die from gunshots. Strangely, however, no firearms were found on campus to account for it.

Some students had reported seeing soldiers, or police, attacking the dorms. It had been these soldiers that had reportedly shot Bryan, and taken several prisoners. Eventually, however, every Wellington student had been accounted for.

But then there were also the wild stories of a winged monster, circling the dormitories. It made it hard to know what to believe.

So many bizarre stories had come out of that evening that at first investigators had dismissed most of them as crazy rantings. It was assumed that they were the result of some yet unidentified narcotic that had been administered to the entire staff and student body. The most likely vector was believed to have been via the kitchen, but so far nothing had been found.

But as evidence was collected, and statements taken as surveillance video had been poured over and the body count rose, an uncomfortable truth had become clear. Not all of the stories, could be disregarded as the product of drug induced hallucinations. Especially after the body of a staff member had been found in the school's pump house, literally torn to pieces.

The deaths that had occurred on that terrible night, had provoked a shit storm of inquiries. As a result, local law enforcement, as well as the F.B.I., and a few other three letter organizations, were digging into every possible angle of investigation.

Thankfully, this insanity had not infringed on Chance's visit. He had very much enjoyed the time he had been able to spend with his fellow Spartans, and now the three friends found themselves chatting in the hallway with Coach McCune.

Chance was distracted however. He could not explain why, but ever since he had arrived at the hospital, he had been experiencing an odd sort of anxiety, a flutter in his chest that had grown stronger as the day had progressed.

As their conversation was wrapping up, and the three boys were discussing where they wanted to go for dinner, an excited voice from down the hall halted their dialogue. A nurse had bolted from one of the rooms, almost knocking over a medication cart as she did.

"Doctor! Doctor!" she exclaimed breathlessly. "The patient is awake!"

A doctor standing at the nurse's station dropped a pad computer on the countertop and walked briskly to meet the nurse. Stopping, he spoke to her for only a moment before quickly entering the room.

Drawn by some unknown force, Chance began to walk slowly toward the treatment room door. Eric and Conor called out to him, but for Chance, their voices were nothing more than distant echoes. For him, the world had shifted into slow motion, making his short journey down the hall seem endless.

Each step he took required every ounce of his strength, and with each step, it seemed that the door slipped further away. Then, in an instant, the distance collapsed, and Chance found himself standing in the room's doorway.

Inside the room the doctor and nurse struggled to hold the patient down on the bed.

"Let me go!" the unseen patient demanded. "He's here! I know he's here!"

As two more nurses squeezed by Chance, and went to assist the others, he stepped further into the room. As he did, the patient suddenly stopped struggling. As he watched, a pair of eyes locked onto his through the tangle of bodies and arms that restrained them.

"Chance!"

"Marina!" yelled Chance, emotion and relief flooding out of him.

Rushing forward, he pushed his way through the attending medical staff to Marina's bedside. Sitting up, Marina threw her arms around him as he crushed her in his embrace.

"I knew you were here," she said, her eyes filling with tears. "I knew you would come."

"I was looking everywhere for you," said Chance, rocking Marina gently. "How did you get here?"

"I don't know. I don't remember," she said.

"She came in with the other victims from Wellington Academy," interjected the doctor.

"Wellington?" questioned Chance, first looking at the doctor and then Marina, confused. "How did you get to Wellington?"

"She's not a student there?" interrupted the doctor.

"No," said Chance, stepping back. He turned to face the doctor, but Marina still clung to his arm. "She's from Havenhurst."

"This girl is a patient at Havenhurst?" asked the doctor, obviously startled by this revelation.

"Yes, sir," said Chance.

"And how is it that you know her?"

"I have been visiting her."

The doctor just stared at him wordlessly.

"It was Dr. Shelby's idea. He said it would be good for her," said Chance, feeling defensive. "Call him, he'll explain everything."

"Mister...?" probed the doctor.

"Jordan. Chance Jordan."

"Mr. Jordan, may we speak privately?"

Marina gripped Chance's arm tighter. "No, don't go," she pleaded.

Chance pulled her close once again, resting his cheek on her head. "Don't worry, I just found you. I'm not going anywhere."

Marina nodded and relaxed.

"I'll be right over there," said Chance, pointing at the door. "You'll be able to see me the whole time."

Marina hesitated, but finally nodded.

Chance bent down and gently kissed her cheek, then stepped away. Immediately two nurses began to attend to her, but her eyes never left him. As the nurses busied themselves around her, she leaned and bent to keep him in sight, seemingly fearful that if she lost sight of him, she might lose him forever.

The doctor led Chance out into the hallway, but as he turned to face him, he was startled to find that they had been joined by three other men. Realizing the doctor's confusion, Chance made introductions

"Doctor, these are my friends, Eric Easton and Conor Jackson, and this rather severe looking man is Coach Phil McCune from Wellington Academy. They are with me."

Coach McCune gave Chance a sideways look, but said nothing.

"I am Dr. Sanchez. You mentioned Dr. Shelby from Havenhurst?"

"Yes," said Chance. "In fact, Coach McCune here can confirm everything I said."

Dr. Sanchez waived off his comment. "Are you aware of what happened to Havenhurst last night?" he asked.

"Yes, it was hit by one of those meteors," said Chance. Then his mind connected the dots. "Was Dr. Shelby in the hospital when it was hit?"

"All we know is that he is missing," said Sanchez somberly. "Did I hear you say that her name is Marina?"

"Yes, Marina Robbins."

"Was she a patient of Dr. Shelby?"

"Yes, she was," said Chance, looking into the room at her. "So, what is going to happen to her now?"

"Well, she has been in a coma since she arrived on Wednesday night," said Dr. Sanchez, crossing his arms in thought. "Now that she's conscious, we will run some tests and try to nail down what caused it."

Upon hearing this, Chance, Eric, and Conor all exchanged glances. Dr. Sanchez caught it, and spoke up.

"Is there a problem?" he asked.

"None of the other Wellington students were in comas?" asked Chance.

"No," confirmed Sanchez, intrigued. "She was the only one. Why do you ask?

Chance took a deep breath, then detailed how everyone who had been found at the White Mountain Research Facility, and transported to Bethesda, had been comatose. He explained how all of these survivors had regained consciousness at the same moment, and with no clear memory of the night before.

Sanchez's eyebrows rose in clear fascination as he digested this new information. "Was this young lady with you at this facility?" he asked, indicating Marina.

Chance sighed then continued. "There's a small amount of confusion about that," he said glancing over at Marina. "Some of us remember her, but where and when has been the source of disagreement. A few do recall her being there, others don't remember her at all. But if she was at White Mountain, I don't know how she could have been found at Wellington."

Dr. Sanchez contemplated this, "I'll call Bethesda and see what they can tell me."

Chance looked at Marina again. "So, what happens next?"

"Assuming all of her tests come back negative, she will be discharged to State Mental Health for evaluation," the doctor said.

"If there is nothing else, may I go see her now?" asked Chance.

"Of course," said Dr. Sanchez, smiling. "Go right in."

"Thank you, doctor," said Chance.

"Gentlemen, if you will excuse me, I have some phone calls to make," said Sanchez. Then nodding to the men, he spun on his heel, and walked down the hall.

Chance turned to look at his friends, an apologetic expression on his face. "Guys, I'm sorry..." he began.

"Dude, shut up and get in there," said Conor.

"I have no idea what the hell is going on," said McCune, "I'm gonna go home, you boys be good."

With that McCune slapped Chance on the back then stalked off down the hall.

Eric and Conor had seen this coming. Every day, as their friend had gone to visit this strange girl at Havenhurst, they had seen him grow more and more attached to her. And though they had never met her before, as they looked at her now, they both felt an odd familiarity with her.

Eric pushed Chance toward the room where Marina waited. "When they finally kick you out, take an Uber over to the Hilton. You can crash with us tonight."

"Thanks bro," said Chance as he hugged his friends. Then heading back into the room, he walked up to an overjoyed Marina, and once again took her into his arms.

FIFTY-SEVEN

The next month was a flurry of activity. The Virginia State Psychiatric Hospital had evaluated Marina, and found her to be well adjusted, and exhibiting a level of maturity and cognitive function appropriate to her age. Finding no reason to hold her, she was released. Because she had been a patient at Havenhurst as a ward of the state at the time of its destruction, the hospital's insurance had provided for Marina's admission into a well-known boarding house for girls.

Chance had wanted to bring Marina home to stay with him, but his father had chosen that moment to act like a responsible parent.

"Son," Nelson had begun in his 'Let me tell you about the world' voice, "you have only known this girl for a few weeks, and you don't even remember all of that. Give it some time, get to know her. If what you say is true, she is changing every day. If in a year from now, you still feel the same way, we can revisit this."

It pissed Chance off. Mostly because he knew his dad was right. It was true, he HAD only known Marina for a few weeks, but that reality was at odds with his heart, which told him that he had loved Marina for what felt like an eternity.

Nelson was also right about Chance's memory loss. Chance, Eric and the others had no clear recollection of the twenty-four hours prior to being found unconscious at White Mountain. Even some segments of time farther back were partially compromised.

It wasn't that their memories were completely blank, but rather that the only things they could recall were disjointed flashes of time, moments of events that, out of context, made no sense at all.

Chance frequently found himself thinking about it, but not this day. Tonight was about Marina. It was an evening he had been planning almost since the day he had found her in Charlottesville.

Pulling Eric's Porsche into a parking space outside Marina's boarding house, he took a deep breath, then set his plan in motion.

Marina's boarding house was a beautiful place. A well maintained and manicured three-story colonial that had been designated a historic landmark. The home's tenants were typically international students enrolled at the University of Virginia, or at the prestigious Virginia Academy for the Arts, and though Marina was attending neither, she nevertheless fit right in.

As the days had passed, and Chance had spent more and more time with her, it had become very apparent that Marina's intellect was staggering. Her memory was nearly eidetic and, as a result, she retained almost everything she read or heard. But Marina wasn't a parrot. She didn't just ingest and regurgitate information. She could process it, and then synthesize new ideas and concepts, and since her awakening upon meeting Chance, she had blossomed.

In the last few weeks Marina had earned her G.E.D. and had taken the S.A.T. exam, nearly maxing it. Chance had been helping her prepare but, while Marina often gushed about what a wonderful teacher he was, he was more than aware that he could take very little credit for her success. Still, he couldn't help but feel a little proud.

Walking up the path to the house, Chance was greeted by a pair of the house's residents as they came down the front steps.

"Hi, Chance," they said in unison, their foreign-accented English sounding musical to his ears.

He just smiled and waved.

As he opened the front door, Chance expected to find the matron of the house seated in her customary position at her desk in the entryway, but Mrs. Henrietta Kapp's seat was uncommonly vacant.

Equally unusual was the sound that filled the room. A beautiful, haunting voice, accompanied by a piano that was coming from the house's parlor room down the main hall.

Following the sound, Chance peered down the hall and saw Mrs. Kapp standing in the entryway of the parlor, holding her hands to her mouth as she wept like a proud mother at her daughter's wedding. When she noticed Chance standing at her desk, she motioned for him to join her.

As Chance approached, he realized that there was a small group of people in the parlor watching the performance. Walking up next to Mrs. Kapp, he looked into the room and saw a woman playing the piano, and standing next to the piano, singing in full voice, was Marina.

Chance was surprised beyond explanation. His first thought was that he had never heard Marina sing before, but then he thought again, and wasn't so sure. In the depths of his mind was a shadow of her voice echoing from a blank moment. It hinted at a memory that refused to show itself.

Looking at the group assembled for Marina's performance, he took stock of them. All were extraordinarily attentive. A woman held out a microphone as she recorded video with a camera on a tripod, and everyone seemed to be enjoying Marina's performance.

As Chance watched, Marina's eyes swept across the faces of her tiny audience until they fell upon him in the doorway. When they did, her face brightened, and she focused upon him all the emotion of her heart that the beautiful song could carry.

It stunned him, and it wasn't until the song had ended that he realized that he had forgotten to breathe. Startled back into awareness by the polite applause of the assemblage, Chance at last took a breath, then looked at Mrs. Kapp with questions in his eyes.

"What's going on?" he asked.

"These people are from the Virginia Academy for the Arts," said Mrs. Kapp, beaming. When she saw Chance was still confused, she elaborated.

"Almost every day I hear Marina singing," she went on, "and I was so impressed by her beautiful voice that I called a friend of mine at the academy...and, here they are."

"So, what does all this mean?" asked Chance as he watched the small group congratulating Marina.

"It means that if they were impressed, Marina could earn a scholarship to study voice at the academy."

"Wow," said Chance. "Full ride?"

"It depends on how impressed they were," said Mrs. Kapp, crossing her fingers.

"Well, if they weren't impressed with that, then to hell with the Virginia Academy for the Arts."

"Mr. Jordan, language, please," said Mrs. Kapp scoldingly, but with a barely restrained smirk on her face and a twinkle in her eyes. Then leaning over to him, she whispered in tones conspiratorial, "But I agree with you."

Chance smiled. "How long before they make a decision?"

"Well, let's see if I can grease the gears a bit," said Mrs. Kapp as she touched Chance's arm, then walked into the parlor to chat with one of the women from the academy.

"Didn't I tell you, Mimi?" gushed Mrs. Kapp.

"You certainly did, Henrietta," said the woman as the two ladies joined arms and walked out of the parlor, "and you told every bit of the truth."

As the two friends walked down the hall to the front room, they were followed by a man talking on a phone. "Yes, I need a meeting with the department chair. Today if possible. And I need to speak to the scholarship committee Chairperson," he said as he passed Chance.

Suddenly Marina wrapped her arms around Chance. "Hi," she said, smiling broadly as she kissed him on the cheek. "You almost missed the show."

Chance smiled back. "That song was beautiful. What was it?"

"It's a song my friend Nikki taught me at Havenhurst," she said softly, a look of sadness on her face.

Chance immediately felt bad. Marina had often spoken of Nikki, and had been devastated by the news of her death when Havenhurst was destroyed.

"I'm sure she would have been impressed," he said embracing her tightly.

Marina smiled bravely, then paused, a look of puzzlement taking over her face. Stepping back, she looked Chance up and down as if inspecting him, and she had good reason.

Chance had come to visit Marina nearly every day since her awakening at the hospital, and every time he had, he had worn jeans and a casual shirt. But on this day, he was wearing a crisp white dress shirt, black slacks and dress shoes. It even appeared that he had shaved.

"Why are you dressed like a Mormon missionary?" she asked, her eyes narrowing in suspicion.

"A little change of pace," he said shrugging. "Why? Don't you like it?"

"I just feel a little underdressed now," she said, pursing her lips.

"You look fine."

"Fine? I look 'fine' now? What happened to beautiful?" she said in mock insult.

Chance smiled. He loved this kind of playful banter that had become so common in their relationship as Marina had matured and grown in sophistication.

"I can't call you beautiful all the time," he said defensively, taking her arm and wrapping it around his as he turned and walked up the hall. "If I did, your head would get even bigger than it already is."

At this, Marina playfully punched him in the arm, then pulled him closer.

Marina was happy. More happy than she could remember ever being. Over the last month, she had bonded deeply with Chance, her love for him growing stronger and more unwavering with each passing day.

"Chance," she thought to herself. She liked the name. She still, from time to time, thought of him as Sari'El, but that name had lost much of its meaning for her. And since Chance seemed only to tolerate it, she just didn't use it anymore.

One thing that had not faded was her love for him. Her love, and her intense feeling that she had loved him long before.

Walking into the front room, they found Mrs. Kapp taking her accustomed seat at her desk, her face still aglow from her little event. When she saw Marina, she jumped up again.

"Oh Marina," she said, hugging and shaking the girl like a rag doll. "I'm so proud of you. They were all so impressed with you."

"I can't thank you enough for setting that up," said Marina, her voice muffled from being crushed into Mrs. Kapp's motherly bosom.

"It was my pleasure," said Mrs. Kapp, releasing her hold. "Just don't forget me when you're a big star."

"Thank you again," said Marina.

Mrs. Kapp took Marina's hands and beamed at her, her eyes brimming with tears. "Well, you two best be on your way," she said.

"I'll have her back as promised," said Chance.

"I'm not concerned. You kids have fun," said Mrs. Kapp, giving Chance a conspiratorial wink, which Marina noticed.

"We will," said Chance as he opened the front door.

As they exited the house and walked down the front steps, Marina rested her head against Chance's arm, then wrinkled her nose.

"Why do you smell like Eric?" she asked.

Chance looked at her, surprised. "And how is it that you know what Eric smells like?"

"Anyone who gets within ten feet of Eric, knows what Eric smells like," said Marina in a deadpan tone.

Chance laughed. It was true, Eric was fond of his Colognes. As they reached the sidewalk, Marina stopped.

"Where is your motorcycle?" she asked, looking up and down the street.

Chance pulled out a key and pressed it, deactivating the alarm on Eric's car with a bright chirp. "Eric lent me his car," he said.

"Ooooo," cooed Marina, running her finger along the Porsche's fender, "I've always wanted to ride in Eric's car."

Chance opened the passenger door for her. "I'm sure he'll be thrilled to hear that," he said dryly. Marina giggled as she slid into the car.

As Chance walked around the driver's side door, Marina's eyes followed him closely. She was sure he was up to something. The way he was dressed, Eric's car, and the obvious collusion between him and Mrs. Kapp, all contributed to her growing suspicion. As they pulled away from the curb, she watched him closely, and he could feel her stare burning into him.

"What?" he asked in mock annoyance.

Marina paused. "So... what was up with all the winky-winky between you and Mrs. Kapp back there?" she said.

"Well, I guess you have a right to know," said Chance seriously.

"What do I have a right to know?"

"It appears," began Chance, obviously uncomfortable, "that Mrs. Kapp is a... bit of a Cougar."

Marina rolled her eyes and sighed loudly.

"No, really. It's disturbing the way she is constantly trying to seduce me with food."

Marina giggled as she thought about the number of times she had watched as Mrs. Kapp had force-fed Chance every conceivable entree and dessert. Smiling, Marina sighed in resignation that Chance was going to hold onto his conspiracy for now, but she consoled herself with the knowledge that sooner or later, she would find out what secrets he was keeping.

FIFTY-EIGHT

After leaving the boarding home, Chance and Marina drove to Charlottesville. He had made reservations at an upscale steak and seafood restaurant where they ate, laughed, and dreamed as they watched the sky turn red over the city. When dinner was over, they walked arm in arm to the car, where Chance paused for a moment to call Eric and let him know they were on their way.

During the drive, Chance put on some music and asked Marina to sing for him. He was astonished by her voice, and by the fact that even after all the time they had been together, he had only heard it for the first time a few hours ago. He was completely enjoying his personal concert. So much so that he almost regretted turning into the driveway of Wellington Academy.

"What are we doing here?" asked Marina, looking at him quizzically. "I thought the party was at the lake."

"It is," he reassured her. "I just need to pick something up."

As the car passed the burned-out shell of the library, Marina put her hand to her mouth and gasped. She had heard about the destruction at the school, but seeing it first-hand made it seem so much more real. So much more, terrifying.

"You don't remember any of this?" asked Chance curiously.

Marina thought for a moment then shook her head.

"No, not really," she said as she stared at the dark ruins. "Just bits and pieces, but I can't tell which are real. I'm not even sure I was here at all."

"Well, this is where they found you."

"Yeah, so they say," she whispered, her mind twisting on that reality.

Turning she looked at Chance. "What do you remember?"

"Like you, bits and pieces," he said.

Marina seemed disappointed by the answer.

"Hey, I have an idea," he said brightly, causing Marina to look at him expectantly. "I remember bits and pieces, and you remember bits and pieces, maybe we should get our bits and pieces together...and...you know."

Marina's eyes narrowed. "Are you talking dirty to me?" she asked.

"No, not at all," he said, unconvincingly pleading his innocence. "I was only suggesting a possible technique to help us recall...stuff."

"I see," said Marina. "So, then you would support say...Eric and I getting our 'Bits and pieces' together in the interest of...recall?"

Chance frowned. "Eric needs to keep his bits and pieces away from you," he retorted.

"But I thought you said. . . "

"You know, this obsession you have with Eric, the way he smells, his car, his...'bits and pieces', is bordering on the unhealthy," he scolded with a smile in his eyes.

"He does have a nice car," said Marina, running her fingers over the Porsche's dashboard leather. "As for his cologne, perhaps you should stop wearing it. I do believe it is rotting your brain."

They were both laughing as Chance pulled up and parked in front of the Grand Foyer. Turning off the engine, he reached behind the seat and pulled out a flashlight.

"Come on," he said, opening the door.

"Where? In there?" said Marina' disbelievingly.

"Yeah, why not?"

Marina looked at the partially burned-out building. Demolition had already begun on parts of it, and debris piles dotted the once flawless lawn.

"Is it safe?" she asked warily.

Chance turned on the flashlight and held it under his chin. "What's the matter? Don't you trust me?"

Marina stared at him a moment. "No, actually, I don't."

Chance smiled broadly and got out of the car. "Come on," he said, closing the door.

Reluctantly, Marina got out and looked up at the massive stone facade. In the moon-silvered darkness she thought it looked like a haunted castle. Pausing, she contemplated waiting by the car, but Chance made up her mind for her as he slipped his arm around her, and urged her forward. As they walked up the front steps, Marina noticed that the massive wooden doors were ajar, and wondered if a bear might have taken up residence in the abandoned school.

Pushing the door open wider, Chance led Marina inside. The darkness was oppressive, so dense that the beam from Chance's tiny flashlight was consumed by it.

"Wait here," he said, stepping away. "I'll find the lights."

"You're just going to leave me here?" complained Marina.

"You'll be perfectly safe as long as you don't move." said Chance smiling.

"Oh, I bet you say that to all the girls," she replied with mock sweetness. But Chance said nothing as he vanished into the inky blackness.

"OK," she said, calling out, "I'll just stand here alone...in the dark...this isn't creepy at all."

But there was only silence, or to be more precise, 'near' silence.

As Marina listened, she was sure she could hear, or maybe it was sense, slight movements in the darkness, but couldn't pinpoint what, or where, they were. Suddenly, Chance's voice called out to her.

"Marina Robins, will you go to the prom with me?"

At this, the lights came up to reveal that the Grand Foyer had been transformed into an elaborately decorated dream in which mere mortals and the gods could play together. Fluted columns had been installed, and they towered above the marble floors that were flooding with wispy fingers of fog from dry-ice machines.

On the ceiling, a vast array of tiny lights created a galaxy of stars, and in the midst of this dream stood Chance. Wearing a tux jacket, and a bow tie, he held a small clear box that contained a beautiful white corsage.

Around Chance stood his friends, Eric, Conor, Kimiko, Bella, and about eight other couples. The men, like Chance, all wore tuxedos, and the ladies in beautiful formal gowns.

Marina looked down at herself, her jeans and sweatshirt, then slowly raised her eyes until she looked upon Chance with an "I'm so gonna kill you" look on her face.

Chance immediately raised his hand in an effort to calm her. "Whoa, whoa, take a breath," he said pleading. "I got you covered."

At this, Kimiko held up a lovely powder blue gown and matching shoes, as Bella walked over to Marina and touched her hair.

"What a mess," she said with an exasperated sigh. "Good thing I'm a miracle worker."

"We better get started. No time to waste," said Kimiko.

Pulling Marina along, Kimiko and Bella led her away. Chance watched as the girls took Marina into the women's restroom. Just then, he felt a hand on his shoulder.

"Join me on the patio," said Eric, smiling.

Chance nodded as he wordlessly turned and walked with Eric and Conor through the large French doors that opened onto a wide flagstone patio. The space was surrounded by stone balustrades that looked out over the valley below. Reaching into his jacket, Eric produced three cigars, and presented one to each of his friends.

"These were supposed to be our victory dance," he said pulling a cutter from his pocket and snipping off the tip of his cigar with a practiced fluidity.

What Eric was referring to was the state baseball championship that should have been played a few weeks prior. Due to the recent disaster, and deaths resulting from it, the game had been postponed. But as the magnitude of the loss experienced by Wellington and its surrounding communities became clearer, as well as the impact on the team members and their families, Wellington had decided to cancel the game.

Chance and Conor snipped their cigars, as Eric produced a lighter and lit his own. He then offered the flame to his friends who leaned in to light theirs. Eric took a satisfied puff, but quickly noticed the sour-faced grimaces of his friends.

"What's wrong?" he asked, bewildered.

"How are these a 'victory dance'?" complained Chance, coughing. "They taste horrible."

Conor waved smoke away from his face, coughing as well. "I know, right? It's like, the losing team should have to smoke these things," he said.

"Are you guys nuts?" said Eric, incredulous. "These are four-hundred- and fifty-dollar Cuban cigars. Rolled on the thighs of beautiful Cuban women, I might add."

"I think the one that rolled this one needed a bath," said Chance, clicking his tongue on the roof of his mouth as if tasting food that had gone bad.

Eric looked at them both stunned, then leaning back against the balustrades, he puffed his cigar and sighed.

"Heathens," he said, talking to the sky. "My best friends are heathens."

At that moment they were interrupted by Bella's voice, calling out to them from the doorway. All three boys turned to see Bella and Kimiko flanking Marina, who they had transformed into a princess from a fairy tale, and her beauty rocked Chance to his soul.

Conor's reaction was uniquely his. "Holy shit," he said, his cigar dropping from his lips.

Chance quickly tossed his cigar away as well.

"Bippity-boppity-boop," said Bella, feigning exhaustion. "Am I not a miracle worker?"

As Chance stood speechless, Eric leaned in close and whispered, "Crazy girls clean up nice, don't they?"

Eric and Conor patted Chance on the back as they left his side to join Bella and Kimiko. Taking the arms of their ladies, the girls smiled and waved to Marina as they were escorted back into the Grand Foyer, leaving Chance and his princess alone, gazing at one another.

Chance was still holding the corsage, and now he opened the clear box and removed it. Setting the empty container on a patio table, he slowly closed the distance between them.

As Marina watched Chance draw closer, she was sure that her heart would pound right out of her chest. Chance looked so dashing, so handsome. He had become the picture of romance, ripped from the covers of the trashy romance novels that Mrs. Kapp had got her hooked on. Except now, instead of imagining it, she was living it.

Reaching out he took her hand and slipped the corsage around her delicate wrist, then taking her hand in both of his, he lifted it to his lips, and kissed it tenderly.

"You are so beautiful," he said, dazzled by the moonlight sparkling in her eyes.

Chance expected some kind of reaction from her. A coy smile perhaps, but what he saw was Marina's face screwing up into that tight-lipped smirk she always got when she was about to play with him.

"But, you said I was beautiful before," she began. "Surely now, I must be even more beautiful... right?"

"Yes, that's true," he said, an amused grin on his face.

"So, what word shall we use to describe my new beauty?" she asked innocently as she stepped closer, biting her lip as she looked up at him, theatrically batting her lashes.

Chance thought for a moment. "Super-beautiful?" he proposed.

Marina wrinkled her nose.

Chance pondered for a moment. "Mega-beautiful?" he offered.

But Marina frowned. "That makes me sound like a transformers robot."

"Uber-beautiful?" he tried again.

"Now I sound like a ride to the airport."

Chance took a deep breath, perplexed. He looked at her lovingly, and then an idea sparkled in his eyes. Reaching up, he lifted her chin slightly and spoke.

"Wunderschön," he said softly.

"Oooo, that sounds nice," she said, lifting her arms to encircle his neck. "What does it mean?"

"It's German. It means 'a wonder of beauty.'"

"I like that," she said, smiling. Then rising up on her toes she kissed him sweetly.

"I love you," she whispered.

"I love you, too," he replied.

"Will you take me dancing now?" she asked.

"It would be my honor."

Marina smiled, sliding her arm under his, as they turned and walked to the patio's door. Chance opened it and watched as Marina swept through, but as Chance moved to follow her, a sibilant sound caused him to pause and look up into the trees for its source. He scanned the bows, but all he saw were dark tenebrous shapes that were both everything, and nothing.

An uneasy sense of malevolence, just out of sight, caused a chill to run through his body. Thankfully, the feeling was interrupted by the touch of Marina's hand on his. Turning, he looked at her, letting her sweet smile sooth his soul. Forgetting everything else, he allowed her to lead him into the building.

In a nearby tree, high up in its limbs, one of the shapeless shadows began to transform. From its center flashed two eyes that glowed like embers fanned in a fire, as it unfolded, taking on the hideous form of a Fallen.

The creature stood on a limb, watching, a glowing vial hanging from a wire around its neck. Spreading its leathery wings, it rose into the moon-scorched sky, then swooping low, just above the tree tops, it glided down the valley toward the river and the coast.

An eerie and suffocating silence fell over the patio, and into the midst of this sepulchral calm stepped Jäger from a shadow on its periphery. His hands in the pockets of his black hooded jacket, he strolled to the balustrades along the edge of the patio, and plucked one of the smoldering cigars from the flagstones.

Puffing on the discarded stogie, he drew in the smoke until its tip glowed like the eye of a Fallen. He watched as the dark shape of the retreating creature grew smaller against the distant horizon, and listened as from far down the valley its preternatural roar sounded in the darkness.

Jäger exhaled, blowing smoke toward the echoing sound, as his eyes flashed electric blue arcs.

EPILOGUE

A heavy Virginia fog had collected in tiny beads on the windshield of Kevin McLawson's eighteen-wheeler, and it annoyed him to the core. He had spent several hours the day before detailing the chrome laden beast, and now all his work had been ruined. From behind the wheel, he fumed silently.

Kevin had been driving trucks for most of his life, and after years of hauling hay for his father, and driving for other transport companies, he had finally saved enough for a down payment on his dream truck, a Peterbilt 379 Conventional.

He had tricked it out with lots of chrome, and a dazzling array of lights that made it look like a U.F.O. as it pushed through the fog. And he kept it polished. Which was why he now sat brooding as his windshield wipers pushed aside the accumulating droplets in lazy intermittent strokes.

As the heavy fog turned to a light rain, Kevin noticed a dark figure walking along the side of the road. The person was dressed all in black with a hood pulled up over their head, and bearing an oddly large backpack.

"Poor bastard," mumbled Kevin as he eased his truck over the center line to give the soaked pedestrian some room. Just as he did, however, the dark figure extended its arm, its thumb up.

Kevin, as a rule, did not pick up hitchhikers. It wasn't from a lack of sympathy, but rather from past experiences. The whole process of inviting a stranger into his 'home' reminded Kevin of the time he had spent in prison.

In prison, when a cellmate, or bunkie, as they were commonly called, moved or went home, he knew a new one would soon arrive. It was always a crap shoot as to whether that new bunkie would be a decent human being, or a babbling, non-bathing, psychopath. Kevin hated that uncertainty.

Now, for reasons Kevin could not comprehend, he felt compelled to help this forlorn creature, who was walking in the rain in the middle of nowhere.

Passing the dark figure, Kevin applied his breaks, and brought his truck to a halt in the empty road, and blew his horn. Reaching across his cab he opened the passenger door, inviting the walker into the warmth of his home on the road.

Kevin could hear the sound of running footsteps as the hitchhiker ran up to the truck, and stepped up onto its running board. He watched as a large black pack came up through the door, followed by his new passenger, who was much smaller than Kevin had expected.

Grabbing the pack, Kevin realized that it was mostly a guitar that had made it look so big. Turning, he placed the bulky pack against the bed in the sleeper. Pulling himself back into his seat, Kevin looked over to his new guest, and was startled as he watched the black hood being pulled back to reveal a beautiful girl with long raven hair.

"Thanks for stopping," she said smiling. "I'm Nikki."

Kevin was stunned, even a bit fearful to discover that his rider was a young, pretty, girl.

Nikki looked at him, her eyes bright and cheerful. "And, you are...," she prompted.

"Kevin," he said.

He didn't mean to be curt, but warning lights were flashing frantically in his brain, and they were screaming 'run!'. The reason was easy to explain.

Kevin had been in prison, true enough. But more relevant to the current situation was the reason he had been in prison.

Around twenty years earlier, Kevin had been in Phoenix, Arizona and had attended a rock concert at a bar. While there he met a girl. She was cute and young, and she seemed to be very attracted to Kevin. Since it was a bar, Kevin had assumed that she was at least twenty-one years old, but after a night together it turned out she was sixteen. What happened next was the stuff of nightmares.

The next morning, the girl told Kevin that she wouldn't tell the cops if he bought her a car. Kevin said no, so she called the cops. When the dust had cleared, Kevin had signed a plea deal and served ten years in an Arizona prison.

So now Kevin was an ex-con and a registered Sex Offender, and had just picked up a young female hitchhiker on a remote country road. The optics of the situation were undeniable, and it was a story line reminiscent of every bull-shit episode of *Law and Order SVU* he had ever seen.

"How old are you?" he asked, more scoldingly than he intended.

Nikki smiled. She could smell his fear and discomfort. Her predatory skills were sharpening, and she could read Kevin's emotions as if they were written on his face. He wasn't the first man to fear or desire her, however. Nikki knew what it was to be sexualized by both men and women. Their lust gave her the power that she would often use to get what she both wanted, and needed.

Nikki looked at Kevin with curiosity. She could sense that he wasn't look-ing at her like that. His discomfort was keeping him at a distance. Not that he didn't find her attractive, he just refused to let his mind linger on that thought. Nikki decided that she liked him. He was a good soul.

"I'm almost twenty-two," she said, smiling. Then she added in a teasing tone, "Don't worry, I don't bite."

"Well, that's not entirely true, now is it?" commented Ray-Ray from the depths of her mind, as he lounged by a pool sipping a cocktail with an umbrella stuck in it.

Nikki ignored him.

'Well at least she's not a minor', thought Kevin relaxing a bit. "Where ya headed?" he asked at last.

"Richmond, for now. Not sure after that," said Nikki, removing her jacket and revealing her tattoo covered arms.

"What are you going to do there?" asked Kevin, shaking his head at all of her ink, "get a tattoo?"

"Gonna be a rock star," she replied nonchalantly, while ignoring his barb.

"Humph," grunted Kevin in his standard judgmental tone.

Nikki smiled again. She could sense that this mountain of a man, with his frowny face, and upper lip that curled in a snarl whenever he wrinkled his nose to hold up his heavy glasses, was a good man. But Kevin obviously had his secrets. Some of them deep, and dark, but all things considered, Nikki decided she kinda liked the grumpy bastard.

As the air brakes hissed and Kevin's truck began to roll down the road, Nikki sat back and relaxed. Her bizarre new life with her Fallen, and her grumpy new friend beside her, was just getting started.

She sensed, however, that it was more than that. Destinies were shifting. The future had become fluid, and the current of fate was now pulling her in a direction she did not control.

Made in the USA
Middletown, DE
24 February 2022

61680228R00227